PATH OF THE
WARRIOR

HE TOOK A crouched step forward, easing into his fighting stance. No longer was he a thing of flesh and blood, a mortal being filled with falsehood and crude passions. He was a warrior. He was part of the Bloody-Handed God, an Aspect of Kaela Mensha Khaine.

Korlandril was no more.

In his place stood a Striking Scorpion of the Deadly Shadow.

A WARHAMMER 40,000 NOVEL

PATH OF THE ELDAR SERIES
BOOK ONE

PATH OF THE WARRIOR

GAV THORPE

BLACK LIBRARY

*For Jes and White Dwarf 127 for
starting me on the Path.*

A BLACK LIBRARY PUBLICATION

First published in Great Britain in 2010 by
The Black Library,
Games Workshop Ltd.,
Willow Road, Nottingham,
NG7 2WS, UK.

10 9 8 7 6 5 4 3 2 1

Cover illustration by Neil Roberts.

A CIP record for this book is available from the British Library.

US ISBN: 978 1 84416 875 0

Distributed in the US by Simon & Schuster
1230 Avenue of the Americas, New York, NY 10020, US.

See the Black Library on the internet at
www.blacklibrary.com

Find out more about Games Workshop
and the world of Warhammer 40,000 at
www.games-workshop.com

Printed and bound in the US.

IT IS THE 41st millennium. For more than a hundred centuries the Emperor has sat immobile on the Golden Throne of Earth. He is the master of mankind by the will of the gods, and master of a million worlds by the might of his inexhaustible armies. He is a rotting carcass writhing invisibly with power from the Dark Age of Technology. He is the Carrion Lord of the Imperium for whom a thousand souls are sacrificed every day, so that he may never truly die.

YET EVEN IN his deathless state, the Emperor continues his eternal vigilance. Mighty battlefleets cross the daemon-infested miasma of the warp, the only route between distant stars, their way lit by the Astronomican, the psychic manifestation of the Emperor's will. Vast armies give battle in His name on uncounted worlds. Greatest amongst his soldiers are the Adeptus Astartes, the Space Marines, bio-engineered super-warriors. Their comrades in arms are legion: the Imperial Guard and countless Planetary Defence Forces, the ever-vigilant Inquisition and the tech-priests of the Adeptus Mechanicus to name only a few. But for all their multitudes, they are barely enough to hold off the ever-present threat from aliens, heretics, mutants – and worse.

TO BE A man in such times is to be one amongst untold billions. It is to live in the cruellest and most bloody regime imaginable. These are the tales of those times. Forget the power of technology and science, for so much has been forgotten, never to be re-learned. Forget the promise of progress and understanding, for in the grim dark future there is only war. There is no peace amongst the stars, only an eternity of carnage and slaughter, and the laughter of thirsting gods.

'Life is to us as the Maze of Linnian was to Ulthanesh, its mysterious corridors leading to wondrous vistas and nightmarish encounters in equal measure. Each of us must walk the maze alone, treading in the footsteps of those that came before but also forging new routes through the labyrinth of existence.

In times past we were drawn to the darkest secrets and ran wild about the maze, seeking to experience all that it had to offer. As individuals and as a civilisation we lost our way and in doing so created the means for our doom; unfettered exploration leading to the darkness of the Fall.

In the emptiness that followed, a new way was revealed to us: the Path. Through the wisdom of the Path we spend our lives exploring the meaning of existence, moving from one part of the maze to another with discipline and guidance so that we never become lost again. On the Path we experience the full potential of love and hate, joy and woe, lust and purity, filling our lives with experience and fulfilment but never succumbing to the shadows that lurk within our thoughts.

But like all journeys, the Path is different for each of us. Some wander for a long while in one place; some spread their travels wide and visit many places for a short time while others remain for a long time to explore every nook and turn; some of us lose our way and leave the Path for a time or forever; and some of us find dead-ends and become trapped.'

– Kysaduras the Anchorite,
foreword to *Introspections upon Perfection*

PROLOGUE

A BLUE SUN reflected from the still waters of the lake while its yellow companion peeked just above the red-leaved trees that surrounded the edge of the water. Red and black birds skimmed above the lake with wings buzzing, their long beaks snapping at insects, their chattering calls the only sound to break the quiet.

A white stone building bordered the water, its long colonnaded veranda stretching over the lake on thick piles. Beyond the portico, it reared up amongst the trees, square in shape, turreted towers at each corner. Thin smoke seeped lazily from vents in the wall, the breeze carrying it away across the forests. Narrow windows shuttered with red-painted wood broke the upper storeys, small balconies jutting from the wall beneath each one.

Armed figures stood guard at the high doorways and patrolled walkways running along the red-tiled roofs. The men were dressed in loose black trousers tucked into knee-high boots, with bulky red jackets buttoned and braided with gold. Their heads were covered by black hoods, with tinted goggles to protect their eyes from the strange light of the local stars. They walked their rounds and chatted with each other, thinking nothing was amiss.

Causing barely a ripple, five green-armoured figures slid from the water, silvery droplets falling from the overlapping curved plates of their suits. They carried pistols and saw-toothed chainswords. Making no sound, the eldar warriors pulled themselves up to the veranda and stopped in the shadows of the pillars, invisible to the group of guards at the doorway.

Patiently, they crouched in the darkness and waited.

THERE WAS A flash of light through the sky and a massive explosion rocked the front of the manor house, shards of stone and cracked tiles thrown high into the air by the impact. A moment later, another blast seared down through the clouds and detonated, destroying one of the turrets in a cloud of dust, spilling mangled bodies to the close-cut lawn beside the mansion.

At the far end of the gardens, black-armoured figures appeared at the tree line, long missile launchers underslung from their arms. A rippling burst of fire sent a volley of projectiles towards the roof of the house while other warriors dashed across flower-filled beds and vaulted over stone benches and ran through bubbling fountains.

Kenainath, exarch of the Deadly Shadow shrine motioned for his Striking Scorpions to stay in the shadows of the lakeside porch, his eyes fixed on the soldiers at the door. As predicted, the men unslung their rifles and dashed from their post, heading towards the attack across the gardens. Kenainath pounced as they passed, his energy-covered power claw ripping through the back of the skull of the closest human.

His warriors followed him, pistols spitting hails of molecule-thin discs, their chainswords purring. Caught by surprise, the soldiers stood no chance and were cut down in moments, dismembered, disembowelled or beheaded by the blades of the Striking Scorpions.

Kenainath crouched amongst the dead soldiers, red-lensed eyes scanning for signs of danger. Other eldar warriors – Dire Avengers in armour of blue and gold – leapt over the veranda and joined the squad. Together they headed towards the back doors.

A creak and a small movement in one of the ground floor shutters alerted Kenainath to danger. He dived towards the cover of a plant holder as the shutters swung open, his warriors reacting instantly to follow him.

The wide barrel of an automatic weapon crashed through the windowpanes and muzzle flare bathed the portico. Bullets whined and ricocheted around the Striking Scorpions sending up shards of stone and ripping splinters from the plant container. There was a shout of pain from Iniatherin just behind the exarch. The Dire Avengers returned fire, unleashing a storm from their shuriken catapults through the window. His body shredded by the fusillade, the man within fell back with a long shriek.

Kenainath glanced over his shoulder to see Iniatherin sprawled across the white stone, armour pierced by a long shard of broken wood, bright blood pumping from a gash to his throat. In moments the warrior was dead, his twitching body falling still as the pool of red spread around him.

More explosions rattled the windows as the eldar forced their way into the building to Kenainath's right. Through the shattered window the exarch saw lithe, bone-coloured figures bounding across a hallway, the air split with piercing wails from the Howling Banshees' masks.

Signalling for his squad to move towards the door again, Kenainath spared another glance for his fallen warrior. He felt no sorrow; it was impossible for him to feel guilt or remorse. Death was no stranger to those that trod the Path of the Warrior. Kenainath's squad was lessened by the loss, but as he looked down at the awkwardly splayed body he knew that the diminishing of the Deadly Shadow's strength would not be for long.

The universe strained for harmony and balance and, as the philosophers claimed, abhorred a vacuum. Another would take Iniatherin's place.

Part One

Artist

FRIENDSHIP

In the time before the War in Heaven, Eldanesh, spear-carrier, hawk-friend, lord of the eldar, faced the armies of the Hresh-selain. Eldanesh was the greatest of the eldar, his spear the finest weapon forged by mortals, yet the king of the Hresh-selain had many warriors. Though he was lord of the eldar and knew it to be his burden alone to protect them, Eldanesh knew also he could not gain victory by himself. He turned to Ulthanesh, second greatest warrior of the eldar, sword-bearer, raven-friend, and asked for his aid in battling the Hresh-selain. Together Eldanesh and Ulthanesh fought, and against their skill and strength the Hresh-selain had no defence. 'Ever shall it be thus', said Eldanesh, 'that when we are most sorely tested, our friends shall stand by our side'.

A STAR WAS dying.

To the eldar she was Mirianathir, Mother of the Desert Winds. She hung in the dark firmament, a deep orange, her surface tortured by frenetic bursts of fusion and rampaging electromagnetic winds. Particles streamed from her body and fronds of energy lapped at the closest planets, scourging Mirianathir's children with their deadly touch. They hung barren around her. For a million years she had been dying and for a million more she would continue to die.

Yet in her death there was life for others.

For the eldar.

Bathed in the radioactive glow of Mirianathir's death throes, a craftworld floated upon the stellar winds; an artificial, disc-like continent of glowing domes and silvery energy sails, arcing bridges and glittering towers. Wings unfurled, the craftworld soaked in life-giving energy, an inorganic plant with mirrored leaves a hundred kilometres long. Surrounded by the ruddy light of the dying star, Craftworld Alaitoc absorbed all that Mirianathir had to offer, capturing every particle and stellar breeze, feeding it through the spirits of its infinity circuit to sustain the craftworld for a thousand more years.

The space around Alaitoc was as full of movement and energy as the star upon which it fed. Ships whirled and swerved, tacking across the stellar winds, refuelling their own energy stores. The webway gate behind the craftworld swirled and ebbed, a shimmering portal into the space between the material and immaterial. Trade ships with long fluted hulls slipped into and out of the gate; sleek destroyers with night-blue hulls prowled through the traffic, weapons batteries armed, torpedoes loaded; slender yachts darted amongst the shoal of vessels; majestic battleships eased along stately paths through the ordered commotion.

With a fluctuation of golden light, the webway portal dilated for a moment and where there had been vacuum now drifted *Lacontiran*, a bird-like trading schooner just returned from her long voyage to the stars of the Endless Valley. Trimming her solar sails, she turned easily along the starside rim of the craftworld and followed a course that led her to the Tower of Eternal Welcomes.

The dock tower stretched five kilometres out from the plane of the craftworld, encased in a bluish aura that kept at bay the ravening emptiness of space. Like a narwhal's horn, the tower spiralled into the darkness, hundreds of figures along its length, lining the elegant gantries and curving walkways. Eldar of all Paths had come to greet their long-travelled ship: poets, engineers, autarchs, gardeners, farseers, Aspect Warriors, stylists and chartmakers. Any and all walks of life were there, dressed in the fineries of heavy robes, or glittering skin-tight suits, or flowing tunics in a riot of colours. Scarves spilled like yellow and red waves and high-crested helms rose above a sea of delicately coiffured heads. Jewels of every colour shone in the glow of the craftworld alongside sparkling bands and rings and necklaces of silver and gold and platinum.

Without conscious thought, the eldar made their way around each other: embracing old friends; exchanging pleasantries with new acquaintances;

steering a private course, never encroaching upon the private space of another. Their voices rose together, in a symphony of sound as like to the babbling of a crowd as a full orchestra is to the murmurings of a child. They talked to and around and over each other, their voices lyric, every intonation a note perfected, every gesture measured and precise. Some did not talk at all, their posture conveying their thoughts; the slightest raising of a brow, the quiver of a lip or trembling of a finger displaying agitation or excitement, happiness or anxiety.

In the midst of this kaleidoscope of craftworld life stood Korlandril. His slender frame was draped in an open-fronted robe of shining silk-like gold, his neck and wrists adorned with hundreds of molecule-thin chains in every colour of the spectrum so that it seemed his hands and face were wound with miniature rainbows. His long black hair was bound into a complicated braid that hung across his left shoulder, kept in place with holobands that constantly changed from sapphires to diamonds to emeralds and every other beautiful stone known to the eldar. He had taken much time to style himself upon the aesthetics of Arestheina, and had considered long the results in a mirrorfield, knowing that his companion was partial to the ancient artist's works.

She, Thirianna, was dressed in more simple attire: a white ankle-length dress pleated below the knee, delicately embroidered with thread just the slightest shade greyer than the cloth, like the shadows of a cloud; sleeveless to reveal pale arms painted with waving patterns of henna. She wore a diaphanous scarf about her shoulders, its red and white gossamer coils lapping across her arms and chest. Her white hair, dyed to match her dress, was coloured with two azure streaks that framed her narrow face, accentuating the dark blue of her eyes. Her waystone was also a deep blue, ensconced in a surround of white meresilver, hung upon a fine chain of the same metal.

Korlandril looked at Thirianna, while all other eyes were turned towards the starship now gracefully sliding into place beside the uncoiling walkway of the quay. It had been fifteen cycles since he had last seen her. Fifteen cycles too many – too long to be away from her beauty and her passion, her smile that stirred the soul. He nurtured the hope that she would notice the attention he had laboured upon his appearance, but as yet she had made no remark upon it.

He saw the intensity in her eyes as she looked upon the approaching starship, the faintest glisten of moisture there, and detected an excited tremble throughout her body. He did not know whether it was simply the occasion that generated such anticipation – the gala atmosphere was very infectious – or whether there was some more personal, deeper joy that stirred Thirianna's heart. Perhaps her feelings for Aradryan's return were more than Korlandril would like. The notion stirred something within Korlandril's breast, a serpent uncoiling. He knew his jealousy was unjustified, and that he had made no claim to keep Thirianna for himself, but still the precision of his thoughts failed to quell the emotions that loitered within.

Set within a golden surround, the opal oval of Korlandril's waystone grew warm upon his chest, its heat passing through the material of his robe. Like a warning light upon a craft's display the waystone's agitation caused Korlandril to pause for a moment. His jealousy was not only misplaced, it was dangerous. He allowed the sensation to drift into the recesses of his mind, closed within a mental vault to be removed later when it was safe to do so.

Thoughts of Aradryan reminded Korlandril why he was at the tower: to welcome back an old friend. If Thirianna had wanted to be with Aradryan she would have travelled with him. Korlandril dismissed his fears concerning Thirianna's affections, finding himself equally eager to greet their returning companion. The serpent within lowered its head and slept again, biding its time.

A dozen gateways along the hull of *Lacontiran* opened, releasing a wave of iridescent light and a honey-scented breeze along the curving length of the dock. From the high archways passengers and crew disembarked in winding lines. Thirianna stretched to her full height, poised effortlessly on the tips of her boots, to look over the heads of the eldar in front, one hand slightly to one side to maintain her balance.

It was Korlandril's sharp eyes that caught sight of Aradryan first, which gave him a small thrill of pleasure; a victory won though no competition had been agreed between them.

'There he is, our wanderer returned to us like Anthemion with the Golden Harp,' said Korlandril, pointing to a walkway to their left, letting his fingers rest upon Thirianna's bare arm for the slightest of moments to attract her attention.

Though Korlandril had recognised him immediately, Aradryan looked very different from when he had left. Only by his sharp cheeks and thin lips had Korlandril known him. His hair was cut barbarically short on the left side, almost to the scalp, and hung in unkempt waves to the right, neither bound nor styled. He had dark make-up upon his eyelids, giving him a skull-like, sunken glare, and he was dressed in deep blues and black, wrapped in long ribbons of twilight. His bright yellow waystone was worn as a brooch, mostly hidden by the folds of his robe. Aradryan's forbidding eyes fell upon Korlandril and then Thirianna, their sinister edge disappearing with a glint of happiness. Aradryan waved a hand in greeting and wove his way effortlessly through the throng to stand in front of the pair.

'A felicitous return!' declared Korlandril, opening his arms in welcome, palms angled towards Aradryan's face. 'And a happy reunion.'

Thirianna dispensed with words altogether, brushing the back of her hand across Aradryan's cheek for a moment, before laying her slender fingers upon his shoulder. Aradryan returned the gesture, sparking a flare of jealous annoyance in Korlandril, which he fought hard not to show. The serpent in his gut opened one interested eye, but Korlandril forced it back into subservience. The moment passed and Aradryan stepped away from Thirianna, laying his hands onto those of Korlandril, a wry smile on his lips.

'Well met, and many thanks for the welcome,' said Aradryan. Korlandril searched his friend's face, seeking the impish delight that had once lurked behind the eyes, the ready, contagious smirk that had nestled in every movement of his lips. They were no longer there. Aradryan radiated solemnity and sincerity, warmth even, but Korlandril detected a barrier; Aradryan's face was turned ever so slightly towards Thirianna, his back arched just the merest fraction away from Korlandril.

Even amongst the eldar such subtle differences might have been missed, but Korlandril was dedicated to the Path of the Artist and had honed his observation and attention to detail to a level bordering on the microscopic. He noticed everything, remembered every nuance and facet, and he knew from his deep studies that everything had a meaning, whether intended or not. There was no such thing as an innocent smile, or a meaningless blink. Every motion betrayed a motive, and it was Aradryan's subtle reticence that now nagged at Korlandril's thoughts.

Korlandril held Aradryan's hands for a moment longer than was necessary, hoping that the extended physicality of the greeting might remind his friend of their bond. If it did, Aradryan gave no sign. With the same slight smile, he withdrew his grasp and clasped his hands behind his back, raising his eyebrows inquisitively.

'Tell me, dearest and most happily-met of my friends, what have I missed?'

* * *

THE TRIO WALKED along the Avenue of Dreams, a silver passageway that passed beneath a thousand crystal archways into the heart of Alaitoc. The dim light of Mirianathir was caught in the vaulted roof, captured and radiated by the intricately faceted crystal to shine down upon the pedestrians below, glowing with delicate oranges and pinks.

Korlandril had offered to drive Aradryan to his quarters, but his friend had declined, preferring to savour the sensation of his return and the casual crowds of eldar; Korlandril guessed from the little Aradryan said that his had been a mostly solitary journey aboard the *Lacontiran*. Korlandril glanced with a little envy as slender anti-grav craft slipped by effortlessly, carrying their passengers quickly to their destinations. A younger Korlandril would have been horrified by the indolence that held sway over Korlandril the Sculptor, his abstract thoughts distracted by mundane labour of physical activity. Such introspection was impossible though; he had put aside self-consciousness in his desire to embrace every outside influence, every experience not of his own body and mind. Such were the thoughts of the artist, elevated beyond the practical, dancing upon the starlight of pure observation and imagination.

It was this drive for sensation that led Korlandril to conduct most of the talking. He spoke at length of his works, and of the comings-and-goings of the craftworld since Aradryan had left. For his part, Aradryan kept his comments and answers direct and without flourish, starving Korlandril of inspiration, frustrating his artistic thirst.

When Thirianna spoke, Korlandril noted, Aradryan became more eloquent, and seemed keener to speak about her than himself.

'I sense that you no longer walk in the shadow of Khaine,' said Aradryan, nodding in approval as he looked at Thirianna.

'It is true that the Path of the Warrior has ended for me,' she replied, thoughtful, her eyes never straying from Aradryan. 'The aspect of the Dire Avenger has sated my anger, enough for a hundred lifetimes. I write poetry, influenced by the Uriathillin school of verse. I find it has complexities that stimulate both the intellectual and the emotional in equal measure.'

'I would like to know Thirianna the Poet, and perhaps your verse will introduce me,' said Aradryan. 'I would very much like to see a performance, as you see fit.'

'As would I,' said Korlandril. 'Thirianna refuses to share her work with me, though many times I have suggested that we collaborate on a piece that combines her words with my sculpture.'

'My verse is for myself, and no other,' Thirianna said quietly. 'It is not for performance, nor for eyes that are not mine.'

She cast a glance of annoyance towards Korlandril.

'While some create their art to express themselves to the world, my poems are inner secrets, for me to understand their meaning, to divine my own fears and wishes.'

Admonished, Korlandril fell silent for a moment, but he was quickly uncomfortable with the quiet and gave voice to a question that had scratched at his subconscious since he had heard that Aradryan was returning.

'Have you come back to Alaitoc to stay?' he asked. 'Is your time as a steersman complete, or will you be returning to *Lacontiran*?'

'I have only just arrived, are you so eager that I should leave once more?' replied Aradryan.

Korlandril opened his mouth to protest but the words drifted away as he caught, just for a moment, a hint of the old wit of Aradryan. Korlandril smiled in appreciation of the joke and bowed his head in acknowledgement of his own part as the foil for Aradryan's humour.

'I do not yet know,' Aradryan continued with a thoughtful expression. 'I have learned all that I can learn as a steersman and I feel complete. Gone is the turbulence that once plagued my thoughts. There is nothing like guiding a ship along the buffeting waves of a nebula or along the swirling channels of the webway to foster control and focus. I have seen many great, many wondrous things out in the stars, but I feel that there is so much more out there to find; to touch and hear and experience. I may return to the starships, I may not. And, of course, I would like to spend a little time with my friends and family, to know again the life of Alaitoc, to see whether I wish to wander again or can be content here.'

Thirianna nodded in agreement at this wise course of action, and even Korlandril, who occasionally succumbed to rash impulse, could see the merits of weighing such a decision well.

'Your return is most timely, Aradryan,' he said, again feeling the need to fill the vacuum of conversation. 'My latest piece is nearing completion. In a few cycles' time I am hosting an unveiling. It would be a pleasure and an honour if both of you could attend.'

'I would have come even if you had not invited me!' laughed Thirianna, her enthusiasm sending a thrill of excitement through Korlandril. 'I hear your name mentioned quite often, and with much praise attached, and there are high expectations for this new work. It would not be seemly at all to miss such an event if one is to be considered as a person possessing any degree of taste.'

Aradryan did not reply for a moment, and Korlandril could discern nothing of his friend's thoughts from his expression. It was as if a blank mask had been placed upon his face.

'Yes, I too would be delighted to attend,' Aradryan said eventually, animation returning. 'I am afraid that my tastes may have been left behind compared to yours, but I look forward to seeing what Korlandril the Sculptor has created in my absence.'

MASTERPIECE

In the first days of the eldar, Asuryan granted Eldanesh and his followers the gift of life. He breathed into their bodies all that they were to become. Yet there was no other thing upon the world. All was barren and not a leaf nor fish nor bird nor animal grew or swam or flew or walked beside them. Eldanesh was forlorn at the infertility of his home, and its emptiness made in him a greater emptiness. Seeing his distress, Isha was overcome with a grief of her own. Isha shed a tear for the eldar and let it drop upon the world. Where it fell, there came new life. From her sorrow came joy, for the world of the eldar was filled with wondrous things and Eldanesh's emptiness was no more, and he gave thanks to Isha for her love.

A SNARL OF frustration rose in Korlandril's throat and he fought to stifle it before it came into being. He glared at the droplet of blood welling up from the tiny puncture in his thumb, seeing a miniscule red reflection of his own angry features. He smeared the blood between thumb and finger and turned his ire upon the small barb that had appeared in the ghost stone, tipped with a fleck of crimson.

It was an affront to every sensibility he had developed, that tiny splinter. It broke the precise line of the arcing arm of his sculpture, an aberration in the otherwise perfect flow of organic and inorganic. It was not meant to be and Korlandril did not know how it had come to be.

It had been like this for the last two cycles. Whenever he laid his fingers upon the ghost stone, to tease it into the forms so real in his mind, it refused to be held sway by his thoughts. It had taken him all of the last cycle just to get three fingers perfect, and at this pace the piece would be far from ready when the unveiling was to be held in just two more cycles.

The pale ochre of the ghost stone sat unmoving, dormant without his caress, but to Korlandril it had developed a life of its own. It rebelled against his desires, twisting away from the shapes he wanted, forming hard edges where soft curves should be, growing diminutive thorns and spikes whenever his mind strayed even the slightest.

He knew the ghost stone was not at fault. It was possessed of no will, no spirit. It merely reacted to his input, shaping itself under his gentle psychic manipulation. It was inert now, but Korlandril sensed a certain smugness in its unwillingness to cooperate, even as another part of his mind told him that he was simply projecting his frustrations onto an inanimate object.

His mind divided, all concentration now gone, Korlandril stepped back and looked away, ashamed at his failing. The shimmering of the holofield around him, erected to conceal the work from admirers until it was unveiled in its finished glory, played a corona of colours into Korlandril's eyes. For a moment he was lost gazing at the undulating view of the forest dome beyond the shimmering holofield, the distorted vista sending a flurry of inspiration through his mind.

'I almost dare not ask,' said a voice behind Korlandril. He turned to see his mentor, Abrahasil, gazing intently at the statue.

'You need not ask anything,' said Korlandril. 'It is Aradryan's return that perturbs me, but I know not why. I am happy that my friend is once again with us.'

'And what of your thoughts of Aradryan in relation to your work?'

'I have none,' replied Korlandril. 'This piece was started long before I knew of his return.'

'And yet progress has been slow since you learnt of it, and almost non-existent since it happened,' said Abrahasil. 'The effect is clear, though the cause remains obscured to you. Perhaps I might help?'

Korlandril shrugged his indifference and then felt a stab of contrition at Abrahasil's disappointed sigh.

'Of course, I would appreciate any guidance you can give me,' said Korlandril, forcing himself to look at the statue. 'I see it clearly, all of it, every line and arc, as you taught me. I allow the peace and the piece to become one within me, as you taught me. I direct my thoughts and my motion towards its creation, as you taught me. Nothing I do has changed, and yet the ghost stone is rebellious to my demands.'

Abrahasil raised a narrow finger at this last comment.

'Demands, Korlandril? It is desire not demand that shapes the ghost stone. A demand is an act of aggression; a desire is an act of submission. The thought shapes the act which shapes the form. Why has desire changed to demand?'

Korlandril did not answer at first, startled that he had not been aware of such a simple distinction, subtle as it was. He repeated the question to himself, searching his thoughts, sifting through his mental processes until he could locate the point at which desire had become demand.

'I wish to impress others with my work, and I feel the pressure of expectation,' Korlandril said eventually, pleased that he found an answer.

'That is not what is wrong,' said Abrahasil with the slightest pursing of his lips, spearing through Korlandril's bubble of self-congratulation. 'Always has your work been expressive, intended to impose your insight upon others. That has not changed. Remember something more specific. Something related to Aradryan.'

Again Korlandril drifted within his own memories and emotions, massaging his thoughts into order just as he manipulated the ghost stone into its flowing shapes. He found what he was looking for, visualised the moment of transition and gave a quiet gasp of realisation.

He looked at Abrahasil and hesitated, reluctant to share his discovery with another. Abrahasil waited patiently, eyes fixed not on Korlandril but on the statue. Korlandril knew that if he asked his mentor to leave, he would do so without complaint, but until then Abrahasil would await a reply. Abrahasil did not need to remind Korlandril that he could be trusted, that the bond between mentor and student was inviolate; that in order to explore and engage the passions and fears Korlandril needed to express himself as an artist, anything he told Abrahasil was in the strictest confidence. Abrahasil had no need to say such things, his patient waiting and the understanding between the two of them was all the communication needed.

'I wish to impress Thirianna out of competition with Aradryan,' Korlandril said eventually, relieved at unburdening himself of sole knowledge of this revelation. He had never spoken of his feeling towards Thirianna, not even with Abrahasil, though he suspected his mentor saw much of Korlandril's thoughts that he did not comment on. After all, Abrahasil had observed them both together on many occasions and Korlandril knew he would not have been able to conceal every sign of affection from his mentor's studied gaze. 'There is a fear within me, and anger that I feel such a fear. Aradryan is a friend. Not a rival.'

Abrahasil turned his head and smiled. Korlandril felt another layer of connection falling into place between them, as if he had stepped across a threshold that he had been poised upon for a long time.

'That is good,' said the mentor. 'And how will you control that fear, that anger?'

Now it was Korlandril's turn to smile.

'That is simple,' he said. 'This sculpture is not for Thirianna, but for me. My next piece… that will be for her. These thoughts have no place in this creation, but they will be the inspiration for another. I can put them aside until then.'

Abrahasil laid a hand upon Korlandril's arm in reassurance and Korlandril gave him a look that conveyed his deep appreciation. Abrahasil stepped out of the holofield without further word and Korlandril watched his wavering form disappear into the miasmic vista of trees.

Feeling refreshed and invigorated, Korlandril approached the sculpture. He laid his hand upon the raised arm he had been working on, delicately running his fingertips along the accentuated flow of muscle tone and joint, rebuilding his mental vision of the piece.

Under his touch, the barb flowed back into the ghost stone and was no more.

THERE WAS AN air of excitement and anticipation in the Dome of the Midnight Forests. Across meadows of blue grass and between the pale silver trunks of lianderin trees, many eldar gathered to await the unveiling of Korlandril's latest creation. Through the invisible force field enclosing the ordered gardens, the ruddy twilight of Mirianathir glowed. The lilt of laughter and the chime of crystal goblets drifted on an artificial breeze that set the jade leaves of the trees rustling; a perfect accompaniment to the swish of grass and the soft conversation of Korlandril's guests.

Some three hundred eldar had gathered for the unveiling, dressed for the occasion in their most fashionable attire. Korlandril mingled with the crowd, remarking upon an elegant brooch or particularly pleasing cut of skirt or robe. For his grand moment, he had decided to dress himself in an outfit that was elegant but austere, out of a desire not to upstage his sculpture. He wore a plain blue robe, fastened from waist to throat with silver buckles, and his hair was swept back with a silver band ornamented with a single blue skystone at his brow. He kept his conversation short, eluding any questions concerning the nature of the piece until he was ready to reveal all.

As he wandered amongst the guests, Korlandril felt a thrill running through him. With each beat of his heart his waystone reciprocated, the double-pulse quivering in his chest. He absorbed excitement from the guests and projected it back to them. He was pleased with the attention, a salve to his pride after the tribulations he had faced completing the sculpture.

Exchanging pleasantries, Korlandril scanned the crowd for Thirianna and spied her with a group of three other eldar in one of the lianderin groves not far from where the shimmering holofield concealed Korlandril's exhibit.

Korlandril allowed himself a moment to admire her beauty from a distance, delighting intellectually and emotionally in the close-fitting suit of red and black she wore. The curves of her arms and legs mirrored those of the branches above her, a natural elegance accentuated by her delicate poise and precise posture. Her hair, pigmented a deep yellow, fell in a tumble of coils down her back, woven through with red ribbons that hung to her waist.

As she stepped to one side, Korlandril saw Aradryan. He was smiling, in the deliberate way maintained by those not entirely comfortable with their surrounds. Korlandril felt the serpent of envy quiver ever so slightly within him, which disturbed him. He thought he had put aside that haunting doubt, that fear lingering at the very edge of his awareness. Seeing Aradryan with Thirianna brought his concerns into stark view and Korlandril's pulse quickened and his thoughts raced for a moment.

Korlandril directed his gaze away as he walked across the meadow, allowing the calm of the garden dome to still the turbulence in his thoughts. Lianderin blossom was just beginning to bud, like golden stars in a deep green night, and the scent of the grass rose up from beneath his tread, cleansing and pure. By the time he reached the group, Korlandril was composed once more, genuinely happy to see his friends in attendance.

Aradryan extended a palm in greeting and Korlandril laid his hand upon his friend's in return. The welcome was repeated with Thirianna, her touch cool and reassuring. As he pulled back his hand, Korlandril allowed his fingertips to brush gently over those of Thirianna, and he allowed his eyes to meet hers for a heartbeat longer than was normal.

'We are all quivering with anticipation,' said one of the group, another sculptor called Ydraethir. He wore a half-gown of deep purple across his waist and left shoulder, cut short on the thighs, exposing skin that had been bleached almost pure white. Ydraethir followed the school of Hithrinair, which saw the sculptor as much a part of the work as the sculpture itself. Korlandril had dabbled with its aesthetic for a few cycles but had quickly found himself to be a dull subject and preferred to express himself through his work at a distance. Korlandril searched for a hint of irony or rivalry in his companion's comment and pose, but concluded that Ydraethir was being sincere.

'It is my hope that such expectation is warranted,' replied Korlandril with a grateful bow of the head. He turned and greeted the fourth eldar, the renowned bonesinger Kirandrin. 'I am very grateful for the interest and enthusiasm you have all shown in my work.'

'I have watched your development closely since I first came upon one of your early works,' Kirandrin said. 'I believe it was *The Blessing of Asurmen*, a life-size piece displayed in the atrium of the Tower of the Evening Melodies.'

'My second ever piece,' said Korlandril with a warm smile of remembrance. 'I am still privileged that Abrahasil saw fit to show my works so early on in my time upon the Path. I have kind regard for that particular sculpture, though my work has moved so far beyond such simplistic formulae now, it feels as if it might have been created by someone else!'

'Is not that the purpose of the Path?' said Ydraethir. 'That we change and grow, and shed that which was before and transform into something new and better?'

'Indeed it is,' said Korlandril. 'To strive for the perfection of body and spirit, craft and mind, that is what we all desire.'

'But is it not the case that we also lose some of who we are?' said Aradryan, his tone one of mild dissent. 'If we are forever moving forward on the Path, when do we stop to admire the view? I think that sometimes we are too keen to discard that which made us as we are.'

Silence greeted Aradryan's remarks. He looked at the other eldar, his face betraying a small measure of confusion.

'Forgive me if I have said something out of place,' Aradryan said quietly. 'It was not my intent to question your opinions, but to merely voice my own. Perhaps my manners have strayed a little while I was away from Alaitoc and the niceties of civil society.'

'Not at all,' Kirandrin said smoothly, laying a hand upon Aradryan's arm in a gesture of reassurance. 'It is simply that such questions are… rare.'

'And the answers far too long to be addressed here,' Korlandril added quickly. 'We shall continue this discussion at a later time. At this moment, I must make my grand unveiling.'

'Of course,' said Kirandrin. Aradryan gave a slow, shallow nod and dipped his eyelids in a gesture of apology.

Korlandril smiled his appreciation before crossing quickly to the holofield and stepping within. Obscured from view, he let out a long breath, releasing the tension that had unexpectedly built up within. There had been something about Aradryan's manner that had unnerved Korlandril. He had again felt that otherness he had encountered when Aradryan had first returned – a subtle desire to be elsewhere. Sheltered within the holofield, Korlandril's waystone was again warm to the touch, reflecting inner assurance rather than anger or embarrassment.

The distraction had taxed Korlandril and with a stab of guilt he realised he had said nothing to Thirianna. He had all but ignored her. He wondered for a moment if he should apologise for his offhand behaviour but quickly dismissed the idea. Thirianna probably had not noticed any deficiencies in his attention and it might be unwise to highlight them to her. If she had recognised any affront at all, she would surely understand the many demands conflicting for his attention on an occasion such as this. Korlandril resolved that he would seek out Thirianna after the unveiling and lavish as much attention as possible upon her.

His mind upon Thirianna, Korlandril's thoughts were awhirl in many different directions, his heart racing, his skin tingling. Ideas flashed across his mind, crashing against the excitement he felt at the unveiling, blending with the disturbance caused by Aradryan, colliding with the apprehension that had been building since he had completed the sculpture.

Korlandril whispered a few calming mantras. As he did so, he ordered his thoughts, pushing some aside for later reflection, drawing on others to reassure himself, focussing on his confidence and experiences to steady his worries. He stood in silent repose for some time, until he was sure he was ready to address the crowd.

When the mental maelstrom had become a still pool, Korlandril stepped out of the holofield to find that his guests had gathered in the clearing outside. Most of the faces were familiar, a few were not. All seemed eager to see what Korlandril had created.

'I am deeply honoured that you have all come to witness the unveiling of my latest piece,' Korlandril began, keeping his voice steady, projecting his words to the back of the crowd without effort. 'Many know that I draw great inspiration from the time before the War in Heaven. I look to our golden age not with regret of a paradise lost, nor with sadness that such times have passed. In the first age of our people I see a world, a universe, that we can all aspire to recreate. Though the gods are gone, it is up to us to make real their works, and through our desire to rebuild heaven bring about the peace that we all deserve. Our civilisation is not lost whilst we still sing and paint – and sculpt – of those times that none of us now remember save in myth. We all know that legend can become truth; that the line between myth and reality is not clearly defined. I would take myth and make it reality.'

Korlandril continued at some length, citing his influences and dreams, expounding upon the schools of thought and aesthetic that had led him to create his sculpture. He spoke smoothly and with passion, giving words to the thoughts that had been streamlined and refined through the long process of sculpting. He talked of the complexities of the organic and the inorganic, the juxtaposition of line and curve, the contrast of solid and liquid.

His eyes roved freely over the crowd as he spoke, gauging their reaction and mood. Most were held rapt by his oration, their eyes fixed upon Korlandril, their minds devouring every syllable. A few stood with expressions of polite attendance, and Korlandril felt a moment of dismay when he realised that one such viewer was Aradryan. Korlandril did not falter in his delivery, sweeping away his concern with his enthusiasm even as he searched for Thirianna. He saw her at the front of the crowd, eager and expectant, her eyes constantly flicking between Aradryan and the holofield that shielded his work.

When he was finished, Korlandril allowed himself a dramatic pause, savouring the anticipation than he had created in his audience. He walked to a small table that had been set to one side, circular and stood upon a spiralled leg, a single crystal goblet of deep red wine set in its centre. He sipped at the drink, relishing its warmth on his lips, the spice on his tongue and a sweet note of aftertaste in his throat, even as he relished the hushed calm that had descended in the wake of his speech.

As he placed the glass back upon the table, Korlandril slipped a thin wafer from his belt and let his thumb run over the rune upon its silvery surface. At his touch, the holofield disappeared, revealing the statue in all of its glory.

'I present *The Gifts of Loving Isha*,' he announced with a smile.

There were a few gasps of enjoyment and a spontaneous ripple of applause from all present. Korlandril turned to look at his creation and allowed himself to admire his work fully since its completion.

The statue was bathed in a golden glow and tinged with sunset reds and purples from the dying star above. It depicted an impressionistic Isha in abstract, her body and limbs flowing from the trunk of a lianderin tree, her wave-like tresses entwined within dark green leaves in its upreaching branches. Her face was bowed, hidden in the shadow cast by tree and hair. From the darkness a slow trickle of silver liquid spilled from her eyes into a golden cup held aloft by an ancient eldar warrior kneeling at her feet: Eldanesh. Light glittered from the chalice on his alabaster face, his armour a stylised arrangement of organic geometry, his face blank except for a slender nose and the merest depression of eye sockets. From beneath him, a black-petalled rose coiled up Isha's legs and connected the two together in its thorny embrace.

It was – Korlandril believed – breathtaking.

Most of the guests moved forward to examine the piece more closely, while Kirandrin and a few others surrounded Korlandril, offering praise and congratulations. Amongst them was Abrahasil, who must have remained out of sight during Korlandril's address. Mentor and student embraced warmly.

'You have nurtured a fine talent,' said Kirandrin. 'It is a masterly work, and one that graces the dome with its existence.'

'It is my privilege to guide such a hand in its work,' said Abrahasil. 'I am very proud of Korlandril.'

His mentor's words brought a flush of happiness to Korlandril and a concomitant throb from his waystone, and he accepted the plaudits of his peers with a gracious bow.

'If my hands have created wonders, it is because others have opened my eyes to see them,' he said. 'Please excuse me. I must attend to my other guests. I am sure we will have many cycles to further discuss my work.'

Receiving smiles of assent, Korlandril sought out Aradryan and Thirianna. They were stood side-by-side in a knot of eldar admiring the statue from a short distance away, the majestic Isha towering above them.

'She is so serene,' Thirianna was saying. 'Such calm and beauty.'

Aradryan made a small gesture of dissent and Korlandril stopped, staying a little distance away from the pair to listen to what they said.

'It is self-referential,' Aradryan explained and at his words the serpent within Korlandril coiled around his heart and gripped it tight. 'It is a work of remarkable skill and delicacy, certainly. Yet I find it somewhat… staid. It adds nothing to my experience of the myth, merely represents physically something that is felt. It is a metaphor in its most direct form. Beautiful, but merely reflecting back upon its maker rather than a wider truth.'

'But is not that the point of art, to create representations for those thoughts, memories and emotions that cannot be conveyed directly?'

'Perhaps I am being unfair,' said Aradryan. 'Out in the stars, I have seen such wondrous creations of nature that the artifices of mortals seem petty, even those that explore such momentous themes such as this.'

'Staid?' snapped Korlandril, stepping forward. 'Self-referential?'

Thirianna looked in horror at Korlandril's appearance, but Aradryan seemed unperturbed.

'My words were not intended to cause offence, Korlandril,' he said, offering a placating palm. 'They are but my opinion, and an ill-educated one at that. Perhaps you find my sentimentality gauche.'

In the face of such honesty and self-deprecation, Korlandril's anger wavered. A rare moment of humility fluttered in his breast, but then the serpent tightened its coils and the sensation disappeared.

'You are right to think your opinion ill-informed,' said Korlandril, his words as venomous as the snake laying siege to his heart. 'While you gazed naively at glittering stars and swirling nebulae, I studied the works of Aethyril and Ildrintharir, learnt the disciplines of ghost stone weaving and inorganic symbiosis. If you have not the wit to extract the meaning from that which I have presented to you, perhaps you should consider your words more carefully.'

'And if you have not the skill to convey your meaning from your work, perhaps you need to continue studying,' Aradryan snarled back. 'It is not from the past masters that you should learn your art, but from the heavens and your heart. Your technique is flawless, but your message is parochial. How many statues of Isha might I see if I travelled across the craftworld? A dozen? More? How many more statues of Isha exist on other craftworlds? You have taken nothing from the Path save the ability to indulge yourself in this spectacle. You have learnt nothing of yourself, of the darkness and the light that battles within you. There is intellect alone in your work, and nothing of yourself. It might be that you should expand your terms of reference.'

'What do you mean by that?'

'Get away from this place, from Alaitoc,' Aradryan said patiently, his anger dissipated by his outburst. Now he was the picture of sincerity, his hand half-reaching towards Korlandril. 'Why stifle your art by seeking inspiration only from the halls and domes you have seen since childhood? Rather than trying to look upon old sights with fresh eyes, why not turn your old eyes upon fresh sights?'

Korlandril wanted to argue, to snatch words from the air that would mock Aradryan's opinion, but just as the serpent within stifled his heart, it strangled his throat. He satisfied himself with a fierce glare at Aradryan, conveying all the contempt and anger he felt in that simple look, and stormed away through the blue grass, scattering guests in his flight.

FATE

At the start of the War in Heaven, all-seeing Asuryan asked the crone goddess Morai-heg what would be the fate of the gods. The crone told Asuryan that she would look across the tangled skein of the future to discern what would become of the gods. Long she followed the overlapping threads, following each one on its course to the ending of the universe, and yet she could find no answer for the lord of lords. All paths took the crow lady into a place of fire and death where she could not venture further. To find the answer she sought, the crone followed Khaine the bloody-handed killer who would wage war on the other gods and the mortals, and took from him a thimbleful of his fiery blood. Returning to her lair, Morai-heg set the burning blood of the war god upon her balance. Upon the other side of her scales she coiled up the thread of fate belonging to Eldanesh.

*All was equal. The crone returned to Asuryan and he
demanded the answer to his question. Morai-heg told
the lord of lords that the fate of the gods was not his
to know. The mortal Eldanesh and his people would
decide if the gods survived or not.*

ROSE-COLOURED WATER LAPPED at the white sands, each
ripple leaving a sweeping curve along the shoreline.
Korlandril followed the ebb and flow, mesmerised;
every part of his mind was directed towards
memorising every sparkle, every splash, every grain.
Sunwings flashed above the waters, darts of yellow
skimming the surface, bobbing and weaving around
each other. Korlandril absorbed every flight path,
every dipped wing, every extended feather and
snapping blue beak.

A sound disturbed his concentration. A voice. He
allowed part of his consciousness to depart the scene
and recall what had been said. He remembered
himself at the same time, sitting crossed-legged on
the golden grass of the lawns in the Gardens of
Tranquil Reflection, listening to his companion.

'I am leaving Alaitoc,' Aradryan said.

Shocked, Korlandril turned all of his attention
upon his friend; sea, sand, sunwings all put aside in
a moment. Aradryan was sat just an arm's length
away from Korlandril, lounging on the grass in a
loose-fitting robe of jade green. He lay on his back,
arms behind his head, while his bare toes, seeming
possessed of a life of their own, drew circular designs
in the air just out of reach of the lake's pale waters.

'You are leaving Alaitoc?' said Korlandril. 'Whatever for?'

'To become a steersman,' replied Aradryan. He did not look at Korlandril, his gaze directed over the waters to the shining silver towers of their homes, and beyond even that, to some vista that only he could see. 'It is time that I moved onwards. I am filled with a curiosity that Alaitoc cannot satisfy. It is like a hunger growing within me, that no sight or sound of this place can sate. I have taken my fill of Alaitoc, and many splendid feasts she has offered me, but I find my plate now empty. I wish to go further than the force shields and domes that have protected me. I feel coddled not safe, stifled not enriched.'

'How soon will you leave?' said Korlandril, standing up.

'Soon,' said Aradryan, his eyes still distant. '*Lacontiran* leaves for the Endless Valley in two cycles' time.'

'*Lacontiran* will be gone for more than twenty passes,' said Korlandril, alarmed. 'Why must you leave for so long?'

'She sails on her own, far from Alaitoc,' replied Aradryan. 'I wish for solitude so that I might reflect on my choices so far, and perhaps divine something of where I should head next.'

'What of our friendship? I am at a loss without your companionship,' said Korlandril, crouching beside Aradryan, an imploring hand reaching out. 'You know that I would be adrift without you to steer me.'

'You will need to find another to guide you,' Aradryan said softly. 'My mind wanders all of the time. I cannot be trusted to watch over you while you dream any more. I cannot walk the Path of

Dreaming with you any longer. I am tired of living within myself.'

Korlandril could say nothing, lost as he was in his thoughts. As he dreamt, as he wandered the paths of his subconscious, it was Aradryan that provided his anchor; a reassuring presence at the edge of his mind, a warmth to which he could return when he came upon the chill and dark places in the corners of his spirit.

'You will find another dream-watcher,' Aradryan assured him, noticing his distress. He stood and took Korlandril's arm, pulling him upright. Now he directed his eyes upon his friend, filled with concern. 'Perhaps Thirianna will join you on the Path of Dreaming?'

'Thirianna the Warrior?' replied Korlandril, aghast at the thought.

'I spoke to her yesterday,' said Aradryan. 'She feels the time is approaching when she will change Paths. You should speak to her.'

A gentle chime broke Korlandril's reverie and he opened his eyes to see a winding road of silver far below him, cutting through gently sculpted terraces. The softest of breezes brushed across his skin and teased his hair. For a moment he thought he was floating far above the landscape. Sliding completely from memedream to reality, he recognised himself on the balcony outside his chambers, bathed in the dying glow of a constructed twilight. He was leaning on a fluted balustrade, looking down at the vineyards that surrounded the Tower of Starlight Majesty.

It took him a little longer to fully recover his bodily control; blinking rapidly, stretching his limbs, quickening his pulse to ease blood back into numbed fingers and toes. He felt a lingering stiffness and wondered how long he had spent exploring his memories, walking back along the Path of Dreaming. He felt an edge of thirst and licked his lips instinctively though there was no moisture in his mouth.

Recalling the alert chime that had roused him, Korlandril turned slowly and reached out his fingertips to a grey, slate-like panel on the wall beside the archway that led into his home. At the moment of contact with the chill slab he felt the presence of Abrahasil outside his chambers and with a brief psychic impulse bid him to enter.

Breaking contact with the infinity link, Korlandril stepped into the shadowy lounge area inside the archway. It was very much like being inside an egg. The wall was a bluish-white, gently speckled with pale green. Curving couches with high backs were arranged facing the centre of the room, and under his feet he felt the thick ply of a heavily woven mat. Sculptures, by Korlandril's hand and others, stood on plinths around the wall. As he looked at each in turn Korlandril felt a flicker of recognition, his mind still tied to the processes of his memedreaming: memories of how they were made or acquired; of conversations concerning them; of moods he had felt whilst looking at them. As each thought bobbed to the surface of his mind he pushed them back, away from direct contemplation. Moving to another infinity terminal, he thought the lights into a soft blue and raised the temperature a little; he felt strangely chilled.

'Perhaps some clothes would warm you quicker,' said Abrahasil, entering the room through the arch from the main foyer.

It was only Abrahasil's observation that allowed Korlandril to realise that he was naked. His nudity caused him no self-consciousness; in his current state of internal awareness – or rather his utter lack of it – such thoughts were impossible.

'Yes, that would probably be for the best,' said Korlandril with a nod. He gestured through another arch to the dining area. 'Please take whatever refreshments you desire, I shall return swiftly.'

Korlandril strode into his robing chamber, still somewhat out-of-synch with himself following his long dreaming. He absent-mindedly touched a hand to a panel on the wall. A door slid aside, revealing a wide selection of attire, from skin-tight bodysuits with glittering metallic sheens to voluminous shirts and long gowns. Korlandril chose a green robe, tight at the waist and flared at the shoulders. He selected a broad belt without thought, his aesthetic instinct guiding his hands to a choice that matched his robe. As he cinched it around his waist, he walked barefoot across the rugs of the lounge area and joined Abrahasil in the dining quarters.

'Six cycles,' Abrahasil said as Korlandril entered. The room was dominated by a long, narrow table extruding from one wall, between eight single-legged stools in a row on either side. Abrahasil sat at the far end. Korlandril saw that he had taken nothing to eat or drink.

'Six cycles of what?' asked Korlandril, opening a crystal-windowed cabinet door. From within he pulled out a blue bottle and two silvered goblets.

'No drink for me, thank you,' said Abrahasil. Korlandril brought both cups to the table nonetheless, in case his mentor had a change of mind. He poured himself a generous helping of icevine juice, keenly aware of the dryness of his mouth and throat.

'Six cycles have passed since the unveiling,' Abrahasil explained. 'I was worried. You left in a hurry. Thirianna explained that you had a disagreement with Aradryan.'

Korlandril sipped his drink, his thoughts of Aradryan fixed on distant memory, another part of him savouring the taste of the icevine with its immediate tang and warm afterglow, while yet another part of his consciousness watched Abrahasil carefully. Korlandril shifted the focus of his memory, replaying events from when Aradryan had returned, reminding himself of what had occurred. After remembering the argument, Korlandril felt the serpent in his gut writhing with anger, hissing and spitting at Aradryan's words.

'Calm yourself!' warned Abrahasil.

'It was to calm myself that I went into my dreams,' Korlandril replied with annoyance. 'Dreams you have disrupted.'

'Six cycles is too long to wander in your mind,' said Abrahasil. 'It is dangerous to indulge in such self-contemplation when treading the Path of the Artist. It can lead to clashes within your spirit – over-analysis of self, confliction between real observation and imagined memory. I have told you this before.'

'I could not think of any other means to hold back the pain, except to return to those times with Aradryan that were more pleasant.'

'You are an artist now, you must express your thoughts, not conceal them!' said Abrahasil. He leaned along the table and poured himself a drink. 'What is the point of creating such great works as you are capable of if you are not going to learn the lessons that underpin them. The Path of the Artist is not about painting or sculpting, it is about controlling your means of expression, of filtering your influences and observations so that you can avoid falling prey to unfortunate stimuli. This argument with Aradryan is a fine example of what you must learn to deal with. You cannot just wander into your dreams and forget the real universe.'

'You think I am juvenile?' said Korlandril, dispensing with all memories of Aradryan as he finished the cup of icevine juice.

'Not juvenile, just rash,' said Abrahasil. 'I have not trod the Path of Dreaming, so I do not know what solace it brings to you. I know that in retreating from your observations you are stepping back from the Path of the Artist. That cannot be healthy by any consideration.'

Korlandril contemplated Abrahasil's warning as he poured himself more drink. The agitated snake within writhed and clamoured for Korlandril's attention and he washed away its nagging with more icevine, for a moment tuning every fibre of his spirit towards savouring the drink, driving away his darker thoughts with a tide of stimuli.

'I need to engage myself in another work,' said Korlandril. 'If I must expunge these feelings with expression, it is best that I not allow myself to dwell on them for long.'

'That would be good,' said Abrahasil.

'I should seek out Aradryan, and listen to him so that I might extract what it is that continues to plague me about his presence.'

'Be careful, Korlandril,' said the mentor. 'You may find Aradryan in an uncertain state, a destabilising influence on your psyche. I sense that you are at a critical stage upon the Path of the Artist. It is my joy to guide you further, but these next steps must be taken with caution. You are on the cusp of realising the full potential of expression, but you must choose wisely those emotions you choose to put on display.'

Korlandril smiled, calmed by Abrahasil's gentle tone. A surety settled in his mind, as if a light had sprung into life to show him the way forward. Under the glare of that light, the devious serpent of his jealousy shrank back into the shadows, cowed for the time being.

Now fully recovered from his dreaming session, Korlandril was filled with purpose once more, his thoughts fixed firmly upon what was to be, the past hidden away where it could do no more damage. Choosing to forget his disagreement with Aradryan, Korlandril lingered for a moment on the happier memories and then allowed those to drift into shadow as well, leaving him nothing but the present and the future.

KORLANDRIL TOOK A skyrunner across the dome, delighting in the rush of air against his skin, the flash of terrace and tree beneath the one-pilot craft as it soared upon the winds, its wings angling and curving in tune with his thoughts. For a short while he allowed himself free rein, forgetting his intent to see Aradryan. Powered by his psychic urging, the dart-like vehicle climbed rapidly, wings tilted back, Korlandril laughing with exhilaration. In his mind his path sculpted a complex web of interleaving arcs and loops and the skyrunner responded, twirling and swooping at his whim.

As the sensation receded and he returned the skyrunner to a stable flight, Korlandril captured the essence of his experience and stored it away. He briefly imagined creating a work of art out of air and fluid, a piece of constant motion illuminated from within, held in slowly uncoiling stasis.

Thinking of his art brought Korlandril back to his current errand. The thoughtwave sculpture was a fine idea, but it could wait. He needed to unburden his spirit of the passion roused by Aradryan's return, and so he angled the skyrunner down towards the silver ribbon of the road, swerving down between the red-leafed icevines on the terraces, darting beneath other craft that zipped to and fro across the dome's artificial sky.

Anticipation grew within Korlandril as he sped through the connecting hub between the Dome of New Suns and out into the Avenue of Starlight Secrets. Here there was more traffic. It was one of the main thoroughfares of Alaitoc where hundreds of eldar moved between the many domes and plateaus that made up the bulk of the craftworld. Some strolled languidly by themselves or with friends, others on skyrunners like Korlandril, many on drifting platforms that eased serenely from one place to the next guided by the group desires of those on board.

Korlandril allowed himself a little amazement at the scene. Rather, not at the scene itself, but at Aradryan's incomprehension of the inherent beauty and intricacy of the craftworld. Aradryan did not look upon the same things as Korlandril with the eyes of the artist, and so perhaps missed the precision of geometry at subtle odds with the inherent anarchy of a living system. He had not developed the senses to appreciate the cadence of life, the ebb and flow of the living and the immaterial and those things that lay in-between.

A hope sprang to mind and Korlandril studied it for a moment, slowing the skyrunner slightly so that its navigation demanded less of his attention. It occurred to the sculptor that he might persuade Aradryan to join him on the Path of the Artist. If Aradryan sought new vistas of experience, then none compared with opening up one's mind to every sensation without hindrance. It bordered on intoxication for Korlandril, and the thought of sharing such delights with Aradryan filled him with energy.

Engines pitching to a constant note that sang in Korlandril's heart, the skyrunner sped onwards. Veering left, Korlandril cut into the Midnight Dome, plunging into near-blackness. His eyes immediately adjusted to the lack of light, seeing shades of dark purple and blue amongst the deep grey. The laughter of lovers lilted above the song of the skyrunner but he ignored them, fearing that to contemplate their meaning would lead him towards thoughts of Thirianna; thoughts he did not want to explore at that moment. He allowed the whisper of the wind to carry away the treacherous sound and instead dwelt on the sensation of motion and the blur of dark trees washing past.

Exiting the Midnight Dome into the twilight of the Dome of Sighing Whispers, Korlandril slowed once more, the engine of the skyrunner falling to a pleasant hum. In respectful quiet he skimmed between the columns that soared up towards the dome roof. While he banked left and right without effort, he pondered how he might broach the subject of Aradryan joining him as an artist.

Slowing further still, Korlandril allowed the skyrunner to drop to ground level and swerved down a tunnelway that led deeper into Alaitoc. Here all pretence of the natural was set aside as he followed the long passage that led towards the docking towers. Oval in cross-section, the tunnel glowed with a warm orange light, flutters of energy pulsing along infinity circuit conduits embedded within the material of the wall. Korlandril felt their ghostly presence all around him as he dived deeper into the craft-world's interior, the psychic energy of the craftworld's spirits merging and dividing around him, whispering at his subconscious.

It was with some relief that Korlandril exited the passageway into the Tower of Infinite Patience, where Aradryan had taken quarters since his return. Leaving behind the psychic susurrance of the infinity circuit, Korlandril brought the skyrunner to a halt not far from a spiralling ramp that led up into the tower.

Dismounting, he allowed the craft to slip away towards an empty mooring niche and with considerable effort focussed on himself. He smoothed crumples in his robe and adjusted his belt, and with a flick of his fingers tamed his wind-tossed hair into something less unruly. Satisfied that he was presentable, he ascended the tower ramp, his long legs carrying him swiftly up to the eighth storey, momentarily revelling in the physical effort after so much recent inactivity.

Finding the Opal Suites, Korlandril touched the infinity plate to announce his presence. He waited for a moment and no response came. Allowing his fingers to linger longer on the psychically conductive slate, he sought for the presence of Aradryan but could not detect it. Only a residual impression of Aradryan remained in this place.

Adjusting his thoughts, Korlandril found that the adjoining apartment was occupied and he made an inquiry to the eldar within. She appeared at the arch-way a little later. She was of considerable antiquity, surrounded by an aura of wisdom and solemnity. From the brief contact he had shared with her on the infinity circuit, he knew that she was Herisianith, a shuttle pilot.

'How might I help you, Korlandril?' she asked, leaning a shoulder against the archway. Her eyes roved quickly up and down Korlandril, looking at him the same way he looked at others. At some point in her long life, Herisianith had been an artist.

'I am seeking my friend, your neighbour, Aradryan,' said Korlandril. 'He came back aboard *Lacontiran* nine cycles ago.'

'Your *friend* has not returned in two cycles,' Herisianith told him. Korlandril did not know why she had used the past-sarcastic form of 'friend', though perhaps she had seen some tiny reflection of doubt in his manner. 'He departed with a companion, Thirianna. Since then I have not seen him or felt him.'

'Did you have any sense of where they were going?'

Herisianith flicked a finger in dismissal, her turn of wrist indicating that she considered such inquiry importune. Not wishing to impose upon her longer, Korlandril gave a nod of departing and turned away. He walked slowly down the ramp, wondering what could have occupied Aradryan for two cycles. Had he spent all of that time with Thirianna?

Korlandril was drawn into a memedream, a small part of his mind guiding his body to a curving bench not far from Aradryan's quarters while the waking vision occupied the rest of his thoughts. His waystone throbbed dully, but he ignored its nagging and delved deeper into the dream.

Sineflower perfume mingled with merecherry blossom. Chatter and laughter. Thirianna standing next to her father, resplendent in a long dress of gold and black, her bronze hair caught up in a floating net of sapphire-blue air-jewels. Her eyes were green with flecks of gold and fell upon Korlandril as soon as he entered the domed chamber. Korlandril felt the warmth of Aradryan by his side: physically and emotionally. His friend had been correct, the daughter of Wishseer Aurentiun was beautiful, a radiant star in a galaxy of light.

Aradryan introduced them. Thirianna smiled and Korlandril melted under her gaze. She complimented him on his moontiger patterned cloak. He muttered a reply, something stupid he had chosen to forget. They danced, exchanging partners, to the skirl of Aradryan's scythe-harp. Korlandril played his light-flute, dazzling the party with the sound and colours conjured by his nimble fingers and playful mind.

A hot cycle followed, the three of them enjoying the artificial sun and lilac beaches of the Dome of Rising Hope. Korlandril revelled in their innocence, reliving the unabashed joy they had shared. Each of them musicians, delighting and teasing each other with their melodies, coming together upon the rhythm of their thoughts and feelings.

The serpent intruded once more, tearing Korlandril from his reverie. Had Thirianna and Aradryan ever been more than just good companions? Quivering slightly from the shock of departing the memedream so suddenly, Korlandril reapplied himself to his current purpose. It would be easier to find Thirianna than Aradryan, and if his wayward friend was not actually with her she might have some better idea where he might be found.

Korlandril found an infinity terminal in a small grove of whisperleaf not far from the apartments. He made a gentle inquiry, seeking Thirianna. She had been on the craftworld longer than Aradryan and her presence in the psychic matrix that powered Alaitoc was stronger. Korlandril concentrated on Thirianna and felt the after-shadow of her spirit moving around the craftworld over the previous two cycles: here, where she met Aradryan, his spirit also registering strongly; the Boulevard of Split Moons, along the arcades of the fashion-sellers and jewelsmiths;

her own quarters – alone, Korlandril noted with some satisfaction – for half a cycle; then to the Bay of Departing Sorrows, where Aradryan was present again, his presence lingering alongside hers for just the shortest time. Now she was back in her quarters, silent, perhaps meditating or composing.

Korlandril voiced thoughts of companionship and directed them towards Thirianna. He waited for her to respond. He allowed the background vibrations of the infinity circuit to occupy him: celebration in the Dome of the Last Sunrise, a disturbing darkness emanating from the Shrine of the Ending Veil.

At this Korlandril withdrew, repelled by the taste left in his mouth from the Aspect Warrior shrine. He had little to do with warmakers, but the Ending Veil was home to one of the Dark Reaper sects; his friends Arthuis and Maerthuin counted amongst their number. He did not pay much attention to military matters, finding it a disagreeable influence on his creations. There was no place for bloody-handed Kaela Mensha Khaine in his work. That his friends might be involved did interest him and he passed on his observations to the dormant Thirianna.

She roused almost immediately, sending him a vision of his Isha statue. The scene was an imagination of the two of them standing beneath it: an invitation. Korlandril reflected the vision back to Thirianna, with a slight adjustment. The night shields were active, dimming the light of the dying star to the twilight of early evening. Thirianna responded in kind and the rendezvous was agreed.

Korlandril broke from the infinity circuit, satisfied with himself. He returned to the Opal Suites and took another skyrunner back to his chambers. His exuberance was muted on his return journey, the lack of Aradryan's touch upon the infinity circuit preying on his thoughts.

THIRIANNA WAS AT the statue, sitting at one end of a curving bench, her eyes directed to the dim glow beyond the dome. Korlandril crossed the grass quickly and Thirianna turned at his approach, a smile hovering on her lips for just a moment.

'Aradryan has left Alaitoc,' Thirianna said quietly when Korlandril was seated beside her.

Korlandril was taken aback and it took him a moment to readjust his thoughts; he had been ready to open the conversation with an inquiry about Thirianna's wellbeing. A flurry of emotions warred within Korlandril: shock, disappointment and, worryingly, a small degree of satisfaction.

'I do not understand,' said the sculptor. 'I know that we had a disagreement, but I thought that he planned to remain on Alaitoc for some time yet.'

'He did not depart on your account,' said Thirianna, though an unconscious asymmetric blink betrayed conflict in her thoughts. She was not lying, but neither was she wholly convinced that she spoke the truth.

'Why would he not come to see me before he left?' Korlandril asked. 'It is obvious that some distance had grown between us, but I did not think his opinion of me had sunk so low.'

'It was not you,' Thirianna said, her tone and half-closed eyes indicating that she believed it was her fault their friend had fled the craftworld.

'What happened?' asked Korlandril, trying hard to keep any tone of accusation from his voice. 'When did Aradryan leave?'

'He took aboard *Irdiris* last cycle, after we spent some time together.'

Korlandril had heard the name of the ship in passing but could not place it immediately. Thirianna read the look of questioning on his face.

'*Irdiris* is a far-runner, destined for the Exodites on Elan-Shemaresh and then to the Wintervoid of Meios,' she explained.

'Aradryan wishes to become a... *ranger*?' Incredulity and distaste vied with each other in Korlandril's thoughts. He stroked his bottom lip with a slender finger, stilling his thoughts. 'I had no idea he was so dissatisfied with Alaitoc.'

'Neither did I, and perhaps that is why he left so soon,' confessed Thirianna. 'I believe I spoke hastily and with insensitivity and drove him to a swifter departure than he might otherwise have considered.'

'I am sure that you are no–' began Korlandril but Thirianna cut him off with an agitated twitch of her finger.

'I do not wish to speak of it,' was all the explanation she would offer.

That sat in silence for a while longer, while littlewings darted amongst the branches of the trees above them, trilling to one another. Deep within the woods a breezemaker stirred into life and the leaves began to rustle gently: a calming backdrop.

'There was something else about which I wish to speak to you,' said Korlandril, having put aside his thoughts on Aradryan. 'I have a proposal to make.'

Interest flared in Thirianna's jade eyes. She indicated with a raising of her chin that they should stand.

'We should discuss this in my chambers, with something to drink, perhaps?'

'That would be most agreeable,' said Korlandril as the two them made their way towards the dome entrance.

Neither spoke as they crossed the dome. They walked a little way apart, the distance a compromise between companionship and decency. Korlandril's heart beat a little bit faster than usual. He tried to contend with a mounting excitement, having not expected such an accommodating response from Thirianna.

It took some time to reach the dome entrance on foot and the night cycle was midway through when they came upon the silvered archway that led into the main thoroughfare around the rim of the craftworld. Here twilight was also in effect, the darkness broken only by a faint red reflection from the dying star and the will-o'-the-wisps of the infinity circuit around them.

The wide passage was quiet; they passed perhaps a dozen other eldar before they reached the turning towards Thirianna's apartments. She had taken up rooms in a poet's commune in the Tower of Dormant Witnesses. It was a place noted for its contemplative atmosphere, with views out to the stars and back across the whole of Alaitoc.

They were about to step onto the sliding walkway up to the towers when a large group appeared from the gloom ahead. Sensing something dark,

Thirianna strayed closer to Korlandril, who put a protective hand upon her shoulder even as his own mood dropped, filled with foreboding.

The group were Aspect Warriors, and an aura of death hung about them as palpable as a stench. They were clad in plates of overlapping armour of purple and black, their heavy tread thunderous in the still twilight. Korlandril could feel their menace growing stronger as they approached, waystones glowing like eyes of blood. They had taken off their war-helms and carried them hooked upon their belts, leaving their hands free to carry slender missile launchers.

Dark Reapers: possessed of the War God in his Aspect of Destroyer.

Though their helmets were removed, they still bore the rune of the Dark Reaper painted in blood upon their faces. Thirianna and Korlandril shrank closer to the edge of the passageway as the Aspect Warriors passed, seeking the faces of their friends. Korlandril realised he had inadvertently pulled Thirianna in front of him a little and the realisation brought a small wound to his pride. For her part, Thirianna was calm but apprehensive. Korlandril could feel her trembling under his palm. It was not fear, it was something thrilling. She had walked the Path of the Warrior, did Khaine even now call out to her? Did the presence of the Aspect Warriors resonate with some part of her buried beneath the layers of civilisation the eldar worked so hard to maintain?

Thirianna pointed, directing Korlandril's attention to Maerthuin. Arthuis walked a little way behind. The brothers stopped and turned their eyes upon

Thirianna and Korlandril. Their gazes were empty, devoid of anything but the remotest recognition. Korlandril repressed a shudder as he smelt the blood upon their faces.

'You are well?' asked Thirianna, her voice quiet and respectful.

Arthuis nodded slowly.

'Victory was ours,' intoned Maerthuin.

'We will meet you at the Crescent of the Dawning Ages,' said Arthuis.

'At the start of the next cycle,' added Maerthuin.

Korlandril and Thirianna both nodded their agreement and the two warriors moved on. Thirianna relaxed and Korlandril gave a sigh of relief, glad to be free of their friends' blank yet strangely penetrating gazes.

'It is inconceivable to me that one should indulge in such horror,' said Korlandril as the two of them stepped upon the moving walkway, still feeling a small aftercurrent of fear from the encounter.

They made a spiralling ascent, languidly turning upon itself as the sliding ramp rose around the Tower of Dormant Witnesses. Korlandril felt a thrill as they emerged into the starlight-bathed sky, nothing more between him and the void than an invisible shield of energy. For a moment he thought he understood something of the lure of the stars that so enamoured Aradryan.

'It is not an indulgence,' said Thirianna.

'What is not an indulgence?'

'The Path of the Warrior is not an indulgence,' she repeated. 'One cannot simply leave anger in the darkness, to fester and grow unseen. Sooner or later it might find vent.'

'What is there to be so angry about?' laughed Korlandril. 'Perhaps if we were Biel-Tan, with all their talk of reclaiming the old empire, then we might have a use for all of this sword-waving and gunfire. It is an uncivilised way to behave.'

'You ignore the passions that rule you,' snapped Thirianna.

Korlandril felt a spear of guilt and embarrassment.

'I meant no offence,' he said.

'The intention is not important,' said Thirianna, her eyes narrowed, lips thin. 'Perhaps you would care to ridicule the other Paths on which I have trodden?'

'I did not mean...' Korlandril trailed off, unsure what he did actually mean, his glibness burned away by Thirianna's sudden scorn. 'I am sorry.'

'The Path of Dreaming, the Path of Awakening, the Path of the Artist,' said Thirianna. 'Always self-indulgent, always about your needs, no sense of duty or dedication to others.'

Korlandril shrugged, a fulsome gesture employing the full use of both arms.

'I simply do not understand this desire some of us feel to sate a bloodlust I do not feel,' he said.

'And that is what is dangerous about you,' said Thirianna. 'Where do you put that rage you feel when someone angers you? What do you do with the hatred that burns inside when you think upon all that we have lost? You have not learnt to control these feelings, merely ignore them. Becoming one with Khaine, assuming one of His Aspects is not about confronting an enemy, it is about confronting ourselves. We should all do it at some time in our lives.'

Korlandril shook his head.

'Only those that desire war, make it,' he said.

'Findrueir's *Prophecies of Interrogation*,' said Thirianna, lips twisted in a sneer, brow furrowed. 'Yes, I've read it too, do not look so surprised. However, I read it after treading the Path of the Warrior. An aesthete who wrote about matters she had never experienced. Hypocrisy at its worst.'

'And also one of Iyanden's foremost philosophers.'

'A radical windbag with no true cause and a gyrinx fetish.'

Korlandril laughed and received a frown in reply.

'Forgive me,' he said. 'I hope that is not an example of your poetry!'

Thirianna vacillated between annoyance and humour before breaking into a smile.

'Listen to us! Gallery philosophers, the pair! What do we know?'

'Little enough,' agreed Korlandril with a nod. 'And I suppose that can be a dangerous thing.'

KORLANDRIL STOOD ATTENTIVELY beside Thirianna while she mixed her preferred cocktail of juices and ground ice. She passed a slender glass to Korlandril and waved him towards one of the cushions that served as seats in her reception chamber. She had rearranged and recoloured her rooms since Korlandril had last visited. Gone was the holographic representation of Illuduran's *Monument to the Glories of Impudence* and the pastel blue scheme. All was white and light grey, with only the hard cushions as furniture. Korlandril looked pointedly around the room.

'It's a trifle post-Herethiun minimalist, is it not?' he said, reclining as best he could.

'You had a proposal?' said Thirianna, ignoring the implied accusation.

Korlandril hesitated. The mood did not feel right. Though they had made up their differences before arriving at the chambers, the comfort he had shared with Thirianna in the garden dome had all but gone. He needed her to be receptive to his idea. He would start by finding some common ground: Aradryan's departure.

'I am sorry that Aradryan has left us again,' he said, meaning it sincerely. 'I had hoped that I could have persuaded him to join me on the Path of the Artist. Perhaps we might have rekindled something of what we shared on the Path of Dreaming.'

Thirianna gave a flick of her hair, a momentary gesture of annoyance.

'What is so wrong with that?' Korlandril asked.

'It was not for Aradryan's benefit that you wished,' said Thirianna, sitting opposite the sculptor. 'As ever, it was because *you* want him to become an artist, not because it would be the best thing for him.'

'He is directionless and lonely,' argued Korlandril. 'I thought that if he could learn to see the universe as I do, with the eyes of the Artist, he might learn to appreciate what the craftworld has to offer him.'

'You are still annoyed that he didn't like your sculpture!' Thirianna was half-amused and half-scornful. She sighed in exasperation. 'You think that if he learnt to 'see' things the proper way he would appreciate your genius all the better. You think his criticisms are invalid simply because he has not shared the same education as you.'

'Perhaps that is the case,' Korlandril said in a conciliatory tone, realising he had chosen the wrong tack. 'I do not want us to be divided by Aradryan's absence. He will return one day, of that I am sure. We have both coped without him, and we will do so again. If we stay close to each other, that is.'

'Your friendship has been important to me,' said Thirianna, warming Korlandril's hopes. He pressed on.

'I have a new piece of sculpture in mind, something very different from my previous works,' he announced.

'That is good to hear. I think that if you can find something to occupy your mind, you will dwell less on the situation with Aradryan.'

'Yes, that is very true! I'm going to delve into portraiture. A sculptural testament to devotion, in fact.'

'Sounds intriguing,' said Thirianna. 'Perhaps something a little more grounded in reality would be good for your development.'

'Let us not get too carried away,' said Korlandril with a smile. 'I think there may be some abstract elements incorporated into the design. After all, how does one truly replicate love and companionship in features alone?'

'I am surprised. I understand if you do not wish to tell me, but what inspires such a piece of work?'

Korlandril thought she was being coy for a moment, but a quick reading of her expression confirmed that she had not the slightest idea that she was to be the subject. That serpent in Korlandril's gut, hissing with annoyance, uncoiled itself. What had been the point of all of his overtures? He had not been obvious in his affections, but neither had he been too subtle in his intent. Was she playing some game with him, wanting him to say aloud what they both understood to be true?

'You are my inspiration,' Korlandril said quietly, eyes fixed on Thirianna. 'It is you that I wish to fashion as a likeness of dedication and ardour.'

Thirianna blinked, and then blinked again. Her eyebrows rose in shock.

'I… You…' She looked away. 'I do not think that is warranted.'

'Warranted? It is an expression of my feelings, there is nothing that needs warranting other than to visualise my desires and dreams. You are my desire and a dream.'

Thirianna did not reply. She stood and took a couple of paces away before turning to face Korlandril, her face serious.

'This is not a good idea, my friend,' she said gently. 'I do appreciate the sentiment, and perhaps some time ago I would not only be flattered but I would be delighted.'

The serpent sank its fangs into Korlandril's heart.

'But not now?' he asked, hesitant, scared of the answer.

She shook her head.

'Aradryan's arrival and departure have made me realise something that has been amiss with my life for several passes now,' she said. Korlandril reached out a hand in a half-hearted gesture, beckoning her to come closer. Thirianna sat next to him and took his hand in hers. 'I am changing again. The Path of the Poet is spent for me. I have grieved and I have rejoiced through my verse, and I feel expunged of the burdens I felt. I feel another calling is growing inside me.'

Korlandril snatched his hand away.

'You are going to join Aradryan!' he snapped. 'I knew the two of you were keeping something from me.'

'Don't be ridiculous,' Thirianna rasped in return. 'It is because I told him what I am telling you that he left.'

'So, he did make advances on you!' Korlandril stood and angrily wiped a hand across his brow and pointed accusingly at his friend. 'It is true! Deny it if you dare!'

She slapped away his hand.

'What right do you have to make any claim on me? If you must know, I have never entertained any thoughts of being with Aradryan, even before he left, and certainly not since his return. I am simply not ready for a life-companion. In fact, that is why I cannot be your inspiration.'

Thirianna took a step closer, hands open in friendship.

'It is to save you from a future heartache that I decline your attentions now,' she continued. 'I have spoken to Farseer Alaiteir and he agrees that I am ready to begin the Path of the Seer.'

'A seer?' scoffed Korlandril. 'You completely fail to divine my romantic intents and yet think you might become a seer?'

'I divined your intent and ignored it,' said Thirianna, laying a hand on his arm. 'I did not wish to encourage you; to admit your feelings for me would be to bring them to the light and that was something I wished to avoid, for the sake of both of us.'

Korlandril waved away her arguments, pulling his arm from her grasp.

'If you have not the same feelings for me, then simply say so. Do not spare my pride for your comfort. Do not hide behind this excuse of changing Paths.'

'It is true, it is not an excuse! You love Thirianna the Poet. We are alike enough at the moment, our Paths different yet moving in the same general direction. When I become a Seer, I will not be Thirianna the Poet. You will not love that person.'

'Why deny me the right to find out? Who are you to judge what will or will not be? You are not even on the Path and now you think you can claim the powers of the Seer?'

'If it is true that you feel the same when I have become a Seer, and I feel the same too, then whatever will happen will come to pass.'

Korlandril caught an angry reply before it emerged, his mind catching up with Thirianna's words. Hope blossomed, bright flowers stifling the angry serpent.

'If you feel the same? You admit that you have feelings for me.'

'Thirianna the Poet has feelings for you, she always has,' Thirianna admitted.

'Then why do we not embrace this shared feeling?' Korlandril asked, stepping forward and taking

Thirianna's hands in his. Now it was her turn to pull away. She could not bring herself to look at him when she spoke.

'If I indulge this passion with you, it would hold me back, perhaps trap me here as the Poet, forever writing my verses of love in secret.'

'Then we stay together, Poet and Artist! What is so wrong with that?'

'It is not healthy! You know that it is unwise to become trapped in ourselves. Our lives must be in constant motion, moving from one Path to the next, developing our senses of self and the universe. To over-indulge leads to the darkness that came before. It attracts the attention of… Her. She Who Thirsts.'

Korlandril shuddered at the mention of the Eldar's Bane, even by euphemism. His waystone quivered with him, becoming chill to the touch. All that Thirianna said was true, enshrined in the teachings of the craftworlds; the whole structure of their society created to avoid a return to the debauchery and excesses that led to the Fall.

But Korlandril did not care. It was stupid that he and Thirianna should be denied their happiness.

'What we feel is not *wrong*! Since the founding of the craftworlds our people have loved and survived. Why should we be any different?'

'You use the same arguments as Aradryan,' Thirianna admitted, turning on Korlandril. 'He asked me to forget the Path and join him. Even if I had loved him I could not do that. I *cannot* do that with you. Though I have deep feelings for you, I would no more risk my eternal spirit for you than I would step out into the void of space and hope to breathe.'

There were tears in her eyes, kept in check until now.

'Please leave.'

Korlandril's anguish was all-consuming. Fear and wrath in equal measure tore through him, burning along his veins, churning in his mind. Dropping beneath it all was a deep pit of shadow and despair, down which he felt himself falling. Korlandril wanted to faint but held himself upright, forcing himself to breathe deeply. The serpent inside him wound itself tight around every organ and bone, crushing the life from him, filling him with a physical pain.

'I cannot help you,' Thirianna said, staring with misery at the anguish being played out in Korlandril's actions. 'I know you are in pain, but it will pass.'

'Pain?' spat Korlandril. 'What do you know of my pain?'

His whole psyche screamed in torment, honed by his practice as an Artist, thrashing for expression. There was no outlet for all of the pent-up frustration; passes upon passes of suppressing his emotions for Thirianna threatened to erupt. Korlandril was simply not mentally equipped to unleash the torrent of rage that whirled inside him. There was no dream he could go to for solace; no sculpture he could create to excise the pain; no physical sensation he could indulge to replace the agony that wracked his spirit. Incandescent, his waystone was white hot on his chest.

Violence welled up inside Korlandril. He wanted to strike Thirianna for being so selfish and shortsighted.

He wanted to draw blood, to let his pain flow out of deep wounds and wash away the anger. Most of all he wanted something else to feel the agony, to share in the devastation.

Wordless, Korlandril fled, his anger swept around by a vortex of fear at what he had unleashed within himself. He stumbled out onto the walkway and stared up into the endless heavens, tears streaming down his face, his heart thundering.

He needed help. Help to quench the fire that was now raging in his mind.

REJECTION

In the time before the War in Heaven, before even the coming of the eldar, the gods schemed their schemes and planned their plans, engaging in an eternal game of deceit and love, treachery and teasing. Kurnous, Lord of the Hunt, was the lover of Lileath of the Moon, and they enjoyed both the blessing of Almighty Asuryan and the friendship of the other gods; save for Kaela Mensha Khaine, the Bloody-Handed One, who desired Lileath for himself. He craved her not for her beauty, which was immortal, nor for her playful wit, which made friends of all the other gods. Khaine desired the Moon Goddess simply because she had chosen Kurnous. Khaine endeavoured to impress her with his martial skills, but Lileath was unimpressed. He composed odes to woo her but his poems were ever crude, filled with the desire to conquer and possess.

Lileath would not be owned by any other. Frustrated, Khaine went to Asuryan and demanded that Lileath be given to him. Asuryan told Khaine that he could not take Lileath by force, and that if he could not win her heart he could not have her. Enraged, Khaine vowed that if he could not possess Lileath then no other would. Khaine took up his sword, the Widow-maker, the Slayer of Worlds, and cut a rent in the void. He snatched up Lileath by the ankle and cast her into the rift in the stars, where her light could no longer shine. For a thousand days the heavens were dark until Kurnous, brave and resourceful, dared the blackness of the rift and rescued Lileath so that her light would return to the universe.

IT TOOK SOME time for Korlandril to restore a small measure of equilibrium. Ashamed and desperate, he hid himself amongst the trees of the Dome of Midnight Forests, no longer weeping or growling. Korlandril detached himself from his physical processes, allowing them to continue without his intervention, losing all sense of sight and touch, smell and hearing. To isolate himself in such a way was a legacy of the Path of Dreaming, shut off entirely from outside stimuli. He was locked up with his own thoughts with no distraction, but resisted the urge to plunge into a memedream and forget everything. On the Path of Awakening he had learnt to divide his attention in the opposite direction, locking away conscious thought, concentrating purely on sensation and response.

The two Paths had complemented well his choice to become an Artist, but now they left him vulnerable. His experience as an adult had been directed towards compartmentalising and controlling his interaction with the world; later, as Korlandril the Sculptor, he had been a conduit for creative expression, turning thought into deed. Now his thoughts were bleak, bloody even, and he could not express them.

Sorting through his impressions and memories, Korlandril tried to make sense of what had happened. He did not understand what had broken the emotional dam that had kept his darker feelings in check. He could not find an answer. Disturbed, he was not sure what questions needed answering. He knew that he could not let these thoughts run rampant, nor could he act upon them. That would be to embrace the mayhem and indulgence that had brought about the Fall.

Korlandril thought for a moment of finding an infinity terminal and contacting Abrahasil. He dismissed the notion. He was in no state to be interacting with the infinity circuit. His emotional instability would be sure to attract attention of the wrong kind, if it didn't do any actual harm to him or the circuit. Even if he could muster enough self-control to navigate the circuit properly, Abrahasil would not be able to help him. This was not some dilemma of form or sensation, or even one of expression. Korlandril simply could not comprehend why he had become so distressed, and why that distress was manifesting itself in such a destructive manner.

Amidst the maelstrom of his thoughts, Korlandril's attention was brought to a small matter that needed resolving. A thought-cycle demanded his attention, a future-memory yet to be experienced. Korlandril analysed it and was reminded of the appointment he had made with Arthuis and Maerthuin. He linked the reminder with a memory and cycled them together with his current feelings. He encountered a shock of recognition, drawing on what he had seen, or rather not seen, in the blank stares of his friends while they had been wearing their war-masks. The deadness that was there, an expression devoid of shock, guilt, shame or remorse.

If anybody could help him understand the turbulence that so unbalanced him now, it would be the Aspect Warriors.

THE CRESCENT OF the Dawning Ages curved out from the starward rim of Alaitoc, bathed in the glow of Mirianathir. The kilometres-long balcony was covered by an arching vault of subtly mirrored material that dimly reflected the patrons below, blending their visual simulacra with the ruddy light of the star to paint an ever-moving scene across the heavens.

The new cycle was just beginning and there were many eldar sat at the tables along the balcony or moving between them and the food bars on the inward side. They ate fruits from the orchards and breakfasted on spiced meats brought back by traders with the Exodite worlds. Drinks of all colours, some luminescent, others effervescent, were dispensed from tall, slender urns or arranged in rows of glittering bottles, regularly replenished by those walking the Path of Service. A dampening field kept the conversation quiet, though there were thousands of voices raised in greeting and debate, departure and conciliation.

One area was sparsely populated, the other eldar leaving an indistinct but noticeable gap between themselves and the patrons that sat at the long benches there. Here were the Aspect Warriors, shorn of their warpaint, together in quiet contemplation.

Korlandril approached cautiously. Even after much meditation and calming mantras, he was still jittery from his recent experience. His nervousness was not helped by the stares of the other eldar as he crossed the pale blue floor, heading towards the Aspect Warriors.

He stopped and poured himself a glass of dawn-water and leaned against the curving counter top as he scanned the assembled Aspect Warriors looking for his friends.

A hand was raised in welcome and Korlandril recognised Arthuis. On his left sat Maerthuin. Around them were several other eldar that Korlandril did not know. They sat with thin platters on their laps, picking at finger food, their voices quiet. Space was made on the bench opposite his friends and Korlandril sat down, agitated by the presence of so many warriors.

'Greetings of the new cycle to you,' said Maerthuin. 'Are you not hungry?'

'I'd skin and eat a narboar if I could,' said Arthuis. His plate was heaped with food and he broke off speaking to cram a handful of scented grains into his mouth.

'This is Elissanadrin,' said Maerthuin, indicating the female eldar sat to his left. She was perhaps eighty or ninety passes old, almost twice Korlandril's age. Her cheeks were prominent, angular, and her nose thin and pointed. When she turned and smiled at Korlandril, her movements were precise, every gesture clearly defined and a little abrupt. She paused as she sensed the identity of the newcomer.

'Pleased to make your acquaintance, Korlandril the Sculptor,' Elissanadrin said. Her tone was as clipped as her motion.

Korlandril opened a palm in greeting. Other introductions were made: Fiarithin, a male just out of puberty; Sellisarin, a tall, older eldar male; others whose names and features Korlandril stored away for future reference.

'There is something different about you, Korlandril,' said Arthuis, placing his empty plate on a shelf underneath the bench. 'I sense something aggrieves you.'

'It is hard not to feel your agitation,' added Maerthuin. 'Perhaps you are uncomfortable with your company.'

Korlandril looked around at the Aspect Warriors. On the face of it, they appeared no different to any other eldar. Without their war-masks on, they were each individual. Some were obviously distressed, others animated, most thoughtful.

'I do not wish to intrude,' said Korlandril. His eyes strayed to one of the warriors, an old female who sat weeping, comforted by her companions. 'I know that recently there was a battle.'

Arthuis followed Korlandril's gaze and shook his head disconsolately.

'Several of us were lost. We mourn their passing, but their spirits were saved,' said Elissanadrin. There were approving nods from others at the benches.

'I shall compose a verse to commemorate their time with us,' said Arthuis.

'I wept like a babe when I unmasked,' Maerthuin admitted with a lopsided smile. 'I think I shall miss Neamoriun the most. He was a good friend and a gifted singer.'

The name flickered with recognition and Korlandril remembered attending a concert in the Dome of Enchanting Echoes.

'I saw him perform,' said Korlandril, wishing to add something to the conversation. 'He sang the *Lay of Ulthanesh*.'

'That was his favourite,' Arthuis chuckled. 'It is no surprise that he joined the Fire Dragons, so full of energy and excitable of temperament.'

'It was only last pass that I saw him, I did not realise he was a Fire Dragon,' said Korlandril.

'One cannot fight all of the time,' said Maerthuin. This appeared to remind him of something and he looked at Korlandril. 'I am sorry that I missed the unveiling of your statue. I will visit it later this cycle.'

A flicker of agitation disturbed Korlandril as he recalled his memories of the event, his disagreement with Aradryan marring an otherwise perfect evening. The others sensed his disquiet.

'I was right, something is amiss,' said Arthuis. 'I cannot think that your work was anything other than spectacular.'

'I had a friend who thought otherwise.'

There were whispers of concern and Korlandril realised he had used not only the past form of friend, but one used to refer to those that were dead. It was a slip of the tongue, but betrayed something deeper. Korlandril was quick to correct himself.

'He has left Alaitoc to become a ranger,' he said, making a reassuring gesture. 'It has been difficult, I saw him only briefly. He is still with us, though I do not think our friendship has survived.'

'It is Aradryan of whom you speak?' asked Maerthuin. Korlandril nodded.

'I always thought Aradryan was a bit strange,' confided Arthuis. 'I half-expected to wake each cycle and discover that he had taken the starwalk.'

Korlandril was shocked. To suggest that another eldar would take their life was one of the crudest notions he had heard. Arthuis laughed at Korlandril's distaste.

'I know that he was your friend, but he was always far too distant,' said Arthuis. 'It does not surprise me at all that he's become a ranger. I have always sensed something of the radical about him.'

'I knew him well and sensed no such thing,' argued Korlandril.

'Sometimes the things that are closest to us are the hardest to see,' said Maerthuin. 'I can sense that you would prefer not to talk about it, so we will change the subject. How is Thirianna, I see she has not come with you?'

The glass shattered into splinters in Korlandril's hand. As one, many of the Aspect Warriors turned their attention to him, a sudden silence descending as they sensed a wave of anger flowing from the sculptor. There was concern in the eyes of several.

'Have you hurt yourself?' asked Elissanadrin, leaning forward to look at Korlandril's hand. He examined his fingers and palm and found no blood.

'I am unhurt,' he said stiffly and made to stand. Arthuis gently but insistently grabbed his wrist and pulled him back down.

'You are trembling,' said the Aspect Warrior and Korlandril realised it was true. He felt a tic under his right eye and his hands were clenched in fists.

'I am…' Korlandril began, but he could not finish the sentence. He did not know what he was. He was frustrated. He was saddened. Most of all, he was angry.

'Our friend is irritable, it would seem,' said Maerthuin. 'Is there a problem with Thirianna?'

Korlandril could not reply. Every time he turned his mind to Thirianna his thoughts folded in on themselves, sending him crashing back into the pit of anger that had swallowed him. The snake within had coiled itself through every part of his body and would not let go, no matter how hard he tried to push it back.

'It is Khaine's curse,' said Sellisarin, intrigued. He reached out a hand towards Korlandril's brow, but the sculptor pulled back.

'Don't touch me!' Korlandril snarled.

Sellisarin made soothing sounds and moved closer, meeting Korlandril's gaze.

'There is nothing to be afraid of,' said the Aspect Warrior, again reaching out his hand.

Korlandril writhed as the serpent whipped and wriggled inside, urging him to lash out. He raised his hands defensively instead, warding away Sellisarin's attention.

'Leave me in peace,' he sobbed. 'I'll… I'll deal with this in my own way.'

'You cannot find peace on your own,' said Elissanadrin, sitting next to Korlandril. 'The hand of Khaine has reached into you and awoken that which dwells within all of us. You cannot ignore this. If it does not destroy you, it could harm others.'

Korlandril looked pleadingly at Maerthuin. His friend nodded silently, affirming what Elissanadrin had said.

'This is part of you, part of every eldar,' said Arthuis. 'It is not a judgement, not something that brings you shame.'

'Why now?' moaned Korlandril. 'Why has this happened now?'

'You must learn to understand your fear and your anger before you can control them,' said Maerthuin. 'Always they have been with you, but we hide them so well. Now you must bring them into the light and confront them. Your rage is growing in power over you. It is not something you can fight, for such desires fuel themselves. Nor can you expunge them from your spirit, no more than you can stop breathing. It is part of you and always will be. All you can do now is find the means by which you can contain it, turn its energy elsewhere.'

'And keep it contained when it is not needed,' added Arthuis.

Shuddering, Korlandril took a deep breath and looked at the faces around him. They showed concern, not fear. He was surrounded by bloody-handed murderers, who not more than a few cycles ago had slain and mutilated other creatures. Yet he was the one that was weighed down by his anger; he was the one who felt a bottomless hatred. How was it that they could indulge that dark part of their nature and yet stay sane?

'I do not know what to do,' said Korlandril, slumping forwards with his head in his hands.

'Yes you do, but you are afraid to admit it,' said Arthuis. Korlandril looked at his friend, not daring to speak. 'You must come to terms with Khaine's legacy.'

'I cannot become a warrior,' said Korlandril. 'I am an Artist. I create, I do not destroy.'

'And that is good,' said Sellisarin. 'It is the division of creation and destruction that you need, the split between peace and war, life and death. Look around you. Are we not peaceful now, we who have killed so many? The Path of the Warrior is the path of outer war and inner peace.'

'The alternative is exile,' said Maerthuin. A sly smirk twisted his lips. 'You could always follow Aradryan, flee from Alaitoc.'

The thought appalled Korlandril. To abandon Alaitoc was to abandon all civilization. He needed stability and guidance, not unfettered freedom. His spirit could no more survive without the protection of Alaitoc than could his body. Another thought came to him. To leave the craftworld would mean parting from Thirianna – in shame, his last act towards her one of anger.

'What must I do?' he asked quietly, resigning himself to his fate. He looked at the warriors. Each had chosen a specific aspect of the Bloody-Handed God to become: Dark Reaper, Howling Banshee, Shining Spear. How did one know which Aspect thrived within? 'I do not know where to go.'

It was Elissanadrin that spoke. She crouched in front of Korlandril and held his hand in hers.

'What do you feel, at this moment?' she asked.

'I just want to hide, to be away from all of this,' Korlandril replied, eyes closed. 'I am scared of what I have become.'

The Aspect Warriors exchanged glances and Elissanadrin nodded.

'Then it is in hiding, in secrecy, in the shadows that you will find your way,' she said, pulling Korlandril to his feet. 'Come with me.'

Korlandril followed her mutely as the other eldar parted for them. He could feel their stares upon his back and cringed at their attention. So much had changed so quickly. A cycle ago he had craved the interest of others, now he could not bear their scrutiny.

'Where are we going?' he asked Elissanadrin when they had passed out of the Crescent of the Dawning Ages.

'In the darkness you will find strength. In the aspect of the Striking Scorpion you will turn fear from enemy to ally. We go to the place where I also learnt to hide: the Shrine of the Deadly Shadow.'

QUIET BUT AGITATED, Korlandril allowed Elissanadrin to lead him to the shuttle vault beneath the Crescent of the Dawning Ages. The wide platform was almost empty, only a handful of other eldar waiting for the cross-hub transport. Korlandril sat on a bench next to Elissanadrin but the two said nothing as they waited for the shuttle.

A soft hum heralded its arrival, pulsing from the tunnelway to the left a moment before the shuttle whispered alongside the platform and came to a standstill, a chain of bullet-shaped compartments hovering just above the anti-grav rail.

The pair found an empty carriage towards the front of the shuttle and sat opposite each other.

'It is not wrong to be afraid,' said Elissanadrin. 'We must learn to live with our fears as much as our hopes and dreams and talents.'

Korlandril said nothing as the shuttle accelerated, plunging into a blue-lit tunnel. For a moment the swiftly-passed lights dappled through the windows until they became a constant stream of colour, blurred together by the speed of the shuttle.

Korlandril tried to relax, to find a dream to take him away from what was happening, but his fists gripped the moulded arms of the chair and every muscle in his body was tense. Closing his eyes did not help. The only memory that came to him was a real dream, a nightmare battle that had plagued his sleep the night-cycle before Aradryan's return.

'Do you dream of war?' he asked suddenly.

Elissanadrin shook her head.

'It is so that we do not dream that we learn to don our war-masks,' she replied. 'Combat is an immediate, visceral act and should not be remembered.'

Her answer only increased Korlandril's anxiety, while the shuttle raced on, heading for the Vale of Khaine, speeding him towards his fate.

KORLANDRIL STOOD IN front of the last of the three gates that led to the shrine. He could see nothing beyond the white portal and was alone. Elissanadrin had left him between the first and second gates and taken another route. The entranceway was physically unassuming, identified by a solitary rune above the outer door. They had passed several such Aspect shrines on the short walk from the shuttle station, along deserted corridors and through empty passageways.

Though the Vale of Khaine looked little different to any other part of Alaitoc – visually bland in Korlandril's opinion – it certainly had its own feel. As soon as he had stepped off the transport, Korlandril had felt it, an oppressive air that filled the space between the curved walls with a pressure that nagged at one's mind.

Fear fluttered in Korlandril's heart as he stood there, not knowing what lay beyond the doorway. The Aspect Warriors never spoke of their shrines and no eldar went to them unless they were destined to join. He could barely feel the infinity circuit in the walls around him, subdued and distant. The spirits within its crystalline matrix avoided this place.

Taking a deep breath, Korlandril stepped forward and the door peeled apart in front of him.

The first sensation was cloying heat and humidity. It washed over Korlandril, sweeping around him with a wet embrace. His skin was slick within moments, a sheen of droplets on his bare arms and legs. The plain white tunic he wore was sodden before he had taken a step forwards.

Dim mist drifted out, swallowing him within its gloom. He could barely see the contorted trunks and drooping branches of trees, overhanging a path ahead. Stepping across the threshold his booted foot came upon spongy ground, his feet sinking slightly into the soft mire. After three more paces the doors silently shut behind him. Korlandril felt closed off. Suddenly panicked, he wheeled around and stepped towards the portal, but the gate would not open.

There was no turning back.

The path itself wound a meandering track between dark pools of thick liquid that gleamed with an oily sheen. Creepers hung down from the branches overhead, sometimes so many of them that Korlandril had to paw his way forwards, their wet tendrils slapping at his face and shoulders.

Not only vines populated the trees. Serpents with glistening green bodies slithered between the large fronds, their red eyes dead of all expression. Insects with wings as large as his hands burred and buzzed around him, skimming over the pools or clinging to the smooth tree trunks, gently fanning their brightly-patterned wings.

The only sounds were the patter of drips on the leaves and the trickle of water through the mangrove roots; and the hammering of his heart. No breeze stirred the trees and the heat grew more oppressive as he followed the snaking path around moss-covered boles. Looking back, all was obscured by heavy mist, the only sign of his passing the coiling wisps left in the air.

He had no sense of how far the chamber stretched. Though he had been walking for some time his route had never been straight and he wondered if he had been circling aimlessly, one stretch of path looking much like any other. He could not feel the pulse of Alaitoc; the inorganic had given way to this artificial wilderness. There was no echo and above him the sky was a distant ochre haze.

For a while Korlandril found himself at peace with this place. Its sombre atmosphere soothed his turbulent thoughts. There was a melancholy air, a primordial stillness that made his anger seem irrelevant. The twisted trees grew larger and larger, almost as old as the craftworld itself. He had no idea how many others had passed along this path before him; hundreds of the Alaitocii had come this way seeking the answers held within the shrine.

A doubt crept into Korlandril's thoughts. Perhaps they had not come this way at all? Perhaps he was lost? His fear returned. Every flitting shadow startled him, every hanging vine a snake in disguise waiting to strike. He quickened his pace, eager to push on to whatever awaited his journey's end. In his haste his foot caught a twining root and he stumbled to a knee. Korlandril thought the root had moved, deliberately tripping him. With fresh dread he stared around at the trees, feeling them coming closer.

He broke into a run. The faster he went, the more the path wound to and fro, the slicker underfoot it became. He thrashed through the creepers, panting wildly, eyes wide, alert for any sign of his destination.

All his other thoughts were put aside, all of his considerable mental powers concentrated on escaping this morass. He flinched at every movement in the shadows, recoiled whenever he strayed from the path and his foot sank into the mire. Whirling, he fell back against a tree, his hand coming against something soft and wet. Looking down, he saw a large-eyed toad leap away, dropping into a pool with a heavy plop. He wiped his hand on his tunic, which was now not only much stained but also tattered in places.

He felt ragged and alone, his mind fraying like his clothes. His boots felt far too tight and he ripped them off, casting them into the mist. Barefoot he squelched along the path again, this time more deliberately, scanning the ground for any sign that he was going in the right direction.

He felt the ground dipping and he pressed onwards, moving down a tree-shrouded slope. The path straightened in front of him and he came upon two thin pillars carved from a grey stone flanking his route, crusted with dark blue lichen. Stopping, he swept aside a patch and saw runes inscribed into the columns, so age-worn he could barely see them. He ran his hands over the rough surface of the left-hand pillar, using his artist's fingertips to read what was written there.

The shadows call and those who answer come here.

On the other column he found more engraving:

Even the deepest shadows cannot hide us from ourselves.

Korlandril stood between the pillars and looked ahead. He saw something concealed in the mists, half-hidden by moss and creepers. Approaching closer he could make out the rough outline of a large ziggurat, made of the same grey stone as the pillars. Trees grew upon its levels, masking it with their leaves. Lichen and vines criss-crossed its blocks, a natural camouflage that had grown over an age.

The path led into a dark opening. Korlandril could see nothing of the interior. Beyond the portal was utter blackness. He stopped just before stepping across the threshold. The darkness was not just the absence of light, it was something else. There was no gradual dimming from the gloom to total blackness, a stark plane of utter shadow marked the boundary. Hands held out in front of him, Korlandril plunged in.

IN THE DARKNESS it was cool. Compared to the heat outside, the inside of the shrine was icy cold and Korlandril's skin prickled. Stretching to either side, Korlandril ran his fingertips across a smooth surface. It was also cold and he snatched back his fingers. He was in a passageway just a little narrower than his outstretched hands. Pressing on, occasionally he would come to an opening on the left or right. There was no sight or sound that guided him and so he kept moving straight ahead. His footfalls were muffled, bare feet padding on a hard surface.

Korlandril felt himself step into a larger chamber. There was no lessening in the intensity of the shadow but he could sense the walls were more distant, his fingers stroking nothing but air. He stood motionless, head turning left and right, seeking something to fix upon.

There was a soft rustle to his left and Korlandril turned his head sharply. He could see nothing.

Then a sound came from the right, a rapid but barely audible drum that lasted for a few heartbeats and then fell silent. He could see nothing in that direction either.

Two lights flared into life ahead of him, pinpricks of yellow that grew quickly in brightness to reveal golden eye-shapes. They illuminated nothing, casting no shadow.

A voice came to him, from behind those glowing eyes. It was quiet, a deep whisper.

'What is this I see, a wanderer perhaps, lost and all alone?'

'I am Korlandril. I seek the Shrine of the Deadly Shadow.'

'And you have found it, seeker of the dark answer, child touched by Khaine's hand.'

Korlandril was not sure what to say and an unnerving silence descended. He dropped his hands to his side and looked at the yellow eyes. They were lenses, of that he was sure.

'Whom do I address?' he asked.

'I am Kenainath, the Deadly Shadow Exarch, keeper of this shrine.'

'I wish you to teach me the ways of the Striking Scorpion. My fear and anger eats at me from within, I must find release for it.'

'What makes you afraid, darkness and shadows perhaps, that which is hidden? What makes you angry, a friend's death or lover's scorn, that drives you to hate?'

Korlandril did not answer, ashamed. Now that he was stood here, in this dark place, it seemed such a trivial thing.

'You give no answer, perhaps you do not know it, that which destroys you.'

'I have been spurned, by one I called friend and one that I loved.'

A sinister laugh came in reply.

'Do not mock me!' snarled Korlandril, taking a pace towards those unmoving eyes. 'My pain is real!'

'We all have our pain, which eats away at our hearts, turns our love to hate. But where is pain now, when anger comes so easy, that you would strike me?'

Korlandril gritted his teeth, sensing that he was being teased. He took several deep breaths and stilled his whirling thoughts, preferring to say nothing.

'Do not fight this urge, the need to unleash your ire, embrace it instead.'

'I do not wish to hurt you,' Korlandril said, and was again laughed at.

'You do not scare me, I am the master of fear, Striking Scorpion. It is you that fears, that which consumes you inside, feeding your desire. You cannot harm me, you have not the skill or strength, nor the will to hurt.'

At that, the shadows receded slightly, revealing an armoured figure crouched upon a step. Its face was a heavy mask, with a serrated grille for a mouth, flanked by bulbous pods, framed with segmented finger-thick black cables for hair, which moved with a life of their own. Green and golden plates slid across each other as it stood, fully a head taller than Korlandril. The ring of its armoured boot echoed around Korlandril as the exarch took a step forward.

It lifted its right hand, gloved in a heavy claw that shimmered with an energy field.

'I could break you now, tear you limb from limb with ease, a work of moments,' said Kenainath, his tone low and menacing.

Korlandril shrank back and took a step away from the exarch as he strode forward, those glowing eyes unwavering. Terror gripped Korlandril, flooding through him like a chill. He fell to his knees, eyes fixed on the mask of the exarch, unable to break from that lifeless gaze.

'I am sorry, I am not worthy,' Korlandril sobbed. Self-loathing mixed with his dread; he had failed, he could not control his fear or master his anger. Kenainath loomed over him, his deadly eyes implacable. 'I do not wish to die, but I cannot live like this!'

The exarch straightened and took a step back, extending his other hand towards Korlandril.

'Then you are welcome. A warrior should fear death, but cannot crave life. Stand up Korlandril, Striking Scorpion at heart, Khaine's deadly shadow.'

Part Two

Warrior

FOCUS

In the time before the War in Heaven, it came to pass that the ambitions of Ulthanesh and the will of Eldanesh were at odds. Eldanesh was greatest of the eldar, and would brook no discord. Ulthanesh could not keep his desires bound within and Eldanesh banished his friend, sending him out into the desert. Ulthanesh was weary from his arguments with Eldanesh and sat upon a rock. He sat for a long time contemplating the wrongs of the universe and the dishonour visited upon him by Eldanesh. Seeing Ulthanesh so distraught the war god Khaine sensed an opportunity for strife. He broke the tip from one of his iron fingers and cast it into the shadows beneath the rock, where the fingertip became a scorpion. The scorpion stole out of the darkness and stung Ulthanesh on the hand. The poison consumed Ulthanesh and for countless days and nights he writhed in the sands burning with fever. Yet Ulthanesh was strong and in time the venom was conquered and the fever passed. When he awoke from his poison-tormented dreams, Ulthanesh found himself at peace. He had survived on his own with no aid from Eldanesh. Ulthanesh realised he had strength enough in himself and no longer needed Eldanesh's protection. Thus was the House of Ulthanesh founded and the strife of the eldar began.

KORLANDRIL AGAIN REMINDED himself that treading the Path of the Warrior would ease his torment. He was, he admitted, at a loss to work out quite how standing on one leg in a swamp would bring about this change. Kenainath squatted on a branch above him, divested of his armour and clad in a close-fitting bodysuit of pale green and golden yellow. Or at least Korlandril thought the exarch was still watching him; the last time he had glanced up to check he had been on the end of a stern admonishment from the master of the shrine. Korlandril kept his gaze firmly ahead, focussed on a knot in the hunched bole of a tree on the far side of the pool.

The warrior-to-be controlled his posture with precision, carefully controlling every muscle so as not to lose balance for a moment. He stood on his left foot, toes sinking into the mud, leaning forward as far as possible without falling, one hand raised in front of his throat in a guard position, the other stretched behind him to offset his forward lean.

It was the seventh cycle since his training had begun and the only other eldar he had seen in that time had been Kenainath. Of Elissanadrin and the other Striking Scorpions, there had been no sign. For seven cycles – and Korlandril was convinced the duration of the cycles were longer here than in the rest of Alaitoc – Kenainath had woken his pupil early and brought him out into the mire surrounding the shrine. The first cycle had been spent learning to breathe – long and low breaths that barely stirred the air. That was all, a whole cycle spent breathing. For the second cycle, Kenainath had commanded Korlandril to hang from a branch by his knees, until he was quite dizzy from the blood in his head, and then led him on a run along the twisting mangrove paths that left the former artist panting and dishevelled. And so on had it continued, each cycle bringing some new yet facile torture to be visited upon him.

'I have no doubt that your methods have been successful in bringing many on to the path of the Striking Scorpion, exarch,' Korlandril said quietly, barely moving his lips for fear of upsetting his delicate state of balance. 'Yet I have not yet seen a weapon nor a scrap of armour. I am quite sure I have no idea how this teaches me how to control my anger.'

'Are you angry now, my young warrior-to-be, standing in the mud?' the exarch replied, his voice a slight relief to Korlandril who thought that perhaps he had been left alone as some kind of mockery. 'Are you frustrated, to be treated in this way, dirty and downcast?'

Korlandril thought about this for a moment and realised that he wasn't angry, nor was he particularly frustrated; not in the same way that thoughts of

Aradryan and Thirianna frustrated him. If anything, he was bored. The physical exertion was considerable – a reminder that even the eldar body had its limits of endurance, speed and strength – but the mental occupation was non-existent. Kenainath had forbidden his student from entering a memedream or any other distraction, insisting that Korlandril be fully attentive to every part of his body and surroundings.

'You wish to have peace, to escape the rage and hate, yet also crave it,' said Kenainath, without waiting for an answer from Korlandril. 'You must learn two ways, the paths to both war and peace, in equal measure. That which we unleash, the face of battle we wear, is as a war-mask. You must put it on, within your spirit alone, and then take it off. Peace must be the goal, war helps us achieve this peace, and then balance comes. It must be a choice, shunning war and death and blood, choosing life and hope. You must make that choice, in every part of life, so that you are free. War is a not a state, it is an absence of peace, a passing nightmare. We awake from it, not remembering its curse, divorced from its taint. We must become death, to protect and to survive, but do not love death.'

Korlandril allowed the words to resonate through his thoughts, glad of something to occupy himself. Something occurred to him, a question, but he was hesitant to ask. The exarch must have sensed something of Korlandril's unease.

'We are here for truth, to find the answer you seek, no question is wrong.'

'You speak of peace, yet you are an exarch. What can you know of peace, who cannot leave Khaine's embrace?

There was a slight creak and a subtle swish of leaves as Kenainath shifted his weight on the branch above. Korlandril wondered if his question had been inappropriate.

'Freedom is not mine, to wander from this temple, out with the others,' the exarch said quietly. 'You do not see me, singing and dancing outside, writing poetry. I stay in this shrine, where my curse cannot harm you, forever trapped here. Though I wear no paint, my war-mask remains inside, clouding all my thoughts. Had you angered me, that first day you came to me, I might have killed you. Even now I hate, filled with my anger always, but I do not strike. It is not madness, not uncontrollable ire, which my war-mask brings. It is an urging, to release what is inside, fighting to get out. I struggle with it, but I am its true master, exerting my will. It is no frenzy, no bloodlust that would swamp me, but a perspective. I see things unseen, pain and misery beneath, which others hide from. It is my duty, the covenant of exarchs, to prepare your mind. You will see horror, witness death and agony, and must confront it. This is my calling, to lead you on that dark path, where others recoil.'

Korlandril's limbs were trembling from fatigue and he fought to remain balanced. The thought of falling into the mud, humiliated in front of Kenainath, stiffened his resolve and he dug deeper into his spirit for strength.

'It is very good, my young but keen disciple, that you do not fall. Look into yourself, tell me what it is you see, what you used to see.'

Korlandril sifted his thoughts, parting a section of his consciousness to keep himself balanced while he danced through his mind. He set aside the physical discomfort and examined his emotional state. He was calm. He hadn't been this calm since...

As soon as Korlandril's thoughts turned to Thirianna, the serpent of jealousy reared, spitting and hissing. For an instant Korlandril's whole body was on fire. Every nerve tingled with vibrant life. He saw the colours of the swamp with a clarity he had not witnessed even as an Artist. Every ripple shone in his mind; every chirrup, scratch and burr of insect sounded distinct in his ears. The faintest breeze on his flesh, the feel of the mud between his toes and the coolness of the water on his skin. His waystone was like a white-hot coal over his heart. Everything stood out in sharp contrast and for that moment Korlandril felt an urge to destroy it all. The need to wreak havoc, shed blood, take life, was overwhelming. He could not take another breath without striking out.

He fell splashing into the muddy pool, his loss of balance so unexpected that he landed face first, unable to break his fall. Spluttering, he rose from the murk, filth dripping from hair, brow and chin.

'A trick?' he snarled, whirling around, still awash with after-eddies from the wave of perfect anger that had swept across him.

The exarch was no longer on the branch. Korlandril cast around for a sign of him but saw nothing, heard nothing. But he could sense the exarch's presence close at hand, subtly mingled with the essence of the swamp. With a shock, Korlandril realised how attuned he had become to his surroundings, unconsciously absorbing its presence, analysing every smell and sound and sight without effort. There was the slightest of disturbances to his left and he turned sharply.

There was nothing; no movement, not even a flicker of shadow.

'Where is your anger, where is the rage from within, which you felt just now?' Kenainath's voice was a distant, echoing whisper, seeming to come from every direction and none, like several voices speaking at once. Korlandril calmed, every fibre relaxing, even his heart quietening as he made himself silent in an effort to attain the sensory state he had briefly achieved.

'It was your anger, bringing heightened awareness, which you felt just now. Our hate is our strength, not some weakness to be purged, if we use it well.'

Korlandril understood the exarch and tried to bring back the moment of pure rage he had experienced after falling, but all he felt was frustration.

'Do not have outbursts, letting your anger fly wild, an unfettered beast. You must learn control, to strike like the scorpion, not the fire dragon. When you can do that, when your anger serves your will, you have your war-mask.'

SLOWLY, CYCLE-BY-CYCLE, KORLANDRIL exerted ever greater control over his mind and body. The two became as one; the physical effort of maintaining the strenuous Striking Scorpion fighting poses narrowed his focus, concentrating his thoughts to a single point. Whenever he deviated from the routines set for him by Kenainath, Korlandril struggled and lost his balance, physically and mentally.

For all that he understood Kenainath's teachings, Korlandril became ever more frustrated by his inability to unleash that moment of primal rage he had felt earlier. He feared that all he was doing was suppressing further and further the anger that had first propelled him towards the shrine.

For forty cycles Kenainath kept Korlandril apart from the other Striking Scorpions, training him alone within the gloom of the shrine and its dismal surrounds. Korlandril longed to see the rest of Alaitoc again. Though it pained him every time he thought of Thirianna, he could not suppress his curiosity and longed to know how she fared. Had she started upon the Path of the Seer? Did she even know what had become of him? How did she feel about her part in his decision to take the Path of Khaine?

As the first glimmer of the forty-first cycle crept through the narrow windows of the upper levels of the shrine, Kenainath appeared as usual. The exarch was clad in his dark green robe, sleeveless, open at the front, a deep yellow bodysuit beneath, his dark red waystone fixed to the centre of his chest. Korlandril looked at the oval of the waystone, noticing the shimmering of its colour, a flickering in its depths as of many lights far away.

'It is time again, to learn the Falling Storm pose, come outside with me,' said Kenainath.

'No.' Korlandril crossed his arms, legs braced apart. 'I do not want to train today. I'm sick of this gloomy swamp. I want to see Thirianna.'

Moving so swiftly that Korlandril barely saw him, Kenainath stepped forward and flicked a hand towards Korlandril's ear. The blow was light enough, but stung quickly. Korlandril lunged, aiming the tips of his fingers knife-like towards the exarch's throat, finishing in the stance known as Sting From Shadow. Kenainath swayed away and retreated with several quick steps.

'It will not be safe, you cannot yet control the hate, and could blindly strike out.'

Korlandril shuddered with the shock of realisation. He had tried to harm Kenainath. He had wanted to cause him injury. Even kill him. He had acted without conscious thought, but he could feel the desire to inflict hurt that had driven the reflex. If he had done such a thing to anyone but another warrior, he would have murdered them.

'Now you understand, that which we are creating, safe here in the shrine,' Kenainath said softly.

'Why would you do this to me?' demanded Korlandril. 'Why turn me into this before I can control it?'

'This is your war-mask, expanding from within you, consuming your mind.' The exarch's tone was unforgiving, with no hint of shame or comfort. 'It is for battle, where you cannot hesitate, but act or react. Do not be worried, you will learn to remove the mask, I will teach you how.'

'You have done this to trap me here, because you cannot leave,' said Korlandril.

'Until you wear it, you cannot remove the mask, it is still hidden. In time you will learn, be free of the mask's control, and then you can leave.' There was no sympathy in Kenainath's voice, but his determined tone eased Korlandril's fears a little. 'Now you have a goal, to leave behind your war-mask, to gain your freedom.'

Korlandril did not know whether it was the mental forces being unleashed by the exarch's training, or the exarch himself, but he despised Kenainath even more. He allowed his anger to simmer inside as he followed the exarch out into the swamp once again. The prospect of finishing his training seemed a distant dream. Yet the exarch's words had struck a chord. If Korlandril truly wanted to be free of this place, he had to rid himself of the cause for his being here – his anger. Kenainath's methods seemed counterproductive, but he had trained many Striking Scorpions and Korlandril had to put his trust in that.

Resigned more than hopeful, Korlandril trailed after Kenainath into the gloom.

'PEACE IS AS it is, unwavering and endless, a constant of life.' The exarch's words were hushed. 'Anger is fleeting, a momentary relapse, when will slips away.'

Korlandril barely heard Kenainath, a whisper on the edge of consciousness. He stood upon a branch of a stooping tree, a greenish pool below him mottled with leaves and algae. A moment's loss of concentration and he would fall into the water.

'The Whisper of Death, and then into Surging Wave, end with Rising Claw,' instructed Kenainath.

Korlandril shifted position with controlled slowness, bending almost double while he eased his left foot forward yet kept his weight on his back leg, left arm raised above his head, right arm crooked by his side. Taking a pace forward, he shifted his balance, thrusting forward with his right arm, sweeping outwards with the left hand. To finish, he straightened, left arm curving up in front of him, right arm held back.

The exarch continued and Korlandril obeyed, moving forwards and backwards along the branch as dictated by Kenainath, making mock strikes and defences as he did so. The motions were effortless, remembered by instinct rather than conscious thought. Korlandril moved gracefully through all twenty-seven basic poses. The branch buckled and swayed beneath him, but his balance remained perfect.

Even as his body moved, Korlandril's mind was still. Seventy cycles now had passed and Korlandril could barely recall his life before coming to the shrine. He knew there were memories inside somewhere, but no longer knew where to look for them. He was little more than a physical vessel moving along a branch, waiting to be filled by something else.

When the exercise was complete, Kenainath signalled for Korlandril to follow him. Korlandril hid his surprise as he leapt lithely down to the path beside the pool. It was early yet in the cycle and it was unexpected to take a break so early.

Kenainath offered no explanation as he turned back up the creeper-crossed path and headed towards the shrine. Korlandril followed close behind, intrigued by this change of routine. The pair plunged into the cool shadows of the temple and then took a turn to the left, down a passage Korlandril had never trod before. It brought them into a long gallery, high and narrow. Along each wall stood five suits of aspect armour, fashioned from many overlapping plates of deep green edged with gold, the red lenses of the helmets dull and lifeless.

Beside four of the suits stood the other warriors of the shrine.

Korlandril recognised Elissanadrin and she smiled in reply to his quizzical glance. The others he had seen around the craftworld, but did not know their names.

'Now to make your choice, to meet your companions, Striking Scorpion,' Kenainath intoned solemnly, taking his place at the far end of the gallery in front of the much heavier exarch armour he had been wearing when Korlandril had first arrived.

Korlandril looked around, wondering which suit to pick. At first they seemed identical, but there were subtle differences; in the placement of gems, the hang of the hair-like sensory antenna-crests of the helmets, the brightly coloured ribbons tied about the armoured limbs.

His first instinct was to stand beside Elissanadrin, seeking the familiar, but he dismissed the urge. It was change and renewal that he needed, not the comfortable. Out of the corner of his eye, Korlandril thought he saw a momentary glitter in the eyes of one suit. He turned towards it. There was nothing to distinguish it from the others, but something about it tugged at Korlandril.

'This one,' he said, striding towards the armour. He stood beside it and turned to face the exarch.

'That is a wise choice, a noble suit you have picked, which has served us well,' said Kenainath. 'You are now ready, in body if not in mind, to don your armour.'

A thrill of elation shivered through Korlandril. For the first time since coming to the shrine he sensed a moment of achievement. He had been dimly aware of the progress he had been making, so subtle had been the changes wrought in him by Kenainath. Now that he was stood beside his armour, Korlandril looked on what had passed with fresh eyes. Just as he had learned to control the ghost stone as a sculptor, now he controlled every muscle and fibre of his body. It was an instrument wholly subservient to his will and whim.

The donning of his armour was not as straightforward as Korlandril had imagined it might be. Just as with the fighting poses, every stage of armouring was precise, each stance and movement strictly defined by Kenainath. With each stage came a mantra from the exarch, which resounded in Korlandril's mind as the Striking Scorpions repeated the words.

First he stripped naked, casting his robe aside as if throwing away a part of himself. He took his way-stone on its silver chain and placed it carefully in a niche in the wall. He felt a quiver of fear at being separated from his spirit-saviour. It was perhaps his imagining, but Korlandril felt a moment of scrutiny, as if detecting eyes suddenly upon him, regarding him from a great distance. He dismissed his unease, knowing that nothing could befall him in the shrine.

'The peace is broken, harmony falls to discord, only war remains.'

Korlandril followed the lead of the others, taking the bodysuit that was folded on a small ledge behind the armour.

'Now we clothe ourselves, with bloody Khaine's own raiment, as a warrior.'

Korlandril stepped into the legs of the bodysuit. It was large and sagged on his limbs and gathered in unsightly bulges between his legs and under his arms, its fingertips dangling uselessly.

'In Khaine's iron skin, we clad ourselves for battle, while fire burns within.'

Korlandril's heart quickened. In his gut, the serpent of his anger stretched slowly. He placed his palms together in front of his face, copying the movements of the other Aspect Warriors. In response, the body suit tightened. As the fabric of the suit shrank against his taut muscles, dormant pads began to thicken, forming rigid areas across his chest and stomach and along the bulge of his thighs, stiffening along his spine.

'The spirit of Khaine, from which we draw our resolve, strengthens within us.'

Korlandril kept his eye on Elissanadrin, following her motions. Reaching behind the armour, he undid the fastenings along its back, letting the lower portion of the torso fall free in his hands. Wrapping it about his stomach and lower back, his nimble fingers worked the fastenings back into place. Its stiff presence around his midsection was reassuring, supporting his back, squeezing against his sides in a firm embrace.

'War comes upon us, we must bear its dark burden, upon our shoulders.'

Following the lead of the others, Korlandril undid the clasps fixing the upper part of the armour to its stand. He lifted it above his head, solid but not heavy. With careful movements he lowered it onto his shoulders. The plates gripped the surface of the undersuit, extending down his upper arms; the rounded bulge of the power generator slipped easily across his shoulder blades. As before, he returned to a stance of repose and the suit shifted slightly with a life of its own, adjusting itself to his body. When it had stopped moving, he tightened the clasps, fixing the armour in place. He felt top-heavy and adjusted his back to stand straighter.

A moment of fear made Korlandril tremble as the bodysuit extended up towards his face, enclosing his throat and neck, the touch of rippling ridges insistent but gentle. The moment passed as soon as it stopped just below his chin. He took a deep breath to steady himself.

'We stand before Khaine, unyielding in our calling, free of doubt and fear.'

The upper leg armour came next, fitting to Korlandril as snugly as the rest of the suit. He found that if he flexed in a certain way, the plates interlocked delicately, strengthening his stance, offsetting the imbalance of the powerpack. Korlandril's pulse was almost feverish, burning along his arteries, hissing in his ears.

'We do not flee death, we walk in the shade of Khaine, proud and unafraid.'

The lower legs were each protected by a single boot-greave piece, which Korlandril slipped over his feet and knees. He fastened these to the thigh armour, fully encasing his legs. Threads of material grew rigid around his ankles, adding additional support, while the boots shortened themselves to fit his feet. A sensation of solidity, of unmoving permanence, filled Korlandril.

'We strike from the dark, as swift as the scorpion, with a deadly touch.'

The vambrace-gauntlets connected to the upper armour, more clasps linking the two as one. Korlandril flexed his arms, feeling cartilage-like tendrils tightening against his flesh, reinforcing his wrists and elbows. Now fully clad save for his face, Korlandril felt incredible, filled with a heat that did not waver. His armour was his skin; it pulsed along with his thundering heart, drawing life from him and returning its strength.

His next act was to retrieve his waystone from its niche, detaching it from the silver surround of the necklace. It responded to his touch, warming gently, suffusing him with delicate reassurance. He placed the waystone into the aperture of the chestplate. It settled home with a soft click. His armour felt the waystone's presence as much as Korlandril, giving a brief, almost imperceptible quiver and then falling still again.

'That is all for now, there is no need of the mask, we are not at war.'

With the donning of the armour complete, Kenainath gestured for the Striking Scorpions to assemble before him. Korlandril took a step forward, the movement feeling awkward in the armour; its weight was evenly spread across him, but its bulk restricted normal movement. In response, he changed the nature of his stride, his body remembering the motions he had learnt while unencumbered. As strange and stylised as they had felt in his robe, they were natural when armour-clad.

The warriors stood in a single line, a short distance apart, facing the exarch. Kenainath led them through the ritual stances and the Striking Scorpions moved together, each replicating his poses without hesitation or variation. Almost like automatons they mirrored the exarch's thrusts and parries, like marionettes all controlled by the same strings.

Korlandril felt a sense of belonging he had not known for a long time, in perfect synchronisation with his fellow warriors. He was as them, and they were as he; of one mind and one function. Every stance brought a fresh thrill, as he learnt anew their purpose. The armour made him complete, his body now perfected.

For most of the cycle they practised their ritual stances. Some were genuinely new to Korlandril, impossible to attain without the support of the armour. He learnt them without effort, swiftly adapting to each challenge. As the session progressed, the stance changes came more swiftly, the tempo of Kenainath's actions increasing with each round of moves.

The exarch spoke rarely, only to reinforce his previous teachings and adding new insights into the way of the Striking Scorpion.

'With balance we strike, not acrobatic Banshees, flailing and screaming. With strength of motion, strike with sure and deadly grace, power from balance.'

Throughout the exercises the hot temper that had filled Korlandril continued to burn. He began to visualise a foe, formless and shadowy, which he gutted and decapitated, countered and eluded. His imaginary opponent had eyes that burned with a red fire, but was otherwise featureless; an anonymous conglomeration of those who had wronged him, an incarnation formed of his anger and fears. In striking at this apparition, Korlandril drew great strength, feeding on his power to destroy that which had tried to destroy him.

Invigorated, Korlandril was somewhat disappointed when Kenainath signalled for them to stop, returning to the stance of repose, palms touching, legs slightly apart, heads bowed.

Korlandril stood there for a while, expecting some new instruction. Footfalls alerted him to the others moving back to their armour-stands and he did the same. Kenainath had left without word.

Reversing the same series of motions they had used to put on the armour, the Aspect Warriors divested themselves of their battlegear. As he removed each component, Korlandril felt a lightening in his spirit as well as on his body. Though he had felt relaxed throughout the practice, he realised he had been functioning at a far higher state of awareness than normal. Colours seemed a little blander, sounds more muted as he brought himself down from the peak of physical attentiveness and assumed a more relaxed demeanour.

'Welcome to the Shrine of the Deadly Shadow,' said Elissanadrin, extending her palm in greeting. She wore a tight-fitting bodysuit with a pearlescent quality, gleaming with tones of white and ivory. Korlandril laid his hand briefly on hers in reply.

'Let me introduce you to your companions-in-arms,' she said, turning slightly, open hand gesturing towards the others.

'Be known to Arhulesh,' she continued, indicating a warrior a little shorter than Korlandril, his long black hair tied into braids with slender dark red ribbons.

'Greetings Korlandril,' Arhulesh said with a lop-sided smile. 'I would have liked to make your acquaintance earlier, but Kenainath is such a stickler for his routines. I must admit, I greatly enjoyed your exhibition, *The Rising of the Heavens*. Did I detect a slight mockery of Khaine in your pieces?'

Korlandril frowned. He could barely remember the sculptures he had created. They were locked away in his memories somewhere, but it was as if he had lost the map and could not find them.

'Oh, Kenainath has drawn you in most conclusively,' Arhulesh said with a raised eyebrow. He turned to the others. 'Careful, we have a real devotee on our hands! I wonder just what, or who, it is that you're hiding from, Korlandril.'

'Hush, Arhu,' cut in Elissanadrin with a dismissive wave of her hand. 'You know that we do not speak of our lives before, unless we wish to.'

Arhulesh directed a nod of apology towards Korlandril, who noted a slight twist to the inclination, a tiny gesture of sarcasm. Elissanadrin laid a hand upon Korlandril's elbow and led him towards the next Striking Scorpion, a serious-faced eldar with gaunt features and stark white hair cropped into a scalplock. He was attending fastidiously to his armour, using a silk-like cloth to wipe away every speck and smear on its surface.

'Speaking of silence, this is Bechareth.'

The name startled Korlandril, for it meant Spirit on the Wind; an appellation given to those whose true identity was not known, usually a stranger. It was also a euphemism for those that had died without the protection of a waystone, their spirits lost to the clutches of She Who Thirsts.

'He doesn't, or can't, speak,' explained Elissanadrin. 'Kenainath brought him to us with that name, and neither has told us anything else. Do not be fooled by his silence, he is a capable warrior.' She paused uncomfortably before continuing. 'I owe him my life.'

Bechareth stood and offered his right hand in greeting; vertical, palm towards Korlandril, a gesture of equality that was rarely used in Alaitoc society except to greet those from other craftworlds. Korlandril raised his left hand in mirror of the gesture, indicating trust, and received a slow blink of gratitude from the warrior. His dark eyes glittered with amusement, and Korlandril felt himself drawn to the mysterious eldar despite his outlandish behaviour.

'Mithrainn,' said Elissanadrin, nodding towards the last of the four. He was of venerable age, probably five hundred passes older or more, with a sharp brow and aquiline nose.

'Call me Min,' he said, eliciting a laugh from Korlandril. The nickname was from the myths of Vaul, after the weak link in the chain that had bound the smith-god to his anvil.

'It is good to meet you... Min,' said Korlandril, touching palms with the elder. 'Forgive my impudence, but I would have thought the Path of the Warrior was more suited to those of less experience.'

'You mean that you think I'm too old for this sneaking about and running around!' Min declared with a grin. He thumped his hand to his chest. 'The heart of a youth still beats within my breast.'

'Powered by the mind of an infant,' added Elissanadrin, rolling her eyes. 'He makes up for Bechareth's silence with his volume. I still think he has some Biel-Tan stock in him, despite his protestations to be pureblood Alaitocii.'

'You may say that, Lissa, but you have yet to catch me in the swamp.'

Elissanadrin conceded this obscure point with a reluctant nod and a pursing of the lips. She smiled when she saw Korlandril's confusion.

'When you have mastered the arts of the fighting poses, you will join us on our hunts. We go out into the surrounds of the shrine and try to sneak up on each other. The Striking Scorpion is stealth as well as strength.'

Korlandril nodded in understanding.

'And how long do you think it will be before I join you?'

'How long is a star's life?' quipped Arhulesh from behind Korlandril. 'Kenainath has a whim of iron. It could be next cycle, it could be not for another two or three passes.'

'Two or three passes?' Korlandril was taken aback. 'Surely my progress has been swifter than that.'

'Whim of iron, remember, whim of iron,' said Arhulesh, shrugging shallowly.

'Is that before or after I get my war-mask?'

'None can say when you will find your war-mask,' said Min. 'For some it never comes and they leave without truly treading the Path. For others, they wear it from the start.'

Bechareth stepped closer and looked intently into Korlandril's eyes, studying every detail. He held up a thumb and forefinger, a little way apart. His meaning was clear: a short time. The gesture turned to an upraised finger of warning.

'He's right,' said Elissanadrin. 'You shouldn't chase after your war-mask, not until you're ready to take it off.'

'I'm not quite sure I still understand what this war-mask is,' confessed Korlandril. 'I mean, Kenainath wouldn't let us wear our helmets today. I don't understand the connection.'

Arhulesh laughed harshly but his face was serious. 'The war-mask is not a thing, it is a state of mind. You have come close to it, or you would not be here. You will know it when it comes. We cannot tell you what it will be like, for it is unique to each of us.'

'Just know that we have all been through the same experience,' added Min. He laid a hand on Korlandril's shoulder. Korlandril was slightly uneasy with a gesture of such familiarity, having only just been introduced. He resisted the urge to pull away but Min must have sensed his reaction. He drew his hand back. 'When it comes, you will share what we all share and my touch will not be so unwelcome.'

'I did not mean any off– '

'We do not apologise to one another,' cut in Elissanadrin. 'Know that in this place, with mask on or off, all is forgiven. The past is the past, the future will be whatever it will be, and we share only the present. Perhaps it is regret that keeps you from discovering your mask. Leave it behind; it has no place in your spirit. As a warrior, regret will kill you as surely as a blade.'

Korlandril pondered this silently. The others turned as one towards the exarch armour at the head of the hall and Korlandril looked over his shoulder to see that Kenainath had returned. He had made no sound that Korlandril had heard and he was at a loss to know how the others had been aware of his arrival. Perhaps they had not been aware at all; the thought that the exarch might have heard the conversation disturbed Korlandril, though he was not sure why.

'It is time for us to depart,' said Elissanadrin.

'Not you,' Min said as Korlandril took a step towards the doorway.

'Enjoy your training, little scorpion,' added Arhulesh, directing a glance towards the exarch, who stood with arms folded across his chest, looking sternly at his disciples.

Bechareth passed Korlandril last, giving a short bow in farewell before leaving with the others. Suppressing a sigh, Korlandril turned towards Kenainath.

'I am yours to teach,' Korlandril said, dipping his head.

'That is well and good, for there is still much to learn, Striking Scorpion.'

ANGER

When the eldar first rose from the bosom of the ground, nourished by the tears of Isha, the gods came to them and each offered them a gift. Asuryan, lord of lords, gave the eldar Wisdom, that they would know themselves. Isha gave the eldar Love, that they would know one another. Vaul gave the eldar Artifice, that they would make their dreams a reality. Lileath gave the eldar Joy, that they would know happiness. Kurnous gave the eldar Desire, that they would know prosperity. Morai-heg gave the eldar Foresight, that they would know their place in the world. Khaine gave the eldar Anger, that they would protect what the gods had given them.

THE TRAINING CONTINUED as before; though now in armour and often in the company of the other warriors of the shrine. Kenainath also turned his attention to introducing the disciplines of stealth and ambush, leading Korlandril through the swamps as silently as a breeze. The pair of them travelled to places new to Korlandril – narrow gorges, winding rivulets and shadow-shrouded caves. Despite the bulk of the Striking Scorpion armour, Korlandril moved as soundlessly as if he were naked. So controlled and effortless was Korlandril's motion, so attuned was he to the swaying of the branches and the slightest ripple of water, he was able to blend his movements to those of his surrounds.

For thirty-eight cycles this continued. Korlandril could discern no pattern to the lessons save for some inner timeline that Kenainath maintained for himself. He did not know against which mark he was being judged or to what standard he might aspire, and so could only follow Kenainath's instructions without question. The exarch made no mention of any change in Korlandril's skills, though he knew for himself that they were steadily improving.

In the carefully choreographed ritual of the shrine, Korlandril could now respond so quickly to the exarch's commands it was if he anticipated them. He kept pace with the other Striking Scorpions without thought. His progress, even if unremarked by the others, gave him some satisfaction and he looked forward to the underlying spirit of sharing he felt when he practised alongside the rest of the shrine. Always he felt invigorated when putting on his armour, but now he was left also with a sense of fulfilment when he took it off.

At the rising of the thirty-ninth cycle, Kenainath, clad in his armour but without his helmet, came to the bare dormitory where Korlandril slept. He instructed Korlandril to don his own wargear and led him into a new chamber. Here were arranged the weapons of the Striking Scorpions, hung upon the wall of the circular room. Ten slender chainswords were paired with matching shuriken pistols.

Not quite knowing how, Korlandril walked directly to the arms that he knew belonged to his armour. He ran his fingers along the cladding of the chainsword, able to feel the entwining decorations through the empathic connection to his gauntlet as if he touched it with bare skin.

'Take up your weapon, let it become part of you, feel it in your hand,' said Kenainath.

Korlandril closed his fingers around the guarded hilt of the chainsword and lifted it easily from the curved wall bracket. Like his armour, it was surprisingly light for its size. It fitted snugly into his palm, like an extension of his arm. He twisted his wrist and examined the narrow blades, each sharp enough to slice through flesh and bone with a single stroke. He saw red reflections of his own admiring face in the jewels along its length.

'How do I activate it?' he asked.

'How does your heart beat, your fingers move at your whim, that is the answer.'

Korlandril stalked to the centre of the chamber and took up the stance known as Sweeping Bite, hunched forward slightly. His right fist was raised in front of his left shoulder, but now he could see that the length of the chainsword extended horizontally in front of his face, just below eye level. He rotated, sliding back his right foot, the weapon flashing in an arc, finishing in Hidden Claw.

Growing in confidence, Korlandril moved through the First Ritual of Attack, pacing steadily across the chamber, cutting back and forth with the chainsword. At the fifth stance – Rising Fang – the chainsword purred into life of its own accord.

Shocked, Korlandril stumbled, the weapon almost falling from his grasp. Kenainath made a strange hissing sound and Korlandril turned, expecting to see scorn on the exarch's bare face. The opposite was true. For the first time since Korlandril had met him, Kenainath was quietly laughing.

'As it was with me, first time I took up a blade, now so long ago.' Kenainath's humour dissipated quickly and he gestured for Korlandril to continue.

The chainsword had fallen lifeless in his grasp. Regaining his focus, Korlandril started afresh from the first stance, and almost immediately the chainsword's teeth whirred into motion, making no more sound than the buzzing of a lava-wing. Unperturbed, Korlandril continued, cutting and slashing, each move increasing in speed until the blade was a green and gold blur in the air. He made backhanded cuts and rounded overhead chops, advancing on invisible foes.

As he weaved the blade around him, the shadowy foe he visualised during his routines came into sharper focus. Its eyes still burned red but it took on a more distinct shape, narrow at the hip, broader at the shoulder. In the eye of Korlandril's mind, his foe bobbed and ducked, parried and countered, advanced and retreated.

With an explosion of breath, Korlandril delivered a killing strike, sweeping the blade up beneath the chin of his imaginary adversary, to come to a perfect standstill in Claw of Balance. Drawing a lungful of air, Korlandril stepped back, assuming the stance of repose. He turned towards Kenainath.

The exarch betrayed nothing of his thoughts. There was neither praise nor condemnation in his expression. The pride Korlandril had felt in his performance evaporated quickly under that inscrutable stare.

'You have now begun, the Path continues onwards, you must follow it.'

Korlandril dared a glance towards the shuriken pistol on the wall, and then looked back at the exarch. Kenainath gave one shake of the head and pointed at the chainsword in Korlandril's hand.

'First master the claw, the venomous bite comes next, the sting is the last.'

Korlandril licked his dry lips and nodded. He returned to the centre of the chamber and took up Claw from Shadow. The chainsword responded to his urging before he had so much as twitched a muscle and within moments he was moving again.

FOR THE FOLLOWING cycles Korlandril trained in isolation, until Kenainath was convinced that he could spar with the other Striking Scorpions without undue danger to them or himself. After twenty-three cycles, the exarch informed Korlandril that he was ready to train armed with the other warriors. Kenainath took his warrior-acolyte to a grove not far from the shrine and gestured for Korlandril to seat himself on a moss-covered log

'What of history, the tale of the scorpion, can you tell to me?' Kenainath asked. 'What myths have you heard, of Karandras and Arhra, the first of our kind?'

Korlandril raked his fingers through his hair as he remembered what he could.

'Asurmen was the first, the creator of the Path of the Warrior,' he said. 'I guess it was Asurmen that discovered how to don the war-mask. He founded the first shrine and gathered disciples to teach, Arhra amongst them, the Father of Scorpions. Some dark fate befell Arhra, of which I do not know the story, and his greatest pupil Karandras took up the mantle and spread the teachings of the Striking Scorpion.'

'That is true enough, the briefest account of it, but you should know more,' replied Kenainath, crouching opposite his pupil, his eyes intent. 'Arhra fell from grace, touched by the dark of Chaos, and betrayed his kin. He turned on the rest, brought daemons to the First Shrine, hungry for power. The Asurya, the first exarchs of the Path, fought against Arhra. They lost the battle, scattered to the distant stars, and Arhra escaped. He strayed from the Path, consumed by his ambition, and found new pupils. His teachings are wrong, a perversion of the Path, the Fallen Phoenix. It is a great wrong, one that we cannot forgive, the worst betrayal. Karandras hunts him, across the stars and webway, for retribution.'

'Arhra still lives?' The tale of the Fallen Phoenix was mixed up with the other myths of the Fall. Not even the eldar had such long lives.

'Who can say for sure, in the warp and the webway, time passes strangely.' Kenainath sighed and his expression was sad, a stark change from his usual indifference or hostility. 'Keep true to the Path, heed Karandras's teachings, remain Korlandril.'

'Have there been others?' Korlandril asked fearfully. 'Warriors that follow the Path of the Fallen Phoenix?'

'Not from my pupils, I have guided them all well, taught them properly,' said Kenainath as he straightened quickly. The exarch's familiar stern expression returned. 'Go back to the shrine, tomorrow you fight proper, tonight you must rest'.

Dismissed, Korlandril walked slowly back beneath the dismal bowers of the trees to the shrine building wondering why the exarch had chosen that moment to reveal the truth about the founding of the Striking Scorpions. As the lights of the shrine dimmed for the night portion of the cycle, Korlandril lay awake pondering what the following cycle would bring.

HE WOKE EARLY, full of nervous energy. The shrine was still swathed in twilight and he swiftly pulled on a loose robe and left his solitary dormitory, feeling confined by its walls. In the gloom outside, the swamp was quiet save for the first chattering of the jade-toads. He took a deep breath, accustomed now to the humidity and heat, though he was far from thinking his present environs were his home.

With that, his thoughts turned to the rest of Alaitoc, as they usually did when he was left with time to think. It was with only a barely intellectual interest that he thought of Thirianna. She was probably upon the Path of the Seer by now. Though it had been a short time, barely a blink in the life of an eldar, that moment when his inner anger had been unleashed by her dismissal seemed distant. Irrelevant. His struggle was not with Thirianna, or Aradryan, or any other eldar. It was with himself.

His body and mind were being perfected for one thing – to slay other living creatures. The thought caused him to shudder. Today he would face one of the other members of the Deadly Shadow, but it would not be a fight to a death. It would be controlled, disciplined, ritualistic. Though he knew nothing of real war, he imagined it to be a desperate, harrowing maelstrom of courage and fear, action and blood. And in that anarchy of battle he would kill. He did not know when, or how, but as surely as he had not been an Artist until he had sculpted his first piece, he would not truly tread the Path of the Warrior until he killed his first foe.

He did not know how he would bring himself to do it. Would it be taken out of his hands? An instinct of defence to protect his life? Would it be cold-blooded, a pre-meditated slaying of another creature defined as an enemy of the Alaitocii by the farseers and autarchs?

Korlandril realised that this was the war-mask Kenainath and the rest talked about. Only on one occasion had he been ready to strike out in anger, truly wishing harm on another individual; that cycle in the swamp, when rage and hate had combined into a moment of pure action. He tried to capture that instance again, but all of his tricks of memory failed him. In that heartbeat his entire being had been focussed on that one effort to hit Kenainath, and nothing else.

For some time he wandered the pathways around the shrine, not straying too far. He knew the twisting trails as well as any other part of Alaitoc, their mysteries unveiled to him through Kenainath. He no longer feared his surroundings. More importantly, he knew that in overcoming his apprehension of this place he had steeled himself against future dread and doubts when confronted by the unknown and unknowable. He was self-aware enough to understand the process being awoken in him by the teachings of Kenainath, weaving layers of the warmask that would, one day, emerge from within his spirit.

The light was considerably brighter when a resounding chime sounded within the shrine, calling him back.

IT WAS BECHARETH. He was armoured save for his helm, and carried his chainsword in an easy grip by his side. There was a tightness to his lips, and fire in his eyes, which spoke of his enthusiasm for the duel about to commence. He appeared relaxed in body, but his eyes were attentive, floating easily but with focus from Kenainath to Korlandril and back again.

As he armoured himself, the mantra of Kenainath flowing through his veins, Korlandril's anxiety slipped away. With each step he became Korlandril less, the Aspect of the Striking Scorpion taking his place. Part of his mind watched the rest with cold detachment, reminding him of the Seven Parrying Sweeps and the Four Rising Attacks. He knew nothing of Bechareth, had only witnessed him performing the practice rituals with the others. Would he be defensive or aggressive? Did he favour a particular style of attack? Korlandril realised that he did not even know how long Bechareth had been treading the Path of the Warrior. He made these observations coolly, without judgement or fear.

He was also unsure of his own strategy. That Bechareth was more experienced seemed certain. Would Korlandril do better to confine himself to fight cautiously until he had more of a measure of his opponent? Or would that hand too much of the initiative to his adversary? Korlandril wondered if he would react well enough to whatever attacks Bechareth made. Part of him considered if the duel would even last more than a few heartbeats.

That thought did bring with it a reaction: a stab of pride. Korlandril had worked hard to learn the fighting stances and the poses of attack and defence. Now was the time to demonstrate that he had learned well. He was determined to give a good account of himself.

At Kenainath's wordless signal, the pair fell in behind the exarch as he led them down a winding ramp to a chamber deep below the pyramid of the shrine's upper storeys. The others followed a little way behind the three of them, walking in single file, clothed only in the undersuits of their armour.

The passageways had a rough, hard-worked surface that seemed odd to Korlandril. The part of him that had been an Artist recognised it for the affectation that it was; nothing on Alaitoc was anything but artificial. Yet the warrior part of Korlandril's mind recognised what the change in surroundings represented. It was tradition, a warrior code that stretched back to the time of the Fall. A shrine dedicated to the teachings of the Striking Scorpion's founder; or rather the teachings of the founder's greatest pupil after his master fell to the darkness.

The ambient light, such as there was in the shrine, was replaced by narrow, flickering tubes. There was pretence here, but one that Korlandril could understand. This was a reconstruction of that first shrine, created by Arhra after learning under the tuition of Asurmen. The Deadly Shadow, as all the other shrines on Alaitoc and the many other craftworlds, was not paying homage to the birthplace of its traditions, but trying to recreate them. Everything was now as it was then. What it was to be a Striking Scorpion had not changed in the thousands of passes that had gone by since that founding.

All of this Korlandril was aware of, with the small critical eye at the back of his mind. The greater part of him, the bulk of his spirit that was now warrior, immersed itself in the atmosphere, heightening his anticipation for the coming duel.

The ceiling was intentionally low, barring the two of them from leaving their feet or swinging their swords too high overhead. The floor was etched with a circle, not much wider than the space the two of them occupied, with the rune of the shrine at its centre. Korlandril knew that the duellists would not be allowed to leave the circle. This was a contest of skill at close confines, of control and precision, the foundation of the Striking Scorpion ethos.

No rules had been explained to Korlandril, but he knew that there would be no actual contact, no risk of drawing blood or damage to the precious armour. He was not even sure this was a contest; he inferred as such from Kenainath's next words.

'This is not a test, a place to prove yourself, to you or to me,' intoned Kenainath, signalling the two warriors into the centre of the oval chamber. The exarch nodded for them to begin and stepped back into the shadows. The other Striking Scorpions watched silently from close to the wall.

The pair shifted instantly, Korlandril assuming Leaf that Cuts, a defensive posture. Bechareth needed no encouragement and stepped forwards and to his left, chainsword humming towards the side of Korlandril's head, the whirring blades stopping short by only the span of a hand.

'Cut!' The word was muffled by the small chamber, coming from the throats of the others at the same time.

Korlandril was taken aback by the speed of Bechareth's attack. The two returned to their positions of repose, staring into each other's eyes. There was intensity in Bechareth's and Korlandril imagined his were the same. This was no war-mask; had it been, the last blow would have sliced off the top of Korlandril's head and Bechareth would not have thought twice about it.

They stood immobile for some time, neither willing to make the first move just yet. Korlandril shifted quickly into Cloud Turning to Storm, feinting high and then spinning low and driving his chainsword toward Bechareth's stomach. His foe deflected the attack, flat of blade on flat of blade, knocking Korlandril sideways by a fraction. Through this miniscule opening, Bechareth stepped forwards again, the tip of his humming blade aimed at Korlandril's throat.

'Cut!' announced the onlookers.

Bechareth stepped back, a flicker of a smile on his lips.

Again and again the same pattern played out: Korlandril countering or attempting an attack, only for Bechareth to manoeuvre into a killing position within a few strokes.

Korlandril shook his head, rapidly losing what confidence he had. It was one matter to execute the strikes and defences he had learnt against thin air, another to perform them against a target that was trying everything to misdirect and unbalance him. His mind, which he had never thought of as particularly slow, seemed unable to register Bechareth's moves quickly enough; any response he might come up with was always too late.

As they paused before their seventh exchange, a sensation of movement, perhaps the slightest sound of a footfall or a breath, caused Korlandril to whirl around, sword cutting the air. He stopped the blade just before it struck Kenainath's outstretched arm. The exarch wore a pleased expression. He moved his gaze from the whirring teeth of the chainsword to Korlandril's stare.

'Do not consider, act without thought or feeling, no hesitation.'

Korlandril understood the lesson, but as he turned to face Bechareth again, he was unsure how to implement the exarch's teaching.

Bechareth flicked up his sword towards Korlandril's thigh, the novice's blade sweeping down and stopping it short. Distracted, he had reacted better than when he had been concentrating. It was not a matter of process, it was a matter of instinct. His body, his inner mind, knew better what to do than his conscious thoughts.

Korlandril focussed on his breathing, relaxing himself, while Bechareth launched a complex assault. At each strike, Korlandril's sword rose to intercept his foe's chainsword with a dull ring. Korlandril could almost see without his eyes, hear without his ears. As never before, he felt enmeshed with his armour, the chainsword an extension of himself and not some foreign object gripped in his fist.

After three more parries, Korlandril took the offensive, sliding a foot forward, lunging towards Bechareth's midriff. Bechareth knocked Korlandril's chainsword downward and flicked his wrist, but Korlandril had already responded, ducking to his left while his blade flashed out towards Bechareth's shoulder. Again the blades met with a brief shudder of contact and then moved on, darting and probing. Korlandril felt like he was standing with the others, simply watching the duel from a distance, amazed at the agility and skill of his body.

'Cut!'

The barked word broke the flow of Korlandril's consciousness. For a moment he felt triumph, for the call had come as he aimed a throat-slashing blow. But Bechareth was smiling, his eyes narrowed. A glance down revealed Bechareth's chainsword barely a finger's width from the inside of Korlandril's thigh – a cut that would have torn through the artery and cut deep into his pelvis.

Kenainath stepped between them, hand raised to halt the duel. He nodded approvingly towards Bechareth, who bowed slightly and withdrew towards the others. The exarch turned on Korlandril, eyebrow raised in question, head tilted ever-so-slightly to one side.

'The lesson is learnt, but you are still a novice, and must practise more.'

'Yes,' replied Korlandril. A moment's reflection and he realised that he was not ashamed of being beaten, he held his head high, his shoulders square. He pondered Kenainath's quizzical expression for a moment, and realised what was expected of him. 'The claw I will master. I am ready to learn the ways of the venomous bite.'

Kenainath nodded in agreement.

KORLANDRIL FOUND THE shuriken pistol – the venomous bite of the Striking Scorpion – more straightforward to use than the chainsword. Like his blade, it responded to his thoughts, firing a volley of monomolecular-edged discs that could slice flesh with ease. Though it could be used at some distance, the shuriken pistol in the hands of the Striking Scorpion was mainly a close combat weapon, complementing the cuts and parries of the chainsword. The sweeping movements Korlandril made with his left hand during the rituals became short bursts of fire, to distract or incapacitate the enemy whilst the chainsword delivered the killing blow.

It was impossible to duel with loaded pistols without risking serious harm, and so Korlandril continued to fight with chainsword alone against the others. His skills improved with each encounter, to the point where he would score a cut almost as often as his opponents. Despite this, there was no word of praise from Kenainath, and of the other shrine members only Elissanadrin ever complemented him on his growing skill.

IT WAS WITH a mixture of trepidation and excitement that, seventy-eight cycles later, Korlandril found himself back in the armouring chamber with Kenainath, about to enter the final stage of his training – the Scorpion's Sting. He suited up as he had done dozens of times before, but on this occasion there was a final line to the mantra intoned by the exarch.

'See not with the eyes, but allow anger to flow, let Khaine's gift guide you.'

Korlandril lifted the helmet above his head and lowered it purposefully, encasing himself fully from toe to scalp. With a hiss of air, the suit sealed itself. He was gripped by a terrifying claustrophobia, trapped inside the helm. It was dark and stifling and he flailed to take it off again, dreading suffocation.

'Be calm warrior, do not let your fears take hold, but extend your will.' Kenainath's voice drifted into Korlandril's consciousness, his tone soothing, patient.

Korlandril forced himself to quell his hyperventilating and took a deep breath, fearing it would be his last.

'See not with the eyes, but allow anger to flow, let Khaine's gift guide you,' Kenainath said again.

The Striking Scorpion performed a mental twist, turning his fear – defence – into anger – attack. He wanted to master the horror creeping up within him, to slay the sly serpent writhing in his gut that threatened to still his heart.

Almost immediately there was light, blinding in its brightness. Korlandril felt the tendrils of the suit's systems reaching into his mind, probing for connection. He fought the urge to resist and instead surrendered himself to its gentle but insistent exploration. The sensation was deeply unpleasant as the Aspect helmet sifted through his memories and thoughts, seeking purchase. Flickers of past events strobed through Korlandril's consciousness, each too brief to recognise but as a sum stirring up long-dead feelings.

With a shriek of anguish roaring from Korlandril's throat, the memory of Thirianna's rejection engulfed him. That primal scream brought forth a hail of spitting fire from the weapons array built into the helmet – the mandiblasters for which the Striking Scorpions were famed and feared.

Plasmic energy crackled along the discharge of conductive needles fired from the helmet-mounted weapons, spraying across the arming chamber in a burst of fury. The anger looped between Korlandril and the suit, sending him staggering, hands raised to the helmet to drag it off. The suit refused him, pulling him down into its dark embrace.

Blackness swamped Korlandril and he collapsed, clattering to the floor in a twisted heap.

* * *

MEMORY, REALITY, HOPE and fear spun with kaleido-scopic chaos within Korlandril's mind. Not even his first Dreaming had been as terrifying. He felt like a mote of dust in a hurricane, a tiny speck of light amidst the furnace of a star. One image burned into his spirit, white-hot in its intensity, inescapable in its magnitude. The rune of the Striking Scorpion seared into his mind.

|Lost|Alone|Pathless|Abandoned|

Laughter – Korlandril dimly recognised it as Aradryan's – turned from humour to taunt. Thiri-anna's eyes – strangely golden – looked at him with pity and scorn. Kenainath's mocking words, his dis-dain. Korlandril was child-like, insecure, exposed to the overwhelming sensations of the universe again. There was nowhere to hide. The shadows brought their own perils.

|Darkness|Rage|Hate|Death|

The need to destroy – to eradicate anything and everything – suffused Korlandril. He would tear the throat from laughing Aradryan. He would pluck the scheming eyes from Thirianna. He would slice the head from Kenainath and take it as a trophy. He would heap ruin upon those that had wronged him, slurred his reputation and scorned his advances.

|Light|Hope|Friendship|Love|

Like the waters of a tidal wave flowing down a whirlpool, the doubt and fear and anger swirled away from Korlandril. He heard the joy in Aradryan's laughter. He saw the affection in Thirianna's eyes. He felt the respect in Kenainath's words.

His hand reached to the spirit stone at his breast, its coolness spreading to each part of him, through his skin, along his nerves, into every organ and bone.

|Calm|Silence|Discipline|Peace|

KORLANDRIL AWOKE ON his cot in the dormitory, unarmoured. He was alone. He could remember nothing save an overwhelming sensation of contentment. The gloom was a comforting embrace, devoid of stimuli to confound and distract him.

Korlandril closed his eyes and slept. He did not dream.

IT TOOK SIX more attempts for Korlandril to finally master the Scorpion's Sting. With each session, he gradually learned to interface with the psychic connections of the armoured suit without suffering the catastrophic feedback of his first encounter. When he finally stood before the others, fully armed and armoured, he was calm and in control.

Bechareth was the first to congratulate him, bowing sincerely and deeply. Elissanadrin came next.

'You have become that which you needed to become,' she said sombrely, her melodic voice tainted slightly by the transmitter of her suit. 'You have achieved the division between your spirit and your war-mask.'

'Which is good news for us,' said Arhulesh, joining the pair.

'How so?' asked Korlandril.

'You will be able to join us outside the shrine,' Arhulesh said. 'The glasses of the Crescent of the Dawning Ages have nothing more to fear from you.'

It was with some shame that Korlandril recalled the incident that had propelled him to the Shrine of the Deadly Shadow.

'Of course,' Arhulesh continued, 'if you feel like smashing anything, make sure you finish your drink first.'

The import of what Arhulesh had first said sank in.

'I will be able to leave the shrine?' said Korlandril. His first reaction was trepidation. What if the others were wrong? What if his anger was not under his control? Korlandril's second thought was of embarrassment. For all that he had discovered about himself as a warrior, he was still ashamed of the journey that had brought him to the shrine's doors. What if he met Thirianna?

'We will be with you,' said Min, laying a comforting hand on Korlandril's arm. 'And if I guess your doubts correctly, you should remember that Thirianna was once a Dire Avenger. In fact, was it not you that judged the warrior more harshly?'

Korlandril had to admit he had confessed as much to the others several times. His views were more conflicted now, but he still felt a certain unease.

'I would like to train for a little more time before I venture out,' he said.

'Nonsense!' declared Min. 'You have learnt too well the art of stealth and secrecy. It is time to step back into the light and enjoy Alaitoc again.'

'Brooding here like Kenainath won't help you,' said Arhulesh. 'What you really need is the company of others.'

'And a carafe or two of summervine!' Elissanadrin added. The suggestion roused in Korlandril a desire to indulge himself a little, to lose himself in talk and wine.

'You are right, this is a time of celebration, not mourning,' Korlandril announced, smiling inside his helm. 'Khaine can keep Kenainath here, but I'm filled with the teachings of Kurnous. Wine and song, and perhaps I might even visit a few old friends.'

The others fell hush and Korlandril felt a presence behind him, a slight chill as if a breeze drifted over his neck. He turned to see Kenainath staring at him.

'I'm sorry, I didn't…'

'No apologies, I would not wish you to stay, who still has freedom. Find happiness now, enjoy your life while you can, you have earned that right.'

Kenainath swung away and then stopped to direct a long stare over his shoulder at Korlandril.

'Do not forget me, and not the Deadly Shadow, who gave you this gift. A pact you have made, with the Bloody-Handed God, he is part of you. Live well and train hard, heed the shrill call to battle, and return to me.'

Korlandril bowed low, humbled by the exarch's words.

'I will return on the morrow, and we will continue. I cannot reject Khaine's gift, and so I look to you to guide me.'

The exarch nodded once and strode away, swallowed by the dark of the shrine.

FEAR

Before the War in Heaven, Eldanesh, sword-brother and hawk-friend, faced the nightmarish horde of the Autochtinii and he was afraid. Countless in number were the foe and the eldar were few. Not for himself did Eldanesh fear, but for the lives of his warriors. As Eldanesh girded himself for the battle to come there was a great tumult of fire in the air. Khaine himself, iron-skinned and fire-blooded, arrived with spear and shield and stood beside the mortal prince. Though Khaine hated Eldanesh and Eldanesh had no love for Khaine, the Bloody-Handed One would protect the eldar from their foes. So it was that Eldanesh's fear was quashed by the presence of the war god and the eldar knew victory over the Autochtinii.

KORLANDRIL SMOOTHED OUT a graceful curve from the ivory-coloured putty, shaping the thigh of the figurine coming to shape in his hands. The old part of him, the essence of the Artist that had survived into Korlandril the Warrior, knew it to be a crude ornament, but the fingers of the Striking Scorpion still recalled the dexterity and skill of his former Path.

The sculpture was of Isha, as were the four others that he had added to his collection since his first departure from the shrine. It helped him to focus on a moment of purity with Thirianna. Korlandril had also come to terms with the rift that had erupted between him and Aradryan, and recognised that the unveiling had not been the start of that division.

It had been childish not to accept that his friend had changed from the eldar he had known before Aradryan's voyage. With the pragmatic eye of the Warrior rather than the idealistic gaze of the Artist, Korlandril could see that he had changed as much during Aradryan's absence. He looked back at the conceited sculptor he had been and wondered why he had so wished to cling to the past.

The door signal chimed and Korlandril stood up, gesturing for the portal to open. He did not look to see who was visiting him as he crossed into the cleansing chamber to remove the vestiges of the putty from his hand. It was probably Min or Elissanadrin, both had visited him regularly.

'Things change again.' The visitor's voice was not Elissanadrin or Min, though it was oddly familiar. Korlandril turned around to welcome the arrival.

It was Aradryan.

He was dressed in a tight suit of shifting greens and blues, his outline indistinct. He wore a belt and sash with many pouches and pockets and a long knife hung at his hip. The garb of the ranger.

'Things change again,' agreed Korlandril. He remembered his manners and gestured for Aradryan to seat himself. The ranger declined with a slight shake of the head.

'I have come out of courtesy to the friendship we once shared,' said Aradryan. 'I thought it wrong to come back to Alaitoc and not see you.'

'I am glad that you have come,' said Korlandril. 'I owe you an apology for my behaviour the last time we met.'

'It was never the case that we wronged each other intentionally, and neither of us owes the other anything but respect.'

'I trust your travels have been fruitful?'

Aradryan smiled and nodded.

'I cannot describe the sights I have seen, the thrill of adventure that has coursed through my veins. The galaxy has been set out before me and I have experienced such a tiny fraction of the delights and darkness it has to offer.'

'I too have been on a journey,' said Korlandril, cleaning his hands.

'I have heard this,' said Aradryan. Korlandril looked at him and raised his eyebrows in question. Aradryan was hesitant, quiet, when he continued. 'Thirianna. I met with her first. She told me that you are now an Aspect Warrior.'

'A Striking Scorpion of the Deadly Shadow shrine,' said Korlandril. He delicately rinsed his hands and dried them under a warm vent above the sink. 'It does not anger me that you saw Thirianna first. My parting from her is an event of the past, one with which I have wholly come to terms.'

Aradryan's eyes swept the living quarters, taking in the Isha statues arranged around the room. He smiled again and darted a doubtful look at Korlandril.

'Well, perhaps not *wholly*,' the warrior admitted with a short laugh. 'But I truly bear you no ill-will concerning your part, unwitting as it was, in the circumstances that engulfed me.'

'Have you seen her recently?'

Korlandril shook his head.

'It would serve no purpose. If I happen to cross her path, it will be well, but it is not my place to seek her company at this time. She and I travel to different places, and we make our own journeys.'

'Someone else?' suggested Aradryan.

Korlandril was about to deny such a thing but paused, his thoughts turning unbidden to Elissanadrin. He was shocked and it must have shown on his face.

'Aha!' laughed Aradryan.

'It is not like that,' Korlandril said hurriedly. 'She is a fellow warrior at the shrine, it would be entirely inappropriate for us to engage in any deeper relationship.'

Aradryan's face expressed his disagreement with this notion more than any words, but he said nothing. The two of them stood in silence, comfortable if not pleasant, before Aradryan's expression took on a more serious cast. 'I have also come to give you advance warning that you will be shortly called to your shrine.'

'How might you know this?' asked Korlandril, frowning fiercely. 'Have you spoken to Kenainath?'

'I would not tread foot in an Aspect shrine! And your exarch does not venture forth. No, it is from first-hand knowledge that I am aware of this. I have just returned from Eileniliesh. It is an Exodite world not so far away. Orks have come to Eileniliesh and her people call on Alaitoc for help. I have come back as their messenger. Even now the autarchs and farseers debate the best course of action. There is no doubt in my mind that they will issue the call to war.'

'And I will be ready to answer it,' said Korlandril.

'I have my own preparations to make,' said Aradryan, taking a step towards the door. 'Other rangers are gathering here to share what they know of the enemy. I must join them.'

Korlandril nodded his understanding. Aradryan was at the door before Korlandril spoke again.

'I am glad that you are alive and well, my friend.'

'As am I of you, Korlandril. I do not know if I will see you on Eileniliesh or before we leave. If not, then I wish you good fortune and prosperity until our next meeting.'

'Good fortune and prosperity,' echoed Korlandril.

He watched the ranger depart and the iris door close behind him. He wondered whether to head directly to the shrine or await Kenainath's command. Korlandril decided on the latter course of action; he was in no haste to put on his war-mask.

KORLANDRIL CONTINUED TO sculpt into the twilight of the cycle, and still no message from Kenainath arrived. He was putting the finishing touches on the sandals of his miniature goddess when he had cause to pause. Something had changed. He was not sure what had distracted him; a glimmer of sensation at the back of his mind.

He dismissed it and returned to his work, only to be disturbed a few moments later by a more vigorous sense of something untoward happening. It was a feeling at the base of his spine and in his gut. His heart was quickening, growing in tempo along with his breathing. Perturbed, Korlandril sat back in his high-backed chair and concentrated, seeking the source of his discomfort.

It felt like tiny vibrations, running through his spirit rather than his body. Something was awakening his nerve endings, stimulating parts of his mind he did not visit outside of the shrine.

For a fleeting heartbeat he thought he could smell burning and blood, and felt a prickle of heat wash over him. He glanced around the chamber seeking the source but could see nothing. The heat was coming from within him.

Unbidden, the apparition of his imaginary sparring partner flickered through his mind. Like a circuit being completed, the image touched off a chain reaction in Korlandril's mind and body. He flushed with a surge of energy even as he felt a tingling behind his eyes as his nerves sought to connect with something that was not there.

He realised that he was seeking his armour. Even as he thought of the shrine, a ghastly roar echoed in the back of his mind, blotting out all other sensation. Korlandril was almost knocked senseless by the sudden assault of rage and hatred encapsulated in that feral bellow. At once, he knew what was happening, and knew also that he had to go to the Deadly Shadow shrine as swiftly as possible.

War had come to Alaitoc. The Avatar of Kaela Mensha Khaine was awakening.

A SMALL BOX had been left at Korlandril's door, a simple white cube no larger than the palm of his hand without wrapping or message. Korlandril bent his knee to pick it up and as his fingers neared the package he felt a sensation of warmth. He pulled back slightly, surprised by the feeling. It felt like Thirianna, though there was something else mixed in with the strange hint of presence that lingered around the gift.

He picked it up and opened the lid.

Inside was a rune, shaped from silvery-grey wishstone. He recognised it immediately, the symbol of the Dire Avengers. It was the martial discipline of this warrior Aspect that had merged with the tender thoughts of Thirianna. Holding it in his palm, Korlandril concentrated, teasing the thought-stream with which the rune had been imbued.

He felt momentary sadness and longing; regret at their parting; pride in his actions. Most of all, he felt the sensation of understanding. Korlandril divined the message. Thirianna herself had once heard her call of Khaine and supported him on his current path. Running a finger along the bars of the rune, Korlandril knew she had taken it as a souvenir from her armour, and now she had passed it to him as a token of her friendship, one that he would be able to understand from one warrior to another.'

He closed his fingers around the gift and smiled.

IT WAS THE first time Korlandril had suited up with the purpose of true battle. Kenainath stood before him with a shallow bowl, a sliver of a blade in his right hand.

'We give of our blood, as Khaine's call roars around us, calling us to war.'

The exarch took the knife and made a cut in the palm of Korlandril's right hand, allowing the lifeblood of the warrior to drip into the bowl and mingle with that of the other Striking Scorpions.

Kenainath then moved around the squad, in turn painting the rune of the Striking Scorpion upon their foreheads. Korlandril was the last and watched with some trepidation as he saw his companions' eyes glaze over, their muscles twitch and their lips curl back from their teeth in snarls.

Then he felt the blood upon his own skin. It felt like the exarch was carving the rune into his flesh with a fiery brand, the pain flaring in Korlandril's mind. The pain turned to anger, welling up from deep within him. The anger drew on the deep-seated frustrations and humiliations Korlandril had put aside, wakening those forgotten emotions.

Quivering, Korlandril did nothing as the war-mask erupted from within him. His blood thundered in his ears and the cut on his palm burned sharply. The air crackled with life and his skin crawled with energy. Like an obscene birth the warrior spirit of

Korlandril burst forth through the barriers he had erected, seething and hungry.

The voice of Kenainath cut through Korlandril's senses.

'The peace is broken, harmony falls to discord, only war remains.'

Korlandril began the ritual of arming, following each step without thought. It was as if he walked towards a burning fire and was preparing to pass through the flames. He steadied himself mentally, concentrating on the exarch's mantra.

'Now we clothe ourselves, with bloody Khaine's own raiment, as a warrior.'

Korlandril could not fight back his excitement. This was the moment he had dreaded and longed-for since completing his training. He felt a moment of shame at his own bloodthirst but the regret soon disappeared as he continued to armour himself.

'In Khaine's iron skin, we clad ourselves for battle, while fire burns within.'

Like no other time, the armour felt a part of Korlandril. He was not simply putting on his suit, he was becoming himself. More than putting on plates of armour, he was stripping away the pretensions of civilisation he used to conceal his wrath.

'The spirit of Khaine, from which we draw our resolve, strengthens within us.'

The rune upon his forehead was now icy cold. Its freezing touch spread through him, until it had almost stilled his heart. With its chilling fingers it brushed away his remorse and pity, crushed his compassion and guilt.

'War comes upon us, we must bear its dark burden, upon our shoulders.'

Khaine's iron skin, indeed! Korlandril felt strong, stronger than ever before. He flexed his shoulders and bunched the muscles in his chest, the armour tightening around him, comforting in its hard embrace.

'We stand before Khaine, unyielding in our calling, free of doubt and fear.'

Korlandril's heart was a drumbeat, endless, martial, driving him onwards. He curled his fingers into fists and felt the power in his arms. It felt good, to be so powerful, to be so alive.

'We do not flee death, we walk in the shade of Khaine, proud and unafraid.'

The armour made a creaking noise as it adjusted further. As it knitted together he felt it bonding to him, infusing his spirit with its own. He heard panting, dimly realising that it was he that was breathing so quickly. He closed his eyes and saw the fire-eyed apparition of his anger swirling around him, encasing him as surely as the armoured suit.

'We strike from the dark, as swift as the scorpion, with a deadly touch.'

Korlandril felt his hands empty, and longed for the feeling of sword and pistol in his fingers. He flexed his gauntleted hands in anticipation.

'See not with the eyes, but allow anger to flow, let Khaine's gift guide you.'

As the darkness of the helm enveloped Korlandril, he was frozen in space and time. The universe paused, holding its breath. He stood there in the darkness, savouring it, remembering with scorn the fear he had felt when first he had come to this place. It had made him whole.

Something was placed in his right hand and he gripped it gently. Sharp blades hummed into momentary life and then fell still. With a click, something was affixed to the relay cord on his left arm and his hand curled around a pistol's grip. Thirianna's rune hung from it, a small decoration of his own.

Then his waystone, sliding into place upon his chest, guarding his spirit against damnation. It was his last armour, his true protection against the thing he was becoming, the creature he *wanted* to become.

The darkness was inside him and outside him, the fiery eyes staring directly out of his head. He had known all along the shadowy figure he had been fighting, but only now truly saw it for what it was. It was himself he had fought. He had strained against the urges and desires that lingered within his heart. He had tried so hard to quell the feelings of rage, but he had fought out of ignorance.

The darkness was no more, save that Korlandril had his eyes closed. He opened them and looked out at the world with a fresh view through the ruby-tinted lenses of his helmet.

He took a crouched step forward, easing into his fighting stance. No longer was he a thing of flesh and blood, a mortal being filled with falsehood and crude passions. He was a Warrior. He was part of the Bloody-Handed God, an Aspect of Kaela Mensha Khaine.

Korlandril was no more.

In his place stood a Striking Scorpion of the Deadly Shadow.

THE MAIN GALLERY of the warship was an immense hall, vaulted with rib-like structures that split into tall, narrow doorways leading to the side chambers. Flickers of energy danced along the wraithbone core, merging with hidden psychic circuitry behind walls of shifting, mottled blue and green. The arched ship chambers rang with booted feet, the keen sound of blades cutting air and now and then an explosion or blaze of laser fire as weapons were tested. Warriors from Alaitoc's dozens of Aspect shrines practised their rituals, each in a separate hall that branched from the main arterial passage, the mantras of the exarchs ringing from the high ceilings in a multi-layered symphony of war.

Korlandril stood in line with the other Deadly Shadow warriors, hearing only the voice of Kenainath and the beating of his heart.

The Avatar was aboard. The Bloody-Handed God walked among them. Korlandril could feel its presence lingering on the edge of his senses. It quickened his pulse and filled every motion with greater energy. His mind was fixed upon a single goal – the annihilation of the orks despoiling Eileniliesh.

The thought of battle filled him with expectation. For all that his rituals as a warrior allowed him to separate his anger from his daily life, it was in war that he would find release. The prospect of blood-shed, the visceral conflict of life and death, thrilled Korlandril. It promised an intoxication even greater and fulfilling than the completion of a sculpture or the climax of a Dreaming, though he could remember these previous victories only dimly.

When the exercises were complete, Kenainath dismissed them. Korlandril hesitated, unsure what to do next. Elissanadrin approached him, removing her helmet. Korlandril's eyes were immediately drawn to the rune of dried blood on her forehead. His ruby-tinted gaze moved to her eyes and he saw the dispassionate stare he now recognised as the war-mask.

Hesitantly, self-consciously, Korlandril took off his helmet, fearful that this act would somehow remove his war-mask. Un-helmed, he felt no different. The rune upon his skin bound him to his mental state, an anchor of anger.

He followed the others as they left the chamber and filed along the central nave of the starship, heading towards the stern. Now and then a glimmer of light would pass along the translucent walls, a bright speck amongst pale orange and yellow shimmering. There was no infinity circuit on the ship, though its wraithbone core pulsed gently with psychic energy, playing upon the edge of Korlandril's senses. It was almost overwhelmed with the far sharper, iron-and-blood-tainted presence of the Avatar.

Other squads were likewise assembling, coming together along the arteries of the battleship on foot and skimming platforms: Dark Reapers in their heavy black armour and vane-flanked helms; bone-coloured Howling Banshees, the manes of their helmets flying with psychic energy; and many Dire Avengers, blue-clad, their exarchs wearing bright yellow and white gonfalons on their backpacks. And many others beside, each representing a facet of the War God; each dedicated to a particular fighting style, brought together in a harmony of destruction.

'It will be eight cycles before we reach Eileniliesh,' said Min, stopping in his enthusiastic stride to allow Elissanadrin and Korlandril to catch him.

It seemed such a long time to wait before the bloodletting would begin, but Korlandril knew that such a journey was short compared to most. He was agitated by the inactivity, wondering how he would make the time pass.

'I see the hunger in you,' said Min, baring his teeth in a grin. 'It will come soon enough, do not fret.'

'How many times have you fought?' asked Korlandril.

'This will be my thirteenth expedition,' said Elissanadrin.

'Twenty,' replied Min.

Korlandril looked around at Arhulesh, who had been trailing behind them a little way, with Bechareth a few more paces even further back.

'Two,' said Arhulesh. 'Including this one.'

Korlandril laughed, and then fell silent, taken aback that he could show humour. Arhulesh growled.

'You gave the impression you were more experienced,' said Korlandril. 'I did not realise you were such a babe-at-arms.'

'It is you that is the adolescent, newcomer,' said Arhulesh. 'Feverish to taste that forbidden pleasure, yet as hesitant as an Iybraesillian maiden on coming to full flower. Be assured that nobody expects you to perform perfectly the first time.'

'My first foray into fleshly pleasures met with success and much gratitude from my partner,' said Korlandril. 'I've no fear my battle-virginity will hold me back.'

'For truth, I am sure you practised equally before both,' laughed Arhulesh.

They walked on for a while longer, the chatter of other squads around them.

'I am hungry,' said Korlandril, even as he realised the emptiness gnawing at him. He felt like an engine that had burned most of its fuel.

'We all are,' said Min. 'Tis a strange thing, for a cycle from now your stomach will feel like an endless knot and you won't want a morsel. Eat as much as you can, while you can. Your body burns energy much faster with your war-mask on, it's important to keep up your energy levels.'

Korlandril nodded in understanding.

Their journey took them past vast hangars where the dark shapes of scout ships loomed in shadow. A few were empty, their ranger pilots escorting the warship through the winding half-real maze of the webway. Other halls were also dormant: places where tanks and other war machines would usually be transported. There was to be no such support on this mission – this was a quick strike to destroy the ork threat in its infancy. Only the Aspect Warriors had been called, the farseers judging the situation not so severe that the citizen militia – the Guardians – needed to be mobilised.

Min led them to an eatery where hundreds of Aspect Warriors were sat at long tables, while others moved busily around the circular counters, helping themselves to the food on offer. A force dome glittered overhead, showing a view of the webway. A curving tunnel of energy enveloped the ship with solid walls of rippling colours, streaked through with flashes of star-lit sky. Engineered from the stuff of warp space, the webway burrowed between and through the immaterial and material worlds, part of both but separate from each.

Now and then they passed a branching route, the webway bifurcating through hanging gateways of gold and wraithbone, inscribed with runes channelling and shaping the psychic energy of warp space. There were other features: small tunnels that cut out great loops of the main channels; huge coils of raw wraithbone wrapped around the insubstantial tunnel in places the only evidence of repairs; occasionally the force walls folded and buckled, rippling with light as some malign creature of warp space intersected with the webway and was thrown back by the psychic wards.

There were no other ships to be seen, the route to Eileniliesh had been cleared by the rangers to allow passage for the large warship.

Thinking about the daemons and other creatures loitering close at hand made Korlandril uneasy. The webway was far safer than open warp space, but it unnerved him to imagine the immaterial beasts held at bay by the translucent walls of energy. He pulled his eyes away and looked at the Aspect Warriors gathered in their squads across the circular hall.

'Why does the Deadly Shadow have so few warriors compared to the other shrines?'

'Kenainath will only take on a single pupil at a time,' explained Elissanadrin. 'It is fortunate for you that he had no acolyte at the time of your... dilemma. I would not have been able to bring you to him had it been otherwise.'

Korlandril also noticed that most of the other shrines had their exarchs with them. Kenainath, as far as Korlandril knew, had remained in the Deadly Shadow's allotted shrine-hall. He spied another group of Striking Scorpions, more than twenty of them. Their exarch sat at the head of the table. A long two-edged chainsword hung on a sling across his back.

'The Fall of Deadly Rain,' said Arhulesh. 'That is the exarch, Aranarha. We should pay our respects.'

The exarch looked up at them as they approached; eyes a deep blue, his features smooth like one of Korlandril's sculptures. His hair was cropped barbarically short, save for two long braids that fell across his face.

'The children of Kenainath, a welcome greeting, and a new member with them!' the exarch said with a lop-sided grin. He stood up and gave a perfunctory bow towards Korlandril.

'My honour,' said Korlandril, returning the bow. 'I am Korlandril.'

'And now a Deadly Shadow, hiding in your shrine, with Kenainath's dark whispers. Why did you not come to me, my door was open, and I am far less fearsome.'

'I–' began Korlandril, but Elissanadrin cut him off.

'It was I that brought Korlandril to the Deadly Shadow, as was right,' she said forcefully. 'Kenainath teaches us well.'

'I do not dispute that fact, but that is not all, there is more to life than war.'

'He allows us to learn those lessons for ourselves,' countered Min.

Aranarha smiled pleasantly and waved for them to sit themselves down.

'You have come here on your own, without your exarch, so enjoy our company.'

Korlandril glanced at the others for guidance.

'Here is as good a place as any,' said Arhulesh, taking a place between two of the Fall of Deadly Rain warriors. He helped himself to a few morsels from the plate of the warrior to his left. 'We have little else to do.'

'We will join you shortly,' said Elissanadrin, turning towards the nearest food counter. Korlandril trailed slightly behind her, bemused by the exchange.

'I detect some enmity,' he said. 'Do you have some issue with Aranarha?'

Elissanadrin shook her head, taking an oval platter from beneath the heated food station. With dextrous flicks of her wrist, she transferred a pile of steaming multi-coloured grains to the plate. Korlandril took up a bowl and wandered to a stand of low bushes growing from a patch of spongy floor. With quick fingers, he twisted the berries from the living branches and then moved on to a small pool where fragrant blossoms floated on the surface. He plucked a couple of blooms and scattered their petals across his food.

'Aranarha and Kenainath have been rivals for some time, but there is no hostility there,' said

Elissanadrin, as Korlandril used a slender knife to fillet slices of meat from the carcass of a shadow-horn. 'Kenainath is old – very old – and he does not approve of Aranarha's methods sometimes. But we are all warriors here, and that is a bond that cannot be broken. For all their differences, they still respect each other.'

'But that does not explain your tone and actions,' said Korlandril, filling his dish with a generous help-ing of split seeds and twists of angel-resin. He was ravenous and had to stop himself over-filling the platter.

'Kenainath sees his entrapment as an exarch as a curse, but Aranarha takes it as a blessing. The older would rather have no pupils, the younger prosely-tises his cult, actively recruiting new warriors.'

'Why does Kenainath want to be free of pupils? Is he that disdainful of us?'

Elissanadrin gave Korlandril a sharp look.

'If Kenainath had no pupils, it would mean that there is no need of him – that others were free from the taint of Khaine's Gift. If you think that Kenainath disdains you, then you see something I do not. Per-haps it is merely a reflection of some residual shame you feel.'

'He does not seem to care too much about me,' Korlandril said with a shrug. 'Perhaps I confuse indifference for disdain.'

'Kenainath digs deep, reaching into the very heart of what takes you to him.' Elissanadrin kept her voice quiet as they moved back towards the table with the other Striking Scorpions. 'Aranarha teaches the rituals en masse, taking no personal interest in each warrior. Which of the two do you think cares more?'

Korlandril considered this as he sat down to eat with the rest. Soon his plate was empty and he returned for more. And then a third helping.

'This fire indeed burns brightly, a feast of Kurnous, would not satiate his need,' remarked Aranarha.

Korlandril looked down at the food piled in front of him. He saw no wrong in it. Min had warned him to eat as much as he could while he felt hungry.

'It would be better that I do not go to my first battle weak with hunger,' he said, before setting to his latest course with relish.

'At least our armour is polymorphic,' laughed Arhulesh. 'It won't feel any tighter!'

Korlandril grinned and reached for a goblet of spiced lodefruit juice. He raised it in toast to Arhulesh and downed its contents in a long gulp. Smacking his lips, he thudded the goblet back onto the table.

'If battle tastes so sweet, the greater banquet is yet to come!' he declared.

THE WAYSEER STOOD in front of an oval, gold-rimmed portal, one of several such gateways extruded from the wraithbone floor in the webway chambers at the rear of the warship. She was swathed in a voluminous robe of deep purple. Her white hair was parted in the middle and fell in two long locks in front of her shoulders, weighted with rings of a metallic blue. About her extended hand orbited five white runes, twisting gently in the psychic breeze of her magistrations as she aligned the entrance with a temporary webway strand into the material universe. The mirror-like skein of energy within the portal's frame shimmered occasionally, causing the runes to dance with more agitation for a moment before settling into their tranquil circling.

'It is almost time, the portal will be open, we are the vanguard,' said Kenainath. He signalled for the squad to don their helmets.

The red-washed taint on his vision made Korlandril think of a film of blood covering his eyes. He was full of energy; not nervous, just eager. This was the culmination of so much time, so much effort in practise, and just as the webway portal was opening, he felt a new door was opening on his life. He longed to race through and grasp whatever opportunities lay beyond.

Fighting the urge to fidget, forcing himself to stand placidly and wait for the wayseer to complete her ritual, Korlandril idly checked his armour's systems. Rather, he allowed part of his consciousness to merge with the suit a little more deeply than usual. He felt nothing amiss.

Slightly bored, he pulled himself back from the suit's rhythms and gently touched the trigger on his pistol, activating the psychic link. Immediately a view-within-a-view appeared in his left eye, like a keyhole in his vision. Through that small opening he could see the green-veined floor of the portal chamber. Lifting his arm, he played the pistol across the webway portal and settled on the wayseer, the image relayed by the seeing-gem of the pistol's sight. A small rune appeared beside the wayseer – the symbol of Alaitoc – indicating she was friend not foe.

It was a precautionary measure, unlikely to be used, but the designers of the pistol perhaps had lived in more turbulent times, when even the craftworlds had raised their weapons against each other. The viewfinder was useful at range but distracting at close quarters. Korlandril dismissed it with a thought and his vision returned to normal.

The faint padding of boots caused him to turn towards the arched entranceway to the chamber. Seven figures entered, shadowy and indistinct; rangers swathed in cameleoline coats, now the white and pale green colour of the chamber, outlines barely discernable. One pulled back her hood revealing a beautiful face, a tattoo of a red tear beneath her left eye, and winked at Korlandril. Yet for all her charming looks and frivolity, there was something about the ranger that disturbed him. His gaze fell to her waystone and he sensed something otherworldly there. She was not on the Path, her senses and spirit free to soar to whatever heights it could, and to plunge to whatever depths awaited.

Like Aradryan, thought Korlandril. Free, but vulnerable.

'You'll be following us onto Eileniliesh,' she said, turning her attention to Kenainath. The exarch nodded without comment.

The other rangers were unrecognisable. Korlandril wondered if one of them was Aradryan. He surreptitiously angled his pistol towards the rangers and activated the Scorpion's Eye, hoping to see their faces. Flicking through various spectra, both visible and invisible, he discovered the rangers' cloaks dissipated not only ordinary light, but also heat and other signatures as might be detected by an enemy. With a disappointed sigh, he switched it off again and turned back to the portal.

The flat plane was now slowly swirling with colours, mostly blues and greens, with occasional twists of red and black. It was mesmerising, and Korlandril felt himself drawn towards it. Out of curiosity he raised his pistol towards the portal, but Min stepped in front of him, placing a hand on his arm.

'Not wise,' said the warrior with a shake of his head.

Korlandril took the warning at face value and lowered his arm.

'The portal is open,' declared the wayseer. The runes floated in a vertical line above her open palm.

The ranger pulled up her hood, her exquisite features disappearing from view. With a gesture made vague by her long coat, she strode into the miasmic plane of the portal and disappeared. Unslinging rifles almost as tall as themselves, the other rangers followed her.

Kenainath moved his gaze from one Striking Scorpion to the next, as if gauging them. He could see nothing of their expressions, but Korlandril wondered if the exarch had senses beyond those of a normal eldar. With no word of instruction, Kenainath plunged in after the rangers.

Korlandril spared a glance at the rest of the squad, but none of them looked back at him. He wondered if they shared the same sense of achievement as he did, about to embark on his first foray into battle. One-by-one they walked into the webway.

His excitement at a crescendo, Korlandril stepped after them.

THE WEBWAY PASSAGE cut towards the surface of Eileniliesh between the real universe and the otherworld of the warp, a flattened tube cutting through what at first appeared to be roiling water. It was impossible to tell the true colour of the tunnel through his lenses, but he would not have been surprised if it had been a sea green or blue. He half-expected to see the red flashes of a firefish going past, or the silver shimmer of a starfin shoal.

The one thing that was strange was the sense of motion, in that there was not any. Though he stalked forwards at some pace behind the others, nothing changed in his surrounds. It felt like he was walking on the spot. The web-tunnel undulated occasionally, but Korlandril could not tell whether this was due to movement in the warp-passage or simply a shift in the energies that were kept at bay by its immaterial walls.

Peering hard through the invisible force wall, Korlandril could make out the indistinct threads of other webway passages, twisting about this one and each other, coming together and parting like the strands of a thread. Of the squads using these other tunnels, he could see nothing.

'How long is this?' he asked, his voice relayed to the other members of the squad.

'Just a temporary burrowing,' replied Arhulesh. 'We'll be down on the surface in a few moments.'

Korlandril peered past the shoulders of those in front, hoping to see something. In his imagination it would be a shimmering veil through which he would be able to see the trees and grass of Eile-niliesh.

Instead, the others flickered out of sight as they passed a certain point, and taking another step, Kor-landril found himself walking on soft turf. He was vaguely disappointed.

'Ready your weapons, battle will be soon at hand, Khaine's bloody playfield.'

Korlandril fell into position at the centre of the squad just behind Kenainath and looked around. Above, the sky was filled with clouds, the light of two huge moons dimly pushing through their gloom. They were on a hillside, gently sloping upwards in front of him, and at the summit there stood a narrow, solitary tower. Light burned within its pinnacle, casting long shadows from the scattered rocks and trees. Korlandril scanned the hillside for the rangers but they were already gone, or so well hidden from view that he could no longer see them.

His mouth was dry and he licked his lips, while he flexed his fingers on his weapons to keep himself relaxed, dissipating a tiny fraction of the energy burning inside him. He wondered how close they were to the orks, but refrained from asking. His question was answered as they crested the hill, revealing a swathe of black smoke hanging low over a forest that grew in the valley beyond.

Korlandril heard a growl of anger from one of the others but he was not sure who had made it. It might have even been himself. The sight of the crude bil-lowings of the orks swathing the beautiful trees darkened Korlandril's spirit. Thoughts of glorious battle dissipated and all that remained was a desire to destroy the creatures that assailed this world.

'Follow the river,' came the voice of the lead ranger from the communications crystal just beside Korlandril's right ear.

Kenainath cut to the right and brought them to a narrow, fast-flowing water course, birthed somewhere within the hill and gushing forth along a rocky defile. The exarch and squad crossed easily at the river head, and moved swiftly down the hillside and into the sparse trees at the edge of the forest.

Aside from the gurgling and splashing of the river, Korlandril could hear the rustling of the leaves overhead and the sigh of the wind through the lush grass at his feet. Of his companions, he could hear nothing, moving as silently as shadows. In the distance, as yet barely audible, there sounded a greater disturbance – the noise of rough engines and cruel laughter.

'The orks have occupied Hirith-Hreslain,' reported the ranger.

Another voice came to Korlandril's ear. He did not recognise it, but it spoke with sombre authority.

'The settlement straddles the river,' intoned the speaker. 'The majority of the enemy are on the webward side, closest to our positions. Their leaders are on the opposite bank. Firuthein, position your warriors along the river behind and prepare to disable any transports crossing from the far side. Kenainath, move your squad towards the bridge to deal with any survivors of the Fire Dragons' strike.'

'It shall be, as you command, with Khaine's will,' replied a sonorous voice, presumably the exarch Firuthein.

'The Scorpions wait, we will strike from the shadow, none will survive us.' Kenainath's tone and cadence were instantly familiar.

'That was the autarch,' explained Min when Korlandril asked who he had been listening to. 'He's coordinating the main attack, and we're to stop any enemy reinforcements.'

'An ambush,' said Arhulesh. 'Exactly our type of fighting.'

THE RIVER WIDENED and shallowed rapidly as it reached the valley floor. The trees grew close to the banks, but now a wide expanse separated the two sides, the dim light of the night sky a deep orange to Korlandril's eyes. The further the Striking Scorpions advanced, the more they were separated from the rest of the army, which was angling towards the greater concentration of orks on the other river bank. Korlandril glanced over his left shoulder and saw the squad of Firuthein's Fire Dragons striding purposefully along the opposite side of the river.

A sudden movement – or rather the sudden stillness of the rest of the squad – alerted Korlandril to something amiss. He froze in place, poised in the stance of Leaf that Cuts.

A ripple disturbed the placid surface of the water, trailed by a thin stream of bubbles. Something was moving towards the squad, just under the waterline. With a thought, Korlandril brought up the wide-spectrum view of his helmet and gazed beneath the water's reflective surface. The 'something' was large and snake-like, five times as long as an eldar is tall, with three pairs of flippers and a wide-fluked tail.

Two large hearts beat beside each other in its chest and Korlandril could see strings of cartilage running the length of its body overlaid with a labyrinth of arteries and strange organs. Korlandril could see the flow of heat from these out to the extremities as the creature swished lazily past, within easy pistol shot.

It gave not a first glance towards the Striking Scorpions swathed from the moonlight by the trees shrouding the bank. Korlandril watched it glide behind him and nodded to Kenainath, signalling that it was safe to continue.

Under the cover of the thickening cloud – the light of the moons now all but gone – the squad made swift progress and were soon within sight of the arcing bridge that connected to the two parts of Hirith-Hreslain. On the far bank – the webward side closest to the eldar army – tall towers rose from amongst the trees. Smoke billowed from narrow windows and soot stained pale walls. On the nearer side the buildings were more widely spaced and a great clearing had been cut into the forest. This had once been pastureland for the grazing beasts of the Exodites. Now it was a ruin, the carcasses of the great reptilian herbivores heaped onto roaring pyres or left in the trampled mud where they had been slaughtered. Crude standards of flat metal icons and ragged banners had been driven into the soil and lashed to the cracked tiled roofs of the outbuildings.

Ramshackle, wheeled vehicles rumbled across the turf, their thick tyres churning up swathes of dirt, cutting gashes into the fertile ground. The air was choked with their fumes. Metal-sided and roofed sheds had been erected over the ruins of farmsteads and barns, where clanging echoed through the night sky and the bright spark of welding torches mingled with the flicker of naked flames and the stark light of artificial lamps. Piles of junk littered the open ground: twisted mechanical workings, badly hewn logs, shredded tyres, the bones of dead food and heaps of steaming dung. Haphazard chimneys jutted from the worksheds spewing oily smoke, leaving a cloud of smog lingering over the filthy campsite.

Through the murk, with the aid of his lens-filters, Korlandril could see the orks, the first he had encountered though he had heard tales from the others of the squad. If anything, their horrific stories did not do justice to the brutal aliens.

There were several dozen of the green-skinned monsters. Most of them were far larger than Korlandril, even hunched and crouching around the fires. Some were enormous, perhaps half again as tall as the Aspect Warriors, and three or four times as broad. They growled and cackled to each other in their brutish tongue, striking out to emphasise their points.

Around and about the encampment scurried a host of smaller creatures, carrying food and weapons, or simply scrabbling about with each other in petty conflicts. Their higher-pitched voices added a dissonant cut through the rumble of the orks' bellows and roars, jarring in Korlandril's ears.

Without thought, Korlandril raised his weapons, disgusted by what he saw.

'It is not yet time, temper your anger and hate, vengeance will come soon,' warned Kenainath.

* * *

THE MOMENTS CREPT past as the Striking Scorpions lay in wait. Korlandril watched the orks, wary of discovery, but not a single greenskin warrior or their diminutive servants spared a glance towards the river. He turned his attention back to the towers of the main settlement. Here the destruction of the orks was even more evident.

The bucket-jawed monstrosities had set up their camp in the ruins of the settlement. Walls had been smashed in to widen doorways and windows, and the detritus of the alien invaders was piled everywhere. They had been here for a short while and had made ugly repairs and 'improvements' with sheets of metal riveted into the elegant stone buildings, and planks of untreated wood lashed into place to form balconies and battlements.

Hundreds of the creatures milled about, arguing and fighting, eating and shouting. With each heartbeat Korlandril came to despise them more. They were an affront to everything he had learnt to appreciate and love. They were an oafish, unsubtle, ill-disciplined rabble. They were incarnations of anarchy and violence, having nothing of culture, wit or art. Their brutality was their strength, their ignorance their armour against the darker things of the universe that preyed on more civilised species.

Though every part of Korlandril strained to unleash the wrath of Khaine, to wipe out these barbaric figures that had survived from the earliest legends of the eldar, a small, reasoning part of his brain told him that it would never be so. If the eldar had been unable to remove the blight of the orks from the galaxy when their civilisation had been at the height of its power, before the darkness of the Fall, they had little hope now. They were so few, so scattered, in comparison to the grunting, seething hordes that now held sway over so many worlds that had once belonged to the eldar.

Korlandril found comfort in a singular thought: by the time the next dawn came, there would be fewer orks to despoil the stars. With skill and determination, some would die by his own hand. The prospect renewed his thrill of being in battle, even though not a shot had yet been fired or a blade swung in anger.

He focussed on visualisations of the combat techniques he would employ against the ungainly monsters. He imagined eluding their clumsy blows while his own weapons cut them down with ease. These brutes had slain other eldar – admittedly backward Exodites, but eldar all the same – and he was in a position to exact red payment for that crime.

No more orders came or were needed. The exarchs knew their roles and the warriors knew how to fight. The only announcement of the battle commencing was a thunderous explosion on the webward side of the river. Thin vapour trails marked the passage of missiles from the Dark Reapers as blossoms of incandescent ruin engulfed the orks. The soft whickering of shuriken catapult fire was soon lost in the tumult of the orks' alarms – blaring mechanical horns, resounding metallic drums and deafening bellows.

Korlandril wanted to join the fray and eased himself forwards to stand beside Kenainath. The water lapped gently at the exarch's knees as he stood motionless in the shallows of the river, eyes fixed on the orks on the right-hand bank. Korlandril turned his attention there and saw the greenskins organising quickly. For all their unsophisticated ways, they responded rapidly to the attack; the promise of bloodshed roused them into a unity of destructive purpose.

Buggies with heavy weapons on pivots slewed back and forth, gathering in makeshift squadrons as they headed towards the bridge. Behind them, two clanking, half-track war engines rumbled into life, each as large as the worksheds and of similar crude construction. Huge tyres kicked up clods of dirt, tracks clanked over rusting wheels as the machines lurched towards the bridge.

The burliest orks clambered up steps and ladders onto their open transport beds while others chased behind. Belts of ammunition were slapped into large-bore guns while smaller weapons dotted across the mobile fortresses were pivoted towards the river. Some of the greenskins wildly shot their weapons into the sky in their excitement, all of them hooted and hollered war cries. The armoured carriers belched forth spumes of thick smoke from their many exhausts, the smog washing heavily towards the river on the brisk wind. The mechanical beasts ground forwards implacably, churning through the piles of rotting carcasses and debris.

The first of the war buggies reached the bridge and raced across, two more not far behind. At the webward end of the bridge, concealed in the shattered ruins of a towering gatehouse that arched over the span, Firuthein and his Fire Dragons moved forwards.

The exarch stepped up to the jagged remains of a window and levelled his lance-like firepike.

A glaring burst of energy erupted from the weapon and hurtled towards the lead buggy. It caught the light vehicle on the nearside above its front wheel, exploding with the power of a miniature sun. Front axle ripped asunder, the buggy flipped dramatically, screeching along the retaining wall of the arcing bridge, trailing a storm of sparks. Korlandril smiled as he saw the buggy's driver dashed against the wall, flopping like a child's doll, while the gunner was broken and smeared along the white stone of the barrier.

The oncoming vehicles swerved around the smoking remnants, their heavy guns chattering, muzzle flare illuminating the orks' yelling, fanged faces. The bullets tore chunks from the walls of the gatehouse, but Firuthein's warriors stood their ground against the wild, sporadic fire. As the closest buggy came within range, the Fire Dragons unleashed their deadly breath, the air churning with white-hot radiation from their fusion guns.

The gunner of the next buggy exploded in a mist of rapidly evaporating organs and blood, his legs and lower torso spilling from the cradle in which he had been sat. The engine of the buggy burst into flames, swiftly followed by a detonation in the fuel tank, turning the vehicle into a careening fireball that ploughed into the ruined gatehouse before exploding into a cloud of debris and mechanical parts.

The larger transports had picked up speed. The nearest had a great plough-like ram on its front and hurled aside the ruins of the first destroyed buggy.

From its back, its cargo of warriors spewed forth a hail of inaccurate fire from their barking guns, streaming bullets in all directions in a frenzy of violence. Heavier arms spat a more staccato beat, thudding their shells purposefully towards the Fire Dragons.

Korlandril watched with horror as one salvo found its mark, tearing great shards of armour from one of the Fire Dragons. The warrior's body – lifeless Korlandril assumed – was flung out of sight into the mangle of the ruined tower.

Korlandril was conflicted for a moment. He was not sure what to think. A distant, whispering doubt told him that this was horrific. He had just seen another eldar brutally slain. Such a thing was perhaps the most traumatic sight he might witness. This quiet voice was drowned out by an altogether more feral roaring, which bayed for Korlandril to avenge the death of the fallen Fire Dragon.

In those few heartbeats of uncertainty, much had happened. At the near end of the bridge the ram-fronted transport had fire licking from under its tracks, gears turned to a molten slurry by Firuthein's firepike. The orks were tumbling over the sides and from the tailgate, gathering around a particularly vast creature with a metal banner pole tied to its back and a necklace of cracked skulls hanging on a chain around its neck. In one hand it carried a short but heavy pistol, in the other a double-headed axe with whirring chainblades.

'The warlord comes out, now it is time to strike swift, and bring down the beast!' cried Kenainath. The exarch was surging forwards through the water even as he gave the shout. Korlandril followed on his heel and the others close behind.

In the darkness and smoke, the Striking Scorpions arrived at the bridge quickly and unseen. The orks had laboured to shove aside the remnants of their transport, urged on by the bellows of their leader and threats from his pistol and axe.

Sudden glimmers of brightness attracted Korlandril's gaze to his right, past the ork warlord and his bodyguard. Like miniature supernovae, sparkling portals were opening up around the orks. Guided by spirit beacons placed by the rangers, the rest of the eldar force was arriving from the webway, surrounding the brutes to ensure none escaped. Squads burst from the ether with their weapons firing; squads of jetbike-riding Shining Spears charged out of the glimmering portals, their laser lances bright with power; caught between the converging squads, the orks died in droves.

Under the bridge Korlandril saw dark shapes, and at first thought they were foes. On closer inspection, he saw more Striking Scorpions: Aranarha's Fall of the Deadly Rain. They moved to cut off the orks' progress at the webward end of the bridge while the Deadly Shadow advanced from the rear.

Beyond Aranarha's squad, battle raged. Bolts of energy and screaming bullets criss-crossed the Exodite towers. The Aspect Warriors attacked with sure and deliberate violence, cutting down all in their path, following in the wake of the Avatar. The shriek of Banshee masks mixed with an unearthly, deafening ululation.

The Avatar of Khaine strode into the orks, the chilling sound coming from the fire-tipped spear in its right hand – the *Suin Daellae*, the Doom that Wails. Twice as tall as the Aspect Warriors surrounding it, the incarnation of the Bloody-Handed One was a nightmarish vision of metal and fire. Its unearthly flesh glowed with a ruddy light from within, its face a moulded visage of pure rage, eyes burning slits of white heat. The Avatar cast its spear through the bodies of a dozen foes before the weapon circled fully and returned to its grasp. Artificial lightning blasts from strange ork weapons crackled across the Avatar's metal hide while bullets pattered and ricocheted all around.

Korlandril had no more time to watch the ongoing orgy of violence – his own desire to shed blood heightened by the sight – for they had reached the winding steps up to the bridge. Kenainath broke into a run, mounting the stairwell swiftly, the rest of the squad following eagerly.

The steps brought them out not far behind the warlord as it advanced towards the main eldar attack, still unaware of the threat emerging from behind. Seven of its brutal subordinates clustered around the alien, shouting encouragement to their smaller minions who were being cut down in swathes by the eldar attack.

Kenainath closed in at a run, his shuriken pistol spitting a hail of razor-sharp discs. Korlandril followed suit, spraying a volley at the closest ork mentor, the salvo leaving a line of shredded flesh across the back of the creature's left shoulder. It turned and glared at Korlandril with beady eyes beneath a heavy, furrowed brow and then opened its fang-filled mouth in a bellow of warning. Its teeth were as long as Korlandril's fingers, spittle flying in heavy gobbets. The creature hefted a large cleaver in both hands, a shimmer of energy playing along its jagged blade. From its eyes to its posture to its roar, everything about the ork signalled murderous intent.

It was a sight Korlandril could never have anticipated and his heart fluttered for a moment, gripped with primitive fear of the gargantuan monster confronting him. As before, Korlandril's response to his fear was a surge of hatred and rage. He pounded forwards, peeling away from Kenainath to close with his chosen foe. The blades of the Striking Scorpion's chainsword blurred into life, fuelled by Korlandril's wrath to such a speed that they screamed as they split the air.

The ork swung its weapon in a long arc towards Korlandril's head. He ducked easily beneath the ponderous attack, his chainsword flashing up towards the underarm of the ork, teeth cutting through muscle and artery. Blood splashed from the wound onto Korlandril's helmeted face as he spun past. Through the Aspect suit he could smell the stench of the ork's life fluid and taste the iron in its blood.

Korlandril's mandiblasters spat laser fire as he sidestepped behind the ork, tearing at the flesh of its back and shoulders. The alien swung heavily around to its right seeking the cause of its pain, blade held overhead. Korlandril did not stand still long enough for the blow to land. He flexed his knees, crouched into Dormant Lightning, and then propelled himself forwards on the tips of his toes, unleashing River of Sorrow. His shuriken pistol fire raked the left side of the ork's face even as Korlandril's chainsword rasped through the thick muscle of its right thigh, gnawing at bone as the Aspect Warrior once again leapt past his unwieldy foe.

The ork collapsed with a grunt, the cleaver falling from its grasp as the alien's muscles spasmed in its death throes. Korlandril performed the coup-de-grace, cleaving his chainsword back-handed into the ork's left temple, shearing through and slicing deep into its brain.

A surge of victory filled Korlandril. The ruined flesh laid out on the stone of the bridge was a greater work of art than any he had ever conceived before. No Dreaming had matched the vitality – the heart-wrenching reality – of combat. Korlandril stood over his fallen foe, admiring the patterns made by the spatters of blood on the pale roadway. He looked at his own armour, smeared with filth, and was jubilant. Korlandril's waystone pulsed in time to the thunderous beating of his heart.

'Korlandril!' Min shouted.

In his ecstasy, Korlandril barely heard his name. He turned to find the rest of the squad.

Something immense loomed in front of him, blotting out the sky with its massive shadow. Korlandril raised his chainsword to Watcher Over Sky, but the defence was pitifully weak against the crushing weight of the warlord's axe. Fang-like chainblades smashed through Korlandril's weapon, sending shards in all directions, and bit deep into the Aspect Warrior's gut.

The force of the blow hurled Korlandril into the air, sending him crashing into the side wall of the bridge.

Horror filled Korlandril as the warlord took a step towards him. The Striking Scorpion was numb with shock and collapsed, his legs suddenly lifeless. He couldn't tear his eyes away from the lumbering ork closing in on him, but could feel his life seeping away through the ragged cut in his belly. His armour tried as best it could to knit the wound, but the damage was too severe.

Kenainath stepped between Korlandril and the ork warlord, the crackling claw of his right fist raised in defiance. The warlord bellowed a wordless challenge and Kenainath responded with offence, smashing the Scorpion's Claw across the chin of the warlord, cracking bone, the fist's powerfield rupturing flesh.

Then the pain hit Korlandril, rippling up his spine, sending a tremor of agony through his brain. He clamped his teeth together to suppress the scream, tears in his eyes.

The rest of the squad wove a deadly dance around their exarch, landing blows upon the warlord, which flailed hopefully at its swifter foes. Blood streamed from dozens of wounds across its chest and upper arms.

The last Korlandril saw was the long blade of Aranarha cleaving into the arm of the warlord, lopping off the limb above the elbow.

KORLANDRIL BLINKED BACK into consciousness. He thought he was drowning for a moment, before he recognised the swirling energies of the webway.

Hands were around him, carrying him. He eased his head to the left and recognised the armour of Bechareth. He heard voices inside his head but could make no sense of them. They were stern, unflinching. The pain was intense, setting his whole body a-tremble.

He could take no more. He was suffering too much.

He passed out again.

PAIN

During the War in Heaven, Khaine the Bloody-Handed One slew a great many eldar warriors. Mother Isha became fearful that the eldar would be exterminated, so she went to Asuryan the all-seeing and begged for him to intervene. Asuryan also feared that Khaine's rage would destroy not only the eldar, but the gods. He consented to aid Isha, but demanded of her to give up a lock of her immortal hair. This tress of hair Asuryan bound into the hair of Eldanesh so that he and all of his descendants could be healed by Isha's love for them.

GENTLE CHIMING AWOKE Korlandril. He found himself lying upon a firm, embracing mattress, warm to the touch. A cool breeze passed over his face. He kept his eyes closed, savouring the sensation of tranquility. At the edge of hearing he detected subtle notes, a drifting music that surrounded him, stroked at his spirit.

As he recovered consciousness, conflict disturbed Korlandril's dream-like thoughts. An image pushed at his memories, insistent but formless. He pushed back, trying to keep the memory at bay.

Through his eyelids Korlandril sensed a pulsing red light. His breath came in time to the surges of crimson energy flowing into his brain. It was slow at first but as it quickened in pace, Korlandril's breathing and pulse became swifter. He had no sense of time passing other than the narrowing gap between each breath and each heartbeat.

The red light had become a flickering strobe, alternating between harsh red and soft yellow. Korlandril hyperventilated, gasping rapidly, his chest aching with the exertion though the rest of his body remained motionless. His nostrils flared as he tried to fill his lungs but the flashing lights made him expel each breath before it had barely entered him.

'Awaken,' said a gentle voice. 'Remember.'

The words trickled into his mind and he was powerless to resist their command.

The barrier in his memories ripped asunder and a vast green beast with razor claws burst towards him. Blood drooled from its fangs. Pain flared.

Korlandril screamed with what little breath he had and fell back into darkness.

HE FLOATED, HIS body weightless, tied to the universe by the most slender tether of his consciousness. The voice returned, but this time there were no other sounds, no light save for a dim and distant pale green.

'You are in the care of Isha's healers,' said the voice. Korlandril could not tell if it was male or female, so softly spoken was the tone. 'Nothing can harm you here. You are safe. You must heal. You must release the power from the Tress of Isha.'

'It hurts,' Korlandril said, numb, barely recognising his own voice.

'The pain will pass, but you cannot heal your wound until you confront it.'

'The pain is too much,' whispered Korlandril.

'The pain is not of your body but of your spirit. The Tress of Isha will free you from your pain. I am Soareth, and I will help you.'

'I do not wish to die,' Korlandril said sombrely.

'Then you must heal,' replied Soareth. The healer was male, Korlandril decided, and young. Soareth spoke with the language of youth. He did not wish to be healed by a novice.

'What do you know of death?' he demanded, growing angry.

'Nothing,' replied Soareth. 'I am an advocate of life. Listen to me carefully, Korlandril. You still wear your war-mask. You cannot have one hand upon Khaine's sword and the other upon Isha's gift. You must take off the mask.'

'You would leave me defenceless!'

'The only enemy that you must fight is yourself.' Soareth spoke so quietly Korlandril could barely hear him. Or perhaps there was something else that made the healer's voice so distant. 'There is no other battle here, Korlandril. Your wound is grave, but you have the strength to overcome it. I will help you.'

'You are little more than a child, I demand to be attended by someone with more experience,' Korlandril said flatly. He felt himself frown.

'I am trained to help you heal, Korlandril. The power to survive does not reside within me, it is within you. Body and spirit are as one. You must strengthen your spirit to strengthen your body. I will show you how you will do this, and guide you to the Tress of Isha. With its power, you will heal. First you must calm yourself, release yourself from Khaine's grip.'

'I cannot,' snarled Korlandril.

'What is it that you love, Korlandril?'

The warrior dismissed the question. There was no love in battle.

Soareth repeated the question, but this time there was a subtle change in the timbre of his voice. Love. The word began to resonate with Korlandril. There had been something he had once loved, before Khaine had taken him. If only he could remember.

A gentle vibration stirred Korlandril's fingers. It was the slightest tremor but it brought feeling to his fingertips. He felt them brushing through something. Something with fine strands. Brushing through hair.

He stroked Thirianna's head as they watched white-plumed snow finches reeling to and fro across the cliffs in the Dome of Infinite Tides. It was an absent-minded gesture, no intent behind it. Her hand was on his knee as they sat cross-legged on the shale beach and looked up at the towering pale rocks. Though there had been no motive behind that soft caress, the sensation stirred feelings inside

Korlandril. Desire rose in him and he stroked her hair again, luxuriating in the closeness between them. He turned his head to look at her, admiring her beautiful face in profile, silhouetted against the low light from the distant wall of the dome. Her gaze was fixed on something far away, seeing something other than birds. Korlandril withdrew his hand, suddenly embarrassed at the gesture. Despite his discomfort, he felt at peace with the feelings now holding sway over him.

Blood sprayed into Korlandril's face, drowning him with a wave of thick red fluid. He sputtered and spat, clawing it from his cheeks, wiping it from his lips and eyes. But the blood kept coming, pouring from his eyes, dribbling from his mouth, seeping from every pore. He coughed, hacking up blood and tissue, despoiling his skin with its sticky gobbets.

KORLANDRIL AWOKE WITH a dull ache in every part of his body, and a sharper pain in his abdomen. He suddenly realised where he was and shouted out, a wordless cry of fear echoing sharply around him. Still he could not open his eyes. He wasn't sure why. Perhaps he couldn't bring himself to look upon the source of his pain, the great wound in his stomach that was leeching the life from him.

'Sleep,' said a quiet voice in his ear. He thought he recognised it, but before he could put a name to the voice he was swallowed up by a gentle somnolence.

A RHYTHMIC BEATING accompanied a slow pulsing of blue light behind Korlandril's eyes. He felt tiny quivers of movement on his skin, like the scampering feet of an insect. It moved simultaneously from the back of his neck down each arm and along his spine, forking at his waist to run down his feet.

'Welcome back, Korlandril.'

Soareth. Korlandril dragged the name from a dark recess in his memories. Something told him not to delve any deeper. He would not like what he saw.

'I am well again?' he asked, surprised by the hoarseness of his words.

'No, not yet,' said Soareth. 'But you have returned to us from the grip of Khaine. You can open your eyes.'

Korlandril prised open one heavy lid, cautious, fearing brightness. The room was softly lit, barely a twilight glow surrounded him. He opened the other eye and glanced around. The shaven-headed Soareth stood at the foot of the bed, a single-piece white robe hanging loosely from bony shoulders. In his hand he held a jewel-studded tablet. His fingers danced over the coloured gems and the room shifted around Korlandril; that is, the colours shifted, creating darker shadows, intensifying the light. The chamber felt smaller.

'Do not be afraid,' said Soareth.

Korlandril tried to sit up so that he could look down at the ruin that he knew his stomach to be. He couldn't move, and said as much.

'I have induced a paralysis for your own safety,' Soareth said. 'The wound has bound but a little. You must help your body complete the healing process. You must draw on the Tress of Isha.'

Korlandril attempted to nod.

'What must I do?' he asked.

'Focus on the ceiling and relax,' said Soareth.

Korlandril looked up, seeing nothing but pearlesque off-white. He was aware of the pain in his abdomen and tried to push it aside so that he could concentrate.

'Do not hide from the pain,' warned Soareth. 'It must be confronted, not dismissed.'

The colours of the ceiling shifted, almost imperceptible at first, a slow merging of pastel colours barely discernable from the white. The colours flowed together and swirled, with no distinct line between them, leaving an impression of a strange meta-colour made up of them all.

'Chant with me,' said Soareth. He started a low intonation, just sounds without meaning, slow and purposeful. Korlandril followed, matching pitch and duration with the healer. His throat hummed with the sound, sending alternating ripples of calm and alertness through his body.

The chanting fluctuated, but Korlandril had the rhythm of it now and matched Soareth exactly. Above the warrior the mottling ceiling was pulsing with life, slow flashes hidden within the maelstrom of colour-energy.

Korlandril shuddered and gave a moan, his synapses flaring from the awakening frequencies pouring into his senses. The tightness in his stomach was sharp, the pain dragging at his thoughts like an anchor. He wanted to fly free of its weight, but the invisible chain held him down.

Eyelids drooping, Korlandril succumbed to the mesmeric influence of the light and sound. He was dimly aware of Soareth moving around him, still chanting, running an angular crystal along nodal parts of Korlandril's body. Psychic energy earthed between Korlandril and the healer, flaring briefly along pain-filled nerves, spasming cells and dilating arteries.

The room went as black as the gulf between stars, swallowing up Korlandril. He could see nothing but inky depths. Raising a hand, he could not even see his waggling fingers. He felt dispossessed of his body and tried to float upwards, buoyed by his own lightness. Something snagged at him, keeping him in place.

A star glittered to his left and he turned to face it. Other pinpricks of light sparkled into life, one at a time, until he was surrounded by a gently revolving constellation of millions of lights. Some were reddish in hue, others bright blue or harsh yellow. He was drawn to a golden star just above him. He reached out and found that he could see the vaguest outline of his hand in the starlight. The stars were close, close enough to touch. His fingers enclosed the warm gold, the light creeping between his fingers, glowing through his flesh.

The star touched his palm and Korlandril was in his chambers, looking up at his mother. Her long silver and black hair hid half her face, but she was smiling. Korlandril played with his animadoll, holding it in his tiny hands, making it wave its flaccid arms with his infant thoughts. The dough-like figure danced jerkily, mirroring Korlandril's own undeveloped movements. Its noseless face creased into a smile.

'This is not where you will find your pain.' Korlandril's mother spoke with Soareth's voice.

He opened his palm and allowed the golden star to drift away. He looked for another, shying away from the baleful ruddy glows behind him, his fingers aiming for a pale blue spark. It bobbed and weaved, trying to elude him, and Korlandril laughed at its antics, still thinking like a child.

Finally his grip ensnared the elusive light.

The lights of the Hall of Inner Harmonies were bright and colourful, dappling the marble-like floor with vitality. Korlandril danced along the line of laughing and singing eldar, linking hands with them as he passed, Aradryan passing down the opposite side of the line. The music was fast and lively, Korlandril's feet skipping quickly across the hard floor, barely touching the ground.

'It is not joy that you seek, Korlandril, it is your pain,' Soareth warned through the mouth of a young, pretty reveller.

Reluctantly, Korlandril spun away from the gala, releasing his hold on the memory-star. He twirled exuberantly a few times more, but his spin brought him closer to the glaring red light that he knew held the memory of pain.

He didn't want to touch it. He could feel its heat, its poison.

'You must,' Soareth told him.

Korlandril's hand trembled as he reached out, arcing his body away from its bloody gleam in fear. His hand closed into a fist, refusing his commands.

'I cannot,' he hissed.

'You will die.' There was urgency in Soareth's tone.

The light of the red star was fading, flickering away into the distance. The constellation around

Korlandril dimmed, the darkness and shadows growing stronger, swathing him. He was torn between two fears, his hand refusing to grasp the memory of his injury while his mind shrank back from the engulfing blackness.

The stars, almost gone, began to oscillate slowly and music stirred Korlandril's thoughts. Soareth sang gently, every note calm and measured, setting up a resonance around Korlandril that filled him with their vibrancy. The stars brightened and Korlandril's hope grew, fuelling them further.

The red star was almost invisible, just the slightest smudge in the darkness. In moments it would be gone.

Korlandril lunged forwards, eyes screwed shut, and snatched at the dying star.

With a jolt he felt crushing weight. Opening his eyes, he found himself bound with silver chains. A huge shadow loomed over him as he wrestled and wriggled with his bonds. It was enormous, silhouetted against a sky of dripping blood. Its eyes were red coals and its hands were fanged jaws. The sky growled at Korlandril as he struggled to free himself, voiceless and impotent. He fell limp and rolled to his side, closing his eyes, waiting for the fatal blow.

'Face your fear!' Soareth's voice was a harsh snarl, stinging Korlandril into action.

With an agonised yowl, Korlandril surged up, the silver chains parting, sending shattered links sailing into the air.

On his feet, Korlandril saw something glowing behind the shadow-ork, its golden aura pushing back the curtain of blood that filled his mind.

Korlandril dodged to his right, hoping to outwit the shadow-ork, but no matter where he moved, the golden glow was always behind his foe.

'I have no weapons!' Korlandril cried out plaintively. 'My war-mask is gone!'

His words echoed dully. Then silence.

'Soareth? Where are you?'

There was no reply.

'I need you, Soareth!'

Desperate, Korlandril cast about for some weapon but could find nothing, just a featureless plain of grey dust as far as the eye could see. There was no way of escaping; Korlandril was trapped with his would-be slayer.

The shadow-ork did not come at him, it just stood glowering between Korlandril and his prize. Its teeth-fingers gnashed occasionally with a ring of metal that jarred Korlandril's nerves.

Korlandril stumbled suddenly and fell into the dust. It was not dust at all, but ashes, and he spat them from his mouth. He could feel his strength fading.

He was dying.

Korlandril's eyes and limbs felt heavy. It would be easy, to slip down into the ash, to lay down his head and wait for his death. His pain would be gone, his fears and anguish with it. There would be peace.

Then he heard it. It was a thunderous thump, but so very far away. He waited an eternity until he heard it again. It was a double-thud, as of a heartbeat. It seemed so slow. But it was not his heart he heard. It was something else, something far greater than he, something as vast as the galaxy. Yet part of it was within him. Unconsciously, his hand went to his naked chest and there he felt a smooth, oval object. His waystone. Glancing down, he saw it bursting through his skin, ruby-bright, slick with his blood.

Death.

'Not yet!' screamed Korlandril, hurtling to his feet. He raced towards the shadow-ork, fists raised. Blow after blow he rained down on its incorporeal form, clawing at it with his fingers, smashing it with his knuckles. His strength was sapped quickly; he could feel the last vestiges of his life fluttering away like moths.

With one last effort, Korlandril drove his fist into the shadow-ork's chest, through the heart. It billowed into formless cloud, swept away by a howling wind.

Korlandril saw then the golden coil that had hidden behind the beast. It appeared as a lock of shining hair wound about the twin stems of a red rose entwined with each other, their thorns sharp. Korlandril cared not for the potential pain. He leapt forward and his fingers closed tightly around the rose and its golden tress.

The thorns pierced his flesh but he ignored them, feeling the white heat of the golden thread.

Light exploded. Korlandril unravelled, streaming away in the wind as a million particles, disintegrated into a galaxy of whirling motes of light.

Each mote became Korlandril. He saw himself from within, racing along nerves and synapses; every fibre and cell, every vein and sinew, every corpuscle and protein. The golden light that was Korlandril raced through the systems of his body, purging and destroying the black stain of infection carried into him by the filthy weapon of the warlord. The cleansing fire of his rebirth burned away a budding neoplasm in his gut and cauterised the frayed blood vessels in his abdomen.

Dissipating, losing energy, Korlandril could hold his mind together no longer and slipped away, allowing the Tress of Isha to do its work.

Soareth was waiting for Korlandril when he awoke. The healer sat at the foot of the mattress, gem-slate in hand, watching the warrior carefully.

'You have done well,' said the healer, smiling warmly.

Korlandril groaned. There was still a pain in his abdomen, but it was not as intense as the sharp agony that lingered on the edge of his memories.

'I will live?' he asked hesitantly. Soareth answered with a nod and a broader smile.

'How long must I stay here?'

'Your physical wound is healing quickly,' Soareth said. He stood and moved beside Korlandril to lay a hand on his arm. 'The wounds of your spirit will take longer.'

Korlandril thought about this, confused.

'I feel well,' he said.

'That is because your fears and your woe are trapped inside that part of you which is your warmask,' said Soareth, sympathy written in his features. 'You must expunge them lest they remain forever, a caustic blight in your psyche that will grow to taint every other part of your spirit.'

'I... I must don my war-mask again to do this?'

Soareth shook his head and gripped Korlandril's arm more tightly for a moment, offering encouragement.

'I can help you explore those parts of your mind now locked within your war-mask. It is not without risk, but I will help you.'

The walls, which had been a steady cream colour, flickered with brief veins of red. Soareth turned towards the door of the small room and Korlandril's eyes followed him.

Dressed in a tight-fitting bodysuit of dark green and orange, Aranarha stood in the doorway.

'Leave!' Soareth said sharply, rising to his feet. The exarch's cold stare passed over the healer and fell upon Korlandril. The room shuddered at the exarch's presence, shimmers of agitation rippling across the ceiling.

'How is our warrior now? I hope he is well, there is much for him to do,' said Aranarha.

'Your kind is not welcome here,' said Soareth, stepping between Korlandril and Aranarha. 'I tell you again, you must leave.'

The exarch shook his head, his twin braids slapping against his shoulders.

'We will deal with pain now, in our own manner, as befits a warrior.'

'No,' said Korlandril. He flinched at Aranarha's scowl but remained strong. 'I will remain here until I am ready. Then I will return to the Deadly Shadow.'

'This is not the place for these words, for these ideas,' hissed Soareth, a hand fluttering across his dark blue spirit stone. 'Do not speak of war in a place of healing.'

'Kenainath failed you before, his way has been wrong, it left you vulnerable. Return with me to my shrine, I will teach you well, make you stronger than before.' The exarch stepped past Soareth, though with care not to touch him, and extended an open hand to Korlandril, as if to help him to his feet.

'No,' said Korlandril, fists clenching by his sides. 'Soareth will help me heal. I trust him.'

'He will destroy your anger, make you weak with fear, and tear away your war-mask. The warrior fights his foes, not parley with them, seeking negotiation. I will show you the true way, the warrior's way, to confront these inner fears.'

Aranarha's tone was implacable and he stooped towards Korlandril, hand still offered.

Korlandril closed his eyes and remained silent. The exarch gave a growl of disapproval and Korlandril waited until his heavy footfalls had receded from the room before opening his eyes. The walls had returned to their placid state.

'I cannot go back, not ever,' he said.

Soareth looked doubtful.

'You think I should return to the shrine?' asked Korlandril, taken aback.

'You have taken only the first steps of your chosen Path,' said Soareth. 'It is unwise to leave early, with issues unresolved, our dreams and desires unfulfilled. Your journey is not yet done. I will help you heal so that you may continue upon it.'

'You heal me to send me back to battle?'

Soareth sighed.

'It is the burden of my Path, far too often, to mend that which will be broken again before too long.'

Korlandril thought about this for a long time before he spoke again.

'It must get depressing. To work in vain so often.'

The healer smiled and shrugged.

'To walk on the Path of the Healer is to give ourselves over to our hopes, to turn our backs on our fear of the future. Hope is an eternal spring from which I drink, and it tastes sweet forever.'

He stood and left the room, the light dimming as he passed out of the door. In the darkness, Korlandril saw vague shapes, moving on the boundary of awareness, looming just out of sight. He shuddered and knew that it would be some time before he was fit to return to the shrine.

RIVALRY

Hawk and Falcon, messengers of the gods both, were close friends. Ever they swept with each other through the skies and danced amongst the clouds. Though filled with regard for each other, they also loved to compete and to set each other dares of skill and bravery. They would race to the moon and back to see who was swiftest. They would goad each other into circling the realm of Bloody-Hand Khaine, daring each other to fly closer and closer to the War God. At dusk one day Falcon and Hawk spied some prey, flying easily upon the mountain winds. Falcon declared that he would be the first to catch it, but Hawk claimed that he was the swifter hunter. The two stooped down upon their prey. Hawk was faster at first, but Falcon beat his wings the harder and dove ahead. Not willing to give up the victory, Hawk surged on, cutting in front of Falcon. Annoyed by his

*friend's manoeuvre, Falcon batted a wing against
Hawk's tail, sending his rival off course. Hawk
returned quickly, flying into Falcon to slow down his
dive. Their wings became entangled and the two of
them fell out of the skies. Their prey flew away,
laughing merrily, and the both of them went hungry
that night.*

THE QUIET OF the shrine was different to the peace of
the healing hall. The Deadly Shadow brooded in its
silence, the stillness stifling, heavy with melancholy
rather than offering solace.

Korlandril walked through the looming trees,
choosing to enter by the way he had first arrived
rather than the more direct passageways that ran
beneath the dome to the shrine building. He had
been away for some time and was not sure what welcome, or lack, he would receive from Kenainath and
the others. Unsurprisingly, none had visited him in
the healing halls. Aranarha's approach had been
greatly against tradition, and Soareth had been agitated by it for several cycles after.

So it was with some apprehension that Korlandril
walked softly along the winding trails, though not as
much as his first coming to the shrine. He began to
recover his feel for the place, sensing the presence of
the shrine seeping back into his spirit, reawakening
emotions that had been dormant. He relaxed as he
realised that it had not been the reaction of his fellow warriors he feared but rather he had harboured
a lingering doubt that he might not be able to
recover his war-mask. The curling mists and strange
groans and coughs from the dismal marshes were

slowly awakening something inside Korlandril, stirring memories he had avoided whilst in the healing halls.

He came upon the black opening of the shrine's main portal and hesitated, peering into the strange darkness that filled the entranceway. It was the Deadly Shadow incarnate, the gloom of death and war that filled the shrine. Once he stepped into it, he would be back again on the Path of the Warrior.

He took another faltering step forward before a noise to his left distracted him. Min pushed his way through the foliage, exiting the ziggurat by some side door. He started upright, surprised to see Korlandril. Recovering quickly, Min smiled broadly and extended a palm in greeting.

'How have you fared?' asked Korlandril, returning the gesture. Min hesitated before replying.

'It is good to see that you are recovered from your injury,' he said.

'I am eager to recommence my training,' Korlandril replied. He studied Min's face for a moment, noting doubt and worry in the lines upon his forehead and the clench of his jaw. 'You did not answer my question.'

Min's eyes shifted defensively for a heartbeat and then resignation showed in his features.

'I will not be training alongside you, Korlandril,' Min admitted. He looked out through the mangrove, away from the shrine. His gaze remained distant as he continued. 'I am done with the Path of the Warrior.'

Korlandril felt a breath catch in his chest.

'How so? I can think of no other warrior, save Kenainath, more dedicated to the Deadly Shadow.'

'And that is the problem,' Min said heavily. 'My war-mask is fading. No, that is not true. My true face is fading, being replaced by my war-mask. I find myself remembering that which should not be remembered. I enjoy the memories of battle, the surge of excitement I feel when fighting. It is not good.'

Korlandril nodded, unsure what to say. The war-mask of the Aspect Warrior served a two-fold purpose. The first was to allow the warrior to harness the energy of his anger and hatred and other negative emotions, giving them vent in battle. The second, and more important in some ways, was to act as a dividing barrier between war and peace. When not in his war-mask a warrior knew nothing of the heinous acts of violence he perpetrated whilst in his Aspect. He could slay and maim without guilt; a guilt that would crush the psyche of an eldar if allowed to dwell on it. That Min was haunted by feelings from his war-mask was a grave matter.

'You have made the right choice, Min,' Korlandril said, stepping forward to pat his companion on the arm. 'I will miss you by my side in training, but I am sure we will still see each other outside. What is it that you plan to do next?'

A fervent gleam entered Min's eyes and he grabbed Korlandril's wrists in his hands and stared earnestly into his eyes.

'It is unlikely we will see each other again, Korlandril. I have sailed close to temptation and to see you and the others would not be wise while you remain

Aspect Warriors. I have come close to being trapped, of becoming something like Kenainath and Aranarha. I need to leave myself for a while, and think I will take the Path of the Dreaming. Promise me, Korlandril, that you should ever despise your war-mask. Do not allow it to become something you crave, as I nearly did. Realise that it has power over you and you should shun its promises.'

Korlandril laughed and gently prised himself from Min's tight grip.

'I have fought but one battle, I think I have many steps to take along this Path before its lures will tempt me to stay.'

'Do nothing rash! Keep that place of peace, which brings you back from the anger, close to your thoughts at all times. Fear lurks inside your war-mask, no matter what healing you have undergone. Do not let it feed your hatred or stir your anger too far.'

Korlandril waved away Min's concerns.

'I bid you good health and a prosperous journey, Min,' said Korlandril. 'I hope to see you again when my time as a Warrior is done. Until then, our Paths run different courses. If you wish to seek a guide for your Dreamings, I recommend Elronfirthir of Taleheac. Speak to the spiritseers, they will find him for you.' He turned his back on Min and strode into the shrine, the chill of its shadow sending a thrill through him.

THE INNER CHAMBERS of the shrine were instantly familiar. Korlandril walked through the darkness without hesitation, navigating through the utter blackness to the armouring chamber. The light within was dim, no more than a ruddy glow from the walls, and in the gloom he saw the suits of armour arrayed along each wall.

Korlandril walked to his armour. The gems set into its plates reflected the dawn-like glow of the room, their light brightening at his approach. He laid his right hand upon the chestplate, over the empty oval where his waystone fitted, and his left hand unconsciously went to the waystone at his breast. Perhaps he imagined the connection or perhaps there was some intangible thread linking him to the suit and back.

'Now you have returned, brought back to us by Isha, whole and well again.'

Korlandril turned his head to see Kenainath crouched upon the dais at the head of the chamber, his elbows rested on bent knees, chin cupped in his hands. The red hue of the room brightened slightly, becoming sharper, causing the shadows to stand out in starker contrast. Korlandril said nothing and returned his gaze to his armour, running the tips of his fingers along the edges of the overlapping parts, dwelling on the fingertips of the gauntlets, caressing gently the mandiblasters on the sides of the helm.

'The armour beckons, seeking its former master, wishing to be whole. Can you feel its will, pushing into your spirit, feeding on your mind?'

'Who made it?' Korlandril asked, stepping away, perturbed by Kenainath's suggestion.

'By me and not me. It was made after the Fall, by First Kenainath.'

The exarch's inflexion and choice of words baffled Korlandril. He switched between tenses, describing himself – Kenainath – as someone both living and dead.

'First Kenainath?'

'I am not the First, though there have not been many, to wear this armour. I am Kenainath, and I am not Kenainath, neither one nor sum.'

'I don't understand.'

'That is for the best, hope that it remains like that, and you stay yourself.'

A dozen further questions came to Korlandril but he stayed his tongue and instead crossed to kneel in front of the exarch in the centre of the chamber.

'I wish to train again.'

Kenainath regarded Korlandril for a long time, a hint of a strange golden glow in his eyes. He looked deep into the warrior's eyes, seeking something of what passed in Korlandril's thoughts, perhaps seeing things even Korlandril did not see.

'Begin tomorrow, this coming night you must rest, training will be hard,' Kenainath said as he stood. He turned towards the shrouded door at the end of the shrine and then stopped and looked back at Korlandril. His lips pursed in appraisal and an eyebrow rose in inquiry. With a nod, the exarch seemed satisfied. 'You are welcome back, Korlandril the Warrior, to Deadly Shadow.'

The exarch faded into the gloom, leaving Korlandril alone with his conjecture and apprehension. For all the worries and anticipation that fired Korlandril's mind, his body was tired. Sleep seemed a very good idea.

* * *

KORLANDRIL ACHED. EVERY part of him was stretched thin, every muscle and tendon quivered and twanged. He realised how honed his body had been before the fight with the orks and how much of a toll his inaction in the Shrine of the Healers had taken. Though his injury had healed it would be some time before he regained the physical perfection he had attained in the shrine.

It was odd to train without Min. It nagged at Korlandril, like looking at a familiar smile with a tooth missing. It was an imperfection in his world, a departure from what he had known as he had become a warrior. In an effort to ignore the distraction, Korlandril turned his thoughts inward during training. His near-death had shown that he was not so accomplished in the deadly arts as he had thought. He strived to find what had been missing from his fighting technique, analysing himself as he made the cuts and thrusts and moved from stance to stance.

As his strength and suppleness returned, so too did Korlandril's precision and style. He was confident that his measured strokes were exact replicas of those demonstrated by Kenainath. It was not his technique that had failed him, it was something else.

It was hard to learn from an experience he could not remember. Objectively he was aware of what had happened to him – the fight with the ork and then the crushing blow from the warlord – but he had no sense of what he had been feeling, what he had been thinking. Those recollections were tied up in his battle persona, hidden behind his war-mask. Though he did not allow them to disrupt his practices and duels, questions surfaced in Korlandril's thoughts when he was outside the shrine; when eating with the others or sculpting in his rooms.

What mistake had he made? Had he made any error, or had it simply been ill fortune that had seen him injured? Had he hesitated or been afraid? Had he been cautious or over-confident?

It nagged at Korlandril that he could not find the answers. His only course of action was to focus everything upon his fighting technique and his decision-making in the duels. The latter was difficult. He fought without conscious effort, allowing reaction and instinct to guide his weapons.

Perhaps that was the problem, he realised. Did his instincts make him predictable? Did he need to intervene occasionally to change his style, to move against instinct? Was it the ritual itself that had been his undoing?

SIXTY-THREE PASSES HAD come and gone since his return to the shrine, during which Korlandril's body had been restored to its peak of speed and strength. His actions were second nature, his weapons once more an extension of his will. He was due to face Bechareth again in a training duel. Korlandril decided that he would try to maintain more of a conscious awareness of his actions during the faux-combat.

The two of them faced off in the chamber beneath the shrine, Kenainath hidden in the shadow, Elissanadrin and Arhulesh calling the winning strikes. Korlandril began as usual, reacting and acting without thought to the attacks and defences of Bechareth. The contest was even, with perhaps Bechareth having slightly the upper hand.

As he ducked and wove, slashed and stabbed, Korlandril allowed himself to engage more closely with his body. He saw it as a globe of light in his mind's eye, his warrior instincts envisioned as a miniature sun, ebbing and flowing with energy, his body moving around and within it. His conscious thought, his reasoning, Korlandril saw as another orb, its surface still and calm. As he fought, Korlandril tried to bring the two spheres together, so that conscious and unconscious might overlap.

He faltered, allowing Bechareth a strike to the abdomen that would have torn open his old wound. Korlandril hesitated, a flicker of memory touching on his thoughts. He retreated into ritual, taking up Hidden Claw, pushing aside the tatters of recollection.

Korlandril began again, forming the globe of tranquil consciousness, but rather than imposing it upon the fire of his intuition, he tried to meld the two, to make them as one. He parried and counterattacked, recognising the move his body had chosen, and the calm sphere slid a fraction closer into place. He lunged forcefully, his unthinking will recognising an opening.

Slowly, atom by atom, Korlandril merged the two parts of his consciousness. His mental exercise was far from finished when Kenainath called for the pair of them to cease their duel. Returning to repose, Korlandril fixed the last image in his mind, a partial eclipse of his warrior instinct by the rational mind, hoping to recreate it the next time he duelled.

Bechareth bowed his head in appreciation and gratitude, a knowing look in his eye. Korlandril mirrored the respect, his gaze not leaving that of his opponent.

'You are taking steps, moving swiftly on the Path, to fulfil your will,' said Kenainath, signalling for the others to leave. 'Your spirit responds; I sense it developing, becoming as one. We are all conflicted, many parts vying to win, yet none may triumph. You must seek balance, in all things not just battle, to be whole again.'

Korlandril nodded and remained silent.

'Practise your focus, see yourself from the inside, and master your will. The Path is wisdom, to control that which taunts us, to find true freedom.'

'And when I am done, will I be free of my anger?'

'We are never free, that is to have no feelings, we hope for control. Our spirits soar high, on a fierce wind of feeling, that ever threatens. Learn to still that wind, to glide on it where you wish, and not become lost.'

'I NEVER THOUGHT I would miss Min's bad puns,' said Korlandril.

His gaze drifted to the empty space on the bench opposite, drawn to the social vacuum created by his former companion's absence. Arhulesh seemed similarly perturbed, sitting next to the void, fidgeting with the scraps of food on his plate and staring absently over the balcony of the Crescent of the Dawning Ages. Korlandril looked over his shoulder. Within a bubble of blue and green captured in an invisible field, shoals of yellow cloudstars bobbed up and down, their slender tendril appendages wafting on gaseous currents. Their motions usually brought a mesmeric peace to those that watched them, but Korlandril was agitated.

'It is a shame that Min had to leave, I feel the squad is incomplete,' he said to break the uneasy quiet.

'It is a good thing that Min has left for another Path,' said Elissanadrin. She looked at Korlandril. 'It is the proper way. We move on, we grow, we change. You have never been comfortable with change, have you?'

Korlandril did not reply, though he knew she spoke the truth.

'It is dread of the future that makes us cling to the past,' said Arhulesh. 'Perhaps Korlandril is scared that he will become an overbearing dullard!'

'And what is it that you fear?' demanded Korlandril, his tone fuelled by sudden annoyance. 'Being taken seriously?'

The hurt in Arhulesh's expression sent a stab of guilt into Korlandril, who reached out a hand in apology. Arhulesh waved it away, his smile returning.

'Harsh, but perhaps true,' he said. His smile faded a little. 'If I cannot take myself seriously, how can I expect anybody else to do so?'

'You are a warrior, it is a sombre responsibility,' said Elissanadrin. 'Surely you can take some respect from that.'

Arhulesh shrugged.

'In my war-mask, that is certain. The rest of the time... I would laugh at myself if it was not so depressing.'

'Surely you became an Aspect Warrior to develop some gravitas,' said Korlandril.

Arhulesh laughed but it was a bitter sound, devoid of humour.

'I joined for a wager,' he said. He lowered his gaze sorrowfully while the others frowned and shook their heads in disbelief. 'It is true. I went to Kenainath for a bet. I thought he would reject me.'

'An exarch cannot send away those that come to them,' said Elissanadrin.

'I wish I had known that now. He kept me there, like he kept both of you, until he'd delved inside my spirit and placed the seed he would nurture.'

'Why did you not leave?' asked Korlandril. 'I mean, after your first battle?'

'I may have stumbled onto the Path of the Warrior by mistake, but I am not so self-centred that I would glibly depart from it. Maybe it was the lesson I needed to learn. Still need to learn.'

Korlandril glanced to his left, across a row of empty tables and benches, to where Bechareth sat looking over the park and lakes beneath the cloud-star bubble.

'And you know nothing of his story?' Korlandril asked.

'Nothing,' said Arhulesh. 'I know more about Kenainath than Bechareth, and that is little enough.'

'I think he was one of the earliest exarchs on Alaitoc,' said Korlandril. 'He told me he was not the first but said that the Deadly Shadow has not had many.'

'That chimes with what I have heard, in rumour and whispers from others that once fought with him,' said Elissanadrin.

'Of all the shrines to go to for your wager, why in all the galaxy did you choose Kenainath's?' asked Korlandril.

'I cannot reason it,' replied Arhulesh, giving another shallow shrug. His brow furrowed. 'He is a hard taskmaster. I have spoken to warriors from other shrines; they train half as much as we do.'

'I would rather be over-trained than under-trained,' said Elissanadrin. 'In battle, at least.'

'Yes, in battle, perhaps, but we wear our war-masks for a fraction of our lives, it seems such a waste.'

'He is serious-minded, I like that,' said Korlandril. 'Take Aranarha, for instance. He seems too eager. I do not think I could trust him.'

'He was once a Deadly Shadow,' Arhulesh confided quietly. 'I have spoken with Aranarha several times, and I think he resents the ancient exarch a little. He is trapped on the Path, dedicated to Khaine's bloody service, but locked away in there is some kernel of anger at Kenainath for allowing him to become trapped.'

'I think there is more the hand of destiny at work here than any ill-doing on the part of Kenainath,' said Elissanadrin. 'It is inevitable that some will become enamoured of battle after much time, as surely as a farseer turns to crystal with the passing of an age. If nobody became exarchs, who would train the generations to come?'

Korlandril pondered this for a time, trying to imagine a universe without the touch of Khaine. The others continued to talk but he did not hear their words. He pictured Alaitoc free of bloodshed, free of the iron beast at its heart, the pulsing blood-wrath fragment of Khaine that dwelt inside every eldar just as it lay dormant in its chamber at the centre of the craftworld.

He then pictured Alaitoc overrun, by orks perhaps, or maybe humans, or some other upstart race. Without Khaine, without war, the eldar would be defenceless. Little enough remained as echoing vestiges of their great civilisation. Without anger and hate, they would be wiped from the stars.

'It is a dream without hope,' he said eventually. 'Peace is merely an illusion, the momentary absence of conflict. We live in an age of bloody war, interspersed with pauses while Khaine catches his breath. I think I understand Kenainath a little better now. It is right to wish that the universe was otherwise, but it is foolish to think that it ever will be.'

'You see?' chuckled Arhulesh. 'You are a warrior now, and fear a future where you will no longer have a place.'

'Things change,' said Elissanadrin. 'You should learn from your healer; there should always be room in your spirit for hope.'

'All things change, and yet nothing alters,' said Korlandril, awash with philosophic thought. 'We know that everything is a great cycle. Star becomes stardust to become another star. War becomes peace to become another war. Life becomes death...'

'...becomes life?' said Arhulesh. 'I hope you're not referring to my spirit meandering around the infinity circuit when this handsome yet fragile body finally succumbs. That isn't life, is it?'

Korlandril had no answer. He was not quite sure what his point had been, and reviewing his words brought back nothing of the momentary insight he thought had occurred.

'As warriors, our deaths may bring life – for other warriors and for those on Alaitoc that we protect,' said Elissanadrin.

'I do not think that was the conclusion I had in mind,' said Korlandril. He stretched and stood up. 'With that being said, I think it suffices for now.'

As he walked across the Crescent of the Dawning Ages, Korlandril felt eyes upon him and glanced back to see Bechareth staring intently in his direction. The Striking Scorpion made no attempt to hide his interest and raised his goblet in wordless toast. Korlandril gave a half-hearted wave in return and hurried out, unsettled by the attention of the silent warrior.

THE CYCLE OF life continued. Korlandril practised and duelled, and when not in the shrine he made an effort to visit his old haunts around Alaitoc – taking the air carriage across the swirling seas of the Dome of Infinite Suns, climbing the cliff paths of the Eternal Spire, swimming in the gravity-free Well of Tomorrow's Sorrows.

He sculpted too, moving on from his Isha fetish to portraits of his shrine-companions that he gifted to each of them, save for Kenainath, whose essence refused to be captured by the psychic clay in any fashion satisfactory to Korlandril. He toyed with the idea of Dreaming for a while, but was hesitant to find a partner to join him, knowing well the dark places such memejourneys might take him. He even met with Soareth a few times, though not within the healing halls. They walked along the sandy shores girdling the circular Sea of Restoration and spoke of things other than Korlandril's injury and Soareth's healings.

Korlandril enjoyed the normality of it all. He knew that at some time, near or far, he would be called again to bring out his war-mask. He did not know what awaited him when that happened. He believed himself content, though he would sometimes wake from sleep with the lingering edge of a dream in mind, a momentary after-image of a shadowy red-eyed figure left in his thoughts.

As the dawn of a new cycle flickered into artificial life, he returned to the Deadly Shadow to find his companions in much agitation. They were gathered in the central chamber, where Kenainath paced aggressively back and forth across his dais. Red-tinged darkness swathed everything, flowing along the chamber in unsettling waves.

'What is occurring?' Korlandril asked quietly as he took his place beside his armour.

'A grave dishonour, done to me and to you all, that must be addressed,' growled Kenainath. 'An insult to us, an affront to our true code, a doubt to be purged.'

Korlandril turned to Elissanadrin for explanation.

'Arhulesh has left the Deadly Shadow and joined the Fall of Deadly Rain,' she replied in a terse whisper, her eyes narrowed. 'He has chosen Aranarha's teachings over those of Kenainath.'

Korlandril redirected his attention to the exarch, who stopped his prowling and crouched at the front of his stage, his eyes roving from one follower to the next. They settled on Korlandril.

'You will represent, champion of this great shrine, against Arhulesh. To end this dispute, affirm the Deadly Shadow, the shrine of first truth.'

'I have no dispute with Arhulesh,' replied Korlandril. 'It seems to me that your division is with Aranarha as much as anybody. If a duel is to be fought, it should be between the exarchs of the shrines.'

'Not my skill in doubt, a question of battle-lore, it mocks my teachings. Pupil faces pupil, this shrine's technique against theirs, to show the true Path.'

'It would be unwise to choose me to represent the Deadly Shadow in an honour-duel,' said Korlandril. He remained calm in demeanour, but inside his heart fluttered at the prospect of representing the honour of the shrine. It was a burden he felt unable to carry. 'Bechareth is the finest warrior amongst us, bar you. He should be your champion.'

Kenainath shook his head.

'It is you I choose, my most recent of students, my faith is certain. It is Korlandril, the newest of our number, who I believe in. No greater lesson, no better demonstration, than your victory.' Kenainath made a slashing gesture with his hand to show the matter had been settled and he would brook no further argument. The exarch's agitation was replaced with satisfaction at this pronouncement. 'Six cycles from now, in a place neither ours nor theirs, you face Arhulesh. Prepare yourself well, fight with bravery and skill, compete with honour.'

Korlandril stood dumbstruck as the exarch stalked from the chamber. He started as Bechareth laid a hand on his shoulder. The warrior winked and nodded his approval. Elissanadrin was less convinced, if her expression was to be judged. She cocked her head to one side, examining Korlandril.

'It would destroy the last remnants of Kenainath's reputation if you fail,' she said sternly. 'It is not only the honour of the Deadly Shadow that rests on your shoulders; it is the shrine's entire future. If you defeat Arhulesh he must renounce his change of heart and return. If you lose to him, he will remain with Fall of Deadly Rain.'

'I see,' said Korlandril, speaking out of instinct. He rubbed his chin with a slender finger. 'Actually, I don't. The loss of Arhulesh is no great thing.'

'Number us,' said Elissanadrin. Korlandril did so: Himself, Bechareth and Elissanadrin, as well as Kenainath. That made four…

'Oh, I *see*,' said Korlandril. 'Unless Kenainath brings back Arhulesh or replaces him quickly, there are too few of us to operate as a squad.'

'Kenainath will be forced by tradition to send us away and the shrine will be disbanded.'

'What would happen to Kenainath? What do exarchs without warriors do?'

Elissanadrin shrugged and shook her head mournfully.

'I do not know, but it cannot be good. For Kenainath, surely it would be the end of him. He has dwindled in reputation for an age; perhaps this will be the blow that finally finishes him.

Korlandril glanced towards the portal that led to the exarch's private rooms. He disliked Kenainath, had done so since they had first met. But he did have respect for him, and for what he had taught

Korlandril. Something else passed across his thoughts. Arhulesh had not only abandoned the exarch, he had walked away from all of them, and the memories of those who had been Deadly Shadow in time past. The thought that the Deadly Shadow would be no more irked Korlandril, and to be sacrificed by the whim of Arhulesh was meaningless. Dormant for some time, the serpent of Korlandril's anger flicked out its tongue, tasting his annoyance. It uncoiled slowly, basking in its return to favour. Korlandril did not fight the creature, but instead allowed it to wind itself into his heart and around his limbs. Its embrace brought resolve, brought strength.

'It will not come to pass,' Korlandril said, fixing Elissanadrin with a stare. 'I will make sure of that.'

THE WARRIORS OF the Deadly Shadow followed their exarch along the narrow tunnel, walking at a measured pace. Kenainath held a sceptre, the head of which was fashioned in a glowing representation of the shrine's rune. It was the only illumination, bathing the close walls with its red glare.

They had departed the Shrine of the Deadly Shadow beneath the armoury through a mist-filled portal none of them had seen before. Korlandril tried to work out the direction they were taking but could come to no clearer conclusion than that they were heading rimward. The passageway was walled with small glassy tiles, of varying shades so dark that they seemed to be black with the barest hint of purple and blue, green and red. There was no pattern to the colours that Korlandril could discern, though on the periphery of vision he was reminded of the mangroves of the Deadly Shadow shrine, their shadows and dismal colours hinted at but not revealed.

The squad's armoured footfalls were stifled by an earthy layer underfoot as they snaked along the straight corridor. The air was chill in comparison to the humidity of the shrine's dome, so that faint breath steamed the air as they advanced.

'Do not allow Arhulesh to take the initiative,' whispered Elissanadrin from behind, repeating the advice she had constantly given Korlandril for the past five cycles. 'The Fall of Dark Rain style relies less on the guile of the Dark Shadow and more on aggression.'

'Yes, I understand,' said Korlandril, keeping his gaze on the back of Kenainath.

'But be careful, Arhulesh is still Kenainath-trained, and he has faced you many times.'

'No more or less than I have faced him,' said Korlandril with a smirk. His joke settled his nerves a little though Korlandril sensed irritation from Elissanadrin and glanced over his shoulder to see that it had brought forth a scowl.

'He will have not changed much in the short time he has been with Aranarha, but perhaps just enough to make things difficult for you.'

'It may be to my advantage, a conflict in his thoughts, in his technique,' said Korlandril, trying to look for something positive in Elissanadrin's warnings. He returned his gaze to the front. He felt Elissanadrin's hand on his shoulder.

'You will be the better warrior,' she said firmly. Korlandril took strength from her conviction, detecting no deception in her tone.

Light flickered ahead, filling Korlandril with the urge to hasten his pace, nervous energy propelling him forwards. He resisted, keeping step behind the exarch. He focussed on the deliberate strides, turning them from a source of frustration to a purposeful meter, regulating his pulse and breathing in time to the solemn steps.

The tunnel led them into a broad octagonal chamber, the walls clad in the same tiles as the corridor. The circle at its centre was built from a low lip inscribed with narrow runes. From three other directions at right angles to each other, more portals led into the duelling chamber. At the same time as Kenainath stepped across the threshold, Aranarha entered from the left, also bearing the glowing sigil of his shrine.

The two exarchs signalled for their followers to take their places along the wall flanking their entrance, and then stepped up to each other, face-to-face within the circle. The Fall of Dark Rain outnumbered the Deadly Shadow by many members.

'Challenge has been set, so that honour is settled, and the truth be known,' intoned Kenainath. There was no anger in his tone, only the solemnity of the occasion.

'The challenge is taken up, to settle honour, to put to rest our dispute,' replied Aranarha with equal gravitas.

They turned to their respective champions. Both bowed and waved their representatives into the duelling area, withdrawing to stand side-by-side a few paces away. Korlandril strode into the circle, chainsword held lightly in his grasp, his eyes intent on Arhulesh as he approached. His opponent's face was set in a serious expression but Arhulesh could not stop the briefest flickers of a smirk from his lips. Korlandril welcomed Arhulesh's amusement; he judged it to be a sign of overconfidence.

The two of them nodded their heads in greeting, eyes fixed on each other, the light from the two shrine-totems casting long shadows across the floor. Slowly, the pair drew up their heads and moved unhurriedly into their fighting stances: Korlandril in Waiting Storm, Arhulesh in a subtly modified version of Rising Claw.

In the back of Korlandril's mind floated the twin spheres of instinct and reason, hovering through and around each other. With his warrior intuition, he sensed that Arhulesh's weight was more balanced to the left, while his reasoning eye calculated that a dropping slash would create the greatest problems from this position.

Without a word, Korlandril flowed into action, stepping forward and twisting into Moon's Falling Wrath, his chainsword flashing towards Arhulesh's chest. His opponent reacted in time, pushing the chainsword aside at the last moment before a strike would be called, but his balance had been shifted to his back foot, to the right.

Korlandril feigned a reverse cut towards Arhulesh's front leg, sending him backwards, and then pivoted on one foot, ducking beneath his foe's blade to bring his own towards the knee of Arhulesh's back leg.

'Cut!' came the call from the surrounding warriors. Korlandril detected a note of triumph in the voices behind him, from the Deadly Shadow. His warrior-spirit throbbed with pride while his reasoning mind told Korlandril that the strike was just reward for a well-worked strategy.

The two exarchs nodded their agreement with the decision, their heads bowing briefly towards Korlandril. The two combatants straightened and returned to repose.

With a flash of foresight, Korlandril guessed that Arhulesh was expecting him to strike first again. Korlandril dropped his left shoulder by the tiniest movement, and as Arhulesh's chainsword swung across his chest in response, Korlandril surged to his right, his feet dancing quickly across the tiled floor. Spinning, Arhulesh barely blocked the cut towards his lower back, and then launched an ill-judged thrust towards Korlandril's throat. The Deadly Shadow warrior delayed his reaction by the tiniest of margins, leaning out of the blow's path at the last moment so that Arhulesh was over-committed. A simple sweep brought Korlandril's blade to within a finger's breadth of Arhulesh's neck.

'Cut!' The call from the Deadly Shadow was excited, that of the Fall of Dark Rain muted. Again the nods of the exarchs conferred the strike to Korlandril.

The third strike went to Arhulesh, who launched a blistering attack from the start, overwhelming Korlandril with the surprise of its feral ferocity. The next onslaught favoured Korlandril, who had expected a repeat, so that he led Arhulesh on a merry dance, defending and parrying but offering no counter-attack until his foe was thoroughly off-balance and unable to ward away the strike.

Korlandril had no idea how the duel was ended. Was there a set limit, a score he needed to achieve? Or was it simply a matter of one exarch giving way to the inevitable?

Distracted by this consideration, Korlandril left himself open to a cut to his left thigh. Inwardly cursing his lack of focus, Korlandril raised his chainsword in salute to gain himself a little time to settle.

From then on, the duel was as one-sided as it had begun. Arhulesh's blows were well-timed, some of them downright devious, but Korlandril had the measure of his opponent. As he fell further behind in the strikes, Arhulesh became more and more aggressive, striving after the victory.

Korlandril tried to be patient, but the ever more desperate attacks of Arhulesh were like a goad to him. The fiery sun of his warrior instinct grew in strength, while the pale moon of his reason shrank. It was enough, Korlandril realised. Arhulesh was fighting on instinct alone now, reducing the duel to a matter of reactions and animal guile.

'Cut!' The call echoed around the chamber once again. Korlandril was eight strikes to Arhulesh's three. Kenainath raised a hand to halt the proceedings.

'The matter is done, the Deadly Shadow prevails: the honour is ours.'

Aranarha's eyes went to Korlandril first and then to Arhulesh. The exarch of the Fall of Dark Rain opened his mouth to speak but Arhulesh cut across him with a strained rasp.

'No! I can do this!' Arhulesh squared off against Korlandril, his expression turning sly. 'If an ork can best him, so too can I…'

Korlandril's eyes narrowed as something surged inside him. Arhulesh launched an attack, aiming a cut towards Korlandril's gut, hoping to capitalise on the distraction caused. Korlandril's weapon swatted aside the predictable blow and he drove forwards, raining down strikes on the chainsword of Arhulesh. The red of his helmet filled Korlandril's vision and there was a strange whirring noise in his ears as he relentlessly pressed forwards, hammering his blade from the left and right, from above and below.

Arhulesh's eyes widened with terror as he desperately fended off each brutal attack.

Hands grabbed Korlandril's shoulders and he was dragged out of the circle whilst others pulled Arhulesh to safety. As Korlandril's back hit the tiles, he was jolted into sensation again. With mounting horror, he remembered that he was not wearing his helm; the red mist had been in his mind. The whirring sound had been the noise of his chainsword, activated by his anger.

He had been heartbeats away from donning his war-mask in a duel.

TRAP

With Khaine by his side, Eldanesh vanquished the foes of the eldar. None could stand before the might of the Bloody-Handed One and his disciple. One evening as the crows feasted on Eldanesh's slain foes, Khaine congratulated Eldanesh on his victories and promised him many more. The War God granted Eldanesh a vision of the future, releasing a drop of his fiery blood onto Eldanesh's forehead. Eldanesh saw what would come to pass under the patronage of Khaine. Enemies unnumbered fell beneath Eldanesh's blade and the might of the eldar grew to its zenith. All creatures were cowed before the strength of Eldanesh and all eldar paid homage to Eldanesh for his rulership. When the vision had passed, Khaine told Eldanesh that the War God would put aside his animosity for the Children of Isha if Eldanesh would simply swear fealty to the

Bloody-Handed One. Eldanesh cared not for the bloody future of Khaine's dreams and refused to give his oath to the War God. Enraged, Khaine struck down Eldanesh and the War in Heaven began.

THOUGH KORLANDRIL HAD lost his control at the end of the duel, it was agreed that he had gained the victory. Korlandril was the first to welcome Arhulesh back, greeting him in the armouring chamber.

'Your place is with the Deadly Shadow,' said Korlandril. 'We are whole with you numbered amongst us.'

Arhulesh studied Korlandril, seeking some hint of reproach or gloating. Korlandril offered neither.

'I am sorry I insulted you,' said Arhulesh. 'It was a sly ploy, one not worthy of the Striking Scorpions.'

'It was ill-judged, but I am glad that I did not make you pay too high a price for the error. I apologise for my reaction, it did not befit the conduct of a warrior facing one of his own.'

Arhulesh extended his hand with fingers outstretched and Korlandril touched fingertips with him, sealing the agreement.

'Kenainath has me training on my own again for the time being,' confessed Korlandril. 'Also I am forbidden from leaving the shrine for the next twenty cycles. I think he trusts me, but he wishes to make a statement. I would not be surprised if he has something planned for you.'

'I'd deserve it,' Arhulesh said heavily. 'Running off to Aranarha to spite Kenainath? I am truly my worst enemy sometimes. Such a fool.'

Korlandril said nothing. Arhulesh's brow creased in a frown of disappointment.

'Was I supposed to argue?' Korlandril asked, keeping the smile from his face.

'I shall become a philosopher next and found a new Path,' said Arhulesh. He lifted a finger to his chin in a pose of mock thoughtfulness. 'On this Path one shall be required to do the exact opposite of what one thinks to be right. I shall call it the Path of the Idiot.'

Korlandril laughed and clapped a hand to Arhulesh's shoulder.

'I shall become your first disciple. While I have dabbled in idiocy several times, truly I should learn its intricacies under a great master. Short of running off to join the Harlequins, I can't think of anything I could do to best your latest exploits.'

'Best not to mock the Harlequins,' Arhulesh said, becoming serious. 'Cegorach still stalks the webway, after all. No point attracting attention to yourself.'

There was something in Arhulesh's tone that betrayed a deeper meaning to his words, though Korlandril could not think what it might be. There was a story here, one that Arhulesh was unwilling to tell.

'You should see the others before Kenainath catches you,' Korlandril said with forced levity. 'And before he sees you with me and extends my penance for another twenty cycles!'

'Good health and prosperity, Korlandril. If we are both fortunate, I will see you in twenty cycles' time.'

Korlandril watched Arhulesh depart. When he was sure he was alone, he took up Rising Claw, continuing his ritual from where he had been interrupted. Out of the corner of his eye, Korlandril saw twin glimmers of red from the darkness of the doorway to the inner shrine and Kenainath's quarters. In a moment, they were gone.

KORLANDRIL ENDURED HIS solitary punishment without complaint. When released by Kenainath, his first instinct was to meet the other warriors. He counselled himself against the urge and decided that he needed to seek less warlike company. It came to mind that he should see someone he had not visited in quite some time.

THIRIANNA'S SURPRISE WAS a reward in itself. After a brief foray into the infinity circuit – the spirits within were not keen to be disturbed by active Aspect Warriors – Korlandril found her in the Garden of Heavenly Delights, poring over a scroll beneath the white-blossomed bower of a snowpetal. Thirianna was dressed in the deep folds of a blue robe, hung with rune charms and bracelets glittering with their own energy. Her hair was swept back in a long plait, coloured a deep auburn and decorated with ruby-red gems. She stood quickly, laying aside her text, and embraced Korlandril. Taken aback, he hesitated before wrapping his arms around her.

'I heard that you had been injured,' Thirianna said, stepping back to regard Korlandril critically, assuring herself that he was well.

'I am healed,' he replied with a smile. 'Physically, at least.'

Korlandril gestured to the bench and the two of them sat side-by-side. Thirianna opened her mouth to say something but then closed it. A flash of concern marred her features.

'What is wrong?' Korlandril asked.

'I was going visit you, as there is something you should know. I would rather we spoke about other matters first, but you have caught me unawares. There is no pleasant way to say this. I have read your runes. They are confused, but many of your futures do not bode well.'

'There is nothing to fear. I have suffered some tribulations of late, but they will not defeat me.'

'It is that which worries me,' Thirianna said. She reached out and laid her palm briefly on his cheek, but he flinched at the touch. 'I sense confrontation in you. You see every encounter as a battle to be won. The Path of the Warrior is taking its toll upon you.'

'It was one slip of concentration, nothing more,' said Korlandril, standing up. He stepped away from Thirianna, seeing accusation in her expression. 'I stumbled but the journey goes on.'

'I have no idea what you are talking about. Has something else happened?'

Korlandril felt a stab of shame at the memory of his mistake during the duel. He did not consider it the business of Thirianna; it was a matter for the Deadly Shadow to resolve.

'It is nothing important, not of concern to the likes of you.'

'The likes of me?' Thirianna was upset more than angry. 'No concern of a friend?'

Korlandril relented, eyes downcast.

'I almost struck a genuine blow during a ritual settlement.'

'Oh, Korlandril…'

Her pitying tone cut sharper than the rebuke he had endured from Kenainath and Aranarha.

'What?' he said. 'You speak to me like a child. It happened. I will learn from it.'

'Will you? Do not forget that I have been a Dire Avenger. Though that time lives in the mists of my past, it is not so old that I forget it entirely. Until recently I trod the Path of the Warlock. As a warrior-seer, I revisited many of my battle-memories, drawing on them for resolve and strength. I recall the lure of the Warrior's Way; the surety of purpose it brings and the comfort of righteousness.'

'There is no fault to be found with having the strength of one's convictions.'

'It is a drug, that sense of power and superiority. The war-mask allows you to control your rage and guilt in battle, it is not meant to extinguish all feeling outside of war. Even now I sense that you are angry with me.'

'What if I am? You sit there and talk of things you do not understand. It does not matter whether you have trodden the Path of the Warrior, you and I are not the same. That much you made clear to me before I joined the Deadly Shadow. Perhaps *you* felt tempted by the power. I have a stronger will.'

Thirianna's laugh was harsh, cutting to Korlandril's pride.

'Nothing has changed with you. You have learnt nothing! I offer comfort and you take criticism. Perhaps you are right. Perhaps it is not the Path of the Warrior that makes you this arrogant; you have always been so self-involved.'

'Self-involved?' Korlandril's incredulity heightened the pitch of his voice. He took a breath and moderated his tone. 'You it was that fluttered in the light of my attention, promising much but ultimately willing to give nothing. If I am selfish it is because you have taken from me that which I would have happily given myself to.'

'I was wrong, you are not selfish. You are self-deluding! Rationalisation and justification is all that you can offer in your defence. Take a long look at yourself, Korlandril, and then tell me that this is my fault.'

Korlandril stalked back and forth for a moment, analysing Thirianna's words, turning them over to divine their true meaning. He looked at her outraged face and realised the truth.

'You are jealous! Once I was infatuated with you, and now you cannot bear the thought that I might live my life outside of your shadow. Elissanadrin, perhaps? You believe that I have developed feelings for another, and suddenly you do not feel you are unique in my affections. '

'I had no idea that you have moved your ambitions to another. I am glad. I would rather you sought the company of someone else, as you are no longer welcome in mine.'

'This was a mistake. You are not worth the grief you bring, nor the time you consume.'

Thirianna began to sob, burying her face in her hands. It was pathetic; an obvious attempt at sympathy and attention. Korlandril wanted no more of Thirianna's manipulation. Without farewell, he ducked beneath the branches of the snowpetal and walked away.

* * *

FOLLOWING HIS ARGUMENT with Thirianna, Korlandril sought to banish the episode from his thoughts with a sculpture. He returned to his quarters to do so but could not settle. He paced about the living space, surrounded by his representations of Isha, each beautiful face a reminder of Thirianna. Every time he sat at his bench with white putty in hand, he could not bring forth a vision to fashion. His mind was full of barbs and edges. Far from creating a thing of beauty that would calm him, his attempts at sculpture brought to mind those things that vexed him the most.

Restless, Korlandril returned to the Shrine of the Deadly Shadow. He found Elissanadrin shadow-sparring in the armour chamber.

'Perhaps you would appreciate something to aim at?' he said, moving to put on his armour.

Elissanadrin smiled and nodded in reply. She spoke quietly as Korlandril armoured himself.

'There is a familiar agitation about you. Thirianna, I would say.'

Korlandril said nothing, his mind focused on the mantra of arming. Pulling on his breastplate, he spared Elissanadrin a brief flicker of a nod.

'It is unfortunate that we grow apart from those we love, but take comfort that as you change, as your life goes on, there will come others with which to share yourself.' said Elissanadrin.

Korlandril activated the suit and he flexed his arms as it tightened around him.

'Is that an offer of congress?' he asked.

'You are very blunt today,' she replied. 'I would not put myself up as substitute for Thirianna. I am not her, so you must take me as I am.'

'I would not want you to be Thirianna,' Korlandril said coldly. He balled his hands into fists and loosened his wrists. 'And you are not. I would very much like to court you and, if all goes well, we could share an intimacy.'

Elissanadrin laughed gently.

'You are so traditional at times, Korlandril. Perhaps we should 'share an intimacy' and then see if we wish to court? I regard physical compatibility highly.'

Neither spoke as they walked to the arming hall and took up their chainswords. They followed the passageway down into the heart of the shrine in silence.

'I already feel compatible with your physique,' said Korlandril. He raised his chainsword to his brow. 'Perhaps the intimacy of the blade will convince you.'

Elissanadrin returned the salute and took her place in the duelling ring. She tossed her hair over her shoulder and smiled coyly.

'I do not doubt your energy or your endurance, but I fear you may be out of practice with your technique.'

'Let me prove to you that I still remember well the tricks and skills hard-learnt in the past.'

Korlandril entered the circle and stood face-to-face with Elissanadrin, so close he could taste her breath and smell her skin. His heart raced, from the prospect of the duel and the pleasures beyond.

The sound of scraping on stone caused both to spin toward the doorway of the duelling chamber. Kenainath stood there, armoured save for his helm.

His dark eyes regarded them both, unblinking, his mouth a thin line.

'No time for duelling, we are summoned to battle; the autarch awaits.'

Shocked from their flirting, Korlandril and Elissanadrin exchanged a glance and followed the exarch hurriedly as he disappeared from the doorway.

'Battle with whom?' asked Elissanadrin. Kenainath gave no reply.

The others were waiting in the main chamber, unarmoured. Kenainath said nothing as the squad fell in behind their exarch. He took them through a narrow doorway and down a long ramp that led into a circular chamber. Lights glowed quickly into life, revealing four sleek transports, coloured the same green as the squad's armour. They hovered slightly above the metallic floor, curved swept-back wings and the high arch of a dorsal stabiliser casting shadows over the squad.

Arhulesh hurried to the closest, touching a rune on its side to open the shallow-domed canopy. He leapt nimbly aboard and moved to the front of the craft. Korlandril waited for the others to seat themselves in the back before taking a place next to Bechareth, thinking it best not to be too close to Elissanadrin considering the playful flirtation they had just been engaged in. Arhulesh closed the canopy and the skimmer breathed into life, a faint hum the only signal that it was now active.

Under Arhulesh's guidance, the craft swung towards an opening at the far side of the chamber, beyond which a row of yellow lights lit the way along a winding tunnel. Arhulesh steered the craft effortless along the concourse, gathering speed until the lights flashing past were a single blurred line.

'Where are we going?' asked Korlandril. Elissanadrin turned from the front and hung an arm over the back of her seat.

'The Chambers of the Autarchs,' she said. 'It is where the shrines usually gather to receive news from the farseers before we don our war-masks.'

Korlandril took this information in silence. He had never heard of the Chamber of the Autarchs and he wondered whereabouts on Alaitoc it was located. The skimmer flew along tunnels and conduits he had never seen before and he assumed that these were in substrata of channels used solely in times of war.

Three other transports of similar design swung into view ahead, coloured in deep blues and black.

'Dark Reapers,' said Elissanadrin. She leaned forwards to study the markings as the skimmers converged. 'Shrines of Dark Moon Waning, Cold Death and Enduring Veil.'

This last one Korlandril knew – the shrine to which Maerthuin and Arthuis belonged.

Craft from other shrines hove into view behind them, joining the line of skimmers converging quickly on the Chamber of the Autarchs. The concourse ended in a wide space, its dome a black hemisphere through which nothing could be seen. The floor stepped down into an amphitheatre. Three figures stood upon a circular dais at the heart of the hall, two clad in heavy robes, the third in blue and gold armour, a crested helm beneath his arm and a long scarlet cloak on his back.

The gathering Aspect Warriors dismounted from their transports on the upper level of the hall as squads took up their places around the autarch and farseers. Korlandril looked at the white stone of the broad steps and saw runes in gold etched into its surface, each indicating the place of a different shrine, arranged by Aspect. Several hundred warriors were already in place and as many again were following their exarchs into position.

'Arhathain,' said Arhulesh, pointing to the autarch. 'He wore the masks of the Dark Reaper, Howling Banshee and Dire Avenger before he became autarch.'

'His name seems familiar,' said Korlandril. Kenainath stopped and Korlandril looked down to see the rune of the Deadly Shadow beneath his feet.

'Commander of Alaitoc during the Battle of Whispers, and co-commander with Urulthanesh at the Thousand and One Storms.' said Elissanadrin.

Korlandril recognised the names of the two battles, both long campaigns that had taken a heavy toll of Alaitoc's warriors.

'I do not know the farseers,' said Arhulesh. Both were male and of stately poise. One was younger than Korlandril, which surprised him. The other was venerable and even at this distance it was possible to see the strange glint of his skin, the first hint of his body turning to crystal, undergoing the transformation wrought upon him by his psychic abilities.

'Time is short, so brevity is required,' announced Arhathain, his voice filling the air, projected by a sonic field to every part of the hall. 'Farseer Kelamith,' the autarch indicated the elderly farseer, 'and his acolyte have foreseen a terrible tragedy for Alaitoc. A silver river turns to black and its boiling waters flow towards Alaitoc. The Dancing Death is seen on the shores of a white sea, her hair braided with the skulls of our children. She Who Thirsts casts her greedy eye upon the stars and in times to come her infernal gaze will fall upon our lives.

'It is vital that we move to prevent this event coming to pass. The Dark Gods have extended their reach once more, into the hearts and minds of the easily-corrupted humans. Though they do not yet know it, they are starting upon a path that will not only damn their own world but will bring forth a host of the Dark Gods' creations. Such is their ignorance that in only three of their short generations they will unleash a cataclysm that will savage planets and bring ruin to the doors of Alaitoc itself. We cannot allow this to happen.'

'The curiosity of the humans shall be their downfall if we do not intervene,' continued Kelamith. His voice was cracked and quiet, weighed down by an eternity of peering into possible futures, all of which eventually led to death and the destruction of Alaitoc. Korlandril wondered what manner of mind could stare into the face of such doom time and again, to avert each disaster as it became known. 'We cannot warn them of dangers yet to come to pass, for in doing so we risk creating the very desire we seek to end. A swift move now, bloody but necessary, will eliminate the threat to Alaitoc and also keep safe the future generations of humans.

'Those we need to eliminate are few, and if we strike hard and with haste they will receive no reinforcement. Overwhelming force will bring capitulation quickly. Those we wish to destroy have in their possession, unwittingly, an artefact that must be retrieved and destroyed safely. You will know it when you are close at hand. On no condition must you approach the artefact itself, and endeavour at all times to keep it from your thoughts lest it ensnares your spirits also. It concerns that which we do not speak of, and so you understand this is no idle caution.'

Korlandril shuddered with the thought of She Who Thirsts. His spirit stone pulsed cold once in sympathy and other Aspect Warriors exchanged glances and gave each other nods of assurance and comfort.

'We will attain orbit secretly and create temporary webway portals in order to strike at the heart of the target's fortifications,' said Arhathain. 'Their army will respond, and we must be prepared to withdraw under attack. Speed is of the essence, lest our ships in orbit be discovered and forced to break their web-way connections. The rangers will gather what information they can about this human planet and the place where they store this vile prize. Detailed battle-sagas will be relayed to each exarch en route to the human world.'

The autarch raised a fist and turned slowly, acknowledging the assembled warriors.

'Alaitoc once again must turn to Khaine's bloody messengers. You will not fail us.'

'It is time to go, to don armour and war-masks, to quicken the blood,' said Kenainath, signalling the squad back to the transport.

Though he had no training as a farseer, Korlandril knew the principles at work: every action had a consequence and it was the duty of the farseers to guide the weapons of the Aspect Warriors to bring about the destiny most favourable to Alaitoc. He felt some small pity for the savage humans that would have to die in this attack, for it seemed that they were unknowing of the harm they would cause. Yet it was a necessary tragedy, the shedding of human blood so that eldar lives were made safe.

He wondered for a moment if killing a human would be harder than killing an ork. The ork was a creature of pure malevolence, of no benefit or advantage. Humans, though crude and unmannerly, were useful pawns and possessed of an innate spirit to be valued. That they were weak and easily corrupted – in body and in mind – was lamentable, but as a species they were more desirable as neighbours than many others in the galaxy. As he took his seat in the transport for the return to the shrine, Korlandril wondered what he would feel when he killed his first human. The thought gave him doubts concerning his chosen Path. Killing orks was simple extermination; killing humans one might consider a form of murder, albeit of a minor kind. Then he realised the ridiculousness of the question.

He would be wearing his war-mask; he would feel no guilt and remember even less.

KORLANDRIL FOLLOWED KENAINATH from the webway portal with chainsword and shuriken pistol ready. They found themselves inside a wide compound surrounded by wood-and-earth walls several times

Korlandril's height. The glimmer of other webway portals crackled in the night air, the shadowy figures of the Aspect Warriors emerging from the gloom. The air was bitterly cold, gentle snow falling from the dark clouds above; a carpet of frost on the cracked slabs that paved the courtyard; frozen rivulets on the brick walls around the open space.

Snaps of laser fire crackled down from the surrounding wall, targeting a squad of Dire Avengers advancing up an inner ramp. They responded with deadly bursts of fire from their shuriken catapults, cutting down several humans wearing thick grey coats and floppy fur-lined hats with flaps that hung over their ears.

The Striking Scorpions, supported by other Aspect Warriors, were to lead the assault against the human stronghold. While other troops secured the outer defences, the Deadly Shadow and others would strike at the central buildings, searching each until they had located the accursed artefact that was their goal. Though a great number of Alaitoc's warriors were to stage the attack, there was to be no long engagement with the enemy; it was a human world and would be home to many times the eldar's numbers. It was imperative that Alaitoc's warhost did not get drawn into an extended battle, which would risk the extraction of the artefact.

Kenainath led the squad away from the walls, towards a complex of four buildings at the heart of the compound. Three were single storey, built of rough grey brick. The fourth was five storeys high, hexagonal in shape, windowless and made of a rock-like substance strengthened with a criss-cross of metallic girders. It towered over the compound, the hub around which everything else was built.

Battle felt different this time. Colder, not just in temperature but also in temperament. There was none of the burning anger Korlandril had felt before, no hatred brought on by the orks or the sweeping bloodthirst of the Avatar to distract him. He watched with detachment as Howling Banshees, bone-coloured and wailing, sprinted towards the nearest compound building, their gleaming power swords slicing effortlessly through the humans spilling from its large gateway.

The Deadly Shadow veered left, alongside the Dire Avengers from the Star of Justice shrine and Fire Dragons from the Rage of Khaine, heading towards the next closest warehouse. Heavy doors rolled together to close off the entrance, sporadic las-fire springing from the narrowing gap but finding no mark amongst the eldar.

With a loud clang, the doors shut. The Dire Avengers directed their weapons against the harsh lamps along the edge of the roof, bringing more darkness. Kenainath motioned the squad to take cover beside the wall of the building as the Fire Dragons closed on the doors with thermal charges in hand.

There was little fire coming from the walls now. A glance around the perimeter showed the Dire Avengers had scoured three-quarters of the wall of its defenders. Black-clad squads of Dark Reapers took up firing positions, their missile launchers directed outside the compound.

With blasts of white fire, the Fire Dragons' thermal charges turned the warehouse doors into a river of cooling slag. The Aspect Warriors ducked through the holes created, the red glare of their weapons sending long shadows back into the compound.

'Strike without mercy, rejoice in Khaine's bloody toll, leave nothing alive!' cried Kenainath, waving the squad forwards with his glowing power claw. Arhulesh was first into the breach, followed by the exarch. Korlandril followed Bechareth through the tangled metal, Elissanadrin at his back.

The inside of the warehouse was empty save for a few metal crates piled neatly to Korlandril's left. A thin wall portioned a separate area to the right. Helmeted heads bobbed up and down at the narrow windows and two small doorways.

The Fire Dragons unleashed their fusion guns' fury, blasts of energy tearing through the flimsy wall. Under the cover of this fire, the Deadly Shadow charged, the occasional las-bolt zinging past them or striking up small clouds of vapour from the floor.

At the closest door, three humans levelled their weapons at Arhulesh and Kenainath. Without thought or order from his exarch, Korlandril raised his shuriken pistol and spewed a hail of lethal discs into the doorway, his fire converging with that of the others. Two of the humans fell back, their chests and faces lacerated; the third fired his weapon, catching Kenainath a glancing blow across the right shoulder. Unbalanced, the exarch took a shortened step to right himself, allowing Bechareth to surge ahead. He and Arhulesh reached the door, chainswords simultaneously decapitating and eviscerating the human remaining there.

Steered by instinct, Korlandril cut to the right of the doorway and hurdled through the shattered remains of a window. The humans within had turned towards Arhulesh and Bechareth, leaving their backs exposed. Korlandril's whirring blade opened the first along the spine from neck to waist, showering the Aspect Warrior with blood and fragments of vertebrae, creating a harmony of wet spatters and bony pattering. He hamstrung a second human, drawing the chainsword swiftly across the back of both knees.

Korlandril turned his gaze on another human and activated his mandiblasters. A flurry of shards spat from the pods on either side of his helm and arcs of blue energy lanced out, earthing through his prey's left eye to send azure coruscations across the blackening skin of the man's face. He collapsed with smoke trailing from his open mouth and ruined eye socket. Almost as an afterthought, the Aspect Warrior turned and drove the point of his weapon into the throat of a fourth human.

Korlandril finished with a flourish, flicking blood from his blade into the eyes of another enemy, blinding him momentarily. In the heartbeat the human flailed at his face, Korlandril slid sideways and brought his sword up and under his target's left arm, chopping through the side of his ribcage and cutting into heart and lungs. The chainsword stuck for a moment, juddering angrily in Korlandril's grasp before he wrenched it free.

Korlandril heard panicked shouts to his right and turned to see three more humans trying to clamber out of the window behind him. One fell to a burst of pistol fire from Korlandril, the other two exploded into ruddy clouds of super-heated matter as the Fire Dragons opened fire from the main floor of the warehouse.

Korlandril paused, eyes and ears searching for prey. There was a groan and he remembered the human he had hamstrung. He turned back to the crippled soldier; he was crawling towards the doorway leaving a smeared trail of blood. Korlandril watched him for a moment, the Artist part of him intrigued by the swirls of red painted on the floor by the human's desperate scrambling. The Aspect Warrior saw himself dimly reflected in the life fluid of his enemies, a distorted portrait in blood.

The moment passed and Korlandril stepped after his wounded foe, only to be beaten to the kill by Bechareth. The Striking Scorpion let his pistol drop to hang from its feed-lanyard and grabbed the human's hair, yanking him up to his ravaged knees. A swift cut separated head from neck, the body flopping into the blood pooling at Bechareth's feet.

Still holding the severed head, Bechareth looked up and saw Korlandril. They could see nothing of each other's expressions, but each realised Bechareth had taken a kill that was rightfully Korlandril's. Bechareth gave a florid bow of apology – face averted, legs crossed – and presented the head to Korlandril.

'There are more than enough foes to spread around,' said Korlandril. 'I do not begrudge you this one.'

Bechareth straightened, nonchalantly tossing the head out of the doorway. He nodded in appreciation.

'The building is clear, Khaine's wrath still waxes strongly, onwards to more death,' announced Kenainath, waving them forward with his claw.

A quick search revealed two back doors to the warehouse, both leading out into a small walled courtyard at one side of the compound's central tower. A metal door set into the side of the tower proved little obstacle; Kenainath's power claw tore through it with two strikes.

Inside was a mess of rooms and corridors. Humans scurried to cover as the Star of Justice squad arrived, salvoes from their shuriken catapults ripping along the olive-coloured walls, cutting down a score of great-coated humans caught in the open. The Striking Scorpions followed behind, despatching any foe that had survived the deadly hail from the Dire Avengers. Room-by-room, the two squads worked methodically across the bottom storey in a circle, leaving nothing alive. Behind them, other squads raced into the tower and up the stairwells.

Detonations sent showers of dust from the pipe-lined ceiling above, indicating stiffer resistance in the upper floors. Korlandril switched to his thermal vision to watch the motes of debris settling on the cooling bodies of his slain foes, the dust draping over them like shrouds.

They found an enclosed spiral stairwell and Kenainath took the lead, the Striking Scorpions surging past the Dire Avengers to take advantage of the close confines. They were only a few strides up the steps when four small objects clattered from the wall above and bounced down the stairs.

Kenainath reacted first, throwing himself forward to get out of the grenades' blasts, while the rest of the squad hastily retreated down the stairwell, using the central pillar as cover. Shrapnel and splinters of wall showered down the stairs, but the Striking Scorpions were left unharmed. The ring of las-bolts echoed from the walls and the squad leapt forwards to rejoin their exarch.

They found Kenainath with the remains of a dead human in the grip of his claw, the soldier's left arm sheared clean off. A headless corpse lay crumpled on the stairs at Kenainath's feet. A few las-impacts had left craters in the exarch's armour, wisps of vapour drifted lazily around him.

Another las-volley shrieked down the stairs, sending the squad back a few paces. Korlandril joined Kenainath and the pair rounded the curve of the stairwell swiftly, shuriken pistols at the ready. A group of humans clustered on a landing above – Korlandril counted eight as he glanced around the turn before pulling back out of harm's way.

'My wrath will go left, direct your fire to the right, and we will slay them,' ordered the exarch.

'As Khaine wills it,' replied Korlandril. He brought back the visual memory of the humans' locations, fixing them in his mind as clearly as if he was standing in front of them. It was a moment's thought to calculate the best sweep of fire to catch them in one burst.

'I am ready,' he told Kenainath.

The two of them sprang around the turn of the stairs, a blur of deadly discs hissing from their pistols. Korlandril's burst struck two kneeling humans across their throats, killing them instantly. He continued to fire as he moved to his left, raising his aim to send a torrent of shots into the stomachs of those stood further back from the steps. They went down with ugly grunts, sprays of blood showing up as bright yellow in Korlandril's thermal gaze.

Korlandril and Kenainath were stepping over the bodies, chainsword poised, before the last of the humans hit the ground.

The landing had two doorways, one to each side. With the tread of the others sounding close on the steps behind, Kenainath flicked his head to the left and signalled Korlandril to stay near at hand.

The open archway led to a series of small cell-like chambers sparsely furnished, with bare walls. Korlandril guessed them to be the quarters of menials; how like the humans to degrade their own kind in an attempt to prove superiority. The true demonstration of civilisation recognised all as individuals, equal and important. An eldar who chose to serve others did so as a means of developing their humility and sense of duty – something that as yet held no appeal for Korlandril.

He brushed aside the philosophic notion as a distraction and quickly scanned the doorways ahead, searching for any heat signature. He registered nothing. The subservient humans had most likely fled at the first sign of attack, perhaps hoping the guns of their masters would keep them safe. Their faith was misplaced. Any who had come into contact with the

Chaos artefact were at risk of corruption, none could be left alive.

A more thorough search confirmed that this storey, complete with kitchens and storerooms, was devoid of foes. Sounds of fighting from above announced more squads advancing ahead of the Deadly Shadow and Star of Justice.

'We shall go higher, ascend to the very heights, catch our foes at bay,' announced Kenainath. Uri-ethial, exarch of the Star of Justice, was quick to agree. The two squads headed back to the stairwell and bypassed the next two storeys, where there was evidence of much heavier fighting. Human corpses littered the landing, but amongst them were broken eldar weapons, pieces of armour and the bright splashes of eldar blood.

Korlandril wondered absently whether he knew any of the fallen. Now was not the time to mourn.

Several more squads joined the attack on the upper level, converging from the third and fourth storeys. As Korlandril ascended the steps, he felt a growing sense of unease. Something tugged at the edge of his spirit and his waystone began to tingle upon his chest.

'Kill them cold and fast, take no joy in the slaying, She Who Thirsts looks on!' warned Kenainath as they reached the last turn of the stairs.

The upper storey was a single open chamber, lav-ishly panelled and furnished. Humans sniped from behind overturned couches and upended bookcases, tomes of simple human script lying ripped and scat-tered across the dark lacquered floor. Flares of blue energy criss-crossed the room, as Dire Avengers and

Howling Banshees boiled up several stairways leading into the chamber.

One particular knot of humans hunkered down behind a large desk set on its side, scraps of paper, crude writing implements and scrawled ledgers piled on the floor where they had fallen. From here, something seeped across the room, touching upon Korlandril's psyche. The thrum of las-fire resounded in his ears and the tight closeness of his armour was a lover's embrace. The scent of the varnish and blood, the whickering of shuriken fire and cries of pain, all combined into a symphony for Korlandril's senses.

Spurred by the thrill, he fired his pistol at a human cowering behind the torn remains of an armchair. The flash of discs buried in his forehead, some slicing through his eyes into his brain. The corpse slowly tumbled to the floor, its gun clattering loudly on the wood.

At the far end of the hall, sheltered amongst a press of drably coated guards, lurked three male humans clad in thick robes of purple and red, edged with fur and gold. The trio were elderly, by human standards, their creased faces twisted in grimaces of shock and terror. The ostentation of their garb marked them as personages of power in the hierarchy of the humans, if not the eyes of the eldar.

Soon this last group were all that remained.

One of them – his thick hood fallen back to his shoulders to reveal a hairless head mottled with blemishes – stood up and shouted in his unintelligible tongue, brandishing a box no larger than his hand, encrusted with pale blue and pink gems. His wide-eyed expression may have been of fear or anger, it was impossible to tell. His contorted face was a grotesque caricature of expression, a gross parody of emotion.

Korlandril's eyes were drawn back to the box, a faint whisper in the back of his mind. The human fell to his knees and his bodyguards threw down their weapons, holding up hands in capitulation. His two magisterial companions fell forwards and debased themselves, looking up imploringly at the warriors surrounding them.

It was the box that called to Korlandril and he stepped forwards, ignoring the human soldiers. The gems upon its surface glittered so brightly, entrancing him. He heard the murmurs of other Aspect Warriors around him.

It would be a sweet prize indeed. Korlandril pictured the bloody ruin he would make of the decrepit creature that kept the beautiful box from him. Korlandril would tear out the human's innards and use them as garlands. His bones would make fine pieces of sculpture, suitably painted and rearranged.

Touch nothing. Free your minds of desire and temptation.

Korlandril recognised the thoughts of Farseer Kelamith. They cut through the strange fog that had clouded his spirit since entering the room.

The air crackled behind the surrendering humans. Where a moment earlier had been empty air, seven heavily-armoured warriors appeared. They were clad in red and black, their backs and shoulders encased in broad, beetle-like carapaces decorated with the designs of white spider webs. In their hands they wielded bulky weapons, deathspinners, glowing blue from within, their muzzles surrounded by spinning claw-like appendages.

As one the Warp Spiders opened fire on the last humans. The muzzles of their weapons flashed with bright blue as gravitic impellers spun into a blur. The air filled with a swirling cloud, indistinct but nebulous. The writhing monofilament wire mesh unleashed by the deathspinners engulfed the humans, slicing effortlessly through skin, flesh and bone. The grey cloud turned red with gore as the humans disintegrated into thousands of miniscule pieces, each small part further sliced and dissected by the streaming wire cloud until only a faint red mist remained.

The sight brought a tear to Korlandril's eye. Such destruction, wrought so quickly and so beautifully. For a moment he entirely forgot the presence of the box, until it clattered to the floor, the remnants of the human's fingers dripping from the enticing gems.

There was a presence and Korlandril stepped aside, sensing new arrivals at the doorway behind him. The Aspect Warriors parted to allow Kelamith and Arhathain to enter. Three dozen runes gently orbited the farseer, intersecting and parting with each other's paths as he strode forward. Arhathain wore his blue armour, in his right hand a spear almost twice as tall as the autarch, its leaf-shaped head inscribed with thousands of the tiniest runes, each burning with its own energy.

With them came a coterie of grim-faced seers, all clad in plain white, heads shorn of all hair. Between them floated an ovoid container, dark red in colour and patterned with silver runes. Korlandril recognised wraithbone – a psychoplastic woven into existence by the bonesingers, the living core of Alaitoc and every other eldar creation. Korlandril's waystone fluttered warmly as the casket slowly glided past him.

From amongst the wreckage to Korlandril's right, a human surged forwards, one arm hanging limply by his side, a long wound in his thigh spraying blood as he sprinted across the room towards the artefact.

Arhathain reacted quickest, his spear singing across the hall to catch the human in the chest, hurling him bodily through the air. A blink later, several shuriken volleys and laser blasts passed through the air where the man had been. Arhathain beckoned to the spear and it twisted, ripped itself free of the dead human and flew back to his grasp. Unperturbed, the autarch approached the box and lowered to one knee beside it, studying the artefact closely.

Whispering protective mantras, the white seers closed around him, their robes obscuring all sight, their sibilant incantations growing in volume. When they parted a moment later, silence descended. The box was gone but the wraithbone casket gleamed with a darker light, an aura of oily energy seeping from it. Korlandril took another step back, unwilling to get too close to the accursed contents now that he was freed from its lure.

The white seers departed with their tainted cargo.

'Humans gather in force to destroy us outside the walls,' Arhathain announced, standing up. 'The garrison are all slain. Return to the webway and we will be away. Take our dead, we cannot leave them in this forsaken place.'

With the others, Korlandril descended to the level below. Here they found several dead eldar, armour pierced by bayonets or cracked by las-blast and bullet. Korlandril stooped and picked up the remains of a Howling Banshee. His faceplate was shattered, revealing an empty eye socket and bloody cheek. Korlandril lifted him gently in his arms and carried him back to the webway portal.

THE SOLEMN NOTES of pipes and a slow and steady drumbeat heralded the arrival of the funeral cortege. Three long lines wound slowly into the Dome of Everlasting Stillness; two lines of eldar flanking the bodies of the dead borne upon hovering biers. The bodies were covered with white shrouds, each embroidered with their names. On the left of each bier the Watcher bore the spirit stone of the deceased: the dead eldar's waystone now imbued with their essence, ready for transference to the infinity circuit. On the right of each departed walked the Mourner in a heavy white veil sobbing and occasionally giving vent to plaintive wails – an eldar who trod upon the Path of Grief. Other eldar of Alaitoc gathered in their thousands to watch the procession, tears in their eyes, memories of the fallen stark and bright in their minds.

They lamented the deaths of those they knew, but could not give full voice to their sorrow lest it consume them. That was for the Mourners, who had devoted themselves to the outpouring of the emotion death brought about, freeing others to remember the fallen with calm regret without being destroyed by guilt.

Korlandril watched sombrely as covered body after covered body slid past, the growls and choking cries of the Mourners falling deafly on his ears. He remembered the sorrow of past occasions, but felt little of it now. It seemed a matter of numbers, though each of those numbers represented a life no more. Twenty-four had died during the attack.

There would be other burials in the cycles to come, but none to match the communal grieving taking place. Twenty more were in the Halls of Healing, some of them fighting with little hope against wounds even the Tress of Isha could not heal. This was for all of Alaitoc to feel its woe. Smaller ceremonies for friends and families would take place after, when the spirit stones of the deceased became one with the infinity circuit.

A shroud marked with the rune of Arthuis passed. Korlandril closed his eyes, memories flooding back.

It was the eve of the Festival of Illuminations. Korlandril danced with Thirianna, while Arthuis and Maerthuin poured large measures from a black crystal decanter.

'What is that you have brought?' Thirianna asked gaily. 'Is it a special treat?'

She had been drinking summervine since midcycle and was a little unsteady on her feet. Korlandril relished the opportunity to hold her close as he supported her, though not so close that it would be inappropriate.

'It is a secret family recipe,' said Arthuis. He proffered two half-full glasses towards Korlandril and

Thirianna. The dancers broke apart and seated themselves at a low table beside the gently bubbling stream that wound through the Valley of Midnight Memories. The dome lights were still bright, shining above like a hundred suns, but soon all would become as black as the deepest shadows between stars, save for the ghost-light of waystones and the glittering ornaments worn in hair and around necks. It was the Time of Shadow, the cycle before the Festival of Illuminations; the night before day, hidden and dark delights before revealing light. It was the night that all could indulge their passions without regret, to expunge themselves of the memories the next cycle.

Korlandril tasted the thick liquid, which was as black as the bottle it came from. There was a hint of effervescence about it and a subtly bitter edge that sweetened into a pleasant aftertaste.

He raised the glass to Arthuis and Maerthuin.

'I congratulate your family on keeping such a delectable tipple a secret for so long!'

'It's just duskwater and nightgrape, mixed with firespice, cloudfruit and dustsugar,' laughed Arthuis. 'Be careful, it tastes innocent, but it hides a sting like Anacondin's spear at its heart!'

'Nightgrape?' said Thirianna, placing her glass on the table untouched. Her eyes flashed with anger. 'That is not respectful. To take the crop from the Gardens of Immortal Solace and use them for intoxication! What would you do if your grave flowers were so used?'

Arthuis grinned, took up the glass and downed its contents in one gulp.

'If it was from my plot, I'd expect you to choke on it!'

The memory disturbed Korlandril. He should not have recalled it – the Festival of Illuminations should have swept away all recollection. What other doors in his mind had he opened when he had drawn on the Tress of Isha?

Korlandril closed his eyes and pictured Arthuis as a statue, immortalised in black gemstone, full of strong corners, but with a hollow within containing a vial of his secret midnight cocktail. It would be a fitting tribute to one who embraced his darkness so openly, and yet strove so hard to bring light to the lives of others.

His death was unfortunate. Sacrificed, like so many others, so that future generations would know peace.

Korlandril opened his eyes and scanned the gathered crowds. Many were Aspect Warriors but the majority were not. None were exarchs, for tradition dictated that the priests of Khaine were not welcome at these ceremonies. Peddlers of destruction were not allowed to mourn their handiwork. To the rest of Alaitoc the exarchs were already dead, and none would mourn their passing, though their deeds would be honoured and cherished. The crowd looked on in demure silence as the glorious dead passed through the Gate of Farewells, a white arc crowned with the golden rune of Alaitoc.

The quiet disturbed Korlandril. These eldar had given their lives, not for quiet contemplation and respectful peace, but for life, for the joys to be experienced by those around them and those yet to

come. Their deaths were sad but the accomplish-
ments of their lives were not rendered obsolete by
such ending. Even their spirits would live on within
the infinity circuit. This was a transition from the
corporeal to the incorporeal, not the ultimate termi-
nation of life, and for the first time Korlandril saw
the funeral rites with different eyes.

'Farewell, Arthuis!' Korlandril called out, raising a
hand in salute to the departing body of his friend as
it disappeared into the glow of the gate. 'You lived as
you wished, and died most nobly! I will visit you
soon!'

Korlandril felt the heat of agitation around him
and the stares of others fixed upon him. He turned
to the eldar next to him, a young male eldar perhaps
only on his first Path. The youth was frowning in
reproach.

'Is what I say not true?' Korlandril demanded. 'Will
you one day be ready to give your life like my friend?
Would you want those you have been cleaved from
to whinge and whimper, or would you want them to
roar out their tributes to you?'

'This is not the place…' said an austere eldar to
Korlandril's left. She laid a hand on his arm and
pulled him closer to whisper in his ear. 'You dis-
credit yourself, and the spirit of your friend.'

Korlandril pulled his arm from her grip and
pushed her away. He had meant the contact to be
gentle, but she fell, landing heavily. Korlandril
stooped to offer her a hand but others pushed him
aside with pursed lips and glares of reproach.

Righted once more, the matriarchal eldar straightened the folds of her robe and faced Korlandril.

'You are not welcome,' she said sternly, and turned her back on him, deliberately and slowly. Others did the same, leaving Korlandril in a spreading circle of isolation.

'What need have I for the fawning attentions of others?' he snarled. 'Once you all craved to be known by me, and I indulged you. You are less than Arthuis. He I called friend and did not judge, and in return he did not judge me and called me friend. Who else here could say the same?'

With a last growl, Korlandril stalked through the flower-studded meadow towards the waiting air-rider.

Part Three

Exarch

LEGACY

During the War in Heaven, Khaine unleashed untold evils upon the eldar. Ulthanesh at first refused to fight, claiming the quarrel of Khaine was with the House of Eldanesh, not all eldar. Khaine's wrath was not so confined and there were those in the House of Eldanesh who remembered the bitter parting with Ulthanesh. Those tainted by Khaine fell upon Ulthanesh's followers and there was war between the Houses. Khaine was pleased, but Ulthanesh finally relented from his pacifism and took up his spear, not to confront the House of Eldanesh, but to bring war to the Bloody-Handed One. Seeing their common foe was the War God, the House of Eldanesh made their peace with Ulthanesh and the two fought side-by-side as the warriors had done of old. But there were those of both Houses so enamoured of war that Khaine worked them against each other, and they would slay

*any foe, regardless of loyalty. They became creatures
of the Bloody-Handed God and turned against their
own kind.*

THE LONGER KORLANDRIL spent at the shrine, the less
he thought of death. He was surrounded by it now,
its messenger and its target. He dimly recalled flickers from the fighting with the humans: brief
vignettes of destruction and slaying lasting no longer
than a heartbeat. The recollections brought no sensation with them, like a play with no words, or a
silent opera. They were simply things that had happened.

One particular cycle after training, Korlandril mentioned this in passing to Arhulesh. His fellow
Striking Scorpion stopped in his stride and directed
a penetrating look at Korlandril.

'You are remembering scenes of bloodshed?'

'Just images,' replied Korlandril. 'Do you not?'

'No! Nor would I wish to. I can feel those memories inside me, down in the shadows of my spirit,
and that is enough to make me sicken with guilt and
woe.'

'I do not understand. We all know that we have
drawn blood and slain. It is irrefutable fact. We are
Aspect Warriors; it is what we have trained to do. I
am no longer an Artist but I can still visit the sculptures I created.'

'There is a difference between intellectual
acknowledgement and emotional connection. Your
sculptures were the product of your actions, not the
memory of them. Tell me, Korlandril, what did it *feel*
like to sculpt your first masterpiece?'

'It was…' Korlandril foundered. He was not sure of the answer. 'There was a sense of achievement, for certain. And release. Yes, definitely a moment of creative release when it was completed. Much like the surge of energy I felt in my first battle.'

'This is dangerous!' cried Arhulesh, backing away from Korlandril.

'Your fright is unwarranted,' said Korlandril, extending a hand to placate his companion. 'What has so shocked you?'

'You compare acts of creation and destruction. That is not healthy. If you continue in this way, you will remember the joy you felt, and that would signal something very grave indeed.'

'Why do you separate death from life, destruction from creation, in such an arbitrary way?'

'Because creation can be undone, but destruction cannot! You may come to hate a statue that you crafted, and can smash it to a thousand pieces, but the memory of it will remain. It is not so with death. You can never bring back those who have been slain; you cannot grant them the gift of Isha. As the act cannot be undone, the memory must not remain.'

'Korlandril still wears his mask, since the last battle, and he cannot remove it.'

Korlandril and Arhulesh spun to see Aranarha walking out of Kenainath's chambers. The Deadly Shadow exarch was close behind.

'It would be too soon, more swiftly than I have seen, I am not so sure,' said Kenainath.

'He has confessed it himself, sees what our eyes see, voiced that which we hear within,' replied Aranarha.

'No, that is not true!' snapped Korlandril. 'I performed the rituals; I removed my war-mask.'

'Then you have nothing to fear, walk from this dark place, go into the light outside,' said Aranarha, his tone challenging.

'I shall!' declared Korlandril. He turned to Arhulesh, who still eyed him warily. 'Come, my *friend*, let us go to the Meadows of Fulfilment and you can tell me more of Elissanadrin.'

He hooked an arm under Arhulesh's and dragged him towards the door. As they walked down the passageway, the admonishing voice of Kenainath drifted after them, his words intended for his fellow exarch.

'That was a mistake, confrontation fills his mind; he will seek a foe.'

'Ignore them,' Korlandril said with a forced laugh. 'They are jealous of our freedom.'

Arhulesh said nothing.

ARHULESH EXTRICATED HIMSELF from Korlandril's invitation shortly after the two had left the shrine, citing a former appointment. Korlandril considered his options.

He felt no desire to sculpt, there were already three half-finished works in his chambers and none of them appealed. He was not hungry or thirsty. His attempt to inveigle Arhulesh into an outing had been borne more out of boredom than a desire for company.

He decided that Elissanadrin would be able to drag him from the ennui that had slowly grown within him since the last battle. She was a Striking

Scorpion and would understand the tedium Korlandril felt.

He found an infinity circuit terminal not far from the shrine portal, hoping to locate Elissanadrin. Placing his hand upon the crystal interface, Korlandril attempted to align with the pulsing spirits within. The connection was fleeting, the energy of the infinity circuit reluctant to conform to his requests. Korlandril was no spiritseer and had no means to commune with the infinity circuit to divine its agitation. He removed his fingers from the crystal, concentrated his thoughts more clearly on Elissanadrin, and tried again.

As before, Korlandril experienced the briefest glimmers of Alaitoc, envisaging the craftworld as a whole, but was not able to detect any presence of Elissanadrin. Perturbed, he stepped away from the interface. The passageway was devoid of other eldar who might assist him, so Korlandril headed towards the Dome of Midnight Forests, the entrance to which was a short walk away.

The bright light of the path gave way to the more diffuse twilight of the dome as Korlandril passed through the wide arch into the trees. This part of the parkland was sparsely traversed due to its proximity to several Aspect shrines. Korlandril headed towards the lakes at the centre, knowing them to be a popular haunt of many Artists and Poets. Perhaps he would see Abrahasil. He had not met his mentor since first going to the Deadly Shadow.

As Korlandril walked through the trees, his thoughts broke in many directions. Memories of encounters beneath the shady foliage flickered through his mind, but he did not linger on any in particular. The shades of the leaves intrigued him, moving into purplish autumnal hue. The softness of the grass underfoot was welcoming. He ran his hands across the craggy bark of a lianderin, his fingers detecting every whorl and knot.

All these thoughts occupied him, but they could not drive out his foremost experiences. A patch of light might reveal him and he kept to the shadows. He changed direction at irregular intervals so as not to approach his target from a direct line. He constantly scanned root holes and branches for signs of danger, though the Dome of Midnight Forests was devoid of any threat larger than a dawnfalcon.

Korlandril's paranoia grew as he heard fleeting voices from ahead. He had covered a considerable distance, unaware of the passage of time. The twilight was darkening through the heavy canopy, signalling the beginning of the dome's night cycle. He had entered not long after the Time of Cleansing at mid-cycle.

The glitter of water could be seen between the trees. There was movement and a figure appeared on a path ahead.

Korlandril was behind the concealing bulk of a tree before he realised it, clinging to the shadow like a spider on its web. From his hiding spot, Korlandril eyed the arrival. She was a little shorter than him, with black and gold hair swept high from her pale forehead. Her soft white tunic had a long tail that danced in the subtle dome breeze, twisting on itself and curving invitingly in her wake. She was laughing, a crystal reader in hand, eyes focussed on its pale display.

'Forgive my intrusion,' said Korlandril, stepping on to the path.

The maiden shrieked and the reader fell from her grasp. She caught it before it hit the wood bark of the path, swiftly straightening as Korlandril approached, a hand held out in apology.

'I did not mean to startle you,' he said.

'Why would you sneak up on me like that?' she demanded. Now that she had been given a moment to study Korlandril, she took a fearful step back. Her voice was subdued. 'What do you want from me?'

Korlandril could not fathom the cause of her disquiet. He had surprised her, but that did not warrant such a guarded reaction.

'I have a question. Have you experienced any problems with the infinity circuit of late?'

'I have not,' she said stiffly. Her tone was clipped, her language formal and cold. Though they were strangers, there was no reason for such bad manners.

'It was a simple enough request,' said Korlandril. 'I do not understand your hostility.'

'Nor I yours,' she said, turning away. 'Leave me alone.'

Korlandril stood dumbfounded as she strode quickly back towards the lakes. He took a moment to review what had happened.

Korlandril was behind the concealing bulk of a tree before he realised it, clinging to the shadow like a spider on its web. From his hiding spot, Korlandril eyed the arrival. She was a little shorter than him, with black and gold hair swept high from her pale forehead. Her soft white tunic had a long tail that danced in the subtle dome breeze, twisting on itself and curving invitingly in her wake. She was laughing, a crystal reader in hand, eyes focussed on its pale display.

'Forgive my intrusion,' said Korlandril, stepping forwards into Claw with Rising Sun, right arm crooked ready to defend, left arm raised for a strike.

The maiden shrieked and the reader fell from her grasp. She caught it before it hit the wood bark of the path, swiftly straightening as Korlandril approached, moving forwards in a crabwise fashion, right arm extended in Lunging Serpent.

'I did not mean to startle you,' he said, shifting to the posture of repose.

Korlandril looked at her retreating back, wondering how it was he had slipped into the ritual postures without effort, and why he had not been aware of it. The two versions of the same event vied in his mind – the one the experience as it had happened, the second his more conscious reflection upon it.

The stranger's fearful and angry reaction proved that his recollection of events was true; it had been his experience of them that was amiss. He had stalked her like prey. Troubled, Korlandril turned away from the lakes and headed back into the woods as the light dimmed and the Midnight Forest earned its name.

KORLANDRIL COULD NOT think. There were too many distractions: rustling leaves, skittering insects, hooting birds, yelping creatures.

He tried to centre his thoughts but every movement triggered his instincts and he was instantly aware, eyes fixed on a snuffling thorn-eater or ears pitched to detect the next beat of a wing overhead. Even the gentle swaying of the trees and the dappling of Mirianathir's light demanded his attention, each shifting shadow requiring his scrutiny before he could settle again.

For most of the night cycle he sat frustrated in the grove, far from the paths used by lovers and philosophers, trying to attain a measure of equilibrium.

Frustrated, as the dome's field depolarised to let through more of the dying star's rays, Korlandril quit his attempts at meditation and headed for the Deadly Shadow.

KORLANDRIL FOUND THE shrine empty, or those parts to which he had access. He suspected Kenainath was present somewhere – where else would the exarch be? – but the chamber of armour and hall of weapons were deserted. In silence, the mantra running through his head, Korlandril equipped himself for training.

He went through his opening routines with ease, stringing together a series of attacks and defences to loosen his muscles, tightened by his unsettling experience in the forest. As he went through these motions, he began to frame the shadow-foe in his mind, readying himself for more extreme exertions.

He found that zone of control and instinct he desired, his chainsword flickering in and out at his whim, weaving a deadly dance of blade alongside imaginary shurikens and bursts from his mandiblasters.

Korlandril stopped, halfway between Rising Claw and Serpent from Shadow.

His shadow-prey had a face. Several in fact. The faces of the humans he had killed. He saw them morphing into each other, eyes dead, mouths agape.

With a laugh, Korlandril slashed at the apparition's throat, taking the head clean off. Its ghost whispered away into cloudy shreds and disappeared. Korlandril continued his training without it. He needed no imaginary foe to fight; he had drawn real blood and taken real lives.

HE PRACTISED FOR most of the cycle and was quite weary by the time he hung up his chainsword and took off his armour. Despite his fatigue, his mind was still aflame, not the least satiated by his exertion. Hunger and thirst gnawed at him, but it was not just for food and drink that he craved. He wanted something to occupy himself. He needed some entertainment.

He found the others at the Crescent of the Dawning Ages and sat with them, a full platter on the table before him.

'I am of a mind to hear a recital, or perhaps see a theatrical performance,' he told the others between mouthfuls of food. 'Something stirring, with drama, and perhaps a little bit of sensuousness.'

'There is a rendition of *Aeistian's Tryst* in the Dome of Callous Winters,' Elissanadrin told him, helping herself to the carafe of summervine Arhulesh had brought to the table.

'Too rhetorical,' Korlandril replied.

'There's a *Weaving of the Filigrees* in the Hall of Unending Labours,' suggested Arhulesh. His eyes flickered between Korlandril and Elissanadrin in a suggestive manner. 'Perhaps the two of you could attend.'

Korlandril considered this for a moment, but dismissed the idea. He did not want to be distracted during his first congress with Elissanadrin. The more he thought about it, the less appealing the notion of physical intimacy with his companion became.

He shook his head.

'We could race skyrunners along the Emerald Straits, I've always wanted to try that,' suggested Elissanadrin.

Korlandril sighed.

'It's not as dangerous or thrilling as it looks, not if you've any experience with a skyrunner at all.'

'I'm not going to waste my time with this,' said Arhulesh, standing up. 'It's clear that you have no appetite for any suggestion I might make. Enjoy the summervine.'

'Wait!' Korlandril cried out. 'I am sure we can think of something. I just want to find something to kill time.'

All within earshot turned towards Korlandril. Across the Crescent of Dawning Ages a shocked silence descended.

'What are you all staring at?' rasped Korlandril, rising angrily to his feet. 'Have none of you ever suffered from a momentary boredom that cannot be satisfied?'

There was a tight grip at his elbow and Korlandril felt himself dragged back to the bench.

'You cannot say something like that!' hissed Elissanadrin. Her expression was a mixture of exasperation and shock.

'Was it my tone? Did I raise my voice too much?'

Elissanadrin's look turned to incredulity and her mouth opened twice without words. Korlandril considered his words innocent enough, but his experience in the Dome of Midnight Forests gave him a moment of doubt. He reviewed the past few moments.

'We could race skyrunners along the Emerald Straits, I've always wanted to try that,' suggested Elissanadrin.

Korlandril sighed, his lips turning to a scornful sneer.

'It's not as dangerous or thrilling as it looks, not if you've any experience with a skyrunner at all.'

'I'm not going to waste my time with this,' said Arhulesh, standing up. 'It's clear that you have no appetite for any suggestion I might make. Enjoy the summervine.'

'Wait!' Korlandril cried out. 'I am sure we can think of something. I just want to find something to kill.'

Korlandril rose back out of the memory with shock.

'Kill time!' he barked. 'I want to find something to kill time!'

Elissanadrin appeared unconvinced. Korlandril was about to argue his point, that it was an innocent slip of the tongue, but he stopped himself.

Korlandril's whirring blade opened the first along the spine from neck to waist, showering the Aspect

Warrior with blood and fragments of vertebrae, creating a harmony of wet spatters and bony pattering.

The moment had been sweet indeed. All he had remembered before had been the faces, but now the artistry with which he had wielded his weapons came back to Korlandril. And the sensation… The hint of it sent a thrill through him, rousing his blood, making every detail of his surroundings stand out in sharp detail. Elissanadrin's breath on his cheek and the scent of gladesuns in her hair. The heat from her body. Even her blood, pulsing though her arteries and veins, flushing just beneath the skin.

What a rich, red paint it would make.

'I do not like the way you are staring at me,' she said, pulling back from Korlandril.

With a shudder, Korlandril forced himself to focus. He stood up, gave a stiff bow of apology, and fled.

THE SHRINE OF the Deadly Shadow would not welcome back Korlandril. He had tried the entrances of which he was aware and none of them would open at his approach. Even the infinity circuit refused to acknowledge his presence. Unsure what this presaged or what course of action to take, Korlandril resorted to returning to the main gateway and banging upon the iris-door with his fist.

'Is this your doing, Kenainath?' he demanded, his voice echoing coldly around the accessway.

His demand was met with silence and he stood fuming and impotent for some time. As he was about to turn away, the door peeled open to reveal Kenainath in full armour, complete with helm.

'You are not welcome; I am exarch of this place, your shrine is elsewhere.'

Kenainath's voice was flat, emotionless. Korlandril took a step forwards but halted when the exarch raised his claw.

'This is where I belong! You cannot cast me out.'

'You have lost your way, you must find another shrine, it is tradition. The Path ends for you; Khaine has taken your spirit, you are an exarch.'

'Nonsense!' Korlandril's laugh was harsh. 'One does not become an exarch after two battles. This is ridiculous.'

'Your journey was short, but now it is completed, you must accept it. There are other shrines, empty and without leaders, one will call to you. As it was with me, as it was with all of us, those trapped on the Path. We will meet again, not master and his pupil, but as two equals.'

'Tha–'

The door whispered shut, cutting off Korlandril's retort. He slumped against the wall, head in hands. It made no sense to him. He had barely taken two steps upon the Path of the Warrior. There could be no way he was trapped. Something had gone wrong, but he was no exarch.

Taking a deep breath, Korlandril straightened, fists clenched. He would not accept this without a fight.

He took several steps away from the door and then halted. Self-realisation blossomed within him. The more he fought this fate, the tighter its grip had become. What was it he was fighting against? Himself? Thirianna? Aradryan? It was senseless, this craving for confrontation. The listlessness that had filled Korlandril since returning from the battle against the humans nagged at him. Would it last forever? Would he ever be rid of the drifting, formless feeling that consumed him?

Kenainath was right. Korlandril craved that dance between life and death, more than anything he had craved in his life – adulation, recognition, self-awakening, all were trivial in comparison to the rush of blood from war and the exquisite delight of a foe slain and a victory achieved.

There was one place left that might provide him with the answers he needed. Moving away from the Deadly Shadow, Korlandril located a bay of skyrunners. Taking one, he turned on the automatic guidance and entered the Chamber of Autarchs as his destination. Thoughts a-whirl, he gunned the engines into life and sped away.

THE MASSIVE AUDIENCE hall was empty save for Korlandril. He paced around the broad steps, looking at the long circles of runes around the central platform, each an Aspect shrine. Some were worn thin by generations of feet, others as bright as the day they had been inscribed. As he circled slowly, he recognised the pattern. The oldest shrines were at the centre, many of them Dire Avengers, Striking Scorpions, Howling Banshees, Swooping Hawks and Dark Reapers. There were duplicates, their runes careful variations of their parent shrines, each moving further from the dais. New runes appeared, of Aspects unknown before – Crystal Dragons, Warp Spiders, Shining Spears. Outwards and onwards the history of Alaitoc's warrior past spiralled.

On the innermost step, Korlandril stopped. He stood on a Striking Scorpion rune. Examining it closely, he read its name in the simple curls and curving cross-strokes. Hidden Death. It was unfamiliar, though he was sure he did not know the name of every Aspect shrine on Alaitoc.

In hiding he had come to the Aspect Warriors, and in death he was trapped. It seemed to make a form of sense. Was this what Kenainath had meant?

Korlandril quickly returned to the skyrunner and entered the Shrine of Hidden Death as his destination. Lifting into the air, the skyrunner turned a half-circle and then darted towards the rimward exit from the chamber. This led into the labyrinth of tunnels Korlandril had seen when coming from the Deadly Shadow. Left, right, and then ascending through a vertical fork, the skyrunner climbed towards the dockside area of Alaitoc, gaining speed. The wind pulled at Korlandril's hair and face and tugged hard at his flapping robes as the skyrunner banked sharply to the right around a curve, spiralling downwards once more, flashing past other junctions.

Even with the considerable speed of the skyrunner, Korlandril was able to memorise the route, ingraining every twist and change of direction into his mind. The further he flew, the greater his hopes surged. It was not the thrill of speed that filled him, but the sense of belonging he yearned for. Along the tunnels and concourses the skyrunner took him closer and closer to his destiny. It sang in his ears with the thump of his heartbeat, coursing through every fibre.

This was the call mentioned by Kenainath.

It was the Time of Contemplation before the skyrunner began to slow, perhaps halfway around the rim of Alaitoc from the Deadly Shadow, nearly as far away as it was possible to get. Was this coincidence? Korlandril was quick to dismiss the idea. There was no coincidence at play. The infinity circuit, the great mind of Alaitoc, had guided him here, by some means or other. Korlandril did not fool himself that he understood everything that was happening, but was content to be buffeted along on its tide for the moment. He had wandered from the Path and become lost; it mattered not who guided him now. Only a single hope remained – to find the peace of battle he so sorely missed.

THE SKYRUNNER CAME to a halt outside an inconspicuous archway, sealed with a solid gate of deep emerald colour. Dismounting, Korlandril dismissed the skyrunner and it sped off around a bend in the corridor. Hesitantly, fearful that this place would reject him also, Korlandril approached the gates.

With a sigh, they swung inwards and a wash of warm air billowed out to engulf Korlandril in an airy embrace. He closed his eyes, savouring the smell of strong spice and the light touch of the breeze on his flesh, the brightness through his eyelids as of a sun close at hand. Opening them, he blinked twice to settle his eyesight and looked upon his new home.

Low dunes of red sand stretched across the dome, their boundaries obscured by distance. Here there grew scrubby patches of candlewood, their violet blossoms small but pungent. A burning orb hung low to his left, like an impossibly close sun, and even as Korlandril watched it sank further and further from view, until all that remained was a dusky glow, though the rest of Alaitoc was perhaps not much past mid-cycle.

Korlandril threw off his boots and robe and undid the ties from his hair, letting all fall free. Bare-footed and naked, he crossed the threshold and walked into the sandy swathes, feeling the particles beneath his soles, sliding between his toes.

Unnoticed, the gates swished shut behind him.

Korlandril wandered this new worldscape for some time, getting a feel for his position and for its atmosphere. It was like no other dome he had seen. The artificial sun disappeared, leaving only a red haze. Far in the distance he could see the glimmer of a forcefield and the glow of Mirianathir. He headed towards it.

Approaching the centre of the desert, his footprints gently swept away by the breeze, Korlandril felt a tremor. Stopping, he located the source of the disturbance, some way off to his left. As he headed in that direction the tremors became stronger, sending waves of sand cascading down the dunesides.

Cresting a particularly high dune, Korlandril came upon a deep crater-like bowl, edged with a thin, high wall. The sands within the wall danced and bounced in agitation. With a rushing of sand, something erupted from the bowl, the red grains pouring from the stepped shelves of its structure. It was a ziggurat, a little smaller than the Shrine of the Deadly Shadow, made of yellow rock. The force of its arrival almost threw Korlandril from his feet as the sands slipped from underneath him.

A white light glowed from the slit-like windows and doorways of the lowest level. With a joyous shout, Korlandril ran down the slope towards the shrine. He paused at the low doorway – barely high enough to enter without stooping – and took a deep breath. The act did nothing to quell the excitement he felt. This place was like a Dreaming made real. Korlandril touched the rough surface of the doorway to assure himself that it was no phantasm. The light spilling from the shrine felt thick in his hands and heavy on his skin, but the stones were real enough.

As he stepped into the doorway, almost blinded, the light vanished, plunging all into darkness. Korlandril's heart quavered for a moment and he stopped, taken aback by the sudden change. As his eyes adjusted, he became aware of a red glow, coming from around a corner ahead. Walking quickly, he followed the patch of dim light, turning left from the main passage into a side chamber. The glow was stronger, coming from an archway opposite, through which seven steep steps led down into the shrine. Coming to a U-shaped landing, Korlandril was confronted by two more archways. The light came from the left, now strong enough for him to see the walls to either side.

Along more corridors and through more arches Korlandril followed the strengthening glow, until it brought him to a low-ceilinged room much like the Deadly Shadow duelling chamber. There was no circle upon the floor but a stand holding an elaborate suit of armour. It was from the red gems encrusting the dark green plates that the light was coming. There was movement in the light; the gems were spirit stones. Seven in all, each containing the essence of a dead eldar.

Korlandril stood before the suit, admiring the curve of its plates, the solidity of its presence. He reached a hand out and touched the breastplate. His waystone flared in response, its glow merging with the spirit stones of the armour. A glimmer of a memory fluttered across Korlandril's consciousness and he snatched his hand back.

The memory was gone. Perhaps he had imagined it.

Walking around the armour, Korlandril studied it closely. It was heavier than normal Aspect armour, the plates reinforced with additional spines and ribbing overlaid in gold. The craftsmanship was exquisite, every curve and line a harmony of functionality and style. Korlandril ran a finger along the back of a gauntlet, shivering with anticipation.

A spark of recollection jolted him away again.

'This is mine,' he whispered, his voice swallowed by the chamber.

Yours…

The voice was not a voice, but a thought. Was it Korlandril's own thoughts, or something else?

'I shall be the Hidden Death.'

Hidden Death…

The thought-echo lasted for a moment and disappeared, leaving no trace in his memory.

Korlandril stared at the armour for a long while, wondering who had created it, who had worn it, which enemies had fallen to its wearers.

Answers…

The time for hesitation and contemplation was over. For good or ill, Korlandril had come to this place – been led to it? – and it was here that things would change. For one who feared change so much it was the final answer. He would change no more. He would become the Hidden Death and remain so until he was slain. He could surrender willingly, leave the doubts behind, the struggle to adapt would be no more, the war within would be called truce.

All he had to do was accept what had become of him and put on the armour.

'War, death, blood, all that remains. I am Exarch Korlandril.'

Exarch Morlaniath.

The name meant nothing to Korlandril, save for the most distant shimmer of a recollection, though he could not place it. It was someone else's memory of a myth Korlandril had once heard, or the name one keeps for oneself and never shares with another.

The time had come.

As he took the armour from the stand, he whispered the mantra that would have him take up his war-mask forever more. Unbidden, the words changed between brain and tongue, but he spoke them surely, as if this was the way he had always meant to say them.

'The peace has been broken, balance falls to discord, only battle remains.'

A shadow-voice joined his as he drew on the first parts of the armour.

'Now we array ourselves, with bloody Khaine's raiment, as a true warrior.'

Now we array ourselves, with bloody Khaine's raiment, as a true warrior.

Images flashed through his mind: memories not of his life. His mind burned with pain, his thoughts stretching to accommodate a whole new lifetime's worth of experiences. Faces of friends he had never met, of parents who had not created him, of foes he had never slain. So many dead faces, thousands of them, in a torrent of anguish and death, and throughout all a jubilant laughter rang in his ears.

And finally a moment of blackness, of agony and ending.

As an automaton, Korlandril continued with the armour, the next line of the mantra barely a breath from his lips, another voice taking it up in his mind.

'In Khaine's own iron skin, we clad ourselves for war, while fire burns hot within.'

In Khaine's Own Iron Skin, We Clad Ourselves For War, While Fire Burns Hot Within.

Another storm of memories, more pain, more death. Korlandril tried to fix upon something he knew to be his own life.

He ran his fingers through Auriellie's sapphire hair, kissing her neck, her sharp cheeks illuminated by firelight.

No! That was not his memory. He had never done that. He had never known Auriellie. He tried again, but the mantra continued to spill from him and he was swept away on another tide of false recollection.

'The iron blood of Khaine, from which we draw our strength, grows greater within us.'

THE IRON BLOOD OF KHAINE, FROM WHICH WE DRAW OUR STRENGTH, GROWS GREATER WITHIN US.

'Battle comes upon us; we bear its dark burden, upon our broad shoulders.'

BATTLE COMES UPON US; WE BEAR ITS DARK BURDEN, UPON OUR BROAD SHOULDERS.

Smaller and smaller, vanishing to a single point. Korlandril's individuality was engulfed by the tide of personalities from the spirit stones. He drowned in darkness, flailing to retain some sense of self against the torrent heaping upon his frail mind.

'Come to stand before Khaine, unyielding in our fate, free from all doubt and fear.'

COME TO STAND BEFORE KHAINE, UNYIELDING IN OUR FATE, FREE FROM ALL DOUBT AND FEAR.

The dead numbered in their tens of thousands. Countless lives extinguished at the hands of those who had worn this armour. Creatures of all races, some warriors, many not. Victims of Khaine's bloody murders.

Korlandril wailed with the last vestiges of his grief, giving his last compassion for those that had been killed, saving none for those to come.

'We do not flee from death; we stride in Khaine's shadow, proudly and with no fear.'

WE DO NOT FLEE FROM DEATH; WE STRIDE IN KHAINE'S SHADOW, PROUDLY AND WITH NO FEAR.

WE STRIKE FROM THE DARKNESS, AS THE SWIFT SCORPION, WITH A MOST DEADLY TOUCH.

SEE NOT WITH EYES ALONE, BUT ALLOW RAGE TO FLOW, LET KHAINE'S GIFT COMFORT YOU.

* * *

KORLANDRIL WAS ALL but gone, a swirl of motes in a far greater consciousness.

MORLANIATH RETURNED. THE exarch opened eyes closed for an age and turned to the great double-handed biting blade upon the wall behind. Taking it up, Morlaniath remembered the weapon's name: *Teeth of Dissonance*. Like two lovers of old meeting, Morlaniath and the immense chainsword became as one, the exarch stroking a hand along the length of the casing. Morlaniath's fingertips danced across the point of every blade. Taking up a ready stance, Morlaniath willed the weapon to life, stirring her from a long sleep. Her purring was as smooth as when she had first been baptised in blood.

Together they would bring death again.

REBIRTH

When the War in Heaven was at its height, the followers of Khaine numbered many. They were dire foes to the Children of Eldanesh and Ulthanesh, for they had given in wholly to their bloodlust. Yet, one-by-one the Champions of Khaine fell. Khaine would not relinquish his servants so easily, and kept their spirits, armouring and arming them to continue the war. Though they were as bloody-handed as their master, these warriors also were defeated and fell. Still Khaine would not release them. Despite Khaine's threats and tortures the Smith-God, Vaul, would forge no more armour and arms for the Bloody-Handed God to rebuild his armies. Khaine would not release his grip on those that had sworn themselves to his cause, and he crushed them together in his iron fist, so that several would fight as one, sharing such weapons as Khaine could spare.

Filled with the wrath of Khaine, the spirit-warriors slew many of Eldanesh and Ulthanesh's children. Yet such was their anger these spirits fell to fighting amongst themselves. Each spirit-part vied for control of the whole and they splintered. Khaine's spirit army fell to ruin as the spirits finally fled his grip.

IT WAS A place of bones and skulls, where blood rained from thunderous skies and the clash of blades and screams of the dying sounded across an unending plain.

He floundered through the bones, slipping and falling with every other step. He cast about for some sense of place or direction, seeing nothing but death. He called out but the wind whipped away his voice as soon as it left his lips. He was lost. Alone. What was his name? Who was he?

He examined the skulls, small and large: eldar, human, threeshan, ork, demiurg, tyranid and many others. Tiny witchlights glowed in their eyes. He picked up a misshapen head, its snout pronounced, the eyes set wide, a ridge of bony nodules across its brow. He stared deep into the eyes, connecting within the remnants of spirit within.

The sky burned with black flames while dazzling yellow beams criss-crossed the ruins of an alien settlement. The Hrekh poured out of their stilt-legged towers, running on bow-legs, guns chattering in their long arms. He sprang easily aside, muddy water splashing up around his legs as he ran through the sluggish river. Vyper jetbikes screamed past, their gunners directing torrents of scatter laser fire into the wood and stone towers, gunning down the Hrekh by the dozen. He leapt up to a walkway above the shallow lake, pulling himself over the rail in one easy motion. The Hidden Death followed, their mandiblasters crackling, shuriken pistols spitting. Pursued by the gleaming jetbikes of the Shining Spears, a Hrekh clan leader hurried around the corner, looking over its shoulder. He pounced, driving the *Teeth of Dissonance* between the creature's swaying paps to erupt from its back. He ripped the biting blade free and kicked the corpse into the water.

The skull dropped from his fingers and the memory disappeared.

How many thousands of deaths were collected here? How would he find one that he recognised?

He picked up another skull, of a human, but in the first flash of recollection he knew it did not belong to him. He threw it to the ground and stamped on it, but the skull only bounced away from beneath his naked foot.

Somewhere there was a memory that was his. He needed to keep looking.

DIM RED LIGHT reflected from the mock-stone walls of the chamber. He looked down and saw sandy footprints on the floor. His footprints. That was confusing. For three generations he had waited in the chamber, waited to be found by the one who answered his call.

Who was he?

We Are Morlaniath.

The thoughts were his, but not his alone. Others stared out of his eyes with him, flexed his fingers around the grip of the long chainsword in his hand, felt the whistle of air into his lungs.

Who was I?

We Were Morlaniath, And Idsresail, And Lecchamem-non, And Ethruin, And Elidhnerial, And Neruidh, And Ultheranish, And Korlandril.

Korlandril.

The name focussed his attention. It was not his only name, but it was his most recent. This body, these limbs and brain and nerves and bone, they had been called Korlandril. With this knowledge, he delved into his memories, seeking the truth of what had happened.

He waited. For a timeless span, there was only spirit. Ultheranish's body had been slain. They had carried the suit here – Kenainath, Aranarha, Liruieth and the other Striking Scorpion exarchs. The sands piled on the doors and the light disappeared. It mattered not. One would come, sooner or later. What was time? A meaningless measure of mortals.

The shrine trembled. Miniscule movement. He awoke. He could feel the anger. The shrine resonated with it. The Avatar had roused. Still none had come. He fell dormant again.

The Avatar was unleashed again, stirring his spirits to awareness. None came. He did not sleep. There was a whisper echoing through the shrine. So far away, so quiet. He listened and learned. One would be coming. He had heard the thoughts of the New One. He shared the New One's anger and rage, felt the pain of his wound. Soon, he realised. Soon he would be coming.

He waited.

The sands shifted. The New One was coming. His thoughts rang like cymbals around the chamber.

Come To Me. I Am Peace. I Am Resolution. I Am The Ending.

The silver chain between them shortened and he pulled harder. The shrine responded, throwing off the detritus of generations. Soon. So soon.

The New One entered. He recognised himself. He touched his armour and the two parts of him became one for a moment.

You are we, and we are you.

'This is mine,' he said, and heard, and replied.

Yours…

The New One spoke and he listened.

'I shall be the Hidden Death.'

Hidden Death…

There was a moment of doubt, of contemplation. He knew what he was seeking. He had always been seeking the same. He was what he was seeking.

Answers…

The New One took up the armour and Morlaniath began the chant. Glorious return was nigh.

He understood now where he had come from. He was not-Korlandril. He was not-Morlaniath. He was both, and others beside. He was all and they were him.

He explored his memories. They were all his, but some he had not seen before. Time passed in a blur of old relationships, battles lost and won, friend-ships long and short, enemies slain and escaped, love and hate, births, romances, disappointments, old hopes and new dreams, and a half-dozen painful deaths. He flitted from one to the next with-out effort, seeking nothing in particular.

He came across one that caused him to stop. A face he knew. He recognised all of the faces, but this was one of the old memories, unknown before to this body. He put a name to the face.

Bechareth.

It did not fit with the other memories. The Bechareth of this body was a Striking Scorpion. The Bechareth of the memory was something else. He searched further back, seeking the genesis of the memory, the start of the story.

He was Ultheranish, the vessel before this current one. They were in the webway, aboard a ship. Through high-arched windows, he watched the glowing rivulets of psychic energy swirling past.

Alarms sounded. Something else was in the webway. He was one of the Hidden Death, just another warrior ready to defend the starship. Not-Neruidh was exarch. He flitted between the two memes-strands, watching himself as exarch and seeing himself through the exarch's eyes. The Hidden Death followed the exarch into the outer corridors, waiting for the attack. Another vessel came alongside, a bladed, sinister reflection of their own warship: the kin of Commorragh. With cutters and forcefields they breached the hull, a swarm of raiders armed with splinter rifles and crackling blades. The Aspect Warriors fought back, the Hidden Death at the fore.

He met sword-to-sword with one of the Lost Kindred, a cruel-eyed wych almost naked save for a few slender straps and curving shoulder armour. His foe was swifter than he, her twin daggers darting and weaving around his chainsword. His armour bore the brunt of her strikes, sparks of energy flying from her blades as they struck. He brought up his pistol to her face and she ducked, to be met by the rising point of his chainsword. Her face split in twain and she fell to the ground, her beautiful features now a gory mess.

Others followed the wyches. They wore armour also, not unlike his, though coloured in black and white. He recognised them immediately. Incubi. A perversion of Khaine's Aspects, debased and immoral. Mercenaries without principle or code.

In a rage he hurled himself at the closest, his chainsword plunging towards the helmeted head. The incubi swayed back, his powered glaive rising to deflect the attack. Spinning, the incubi delivered a kick to his midriff, sending him staggering. His chainsword flashed up to ward away a strike towards his chest, sending the glaive's gleaming head screaming past his right shoulder.

The pair parted and circled, feinting and jabbing with their weapons. The incubi's eye lenses gleamed with a yellow, ghostly light. Sickened with rage, he launched another flurry of attacks, mandiblasters spitting, chainsword weaving left and right. The incubi ducked and swerved aside from each blow, the tip of his glaive carving figures-of-eight in front of him.

A chance salvo from the Striking Scorpion's pistol caught the incubi in the thigh. He followed up with a blistering series of strikes towards the head and throat, each caught at the last moment on the haft of the incubi's weapon. A sudden change of direction and a twist to the left sent the chainsword's teeth into the incubi's lower back, slivers of torn armour spraying to the floor.

A backwards sweep caught the enemy a glancing blow to the side of the head, shearing away part of his armour, splintering the eye lens on the left side of his face to reveal a glimpse of the creature within.

The incubi looked up at him with a horrified eye, hand thrown up defensively in front of him. It was the face not-Korlandril knew as Bechareth.

The Striking Scorpion had no time for the death-blow; more warriors swept from the pirate vessel, engulfing the Hidden Death in a swirling melee.

The memories of Ultheranish and not-Ultheranish shed no more light on what had happened. He delved into the past of not-Neruidh.

'He must be accepted, pupils are not turned away; it is not a choice.' Kenainath stood in the Chamber of Autarchs with not-Neruidh, Aranarha, Liruieth, Kadonil and Elronihir. Beside the Deadly Shadow exarch stood the former incubi, Bechareth, eyes downcast, demure and silent. He wore a plain white robe from the Halls of Healing, several spirit-aligning gems hung about his person to aid his recovery.

'He is the enemy, one of the dark kin. He cannot be one of us!' Kadonil was vehement.

'This is no debate, I have made my final choice, I will not change it.'

'What you say, it is true, he is yours,' said Liruieth, her voice quiet but firm. 'Watch him close, tell no one, work him hard.'

'He will be silent, none but us shall ever know, a Scorpion's secret,' Kenainath assured them.

Kadonil whirled away in disgust. Aranarha stalked off without a word. The remaining exarchs nodded in compliance, and departed.

Though he had always known it, the memory was a shock. Bechareth, who he had befriended, who he had trusted in battle, was not of Alaitoc. He was not even of the craftworlds.

He felt betrayed. Kenainath had kept this secret from them all, swearing Bechareth to silence to protect his own reputation.

Rash.

It Was Decided. The Vote Was A Majority. You Cannot Revisit That Decision.

I Was Always Dubious, But You Would Not Listen To Me.

You Are Dubious About Everything.

Quiet! thought not-Korlandril.

The voices fell silent as Morlaniath strained his senses. Someone was approaching the shrine.

'Hello?' a quavering voice called out.

Greet Him.

Let Him Wait.

Who is it?

Your First Pupil.

One To Be Taught.

So soon?

Always It Is So. A New Exarch Needs Followers. The Shrine Calls To Them.

Stirs Their Blood. Most Are Deaf To My Call.

There Will Be More In The Times To Come.

How do I teach him?

We Have Taught Many Already.

Remember.

The First Of Many. Hidden Death Will Rise Again.

* * *

WITH TREMBLING HANDS Morlaniath took off his helmet. Slowly and precisely, he unfastened the clasps of his armour and took it off piece-by-piece, reverentially placing each part back on its stand.

The other voices subsided, but their presence remained. His head still contained names of those he had never met, faces he had never seen with these eyes, foes slain in bloody combat by hands other than his.

Clad in the undersuit, Morlaniath turned to his left, knowing that the steps through the archway there led directly to the main chamber of the shrine. He could feel the presence of his first acolyte; nervous, frustrated and angry. Just as he had been.

He ascended the stairway swiftly and silently, entered the main chamber behind the aspirant. The newcomer was young – younger than he had been when he had approached Kenainath. He could feel his anxiety, pouring out in waves.

'We are the Hidden Death; you hearken to our call, who is troubled in mind.' Morlaniath barely recognised his own voice and was unsure if he had spoken the words. There was a ritual cadence to them, phrases so oft-spoke in times past that they spoke themselves.

'I dreamt of a river of blood, and I bathed in it,' said the young eldar, his voice querulous, his eyes fixed on Morlaniath as he stepped slowly across the chamber floor.

'Dreams of death and bloodshed, Khaine's hot touch on your mind, a hot thirst for battle. These have brought you to me, Exarch Morlaniath, the keeper of this shrine. I will lead you to truth, take you on that dark path, into your mind's shadows.'

'I am afraid, exarch.' The youth's subservience was both refreshing and yet familiar. As an Aspect Warrior, Morlaniath had quickly grown used to suspicion and dismay from others not on the Warrior Path. Now he was exarch, feared but revered.

He took the other's arm in his grip and pulled him to his feet. He fixed the warrior-to-be with a long stare, gauging his mood. He wondered if he had appeared as pitiful to Kenainath. So full of ignorance, so afraid of himself.

'The Path will be bloody. You walk alongside Khaine, and may not make the end.'

The eldar nodded dumbly, fingers fidgeting at the loose robe he wore.

'The urge is strong in you, to shed blood and bring death; you must strive for control. We will bring your war-mask, unleash your death-spirit, so that it cannot hide. You will control its wrath, it will hold you no more, you will gain your freedom.'

'Why has this happened to me?'

Such a familiar question! He remembered it from his own lips and from dozens like him. All faced the same shadows in their spirits, all had to deal with Khaine's double-edged gift. Why did each one of them believe themselves different? Did they truly think they were free of Khaine's touch, or that there would be a time when Khaine's hold on the eldar would be broken for good?

'You are not so special, to feel these darkest moods, and wish to act on them. You are but a mortal, with a mortal's nature, for the good and the ill. Learn to embrace this gift, love Khaine's dark legacy, and you will master it.'

'I… I am so weak…' the eldar sobbed.

'You are at your weakest, so we will make you strong, strong enough to prevail.'

Morlaniath headed towards the archway leading to the shrine's central corridor, beckoning his aspirant to follow.

'Weak in body and mind, full of doubt and sorrow, but we will remove them. A farewell to your guilt, no remorse or lament, a warrior in truth.'

He led the youth out into the heat of the desert, the warmth on his skin like a homecoming. Here he had first learnt the ways of the Striking Scorpion from Nelemin, who had been taught by Karandras the Phoenix Lord. For life-after-life he had come to this place, first to learn, and then to teach, reinventing himself with each episode, an unending link to the founding of the Striking Scorpions.

'I am Milathradil.'

Morlaniath regarded the youth without expression.

'You are Milathradil, of the Hidden Death Shrine, a Striking Scorpion.'

THE NIGHT-CYCLE OF the desert dome was dry and frigid. Morlaniath stood at the gate of the shrine and looked out over the sands, feeling at home. The dome's fields dampened the dying star, leaving only the faintest glimmer of scarlet to light the dunes, ever-shifting in the artificial winds. Constant but changing, like Morlaniath. Every cycle-start, at the Time of Wakening, he looked over his domain. For an age this had been his place. It was still his place, through this new body.

The shrine alerted him to the presence of Kenainath and Aranarha. He felt them crossing the threshold from the sub-strata tunnels. He turned and made his way to his chambers, walking along feet-worn corridors and down ancient steps without thought.

The two exarchs waited for him in his private arming room, clad in loose robes, their spirit stones lighting the gloom.

'A welcome return, from the void of somnolence, with new life inside,' said Kenainath, giving a polite bow.

Morlaniath smiled.

'It is good to return, you trained this body well; I am fully restored.'

'Yet the spirit was weaker, it is trapped with us, doomed to tread this path with us,' said Aranarha.

'Another always comes, be it soon or later, the nature of Khaine's gift.'

Morlaniath felt his newest disciple stirring in the chambers above. Out across Alaitoc, others were responding to his presence, troubled by their thoughts, fearing their own anger. They did not yet know it, but they would come to him soon.

'Do you feel his anguish, sense his dark destiny, the burning in his blood?'

The others nodded.

'He will make a fine pupil, so full of anger, his resentment is his key,' said Aranarha. 'He will train ferociously, you must watch him close, temper him with much patience.'

Morlaniath nodded in agreement. The three exarchs exchanged gestures of parting and then Morlaniath was alone.

He felt nervous inquiry resonating through the shrine. Milathradil was awake and seeking him. It would not be well for him to wander the shrine without a guide. Invigorated by his fresh life, Morlaniath headed up the stairs to find his new pupil.

THE STUDENTS WERE willing and growing in number. Over the last sixty cycles, Milathradil had been joined by Euraithin, Lokhirith and Nurianda and the four of them were attentive to Morlaniath's instruction as he taught them the rituals of combat. Much of the teaching was in the style of the Hidden Death, but in places the stances and strikes were subtly evolved, incorporating Deadly Shadow techniques from not-Korlandril's experiences.

The Hidden Death desert was the opposite of the dank swamps of the Deadly Shadow, but Morlaniath's previous lives had been spent in this arid dome and he adapted to the environment without hesitation. He learned afresh what he already knew, the instinct of the residual spirits dwelling within him guiding him effortlessly across the dunes, leading him to the training areas and the tests to put before his acolytes. He knew the haunts of the sand-serpents that burrowed beneath the dunes; the piping calls of the windhoppers; the trails of the scurrying worm-hunters and the coiling casts left by their prey.

Without his armour, he walked across the drifts, comforted by his sense of place and the residual presence of his other selves. They were always there, though speechless, guiding him indirectly, steering him this way or that.

The former exarchs were stronger when Morlaniath wore his armour. Nagging doubts and unconscious knowledge were given voice by their spirit stones. Their counsel was sometimes at odds with Morlaniath's own inclinations, and even with each other, though all professed a common goal.

At night Morlaniath did not sleep, but instead retreated to his private chamber and donned his armour, to rest his body and commune with his other selves. It was one such night-cycle that Morlaniath pulled on his armoured suit, his thoughts on the progress of his nascent squad.

You Are Too Lenient With Your Pupils. They Are Not Focussed. They Chatter Aimlessly When You Do Not Attend Them.

Nonsense! It Is To Attain Balance That We Strive, Not To Create More Exarchs. Their Division of War And Peace Is Proceeding Well.

An exhausted mind makes mistakes. I show them the rewards of control, the freedom they will earn for themselves when they have separated their warrior spirits, when they have grown their war-masks.

I Sense Kenainath's Hand In This. He Has Too Much Influence Over You.

I Too Learned At The Deadly Shadow. Kenainath's Teachings Grant Perspective And Offer Challenge.

I will teach as I see fit.

Foolish, To Dismiss Our Experience So Quickly.

I share your experience, it is mine also. The Hidden Death is being reborn, but it will take some time. I will show patience, as Aranarha suggested.

Another Upstart!

You Are Jealous Of Him. He Is Popular With His War-riors. Your Aloofness Was Always Your Weakness.

Some Will Die. It Does Not Benefit Master or Pupil To Grow Too Attached To Individuals. Warriors Come And Warriors Go. The Hidden Death Is Eternal.

And it shall remain so under my leadership. I am now the Hidden Death.

We Shall See.

FOR ALL HIS patience, Morlaniath was eager for his squad to complete the first stages of their training. Heedful that rushing matters could risk everything, he waited until all four of his students were ready to take the next step. He introduced them to their armour, allowing each to pick their suit. He felt a perverse delight when Milathradil picked the suit once worn by not-Ultheranish when he had been a simple Striking Scorpion. It stirred something in his memories, a nugget of information he had not examined before, when he had chosen his first suit of armour, which now concurred with an older fragment of knowledge.

His first instinct was to stand beside Elissanadrin, seeking the familiar, but he dismissed the urge. It was change and renewal that he needed, not the comfortable. Out of the corner of his eye, Korlandril thought he saw a momentary glitter in the eyes of one suit. He turned towards it. There was nothing to distinguish it from the others, but something about it tugged at Korlandril.

'This one,' he said, striding towards the armour. He stood beside it and turned to face the exarch.

'That is a wise choice, a noble suit you have picked, which has served us well,' said Kenainath. 'You are now ready, in body if not in mind, to don your armour.'

'Which has served us well?'

Kenainath was referring to himself, the exarch, not the shrine as an entity. He had once worn the armour that Korlandril had picked. The thought gave Morlaniath pause, to wonder if perhaps he had been destined to become himself at the moment he had first stepped into the Deadly Shadow.

He led the others in their armouring, teaching them the Hidden Death mantra, which had been passed to him by his fore-spirits when he had donned his exarch armour.

It was intriguing to watch the reactions of his pupils, and to see himself again as that novice wearing armour for the first time, more than half a dozen times over. He felt again the surge of power, of strength, that had flowed through him, the first glimmerings of his war-mask shining through.

Milathradil was the most eager. Morlaniath could feel his war-mask just beneath the surface. It resonated with the exarch, feeding him and drawing on him at the same time. Morlaniath would have to watch Milathradil closely; his passion could be his undoing.

Nurianda and Euraithin were more hesitant, sharing excitement and fear in equal measure, as it should be. Lokhirith was afraid. He was fearful of his own power, afraid to embrace his war-mask, holding back on the tide of emotions that needed to be given freedom before they could be controlled. Morlaniath decided he would pair Lokhirith with Milathradil for a while; they were in an odd balance together and would bring each other closer to internal harmony.

When the warriors were full-clad, Morlaniath began the rituals again. He moved without thought, called out the names of the poses. With that part of his mind not occupied by the training, he wondered which of his followers had shadow-foes and which did not. They moved with poise and precision, but it was not their technique that Morlaniath examined as he called out Rising Sting from Darkness. He was connected; connected to the shrine and through it to the Striking Scorpions, those in front of him now and all of those that had come before.

He read the micro-expressions in their faces and sensed their emotions. Euraithin was too focussed on his body, tightly controlling every motion. He needed to allow his instinct to prevail so that his attention to his environment was not lacking. Nurianda, she was a study of balance, at once a whirling maelstrom and a tranquil lake. Milathradil was distracted, too intent upon the creation of his shadow-foe. Morlaniath could read the fierce visualisation in his gestures, in the determination of his thoughts and the slightly curtailed, clipped nature of his technique. Lokhirith was still uncertain, second-guessing his body, his eyes straying to Morlaniath or his companions, seeing too much of the real world to lose himself entirely in the battle.

Progress had been made, but there was still a long way to go.

Morlaniath communed, resting his body in his armour while his spirits digested the events of the cycle. There came a sudden interruption to their deliberations.

One Is Coming.

Morlaniath sensed a presence at the borders of his domain, at the main portal to his desert dome. It was not an aspirant, though he felt a great deal of tension from his visitor. It was not an exarch: he would recognise his kin instantly. There was something familiar in the presence; a similarity to someone locked away within his memories, but dissimilar enough that he could not locate it. The person approached and then went away, and then approached again. There was hesitancy, a mixture of fear and doubt.

He opened his eyes, feeling change afoot.

Still armoured, Morlaniath took a skyrunner from the shrine's depths and sped across the desert leaving a plume of sand in his wake. He flew directly to the main portal, the nagging sense of recognition tantalising in its closeness but still eluding him. Dismounting, he opened the wide gateway with a thought command.

A farseer turned quickly, taken aback by his arrival. She was dressed in a long robe of pure black, embroidered sigils of silver and white decorating the hem and cuffs of her gown. She fidgeted with a pouch at her waist, while her eyes widened with a mixture of surprise and disgust.

He recognised those eyes. It was Thirianna.

Oh, It's Her. Troublemaker, That One.

'It that you, Korlandril?' she asked.

'I am not Korlandril, though he is part of me, I am Morlaniath.'

You Should Say 'We'. It Is Very Rude To Ignore The Rest Of Us.

We Are One. 'I' Is Correct.

Ignore Them Both. This Argument Never Ends.

Thirianna took a step away, shoulders hunching.

What Does She Want?

She Doesn't Belong Here. Send Her Away!

Look How Scared She Is Of Us.

'Why do you disturb us, coming here unbidden, breaking the gold stillness?'

She took a few steps further back, shaking her head.

'This was a mistake. I should not have come. You cannot help me.'

Good Riddance.

She Has Already Roused Us. We Have Nothing To Lose By Letting Her Speak.

We Have Wasted Enough Time. Let Her Go.

She might return and disturb us again.

'Now that you have come here, seeking guidance and truth, speak your mind with freedom. If I can assist you, if you have hard questions, perhaps I can answer.'

Thirianna approached and stared past Morlaniath, taking in the wide vista of the desert. Her gaze turned to the exarch.

'Is there somewhere else we can speak?'

Always the Same. Farseers Want To Know Everything. Do Not Let Her In. She Is Not Welcome.

The Shrine Is Soaked In The Memories Of Blood. She Cannot Go There.

'The shrine would not be fit, farseers enter with risk, and I am loathe to leave.'

'Can we perhaps walk awhile? I do not feel comfortable discussing matters on your doorstep.'

Morlaniath turned away, assuming she would follow. The sands shifted under his booted feet but he walked with purpose and balance, heading towards a shallow oasis gently fed by irrigation webs beneath the sands. Clusters of red-leaved bushes hid the water's edge, bright white stars of blossom poking from the foliage.

The water was still. Sometimes he came here to contemplate without his companions. This was the first time he had come here in the full presence of the others. Memory came without asking, swamping him for a moment with recollections of this place as each spirit clasped to some distant event, seeking to relive them. He pushed them away and gestured for Thirianna to seat herself beside the still pool.

'This is… pleasant.' She looked at her surrounds and sat down, gathering her robes to one side, her black hair tossed over her shoulder, head tilted away from Morlaniath.

'It is the birth in death, the hope in hopelessness, life amongst the barren.' She did not look at him when he spoke. She gazed thoughtfully into the waters. Insects skimmed the surface, sustained by its tension.

'I have foreseen troubling times for Alaitoc, perhaps something worse.'

A Farseer Foresees Trouble? That Is The Nature Of Things.

Listen To What She Has To Say.

This Is A Waste Of Our Time. We Should Wake The Warriors And Begin Their Training In The Dark Stalking.

'You are now a farseer. Such things will be your life, why do you come to me?'

'I am told that I am in error. The farseers, the council of Alaitoc, do not think my scrying will come to pass. They say I am inexperienced, seeing dangers that do not exist.'

They Are Right.

Pompous And Conceited, All Of Them. She Thinks She Sees Something They Cannot. They Cannot Conceive Of Being Blind To Anything.

Not all of them.

Yes, All Of Them.

'Likely they are correct, your powers are still weak, this path is new to you. I do not see my role; I am the exarch here, not one of the council.'

'You don't believe me?'

'You offer me no proof, and there is none to give, belief alone is dust.'

Thirianna stood and walked to the pool's edge. She dipped her booted toe into the waters, sending a ripple across the surface. The ripple disturbed Morlaniath. This was a place of calm and Thirianna had brought disquiet. He said nothing and watched as she allowed the droplets to fall from her boot, moving her foot so that they dribbled a swirl in the sand.

'I followed the fate of Aradryan.' Morlaniath spent a moment recalling the name. One who had been friend to Korlandril, unknown to not-Korlandril. He had started Korlandril on his path to this place. Thirianna continued without pause. 'Our three destinies are interwoven. More than we have seen already. Yours is not ended, but will soon; his is distant and confused. Mine... Mine is to be here, to tell you these things to set in motion future events.'

Fanciful And Untrue. All Destinies Are Interwoven.

'What is it you have seen, what visions bring such woe, what do they mean for us?'

'Aradryan dwells in darkness, but there is also light for him. But his darkness is not confined to him. It spreads into our lives, and it engulfs Alaitoc. I do not know the details; my rune-casting is very crude at the moment. I feel he has done something gravely wrong and endangered all of us.'

'Your warnings are too vague, they contain no substance, we have no course of action.'

Thirianna snorted, a sound of bitter resentment and dark humour.

'That is what the council says. 'How can we prepare against something so amorphous?' they asked. I told them that more experienced seers should follow the thread of Aradryan. They refused, claiming it was an irrelevance. Aradryan is gone from Alaitoc, they told me, and he is no longer their concern.'

Who Are We To Argue?

This Is Not Our Concern. We Are Warriors, Not Philosophers.

Morlaniath listened to this, perplexed. The council were correct. They could no more act on such a vision as they could an unfounded rumour. Other memories came to mind, rebuilding his picture of Thirianna. She was always seeking attention, always looking to be the centre of things. It was no surprise that she had not yet removed this flaw from her character, and now sought to garner an audience by claiming some personal insight into Alaitoc's doom.

'Continue your studies, delve further into this, to seek your own answers.'

'I fear there is no time. This is imminent. I lack the strength and the training to see far ahead.'

If She Is So Weak, How Have Others Not Seen This Disaster?

That Is A Good Point. Her Story Is Incomplete. Send Her Away!

'Others have not seen it, your fresh cataclysm, who are stronger than you. I must concur with them, who have trodden the Path, who see further than you.'

'It is such a small thing, whatever it is that Aradryan does.' She stooped and took a pinch of sand, rubbing her fingers to spill it to the ground until she held a single grain. She flicked it into the waters of the pool. 'Such a tiny ripple, we can barely see it, but a ripple nonetheless. The anarchy of history tells us that momentous events can start from the most humble, the most mundane of beginnings.'

'I have no aid for you, no council influence, and I agree with them. Go back to your studies, forget this distraction, I will not assist you.'

She looked at him for the first time, eyes misted, lips trembling.

'I feared the worst, and you have proven me true. Korlandril is not dead, but he has gone.'

'Which you once predicted, that both of us would change, for better or for worse. I am Morlaniath, you are Thirianna, Korlandril is no more. Seek contentment from this, do not chase the shadows, only darkness awaits.'

'Do you not remember what we once shared?'

'I remember it well, we shared nothing at all, I have nothing for you.'

Thirianna straightened and wiped a gloved finger across her cheek, a tear soaking into the soft fabric.

'You are right. I will leave and think of you no more.'

She bunched up her robe and strode up the encircling dune, heading towards the main portal. Morlaniath followed a short way behind and stopped on the dune's crest to watch her retreating back. She reached the gateway and Morlaniath willed it open. Then she was gone and with a thought he closed the gate behind her.

THE TEETH OF *Dissonance* thrummed in Morlaniath's hands, carving the air with beautiful sweeps. All in the shrine was quiet save for the sound of the blade and the tread of the exarch's booted feet on the stone. His followers were all asleep, exhausted by the day's training. Only their dreams broke the stillness, edged with blood, tinged with death. Morlaniath smiled.

He finished his practice and returned the blade to its rightful place. Taking up the stance of repose, he thought about Thirianna's visit.

Were we too dismissive?

You Gave Her Full Chance To Speak Her Case. We Are Unconvinced.

We Have Other Concerns. It Is Not Our Place To Debate With Farseers. Let The Autarchs Do That.

She came to us as a friend.

We Are Exarch. We Have No Friends. She Came To Us In Desperation When All Others Had Turned Her Away. It Is Shameful.

Then I ask not for her sake, but for Alaitoc. If what she says is true, it bodes ill for us.

What She Says Is Fantasy. Do Not Give It Further Consideration.

If There Is To Be War, We Will Fight. We Train Our Warriors For Battle. There Is No More That We Can Do. That Is What It Is To Be Exarch.

There It Is Again: 'I'. This Individuality Is Unbecoming.

I am still myself, Morlaniath and not-Korlandril both. I will make my own decision.

To Be Exarch Is To Know Sacrifice. Not For Us The Twilight Of The Infinity Circuit. Darkness Is Our Domain. If It Comes To Pass That This Body Dies, We Will Endure. That Is The Reward For Our Sacrifice.

Do Not Meddle In The Affairs Of Others. It Is Not Welcome And It Is Not Our Duty.

We Do Not Understand Her Motives. If What She Says Proves True, We Will Be Informed. If It Is Untrue Our Interference Risks Bringing Disharmony.

I am unsettled by this. If my fate and Aradryan's is still entwined in ways not yet revealed, it would be wise to heed her warning.

Farseers Always Speak Of Fate. It Is Their Reason For Everything. Sometimes Things Happen Without Purpose. All Warriors Know This. We Train, Perfecting Our Art, But It Is In The Nature Of War That The Random And The Uncontrollable Appear.

It was Thirianna and Aradryan that set me on this course, to our rebirth, to the return of the Hidden Death. I conceive that it is possible my future and theirs are not wholly separate.

Then What Will Happen, Will Happen. Let The Farseers Chase The Possibilities, We Will Deal With The Consequences.

Now it is you that is willing to surrender to fate.

This Debate Is Inappropriate. She Is A Distraction. Ignore Her.

I Concur. Concentrate On The Training Of Your Warriors.

Morlaniath stripped off his armour, unable to shake the disquiet, annoyed by the conflict of thoughts raised by Thirianna. While the direct thoughts of Morlaniath faded into memory, their effect lingered on, confusing him. The question of faith vexed him the most. He had seen her conviction, but had ignored it. Whatever the reality, *she* certainly believed something terrible was going to happen.

It irked him that he was powerless, or so it seemed. He was entirely in the hands of the farseers, and they had chosen to ignore her.

He focussed on this train of thought. His distaste was not with the actions of Thirianna but with the inaction of the council. Part of him was too willing to simply accept their judgement. It was against his nature to submit, to blindly concur, now more than ever. The vestiges of not-Korlandril struggled against Morlaniath, urging him to do something.

STILL IN A state of conflict, Morlaniath gathered his squad at the start of the next cycle and led them in the combat rituals. It diverted his attention away from the dilemma posed by Thirianna.

Nurianda was proving to be the most capable of his students. Her technique was impeccable and she had found her war-mask without trauma. She had mastered the chainsword and the pistol without drama, and was at one with her suit. The others still struggled. They seemed reticent to lose themselves fully, still clinging to fragments of their past lives, gripping tight to the last vestiges of their former selves. While they resisted their own temptations they would never be able to progress.

Morlaniath tried to remember what it was like when he had been Korlandril. It was unpleasant, full of conflict and fear. The memories of the other Morlaniaths intruded upon his recollections, blurring the line between what had been his life and theirs. He had welcomed becoming the Hidden Death, yet the vestiges of his former life clung to his mind; or perhaps he clung to them. It occurred to him that perhaps he had been right to dismiss Thirianna. She was a tie to the past that no longer held any relevance for him.

He dismissed the squad and was about to leave when he noticed Nurianda lingering next to her armour.

'There is something amiss, you are free to leave here, yet here you still remain,' he said, approaching the Striking Scorpion.

'I find it difficult,' she admitted, eyes downcast. 'I tried to speak to my father, but he does not understand.'

'He cannot understand. Each of us has a Path, which only we can walk. I am merely a guide, the journey is all yours, you must walk it alone.'

'What if... What if the journey does not have an end?'

'It ends eventually, at one place or other, though I do not know which. Do not dwell on the end, but move along the Path, striving for your own goal. Know what you leave behind, the suffering and fear, seeking a place of peace. The love for your father, his affection for you, should act as your anchor. While you drift it remains, as it was at the start, so too at the ending.'

Nurianda smiled, wistful and thoughtful.

'Thank you. I will be patient with him.'

Morlaniath waved her to leave and stood for a while longer, gazing at the empty suits of armour. Each had belonged to many warriors. He could remember all of them – the ones that had lived, the ones that had died; the ones that had moved on, and those who had become him. He was all of them and none of them. What was he? Nothing more than dis-membered spirits sharing a corporeal prison, unable to welcome the peace of the Infinity Circuit, unable to die because She Who Thirsts would claim him. He was nothing if he was not his experiences, his mem-ories. He was the walking dead, stuck in the limbo of this body.

He could sense himself losing touch. This fresh body, it had stirred old feelings and old thoughts: memories of freedom and love; moments of plea-sure and pain; moments of mortal senses and mortal thoughts. Its touch remained for the moment, but Morlaniath knew from several experiences that it would not last. Not-Korlandril invigorated him for the time being, but soon that spark would gutter and he would be Morlaniath wholly, the immortal ser-vant of Khaine.

Let go of the past? That was foolish. Though many were the ways he had become Morlaniath, each was unique to him, each was a journey he had made. The Path had ended for him, but that did not eliminate the route he taken to reach this point. That route had meaning, and the people who had walked beside him for a while also had meaning. He had no future, save an eternity of violence and death, but they did.

He did not like unfinished business. The past was not irrelevant, but he had to leave it behind. Morlaniath made a decision and headed for the skyrunners.

'Perhaps you seek war, for that is your nature,' said Arhathain.

'I cannot make a war, if that is my desire, it is the council's choice,' replied Morlaniath.

He knew the autarch well; had fought beside him on many a battlefield. Like all autarchs he was strong-willed, determined enough to tread the Path of the Warrior several times without being ensnared by Khaine's curse. He remembered Arhathain as a young Dire Avenger, and a Howling Banshee in more recent memory. As an exarch he was far older than Arhathain, but not-Korlandril had been less than half his age. A dichotomy of feelings warred within Morlaniath, causing him to feel ancient and infant at the same time, unsure of his place and his time.

He had called Arhathain to the Chamber of Autarchs and spoken of Thirianna's predictions. Arhathain defended the council's decision, as was to be expected. Morlaniath tried to find the words that conveyed his thoughts, but it was difficult; he wanted to seize the autarch and force him to agree.

Keeping his temper in check, he listened to what Arhathain had to say.

'Every day our seers uncover a thousand dooms to Alaitoc. We cannot act on every vision; we cannot go to war on every doubt. Thirianna herself cannot provide us with clarity. We might just as well act on a superstitious trickle of foreboding down the back of the neck.'

'She lacks the proper skill, the means to give you proof, hold that not against her. Give her the help she needs, to prove her right or wrong, she will keep her silence. This doubt will hold her back, it will consume her thoughts, until you release her. You have walked many paths, seen a great many things, lived a great many lives. That life you owe to me, I remember it now, so many cycles past. I was your guardian, the protection you sought, a true companion. I remember the debt, the oath you swore to me, it is now time to pay.'

Arhathain frowned and turned away, pacing to the far side of the rostrum at the centre of the hall.

'The one I made that promise to died ten passes and more ago,' he said softly, looking up at the circular opening at the top of the dome. A distant swathe of stars was strewn across the blackness of space. 'I did not swear that oath to you. It is not Elidhnerial that asks me to repay that debt, it is Korlandril.'

'I am Morlaniath, Elidhnerial too, and also Korlandril. The debt is owed to me, to all the parts of me, united in spirit. Who save me remembers, can repeat the words used, heard them spoken by you?'

'If I do not do this?'

'Your honour is forfeit, and others shall know it, I will make sure of that.'

The autarch turned and directed an intent stare at Morlaniath.

'You will not call on me again in this way?'

'Your debt will be repaid, to Elidhnerial, and we shall speak no more.'

Arhathain nodded reluctantly and stalked up the shallow steps of the chamber.

Morlaniath smiled at his departing back; the part that was not-Korlandril was pleased. He did not know what would become of his intervention, what the future would hold for him or Thirianna. Yet he was content. As a last act before he wholly became Morlaniath, it was worthwhile. Soon she would be unimportant, just another one of the memories, no greater and no less than the thousands of others he had met and loved and hated and been indifferent to. This was his parting gift. Even now the memory was becoming lost in the haze.

By the time he returned to the shrine, he would no longer care.

TRANSFORMATION

When the Great Enemy was born, the Bloody-Handed God brought war against She Who Thirsts but was quickly vanquished by the newborn horror. The Prince of Pleasure and the Lord of Skulls fought over possession of Khaine's spirit, for the Bloody-Handed God was a child of both but belonged to neither. Great was the struggle in the remnants of heaven, but neither She Who Thirsts nor the Master of Battle prevailed. When both the rivals were exhausted, they drew up their boundaries and in the calm eye of their wrath Khaine fell into the world of mortals. Here the Bloody-Handed One shattered into many fragments, unable to exist as a whole in the material realm. His power spent, his body divided, Khaine's wrath was finally diminished. Though suppressed, his rage lingers on in these fragments, drawn to war and strife, awaiting the time when blood *awakens him and his vengeful essence gains form once more.*

THE SHRINE THROBBED once, a frisson of rage that peaked in less than a heartbeat and was gone; a spasm of energy that distracted Morlaniath for a moment, causing him to almost miss his next instruction. He put the tremor to the back of his mind and completed the training period with his pupils, dismissing them abruptly when they were done.

He was uncertain of the cause for the momentary flux of psychic energy that had disturbed him, though he had strong suspicions. He took a skyrunner from the shrine and flew through the bowels of Alaitoc, following an instinct.

The tunnels he navigated were lit by the solitary beam of his skyrunner, a circle of light in the blackness. In the darkness around him, strands of wraithbone glittered occasionally with psychic force as the spirits of the infinity circuit pulsed to and fro. This was the life of Alaitoc – the heart and arteries, skeleton and nervous system, thoughts and feelings of the craftworld. The disturbance that Morlaniath had felt did not come again as he rode, though he sensed a residual after-shock of its occurrence, a tension that filled the air.

At the hub of Alaitoc, where the many psychic veins and nerveways of the craftworld converged, Morlaniath exited the service passage and brought his skyrunner to a halt inside a darkened chamber. The infinity circuit glowed with a ruddy light, the red of a womb. A gate was open before him, its two huge doors opened wide to reveal a wraithbone-wrapped chamber. At the centre of that room was a great throne of iron. Upon that throne sat a statuesque figure, twice Morlaniath's height, its skin fused metal, its eyes black, empty sockets. The immense figure brooded, sucking the light from the throne room, iron fingers in fists, face contorted in a silent roar.

He felt the approach of someone behind him and turned.

'You felt it also, a heartbeat of Khaine, the Avatar stirs?' asked Iriethien, Dire Avenger, exarch of the Light That Burns.

'I felt something stirring, the Avatar still sleeps, the time has not yet come,' Morlaniath said.

'War is approaching, Khaine knows of these things, he senses battle,' said Iriethien. He gazed at the immobile giant, seeking any sign of life.

'We will know soon enough, there will be no doubting, when the war god calls us.'

The presence of Iriethien had confirmed Morlaniath's suspicions. As he returned to his skyrunner, a single thought troubled him: his warriors were not yet ready for battle.

THE TREMULOUS SENSATION from the Avatar of Khaine did not repeat itself, but Morlaniath knew that it had not been an aberration. Once it began to waken, the Avatar did not fall into slumber again without blood being shed. The other exarchs felt it also, and sent warning to the council of Alaitoc that events were unfolding that would take the craftworld to war.

Filled with a new urgency, Morlaniath pressed on as quickly as he could with the training of the

Hidden Death Striking Scorpions. All of them had now progressed to mastering the helmet and mandiblasters but progress seemed slow to the exarch. He had to be certain that they were ready for battle and was still unconvinced. If their training was insufficient it might mean disaster, not only for themselves but for the other warriors that would be relying upon them.

Morlaniath did not fret, did not waste time worrying about this state of affairs. The matter was a simple one: when war came they would either be ready or they would not. If they were not suitably prepared, they would not fight.

THE VOICES WERE no more. The nights brought silence and solitude, a time for contemplation. Morlaniath found peace in the memories of battle, reliving the glories of his past, sometimes even dwelling upon the moments of his deaths, learning from them, seeking ever to improve himself.

He found his memedreams lingering more frequently on his bloody encounters with humans. Was it because his last battle had been against the followers of the Corpse-Emperor? Was there some deeper force at play that led him to relive these wars?

His pondering was interrupted, seven night-cycles after he had felt the tremor of the Avatar. Through the strands of the infinity circuit he was aware of a new arrival coming to Alaitoc, a presence that resonated through all of his lives, all of his spirits. There was a counter-echo in the midst of his consciousness, a responding tremble of awareness from the other shrines, and again the great pulse of

Khaine's heartbeat thudded briefly across the infinity circuit.

THE DOCKING BAY glimmered with light from the webway portal, swirling purple and blue dappling the curved walls and the armour of seventeen exarchs. They waited in silence, each called from his or her shrine; Swooping Hawk, Dark Reaper and Striking Scorpion. Morlaniath felt the same as the others, a primal instinct to gather, to greet their arrival.

They had been brought to the Star-Wreathed Stair, the docks where warships came and went, keeping their taint of blood from ships of peaceful purpose. This was the place where the Aspect Warriors boarded their vessels. It was where their remains were brought back. From here Alaitoc had launched its warriors into the Night for an age, sending them to slay or be slain. This was a place of destiny, from whence the fate of Alaitoc had been steered: expeditionary forces to uncover rising threats; fleets bent on vengeance for eldar deaths; armies that had destroyed worlds; missions to kill the ignorant and the innocent; warriors sent to slaughter inferior races, whose only crime had been their existence.

Death stained the twining branches of wraithbone around the dock, the infinity circuit singing a mournful dirge at the back of Morlaniath's mind. It nourished him and he drew a deep breath of satisfaction.

The bow-wave of psychic energy from the webway grew stronger, the arrival of a ship imminent. It carried with it a sensation of belonging, of acceptance and stability. These thoughts were touched with blood, images of destruction played out in bursts of mental activity. It was similar to the sensation he felt from other exarchs, though greater in its intensity, increasing in its power the closer the ship came.

As when Thirianna had come to the shrine, Morlaniath knew who it was that came to Alaitoc, but could not recognise him. The whole had changed but parts remained familiar, much in the same way as an exarch's spirit slowly evolved into a new personality with each warrior that took up the armour.

Ageless immortality was the backdrop to each of the sensations, older even than Morlaniath, a spirit so deep that it swallowed everything that touched it.

The webway portal pulsed, readying for the ship's exit. A surge of psychic energy swept through the assembled exarchs, bringing flashes of insight, visions of distant worlds and ancient places.

The ship broke through the portal at incredible speed: one moment the bay was empty, the next the sleek black hull filled the void. Its surface rippled with faint colour, waves of dark purple and blue shimmering from shark-like nose to slender tail fins. It lowered silently to hover just above the deck, merging with its own shadow.

A circular portal opened, creating a disc of faint white light. Morlaniath strained forward, pulse racing.

Three figures appeared at the portal as the tongue of a ramp extruded itself to the floor. They wore armour, their suits versions of the exarch armour of those that waited but far heavier and more elaborate, and even more ancient: Swooping Hawk, Dark Reaper, Striking Scorpion. Their weapons were ornate artefacts of the time before the Fall when eldar power had been at its height; beautiful instruments of destruction salvaged from the ruins of an entire civilisation.

The first wore wings that shimmered in a thousand colours, a curved blade in one hand, a multi-barrelled las-blaster in the other, helm adorned with a single feathered crest, his armour a mottle of summer blue and winter grey. The next had armour of black, sculpted with golden bones, his helm a red-eyed skull, the image of Death itself, a scythed shuriken cannon in his grip. Last came the Scorpion, and upon him Morlaniath fixed his gaze, the flow of connection between them strengthening as the new arrival approached. His yellow and green armour was banded with obsidian ribbing, his helm curved back in a series of plates like a scorpion's tail, crackling mandiblasters pods to either side. One hand was an elegant claw wreathed with energy, the other gripped the hilt of a biting blade, its teeth so sharp that rainbows of cut light danced around them.

They were the first exarchs, those who had walked the Path of the Warrior in the wake of the Fall and studied under the guidance of Asurmen. Morlaniath knew them immediately, remembered them from previous encounters while legends of their deeds surfaced in his mind.

Three founders of the Aspect shrines: The Cry of the Wind, Baharroth; The Harvester of Souls, Maugan Ra; The Shadow Hunter, Karandras.

Three Phoenix Lords, almost without precedent, had come to Alaitoc for a single purpose: war.

* * *

THE ARRIVAL OF the Phoenix Lords was both a reaction and a catalyst. They had sensed a new doom approaching Alaitoc and had been drawn to the coming conflict. Their presence reacted with the somnolent essence of Khaine's Avatar, speeding its wakening. Morlaniath's memories were clouded with blood, his training sessions with his warriors interrupted by waves of bloodthirsty sensation. The other exarchs felt it too, and the Aspect shrines and infinity circuit gently thrummed with the nascent rage of Kaela Mensha Khaine.

Faced with these events, the council of Alaitoc summoned its greatest seers to divine which potential cataclysm was most likely to engulf the craftworld. They studied the runes of Thirianna, ready to listen to her half-formed tale of approaching death. Eyes more ancient than hers scanned the skeins of possibility, following the threads of Aradryan's life and the interwoven fates of Alaitoc.

All agreed: a great darkness was descending upon the craftworld. The rune of the humans blackened when touched and the farseers felt the irrational hatred of mankind directed at Alaitoc.

The autarchs called the exarchs to assembly in their circular hall, Alaitoc's deadliest warriors all gathered in one place. The air seethed with their fierce pride and lust for battle. Morlaniath was drenched in their growing anger and strengthening hatred, soaking it into his spirit, elevating his own anticipation to a peak.

Arhathain, accompanied by Alaitoc's three other autarchs, addressed the restless throng of shrine leaders.

'It is the humans,' he said solemnly. 'The followers of the Emperor will come to Alaitoc intent on conflict. Why they choose to do so is unclear, but some slight against them has stirred their wrath. As a single pebble may start a landside, so the act of one has led the humans to Alaitoc. Though the farseers have travelled the strands of destiny, there is but one consequence that cannot be averted: Alaitoc will be attacked.

'It is not our place to speculate on the shortsighted decisions of humans. It is our task to prepare for war and deal with the consequences. Rangers have returned to Alaitoc, bearing grave news. Imperial ships forge their way through the Sea of Dreams, heading in our direction. There is insufficient time to elude them; they are too close and Alaitoc is not yet at full energy peak. Our starships will intercept them, deter them from coming, but humans are ill-counselled and stubborn. It is likely they will attempt to breach Alaitoc and bring battle to our homes. Though they think that they come with surprise as their weapon, we have not been taken unawares.'

The autarch had calmly relayed this information, but now his voice rose, stoked by feeling.

'We will not allow this absurd action to go unpunished! The temerity of the humans staggers belief, even if their ignorance is well-recorded. It is not just Alaitoc that we must fight to protect, but all of our people. If the humans think that they can attack craftworlds with impunity, it will signal the end of our species. They must learn the folly of their action, through the bloodiest lesson we can give them. They are cowards, and superstitious. We will write new legends for them; myths of how the eldar slaughtered them for their stupidity; stories written in their entrails and blood.'

Arhathain walked slowly around the circumference of the podium, bright blue eyes passing over the circles of exarchs. His lips formed a snarl.

'We abhor you! We who are free are fearful of you, the living reminders of the consequences of weakness and indulgence. Rightfully you are shunned, for your spirits are cursed by Khaine. You are warmongers and murderers. Those of us who have passed along the Path of the Warrior stand absolved of the atrocities we have committed and have found peace. You are trapped, relishing your bloody deeds, glorying in your hatred and rage.

'But we who are free also need you. Without the exarchs, we would all be lost. You carry the burdens of our guilt. You stand between our fragile spirits and the degradations of war.'

His voice became a harsh whisper as he continued to circle, tense, shoulders hunched, fists tight.

'This is your time! The humans seek to violate our beautiful homes. They *dare* to bring war against us! You are our bloody messengers. You are Kaela Mensha Khaine's anointed slayers, our vengeance incarnate, our anger given form. You are merciless, and rightly so. Our survival allows no compassion; our continuing existence depends upon the unthinking doing the unthinkable.

'Feel now the pulse of Khaine throbbing through your veins. We who are free, we feel it also. But it is but a cold trickle in our veins compared to the white heat of its ferocity in your hearts. The Avatar awakens. Feel his call. Take to him that which he needs.'

The autarchs and exarchs turned as one to the main gate at the height of the stepped auditorium. A lone figure stood there, silhouetted against an orange light beyond. It was the Shining Spear exarch, Lideirra of the Midnight Lightning shrine. She wore her silver and gold armour and carried an immense spear, its head as long as her arm and as broad as her face – the *Suin Daellae*, the Doom that Wails, the weapon of the Avatar.

'Behold the Young King!' announced Arhathain. 'Your gift to Khaine in return for the awakening of his Avatar.'

With a fierce shout, the exarchs raised their right fists in salute to the Young King. Chosen from amongst their number, the Young King served as their spiritual leader for five hundred cycles and then passed on his or her crown to another. For most, their rule passed without sacrifice; for a few their reign would end in blood, their spirit offered up to Khaine to breathe life into the metal husk of Khaine's Avatar.

Lideirra stood calmly in the archway, accepting of her fate. It was not only a great honour to be chosen as Young King – named after Eldanesh's epithet as a child, though the chosen exarch could be male or female – it was also a promise of release. To be consumed by the rage of Khaine's fiery spirit was a release from immortality, one that few exarchs would ever know.

The six exarchs of the innermost ring, the oldest of their Aspects, headed up the steps to the Young King:

Morlaniath, Striking Scorpion; Iriethien, Dire Avenger; Lathorinin, Howling Banshee; Faerthruin, Fire Dragon; Maurenin, Dark Reaper; Rhiallaen, Swooping Hawk.

They formed an honour guard around the Young King, three on the left and three on the right, and walked slowly from the hall. Another triumphant shout echoed behind them as they passed from the sight of the exarchs.

The walls of the passageway were covered with holographic images of the oldest myths of the eldar, the tales that had inspired the Aspects. Scenes of destruction from legend enveloped the entourage as they paced slowly towards the shrine of the war god. The doors closed silently behind, leaving them bathed in the soft glow of the projections. This was the Bloodied Way. It wound gently downwards, bringing the procession to the antechamber of the Avatar's throne room. The great bronze doors were closed, a thick trickle of ruddy light creeping from beneath it.

Morlaniath could feel the presence of the Avatar; its heat on his body, its spirit in his mind. The ground reverberated beneath the exarch's feet with a sonorous beating. His heart matched the rhythm.

From hidden doorways, masked and robed seers entered: the warlocks. Former Aspect Warriors, the seers too felt the pull of Khaine. They brought with them a long cloak of red and a golden pin fashioned in the shape of a dagger. The two bearers stood before Lideirra as the exarchs slowly removed her armour. They handed each piece to one of the remaining warlocks.

When Lideirra was naked, Iriethien took the dagger-pin in his left hand. Another warlock garbed in white robes came up next to him, an ornate golden goblet in his hands: the *Cup of Criel*. The myths of the eldar held that when Eldanesh had been slain by Khaine, his followers had caught his blood in seven cups, to keep it from the war god. Khaine fought hard to reclaim the life and spirit of his victim, but Eldanesh's people had held the war god's armies at bay, preserving Eldanesh's spirit forever.

Standing behind the Young King, Iriethien used the point of the pin to cut the rune of the Dire Avenger into the flesh of Lideirra, beneath her left shoulderblade. The dagger-pin cut through skin and flesh effortlessly. Blood ran in rivulets across the Young King's pale flesh, dripping from her buttock to be caught by the cupbearer.

When he was done, Iriethien passed the knife to Morlaniath, who drew out the sigil of the Striking Scorpions on the other side of Lideirra's back. He passed the knife to Lathorinin, who carved the rune of the Howling Banshee beneath Lideirra's left breast. Next came Faerthruin, making the mark of the Fire Dragon on the Young King's right side. Maurenin and Rhiallaen cut Lideirra's arms, inscribing the runes of the Dark Reaper and Swooping Hawk respectively.

All the while Lideirra stood in silence, trembling slightly but not once flinching from the blade worked upon her flesh. Her eyes were bright with anticipation, fixed upon the bronze doors in front of her. Her white skin was criss-crossed with trails of blood.

One of the warlock attendees brought forth Lideirra's waystone, clasped into a fixing upon a pale silver chain. This was hung around her neck. The stone bearer then took up the dagger-pin and delicately cut the rune of the Avatar into Lideirra's forehead. Crimson trickled into her eyes but she stared unblinking, red tears streaking her cheeks.

The mantle of the Avatar was hung from her shoulders, fixed with the bloodied dagger-pin. Its great length was wrapped about her body twice, and still it trailed on the floor behind her. Darker shadows spread across the red cloth as her blood soaked into the tightly-woven fibres.

Next she was presented with the *Suin Daellae*, taking the immense spear in her right hand. Into her left was placed the *Cup of Criel*, now brimming with her blood.

The warlocks formed a circle around the Young King and her honour guard. One of them raised her voice, giving vent to a piercing wail which flowed into the opening words from the *Hymn of Blood*. Another took up the refrain, adding a discordant tone beneath the first, and then another and another until the warlocks filled the antechamber with the sound of harsh singing.

Morlaniath turned his attention upon the throne room doors. The light from beneath was growing bright, flickering, reflected from the entwined wraithbone of the antechamber. The heat from the bronze portal increased steadily, until the air shimmered and Morlaniath blinked sweat from his eyes inside his helmet. Crackles and splintering noises sounded dully from within the throne room. Hisses of steam and the snap of flames grew louder.

. The exarchs joined their voices to the chants and shrieks of the warlocks, adding another discordant harmony to the hymn.

Morlaniath felt the stirring of the Avatar at the base of his spine, its presence tingling up to his neck and then flowing along into his fingertips, into his gut and down to his toes. Energy suffused every part of him, setting his nerves alight.

He sang on, roaring the praises of Khaine, his voice cutting across the ululations and wails of his companions.

In the midst of the ritual, Lideirra stood immobile, skin stained with blood, a thickening crimson pool around her bare feet. Cup and spear were unmoving in her hands, and save for the subtlest rise and fall of her chest she was no more than a statue.

Another reverberating heartbeat throbbed through Morlaniath. Then another, and another. The bass pulsing fitted with the tempo of the strident hymn, both quickening with each other.

With a rush of heat, the bronze doors opened, bathing the antechamber with dazzling light. Morlaniath could barely make out the form of the Avatar in the brightness, a hulking ember sat on its throne, a shadow amongst the light.

The Young King paced into the throne room, spear and cup held before her. She was swallowed by the light and then briefly appeared before being engulfed again by the shadow of the Avatar.

With a dull thud, the doors slowly closed, ending the hymn, the quiet that followed eerie, full of febrile tension. Still the sounds of metal melting and fire burning came muffled through the doors. A rumble as of distant thunder gently shook the bronze barrier.

The warlocks departed wordlessly as the exarchs formed a circle, standing hand-in-hand with each other, Iriethien to Morlaniath's left, Lathorinin to his right. The ring thus formed, the exarchs' spirits flowed into one another, mingling and swirling together. Their voices were raised in a single chant, a soft, bass humming that set the chamber to vibrating. Morlaniath drifted away, losing himself in the maelstrom of spirits created by the conjoined exarchs.

MORLANIATH'S NEXT MOMENT of awareness came as he stepped back from the circle. Aranarha had taken his place at the vigil. Morlaniath returned to the Chamber of Autarchs where the other exarchs waited.

He rested, waiting for his time to come again. Around his dormant form, exarchs came and left, but he did not notice them. He dreamt, wandering in his memories of battle, delighting in the recollections of previous times spent fighting alongside the Avatar. The dreams became more vibrant, more distinct and he knew the Avatar's awakening was coming closer.

The exarchs began to drift away from the chamber, singly at first, and then in small groups, returning to their shrines. Morlaniath lingered a while longer, revelling in the life that flowed into him.

His contemplations halted abruptly. He sensed Kenainath behind him. Opening his eyes, he turned to his fellow exarch.

'There is something amiss, I feel a disturbance, your spirit is troubled.'

'Your thoughts are correct, I have need to speak with you, come now to my shrine.'

Morlaniath felt for the presence of the Avatar, knowing that he would have to return soon to the Hidden Death and ready them for the Avatar's awakening. He knew that there was yet still time. He nodded his acquiescence and accompanied Kenainath from the hall.

MORLANIATH FOLLOWED THE other exarch into the armouring chamber of the Deadly Shadow. Silence reigned, the squad not yet called to war by their leader, though surely they felt the coming of the Avatar.

'Where are your warriors? The time is approaching, they must soon be ready,' said Morlaniath.

Kenainath took off his helmet and placed it upon the top of its stand. His face was emaciated, his eyes sunken and dull, his dry skin clinging to the sharp bones of his cheeks.

'I cannot lead them, I will not see this battle, my time here is short.' Kenainath's voice was barely a whisper. 'This body is old, the time of its end draws close, and will pass away. No other comes here. The Deadly Shadow will sleep, waiting for rebirth.'

'It is a cruel ending, on the eve of battle, one more glorious war,' replied Morlaniath.

Kenainath gripped Morlaniath's shoulders and fixed him with a penetrating stare.

'There is not much time; I have something to ask you, a boon to request. Your squad is untested, your warriors not ready, you cannot lead them.'

Morlaniath opened his mouth to argue but Kenainath ignored him and continued on.

'You need warriors, take on the Deadly Shadow, lead them in battle. They need an exarch, let them be the Hidden Death, with you their exarch.'

A reflex shimmered through Morlaniath's consciousness: the Avatar's awakening was approaching. Time was short. He looked at Kenainath, seeing him through a hundred different memories. It was a harsh fate that took his life from him, at the brink of Alaitoc's greatest need. Yet this body had fought longer than any other exarch. Perhaps he deserved peace for a little while; perhaps this was a battle others needed to fight for him.

'It shall be an honour, to lead your warriors, to make them Hidden Death.'

A thin sliver of a smile twisted Kenainath's cracked lips.

'The honour is mine, to stand in such company, to be found worthy.' Kenainath looked sharply past Morlaniath's shoulder, as if someone had entered the room. 'My pupils approach, I will send them on to you, at the Hidden Death. The Avatar comes, make them don their masks swiftly, take me from their minds.'

Morlaniath nodded in understanding. There should be no time for the Deadly Shadow to dwell on the passing of their exarch, and there would be time enough for them to mourn after the coming battle. He clasped Kenainath's hands for a moment, their spirits mingling for a moment before he broke the contact.

'Enjoy your coming rest, it will not be forever, and we will fight again.'

Morlaniath turned away and headed to the skyrunners below, sensing others approaching the shrine.

As he straddled the skyrunner, he felt a surge of power coursing through him. He would have to be swift: the Avatar was almost awake.

MORLANIATH SPED FOR the throne room of the Avatar, dragged on by the call of the war god incarnate. He had readied his own shrine, joined shortly after his arrival by the warriors who had been the Deadly Shadow. Though Elissanadrin, Arhulesh and the others had been full of questions, Morlaniath had allowed them no time to ponder the turn of events. He had left them ready to bring forth their war-masks; waiting in silent expectation for the Avatar's coming, along with the dozens of other Aspect Warrior shrines across the craftworld. At the moment of his awakening they would don their helms and be suffused with his bloody power, ready to bring death to the humans.

He took his place in the circle of founders, heart racing, breaths coming in short gasps. The doors of the throne room shuddered violently, smoke and flames licking beneath them. The humming incantation of the circle was drowned out by a metallic pounding and the roar of flames.

A piercing scream cut through the chant, and silence fell. Morlaniath shuddered in the grips of ecstasy, the rage and hatred of the Avatar coursing through his body. Through the infinity circuit, the war-call of Khaine echoed through the Alaitocii, bringing everything to a stop. For a single instant every eldar on the craftworld, alive and dead, were joined as one, their psychic energy bringing forth the incarnation of their rage, their living idol of violence.

In a quivering rapture, Morlaniath watched the bronze doors crash open.

The Avatar's eyes burned with dark fire, glowing coals of hatred. Its iron skin was blistered, cracked and pitted, molten rivulets dribbling over the plates. Between them, fiery hide burned bright, tongues of flame licking along metal muscle, flickering within immortal joints.

In its right hand it wielded the *Suin Daellae*, the arcane weapon glittering with power, the runes upon its haft and head writhing with flaming sparks. Upon its shoulders it wore the ruddy cloak, its cloth and dagger-pin still stained with blood. Of Lideirra there was no sign, save for a gory slick of blood encasing the Avatar's arms from burning fingertips to sharp elbow. The blood hissed as it dripped to the floor.

All of this Morlaniath saw in a moment before the Avatar swamped his mind. The exarch relived every death he had inflicted, his joy reaching a crescendo. It was almost too much, a blurring kaleidoscope of pain and bloodletting, every flitting image heightening Morlaniath's pleasure until he could restrain it no more.

He arched his back and let loose a roar of rage, venting every atom of his hatred, his call joined across the craftworld by thousands of throats.

WAR

In the time following the Fall, Asurmen rallied the shattered remnants of Eldanesh and Ulthanesh's children. Upon the craftworlds they fled, the ravages of She Who Thirsts following them swiftly. Asurmen knew that the children of Eldanesh and Ulthanesh could not flee forever, for the obscene god that had been born out of their lustful desires and perverse nightmares was still a part of them. Asurmen led a handful of his followers to a barren world free of distraction and temptation. Here Asurmen founded the Shrine of Asur. Dedicating his life to the preservation of the domain of Asuryan, king of the gods and arbiter of heaven, Asurmen taught his followers that they must give up their love of the gods, for indulgence had led to decadence and wickedness. The destructive impulses of Khaine had to be tempered with wisdom, and so Asurmen taught his followers

*how to forget the joy of slaying and the thrill of
battle. At the Temple Shrine of Asur, his pupils each
developed their own fighting technique, channelling
only a part of the Bloody-Handed God's rage. They
were the Asurya, the first exarchs. When the treachery of Arhra destroyed the Temple Shrine of Asur, the
Asurya escaped to the craftworlds to found new
shrines to pass on their disciplines of war. The Asurya
created the Path of the Warrior and would be known
in ages to come as the Phoenix Lords, each reborn out
of death until Fuegan of the Burning Lance calls
them to the Rhana Dandra, the final battle, ending
of the children of Eldanesh and Ulthanesh.*

ALL WAS STILL in the Dome of Crystal Seers. Trees of
multicoloured wraithbone jutted from the exposed
infinity circuit, their glass-like leaves casting rainbows across the white sand-covered ground. Beneath
their contorted limbs stood the immortal seers, flesh
turned to ice-like crystal, their robes hung upon
glassy bodies, their spirits long departed.

The dome throbbed with the energy of the infinity
circuit as Alaitoc readied to defend itself. Morlaniath
and the Hidden Death had been stationed to guard
the dome alongside four other squads: Shining
Spears on their silver jetbikes; Howling Banshees
with their flowing manes and screaming masks; Dire
Avengers in their blue and white; Warp Spiders with
their glowing deathspinners.

Behind them hovered three Wave Serpents, elegant
troop transports coloured in the blue of Alaitoc with
purple thorn patterns wreathing across their sleek
hulls. Energy vanes crackled with power along their

bows, distorting their shapes with a shimmering protective field. Each had a turret sporting shuriken cannons or pairs of brightlances that swivelled watchfully.

Morlaniath spared no time for these sights. His attention was fixed far above, through the transparent force dome. Here the first battle for Alaitoc was being waged in the cold vacuum of space.

Bright flares of light from crude plasma engines betrayed the positions of the Imperial ships. Ghost-like, the warships of the eldar flitted past, only the shimmer and glint of their solar sails giving them away, their hulls as dark as the void.

Trails of fire criss-crossed the starry sky, as missiles and torpedoes streaked across the firmament. The blinding flash of laser weapons flitted through the darkness, while blossoms of brief flame erupted in the void. Squadrons of graceful destroyers tacked effortlessly to bring their weapons to bear while battleships slid gently through the maelstrom, their batteries unleashing salvoes of destruction, open bays spewing wave after wave of darting fighter craft and wide-winged bombers.

An Imperial frigate hove into view, so close that Morlaniath could see its white hull and golden eagle-headed prow. It was a slab-sided, brutal vessel, encrusted with cornices and buttresses, its prow a giant golden ram shaped like an eagle's beak. Flashes rippled from bow to stern as it opened fire with deck after deck of guns, the flashes cut through by the searing beams of laser turrets arranged along a crenulated dorsal deck. Alaitoc responded, a storm of lightning and laser leaping from the craftworld's defence turrets and anti-ship guns. The human ship was engulfed by a torrent of fire and its hull quickly broke, sending plumes of burning air into the vacuum. Wracked by the eldar weapons, the frigate's plasma reactors detonated in a blossom of white.

It was as if the stars themselves fought, and Morlaniath stood entranced by the spectacle of destruction.

The eldar ships glimmered with holofields, appearing as shimmering ghosts to open fire before disappearing against the star-filled backdrop. Human void shields sputtered with blue and purple flares as they unleashed bursts of energy to shunt the attacks of the eldar into warp space.

For all the skill of the eldar crews and the agility of their ships, the humans drew inexorably closer, their coming heralded by fresh waves of torpedoes and the glare of attack craft. Burning hulks drifted in their wake, both human and eldar, debris gently spiralling away from shattered wrecks. The humans seemed bent on their course, coming straight for Alaitoc like armoured comets, punching through the craftworld's fleet, heedless of the damage inflicted upon them. Morlaniath had to admire the humans' single-mindedness, misguided as it was. Blind faith in their decrepit Emperor gave them a zeal that overrode all logic and sensibility.

A massive shape loomed through the dome, dozens of armoured doors opening along its side to reveal bristling gun batteries. Defensive fire converged on the cruiser and its shields rippled, dissipating the blasts with actinic flares. Its bow erupted with blossoms of orange and moments later the streak of torpedoes hurtled towards Alaitoc, breaking into hundreds of smaller missiles as they crashed into the craftworld.

Morlaniath felt the tremor of their impact, not through his flesh but in his mind, the infinity circuit reverberating with a spasm of pain. More salvoes from the cruiser's gun decks slammed into Alaitoc, crashing against the energy shields that protected the domes. This time the ground did shudder, so close were the impacts of plasma and rocket. The barrage continued for some time and then fell silent, the flare of laser and shell replaced by the small pin-pricks of assault craft engines.

The humans were sending their boarding parties.

'THE TOWER OF Ascending Dreams is under attack.' Arhathain's voice cut through Morlaniath's trance. 'Stand ready to respond on my command.'

The exarch signalled to his warriors to mount up in the Wave Serpent. As they ran up the ramp at its back, he saw the Warp Spiders wink out of existence, while the Shining Spears gunned the engines of their jetbikes and sped out of sight between the wraith-bone trees.

Morlaniath crouched in the back of the Wave Serpent as the ramp closed, sealing them inside. Above him motors whined quietly as the turret lowered into the hull, the pilot readying the transport for departure.

The Striking Scorpions waited for the autarch's orders, every heartbeat slowly tickling past. Arhulesh fidgeted with anticipation, flexing his fingers around the grip of his chainsword. Elissanadrin crouched next to Morlaniath, forearms gently resting on her knees, head bowed in concentration. Bechareth remained as silent as ever, his gaze fixed on Morlaniath. The exarch stared back, wondering what passed through the former incubi's mind. Did he confuse Morlaniath with Korlandril, thinking perhaps that they shared some kind of bond? Did he ponder his fate now that Kenainath's protection was no more? Morlaniath had questions of his own; questions that only time would answer. Was Bechareth truly reformed? He had fought as Hidden Shadow many times, but would he be willing to lay down his life for Alaitoc, an adopted home? Could he be trusted to fight if it seemed that Alaitoc was waning?

'The humans have broken into the lower levels of the Tower of Ascending Dreams,' announced Arhathain. 'Move forward to contain them. Do not over-commit. More human ships are closing along the starward rim. Be ready to fall back and redeploy. Guardian forces moving in support.'

The thrum of the Wave Serpent's engines filled the cabin as it lifted higher and turned on the spot. There was little sensation of movement save the slight pull of inertia as the transport accelerated, but on internal screens Morlaniath saw the crystal seers skimming past as the pilot steered the Wave Serpent towards the main artery to the docking area being attacked.

They passed through the low portal at high speed, veering onto a thoroughfare lit by bright bands of green and blue. The lights flashed past the screen, increasing to a rapid strobe as the Wave Serpent picked up speed. Other vehicles joined them at intersections; several Wave Serpents fell in behind them while two Falcon anti-grav tanks sped past, their helmeted pilots and gunners glimpsed briefly through armoured canopies.

Suddenly deceleration pushed at Morlaniath as the Wave Serpent cornered sharply. He swayed with the momentum, readjusting himself on his haunches to keep his balance. The Wave Serpent picked up speed again as it accelerated along the ramp leading towards the dock towers.

They burst onto the broad plaza of the rim, the whining of the engines lost in the cavernous space of the empty docks: all of the ships had let slip from their moorings as soon as the Imperial fleet had broken out of warp space.

The Wave Serpent slewed to a halt and the ramp lowered even as the transport settled down into a low hover. Morlaniath raced down the ramp, the squad close behind. The outer part of the dock was deserted. Only the occasional flash of a laser or torpedo trail beyond the shimmering force curtain betrayed the battle that was raging.

A spiralling rampway led up to the lower levels of the Tower of Ascending Dreams. The building formed a tapering curve into a soaring pinnacle that jutted out from the craftworld's rim. Slender windows pierced the walls, sometimes lit by a flash of energy from within.

Their armoured boots thudding softly on the rampway, the Striking Scorpions entered the lower level – several storeys of arched rings surrounding the central core of the tower – with the sounds of other squads just behind. Morlaniath looked over his shoulder to see Erethaillin's Maidens of Fate catching quickly, the lightly-armoured, swifter Howling Banshees passing the Striking Scorpions as they turned a loop of the ramp onto the second level.

Morlaniath could hear gunfire; the chatter of barbaric solid-shot weapons, the zip of laser fire and the air-splitting shriek of shuriken ammunition. He pulled free the *Teeth of Dissonance* from where the blade had been hanging across his back, wielding it in both hands as the spiralling passageway took them up another level.

The Hidden Death ran onto a wide concourse that curved gently along the rim of the craftworld. A sea of stars spread out beyond the blue-tinged force wall, burning debris floating across the starscape.

The whirr of wings caught the exarch's attention and he glanced up to see a squad of Swooping Hawks flying above him, the wings of their flight-packs a multi-coloured blur in the dim yellow glow of the chamber. He saw Phoenix Lord Baharroth gliding amongst his followers, his las-blaster sending shafts of brilliant energy into the upper levels of the docking tower.

Ahead, through an archway that arced far above him, Morlaniath could see blue-clad eldar with yellow helmets gathered in a defensive semi-circle: Guardian squads protecting the landing beyond the arch, shuriken catapults spitting salvoes into a foe that the exarch could not yet see. Amongst the Guardians glided heavy weapons platforms, their crews close at hand with psychically-linked controls.

Brightlances spat blasts of laser, starcannons unleashed torrents of blue plasma and missile launchers filled the air with screaming trails. The Swooping Hawks dove through the arch, their weapons criss-crossing the chamber beyond with white ripples of fire.

Morlaniath reached the archway and looked up at Alaitoc's attackers.

They had taken cover on a sweeping gallery above and opposite the archway, hiding behind rows of slender columns that rose to the ceiling far above. The stunted, thick-limbed enemy were clad in rumpled suits, grey and black camouflage, skull and eagle insignias stitched onto arms and chests, their flat faces hidden behind silver-visored helmets. In fat, gauntleted hands they carried crude laser weapons that fired bolts of red. Pinned back by the eldar counter-attack, the humans clumsily bobbed into view, loosing off scattered shots before hiding again.

The Swooping Hawks swept majestically up, slaloming between the pillars, grenade dispensers on their thighs showering the humans below with blasts of plasma and shrapnel. The Maidens of Fate – Erethaillin's Howling Banshee squad – were already at the left-hand end of the rampway that led to the human-occupied gallery, the exarch at the forefront of their charge, a gleaming, curved sword in each hand. Forced back by the heavy weapons of the Guardians, the grenades of the Swooping Hawks and the approach of the Howling Banshees, the humans directed no fire towards Morlaniath and his squad as they raced across the tiled floor between the arch and the right-hand access ramp.

Morlaniath could see human officers amongst the throng of their men, swathed in long dress coats with golden epaulettes, wearing silver-peaked caps with winged skull badges. None of the humans noticed the Hidden Death quickly but quietly stalking up the ramp, keeping to the long shadows cast by the pillars above.

Morlaniath broke from the ramp at a full run, the others directly behind him. Their shuriken pistols spat a blurring volley into the nearest humans, shredding grey fatigues, cracking mirrored visors. Their sergeant turned in dismay, a moment before the *Teeth of Dissonance* separated his head from his shoulders in one sweep.

The Hidden Death did not pause to finish off the wounded, following closely as Morlaniath charged into the group of humans huddled behind the next column. The exarch's mandiblasters exploded across the face of a black-coated officer, the human's face twisting into an agonised, wordless scream as energy flared across his swarthy skin. Morlaniath swept his biting blade across the officer's left arm, severing the limb at the shoulder.

A flash and a roar at close range heralded a shotgun blast, a moment before a storm of pellets crashed into Morlaniath's left side, staggering him for a moment. He turned quickly and saw the panicked human trying to load more shells into the gun's slider, his movements slow and fumbling in Morlaniath's eyes. With a laugh, Morlaniath gutted the impudent creature, spilling his intestines over the white-and-gold tiles of the gallery. Around him, the Hidden Death chopped and hacked, coating the floor with blood and limbs.

The Striking Scorpions and Howling Banshees converged from opposite ends of the gallery, cutting down all in their path. The humans got in each other's way, the few shots they fired woefully inaccurate. Six more of their number fell to the blade *Teeth of Dissonance* and Morlaniath growled in tune to his weapon, relishing every death.

Las-blasts and the thudding of feet heralded the arrival of more humans coming down the broad stairway that swept down to the gallery from the docking spire above. The Swooping Hawks greeted the reinforcements with las-fire, shrouding the steps with a fusillade of deadly light. Guardians poured along the gallery from either end, adding their own fire to the defence.

The snap of the humans' lasguns was drowned out by the piercing shriek of the Howling Banshees as they charged again, their masks projecting a psychosonic wave before them. Some of the humans fell to their knees, ears and eyes bleeding, others dropped weapons from numbed fingers or simply collapsed with spasmodic fits. Even those that were not incapacitated stood in quivering shock, unable to defend themselves as Erethaillin and her warriors closed for the kill, power swords cutting through flak jackets, flesh and bone without resistance.

Morlaniath was about to lead his squad forward in support of the Howling Banshees when Arhathain's voice cut through his thoughts.

'Enemy numbers are strengthening. They have breached our defences in several positions and are establishing a landing zone. Stage a withdrawal from the Tower of Ascending Dreams to avoid being isolated. Bring the enemy into the Concourse of the Suffering Heart. Additional forces will join you at the Plaza of Alaithir.'

In response to this new plan, the entirety of the tower plunged into darkness, the dim light of the walls extinguished by Alaitoc. Through the augmented vision of his helmet, Morlaniath watched the Imperial soldiers toppling down the stairway, tripping over each other, flailing in the blackness for balance. The bright flash of the Swooping Hawks' lasers and the flare of missile detonations highlighted faces contorted in terror at this sudden change of environment.

The eldar withdrew from their foes behind the fire of the Swooping Hawks and Guardian weapons platforms. With their attackers thrown into disarray, the Alaitocii withdrew from the Tower of Ascending Dreams into the concourse outside, squads taking it in turns to stand rearguard while the rest retreated. Outside once more, the Striking Scorpions boarded their Wave Serpent and turned to speed along the rim, heading for the Plaza of Alaithir, a broad junction between the Concourse of the Suffering Heart and the Mourning Way. Behind them, the Imperial troops staggered out into the lighted concourse to be cut down by Falcon tanks and soaring Vyper jetbikes.

AT THE PLAZA of Alaithir, forces were converging from three directions, falling back from all across the starward side of the craftworld. Silhouetted against the orange glow of the dying star, Falcons hovered at each intersection, weapons trained above the incoming squads of Aspect Warriors and Guardians. Wave Serpents converged on the immense fountain at the centre of the plaza, from which reared an enormous statue of the autarch after whom the plaza was named. The marble warrior stood with sword and fusion pistol at the ready, glaring balefully down the Mourning Way towards the Spire of Tranquillity.

The Hidden Death disembarked to join the line defending the concourse along which they had just travelled. The Vypers and Falcons slid back into view occasionally, firing their weapons at foes hidden behind the curve of the craftworld's rim. Eventually the humans came into view again, resolutely advancing in a column hundreds-strong. Gawky walkers strode on double-jointed legs beside the squads of infantry, their multi-barrelled lasers spewing a torrent of fire at the eldar vehicles. Human heavy weapons teams ran forward, dragging wheeled lascannons and bulky autocannons behind them. They set up firing positions alongside the advancing companies, adding the fury of their fire to the walkers' as cover for the advancing soldiers.

As shells cut dark streaks through the air, a Vyper was clipped by a salvo, losing a control vane. It careened out of control into the jade-coloured interior wall. Another volley ripped into the armour of a Falcon, which listed sideways before grinding into the ground with a crumpling of armoured plates. More shots punched through the wreckage, cracking sensor gems and showering pieces of shattered canopy across the tiled floor. Its anti-grav engines destroyed by a laser blast, another tank flipped awkwardly upwards, pulse laser still firing burning bolts of light. The turret of a third Falcon erupted in flames from a hit and the tank spun crazily about its axis until it crashed into the energy field on the spaceward side of the plaza, ripples of lightning spreading across the force shield.

Faced with the continuing onslaught, the Falcons' and Vypers' pilots increased the speed of their retreat, eventually turning completely and boosting away from the Imperium's soldiers on plumes of light. The throb of their engines vibrated through Morlaniath as they soared overhead into the relative safety of the plaza.

To the advancing humans it must have seemed as if they had their foes at bay, trapped in the open space of the plaza. The grass-covered hills and marble-like roadways provided little cover for the sheltering troops. The eldar waited in silence while the angry orders and triumphant shouts of the Imperial officers echoed along the concourse.

A shimmering force wall blazed into existence barely a dozen paces in front of Morlaniath and the other squads at the concourse edge of the plaza. Everything beyond was tinted by the blue of the field, as if the army marched along the bed of a shimmering sea. Las-bolts and bullets sparked from the force shield, which quivered with each impact but held firm. Morlaniath smiled. The shield wall was not to protect the eldar from attack. It had another, far more deadly purpose, as the humans were about to discover.

The fine tendrils of the infinity circuit within the inner wall of the concourse flickered and then darkened. Deprived of energy, the outer force wall collapsed with a flare of light. Exposed to the ravening vacuum of space, the humans were swept from their feet by the explosive outrushing of air, hundreds of them hurled out of the craftworld in moments. Their screams were lost in the void as their skin froze and blood vessels tore open while weapons and helmets spun around them. Even the walkers could not fight against the explosive depressurisation, their awkward metal legs flailing as the sudden hurricane hurled them out into the stars along with their dying comrades.

The massacre lasted only a few moments and silence descended. Glittering particles of frozen blood lingered in the air, before falling like rain in the artificial gravity of the craftworld. With a grim fascination Morlaniath watched the red pattering, interspersed with plummeting corpses that thudded upon the tiled concourse in mangled heaps. Though the depressurisation had been done out of necessity and lacked the true artistry of a well-placed shot or cut, there was a simple beauty to be found in its effective results.

'Human forces have pushed into the sub-levels beneath the docking dome,' Arhathain informed the warriors of the craftworld. 'More assault craft are inbound. They must be driven back.'

Morlaniath gestured for his warriors to follow him back to the Wave Serpent.

'No overconfidence, this is but the first strike, the humans will fight hard,' he told them as they strode up the boarding ramp. 'We will be pitiless, make them pay heavily, every step shall be pain. Look to one another, strike with single purpose, fight as the Hidden Death.'

The ramp closed behind them and within moments the Wave Serpent was moving again, angling towards the Mourning Way.

'How do we fare in other battles?' asked Elissanadrin.

'That is not our concern; we fight the foes we face, to their destruction. Focus on this sole task; allow no distraction, until our foes are slain. Listen for the autarchs, they will guide our swift hand, to land the deadly blow.'

'Their looks of terror when the darkness came, that is something I will treasure,' said Arhulesh with a sharp laugh. 'Did you see their surprise? Such stupidity, to think that Alaitoc would tolerate their filthy presence.'

'It is a shame that those who knew such fear are now dead,' said Elissanadrin. 'Terror is a disease; it spreads through an enemy as swift as a plague.'

'Let us hope that they communicated some of their dread before they perished.' Arhulesh turned to look at Bechareth. 'How can you keep your delight to yourself? Does it not eat at you, to hold in that delightful moment of death, when an enemy's spirit is extinguished?'

Bechareth's helmeted head cocked to one side. His gaze moved between Arhulesh and Morlaniath. The Striking Scorpion shrugged and shook his head. He raised a finger to the grille of his helmet and pulled free his chainsword. The bloodstained blades of its teeth gleamed in the light of the compartment.

'Though his voice is silent, Bechareth speaks to us, his blade's words come loudly,' explained Morlaniath, eliciting a laugh and a nod from Arhulesh.

'It certainly does,' said the Striking Scorpion. 'I slew thirteen of them, but could not match your tally. Eighteen, was it not?'

Bechareth nodded.

'We shall see who has the greater score when the humans have been driven from Alaitoc. I think I may even beat you this time.'

'The count will be many, the humans come in force, plenty for each of us,' the exarch assured his squad.

As their minds turned to the prospect of much death to come, the squad fell silent. Morlaniath allowed himself to briefly recall his latest slayings, while part of him kept an eye on the crystal screen displaying the Wave Serpent's position. Along with many others, the Hidden Death had dropped several layers beneath the main inhabited zone of Alaitoc; the Wave Serpent raced along an arterial supply route usually used to transport wares from the Exodite colonies and other craftworlds to the various parts of Alaitoc.

These depths were totally enclosed, divided from the emptiness of space by solid walls and floors, not force shields that could be switched off. Listening to the irregular comments from the autarchs, Morlaniath learnt that the humans had been over-confident in their speedy assault, but now they advanced with more caution. This did not make them any less dangerous. They would gather their strength and attack relentlessly, knowing that they had the advantage of numbers. They could not be allowed to gain a worthwhile foothold on Alaitoc. If they did, it could well herald a slow doom for the craftworld.

As Morlaniath considered this, he felt a ripple through the wraithbone skeleton of the Wave Serpent as it connected to the infinity circuit with a flutter of psychic energy. He felt another mind touch upon his thoughts and instantly recognised Thirianna, remembering the sense of her from their encounter at the shrine. Through the psychic connection Morlaniath felt the fleeting presence of other eldar: exarchs and Guardian squad leaders, vehicle pilots and support weapon gunners. All were joined together for a moment.

The enemy make progress along the Well of Disparate Fates. Walk the red path with them, drive them back to their landing craft. There followed a flutter of brief images: Imperial soldiers setting up crude barricades; the small one-man walkers stalking through unlit corridors, searchlights playing across curving walls; an officer with a pistol in hand bellowing at his troops.

She was gone, leaving only an aftertouch in Morlaniath's mind. The exarch opened up the communications channel with the Wave Serpent's pilot, Laureneth.

'Put us down close to them, we will advance on foot, cover us with your fire,' he told the driver.

'I understand, exarch,' the pilot replied, his voice flat. The telemetry display close to Morlaniath changed to show a schematic of the conduits and tunnels beneath the docks. A rune flashed at an intersection a short distance from the place they had seen in Thirianna's message. 'Will that be suitable, exarch?'

'That will be suitable; a bloody trail follows, as we walk in Khaine's shade.'

THE DEADLY STRUGGLE between the Alaitocii and the invading humans filled the sub-strata levels of the docks. The Imperial forces were desperate to gain a foothold into which they could move their heavier materiel. Despite the Alaitoc fleet taking a serious toll of the transports attempting to reinforce the landing zone, with perhaps only one in every three of the human's craft making fall at the craftworld's rim, the enemy continued relentlessly. A growing field of burning craft, debris and corpses coalesced around the dock facilities in ponderous orbits, kept close by Alaitoc's artificial gravity field.

The eldar held their ground in a large nave-like intersection between three transit routes from the docks to the central arterial concourses. The humans advanced along two vaulted tunnels, scampering from pointed arch to pointed arch, sometimes using the mounds of their own dead as cover. They offered little in the way of fire – by the time they had closed the range, their numbers were so low they were swiftly eliminated by the Guardians. On levels above and below, to the left and right, similar firefights wracked the craftworld.

'They fight like maniacs, not counting any cost, the price paid by fanatics,' Morlaniath commented to his squad as he watched the grey-clad soldiers charging headlong into a volley of missiles fired by several squads of Dark Reapers. With the Hidden Death, other squads of Striking Scorpions, Howling Banshees and Warp Spiders were positioned a little way behind the fighting, ready to move forward to stave off any breakthrough or counter-attack if an opportunity presented itself. Occasionally the Wave Serpent behind the squad unleashed a torrent of plasma from its starcannons, the flickering shots disappearing into the gloom of the passageway.

'Numbers are no tactic, to be hurled like bullets, a limitless supply,' the exarch continued. 'They render death pointless, each life a statistic, that no one is counting. They use the hammer, to smash at formless fog, to destroy only air.'

Though Alaitoc could not empty the air from this section, the craftworld did not permit the humans easy advance. The light dimmed and changed, from bright mid-cycle glare to late-cycle twilight, interspersed with brief periods of blinding whiteness and utter darkness.

Infinity circuit energy coursed through the walls; Morlaniath could feel the spirit energy within rippling on the edge of consciousness. Amidst the turmoil, ghostly apparitions, brief psychic phantasms, appeared amongst the enemy ranks, no doubt guided by the seers: raving, fire-wreathed monstrosities; weeping human mothers cradling the bloodied swaddling of children; fluttering flocks of giant wasps; shimmering lights that contained the screaming faces of the humans. Locked inside the walls of the craftworld the enemy had no gauge of time passing and could not know whether they fought for a heartbeat or a lifetime; the eldar were free from such doubts, subconsciously attuned to the internal rhythms of Alaitoc.

The terrifying assault on the senses of the humans had only a limited effect. Occasionally a soldier would break and run screaming from the fight, but more often the bellows of the humans' leaders cut through the clamour, urging the soldiers forwards. Morlaniath watched a robe-clad human with a bald head raising a book in his right hand, frothing and shouting, his homilies keeping the soldiers at their positions despite the horrendous casualties. Grim-faced officers with peaked caps and skull-shaped badges instilled discipline with more brutal means, turning their pistols on their own warriors when they showed signs of cowardice.

'Their faith is a façade, layered onto cowards, driven by fear more than hate,' Morlaniath observed. 'Superficial hatred, falsely righteous anger, is no motive for war. Our hate and rage is pure, Khaine's lasting gift to us, a true strength of spirit. Do not pity these fools, they can learn nothing new. Any mercy is wasted. They die without meaning, no one counting the toll, no one heeding their deaths. Their lives are meaningless, no lasting potential, short spans easily spent. No true aspirations, just fear and resentment, minds filled with hollow thoughts.'

Crude as the humans' techniques were, they were slowly gaining ground by sheer weight of numbers and raw belligerence. The autarchs had acknowledged as much when Arhathain next communicated to the exarchs and Guardian squad leaders.

'A new wave of forces is closing on the humans' landing area. These reinforcements cannot be allowed to bolster the attack. Push the humans back to their ships and eradicate them.'

A flash of awareness from the infinity circuit brought Morlaniath's attention to a circular opening in the curving wall behind him. The covering melted away, revealing a narrow but navigable conduit that ran alongside the main passage.

Erethaillin and her Howling Banshees were already at the tunnel mouth, ducking their maned helms into the service duct. Morlaniath and the Hidden Death followed as swiftly as their heavier armour allowed, the iris-door coalescing across the gap behind them, plunging the passage into gloom. The glow of psychic energy trailed along crystalline fibres in the wall and by this witchlight the two squads advanced quickly. There was no need to guess the relative positions of the enemy in the parallel corridor; Alaitoc would lead them to where they were needed.

Bent over, the Howling Banshees sped along the conduit on light feet, their bone-white armour cast with a blue gleam from their power swords. Morlaniath watched them getting further and further ahead until the glow of their weapons and eyes was no more than a quickly receding haze in the distance.

The tunnel curved gently upwards, taking it away from the main route by which the humans were attacking. Morlaniath surmised that they were being taken direct to the landing zone, but wary of the limits of estimation, sent a message to Arhathain.

'Into the foes' dark heart, a fatal blow unseen, is that our new purpose?' he asked. It was but a few heartbeats before Arhathain responded.

'The enemy will be caught twixt doom and death, with no escape. The new arrivals are imminent; do not allow them to join the ongoing attack.'

The glow ahead grew bright again, and soon the Striking Scorpions saw the azure-dancing blades of the Howling Banshees squad, crouched around another iris door having been told to wait for the following squad.

'Strength in our unity, together we fight, in victory renowned,' said Erethaillin.

'With the Maidens of Fate, the Hidden Death will fight, doom and dark together!' laughed Morlaniath.

They waited in silence, eyes fixed to the closed portal. The sound of booted feet reverberated through the conduit from the passageway on the other side of the door, an occasional guttural human command added to the noise.

The iris door widened and the Aspect Warriors streamed through, pistols blazing.

They were at the skin of Alaitoc itself, a large domed hallway filled with humans. Blunt-nosed landing craft squatted on the curving star-quays, the air shimmering with cooling engines. Dozens of humans marched down the ramps from these assault boats, utterly unprepared for the sudden attack.

As a human fell with a volley of shurikens in the back of his neck, Morlaniath saw Aranarha and his squad attacking from close to the rim wall. Warp Spiders materialised in the midst of the foe, their deathspinners ripping through whole squads. From above, Swooping Hawks dropped down through the arching arms of loading cranes, plasma grenades blossoming beneath them, their las-blasters sending streams of white death through the milling humans.

Morlaniath spared no more thought for the other squads as he chopped the head from an Imperial soldier with a twist of his wrists. One of the peak-capped officers bellowed incoherently at him, raising a fist sheathed in a crackling mechanical gauntlet. Morlaniath sliced the human's arm at the elbow, the powered glove clanging to the floor. Las-bolts sprayed from the officer's pistol, catching the exarch on the right side of his chest, leaving smoking holes in his armour. Annoyed, he flexed his arm and sent the *Teeth of Dissonance* through the officer's other elbow, leaving him literally disarmed. The officer collapsed to one side, still shouting, kicking out with his legs in hopeless defiance. Morlaniath ended him with a surge from his mandiblasters, the laser bolt punching through the human's gilded breastplate. The whole affair had taken less than three heartbeats.

A human crouched over a buzzing piece of equipment looked up in horror as Morlaniath loomed over him – on the end of a coiling wire he held a cup-shaped receptacle to one ear. The *Teeth of Dissonance* cleaved through the human's upraised arm and came to rest halfway through his skull, showering the fizzing electrical box with blood. Morlaniath let go of his sword with one hand and stooped to pick up the receptacle and hold it close to his helmet's auditory pick-up. Between bursts of static, meaningless human gibberish rang tinnily in the exarch's ear.

Being overrun at sector six – by the Emperor's holy shrivelled gonads, we need more ammunition – did you see what they did to the captain? Is that him over there? Where did the rest of him go? – Remain at stations, reinforcements incoming – The door won't open, Command. It swallowed Sergeant Lister – Say again, corporal, report position – Reinforcements imminent, the Asta–

Morlaniath dropped the comm-device and looked across the wide hangar. A few pockets of humans held out, defending their shuttles to the last soldier. His squad was too far away to intervene, there would be none left by the time the Hidden Death reached the landing craft. He watched with a twinge of envy as Aranarha boarded one of the assault boats with his warriors.

'Enemy reinforcements have reached the docks,' announced Arhathain. 'All units fall back to the Dome of Midnight Forests. Do not engage the enemy, fall back at once.'

Morlaniath was confused. The hangar and docking platforms were in eldar hands. Heavy weapons were moving up the access ramps. Any enemy foolish enough to make a landing in the teeth of the eldar squads would be cut down as soon as they set foot on the craftworld. He turned towards the glimmering one-way field that protected the dock opening. There was no sign of approaching craft outside, just a swathe of stars.

Of the attacking ships, there was nothing to be seen save for a handful of flaring plasma drives against the darkness. Morlaniath could not see how so few reinforcements had so unsettled the autarchs.

THE DOCKS SHOOK with a thunderous impact as a torpedo-like craft smashed through the outer wall to Morlaniath's left, the nose cone of the boarding vessel surrounded in a red haze of energy. Two more slammed into Alaitoc to either side of the first, sending cracked shards of wall flying across the docks. Light within recesses around the torpedoes' noses flared and Morlaniath dropped to his belly in an instant, warned by instinct. A barrage of rockets filled the dockside, a mass of fire and smoke trails and deafening blasts that cut through the eldar. Secondary detonations tore apart the human landing craft, creating a fresh storm of shrapnel.

Morlaniath jumped back to his feet and checked on his squad. Arhulesh held his arm where a long gash had ripped through his armour, and there were minor cracks and scratches in the suits of the others, but no serious injuries. The same could not be said for other eldar forces. The limp forms of Guardians lay sprawled across walkways, sparks fizzing from the remnants of their heavy weapons. Erethaillin's squad had been close to the wall and bloodstained armour littered the hangar floor, the tattered strands of the Howling Banshees' helmet manes floating around their corpses.

In every direction Morlaniath looked, he saw dead and dying eldar.

His gaze was drawn back to the three glowing projectiles jutting through the wall surrounded by a lingering haze of smoke. Though scorched, they were painted in white and red. In unison, the noses broke into four petal-like segments, opening up to reveal a harsh white interior. The bottom petal touched down like a ramp and in the dizzy aftermath of the rockets blasts, the dock rang with heavy feet.

A dozen fiery trails snarled from of the opening portals, followed by the sharp crack of detonations, the bloodied remains of eldar warriors flung across the hangar floor. With morbid curiosity Morlaniath focussed on one, seeing a miniature rocket at least the size of his thumb propelled out of the white light. It hit a Guardian in the leg and punched through the thin armour into flesh. A moment later it detonated with a blossom of bone and blood, ripping the limb apart from the inside.

Morlaniath knew this weapon.

He had faced it once before: the time when not-Lecchamemnon had been slain. The memory of his death was unpleasant and the exarch looked at the boarding torpedoes with a disconcerted feeling as more of them burst through other parts of the dock wall. Hugely armoured figures ran down the ramps, their guns spitting fury.

Imperial Space Marines!

DEATH

In the moment between Khaine's sword blow and Eldanesh's death, Asuryan the Phoenix King came down from heaven. Eldanesh asked why it was that the eldar had to die. Asuryan laughed at the question. He told Eldanesh that he could not die. The father of the eldar would live on in the spirit and memory of his children, reborn anew in every generation. While his children prospered, Eldanesh would be immortal. As death's grip tightened on Eldanesh and the stars dimmed, Asuryan gave him one last message. The gods had no descendants, only they could truly die.

THE RETREAT FROM the docks was swift. Faced with the devastating onslaught of the Emperor's most fearsome creations, the eldar melted away into the inner corridors and halls of Alaitoc. The craftworld secured their retreat, delaying the pursuing Space Marines with closed doors and energy fields. Driven by the energy of the infinity circuit, Alaitoc remapped entire parts of its layout to stall the enemy advance, sealing corridors and collapsing walkways to strand the enemy and separate them from each other. When all was done, the infinity circuit shrank back from the docks, rendering the crystal network dead, leaving no means for the foe to exploit or infiltrate its energies.

As the squad boarded their Wave Serpent in silence, Morlaniath sensed the numbed shock of his warriors, the realisation that there existed foes in the galaxy that were the match of them.

'It is not the right place, to face our foes head on, standing with blade-to-blade,' he said as the Wave Serpent lifted off and turned sharply, heading for the Dome of Midnight Forests. 'We are part of the whole, a sole Aspect of Khaine, not complete of itself. With others we will fight, much greater together, victorious in time. Space Marines are dire foes, deadly in their own right, but so few in number. They are strong of body, they know not dread or doubt, yet still they can be killed. No swift victory comes, this is a war of will. Alaitoc must prevail.'

'The enemy have secured many landing points behind the spearhead of their finest warriors,' Arhathain cut through Morlaniath's encouragement. 'Their numbers will swell and they will bring vehicles and heavier weapons. We cannot be dragged into their crude way of war, meeting them headlong. They will lumber after us with great crushing blows; we must be the blade that cuts a thousand times. We have killed many of the humans and we must kill many more before we know victory. There will be no swift road back to peace. The true war for Alaitoc begins now.'

The exarch sensed lingering doubt in the minds of his followers.

'The autarch speaks the truth: we fight for survival, to avoid extinction. Harbour no weaknesses, dispel the seed of doubt, harden yourselves for war. Know there is no retreat, we fight to guard our home, to keep our future safe.'

'Space Marines, tanks, countless soldiers, how can we fight against such things?' asked Arhulesh.

'With blade and with pistol, we fight what we can kill, trust others for the rest. We are not without arms. We have our own weapons, to meet these kinds of threats. Defeat is not our fate, not by the hands of men, not in this place and time. Let hate be your courage, let anger be your shield, let Khaine watch over us.'

Their disquiet receded as the Wave Serpent sped on. In silence, they each fell into a meditative state, drawing on their resolve to quench the fear that had risen. Morlaniath had no need to bolster his convictions with abstract contemplation. He had a very real reason to despise the Space Marines of the Emperor.

THE FIELDS AROUND the town burned, pockmarked with craters. The bodies of gigantic miradons lay in burning heaps, their scales glistening in the flame-light. More blasts rained down from the skies, crushing the buildings of Semain Alair. Charred corpses were flung high into the air by the plasma impacts, while the screams of the burning Exodites mingled with the agonised bellows of their herds.

The exarch watched the devastation from a stand of burning trees on a hill overlooking the farming settlement, the canopy overhead a crackling inferno. In irrigation ditches and hollows, others lay in wait.

He turned to Farseer Alaitharin.

'We have arrived too late, the slaughter has begun. Now we must count the dead.'

The seer's ruby-like eye lenses fixed him with a stare. She reached into the pouch at her waist and drew forth a handful of wraithbone runes. They lifted from her open palm and arranged themselves into a circling pattern, slowly revolving around the farseer.

'It was not our fate to protect them,' she said slowly. 'We cannot stop the humans from taking this world.'

'I do not understand, what is our purpose here, if not to drive them back?'

'One is coming who will become a greater military leader. In a generation from now, he will lead his forces against the fleet of Alaitoc in the Kholirian system and destroy many of our ships. I have followed his strand. He is most vulnerable here, during this conquest. Extinguish his light now and it will never burn our people.'

'Who is this great leader, a threat to the future, no human lives so long?'

'He is no human,' replied Alaitharin. The runes ceased their orbit and floated back to her hand. She looked up into the evening sky. 'He comes upon a shooting star.'

Morlaniath and the other Hidden Death warriors followed her gaze. Pinpricks of light appeared in the sky, swiftly growing larger. As they neared, Morlaniath could see black liveried craft falling through the atmosphere, the glimmers of light the glare of their heat shields. The exarch counted them, fourteen in all.

Dart-like shapes appeared over the hills in front of Morlaniath, closing fast: Nightwing fighters. Lasers lanced from their prows, striking the falling drop-pods. The armour of many shrugged aside the attack, but three exploded into clouds of fire and debris, exploding into parts that burned away into nothing. The Nightwings twisted and fired again, destroying two more.

Bulkier shapes appeared in the twilight, rockets flaring from their wings – the gunships of the enemy. They were high-sided, clumsy craft, laden with weapons. The Nightwings were forced away from the falling pods by the weight of fire as they turned to meet this new threat.

With blazes of plasma, the drop-pods slowed their descent and slammed into the soft earth of the farms. Heat shimmer disturbed the air but Morlaniath could make out white cross-shaped markings on their sides. Explosive bolts crackled and ramps crashed to the burnt ground, disgorging squads of bulky, armour-clad warriors.

'This one,' said Alaitharin, pointing to a squad sergeant forging up the slope towards the burning settlement, his squad in close formation behind him. A rune – the symbol of fate sealed – appeared in Morlaniath's vision, dancing over the head of the Space Marine. Even when he disappeared into a dell, the rune betrayed his whereabouts. 'It is destined that you slay him. Go now, bring his doom swiftly.'

Morlaniath headed towards the burning buildings with his squad in tow while other eldar forces formed a ring around the disembarking Space Marines. The rune of fate was a constant presence, dragging him on. Gunfire erupted across the devastated field but he did not spare a glance backwards, intent only on the prey he stalked.

The outskirts of the settlement were as ruined as the centre, the high towers and long halls crushed to piles of rubble. Morlaniath skirted around a complex of half-fallen walls that had once been a storehouse. Twisted harnesses and saddles jutted from the shattered masonry. Here and there an arm or leg could be seen, dust sticking to the drying blood.

He found it hard to understand the farseer's attitude. Surely this warrior could have been killed before the attack was launched? It was one matter to expend the lives of lesser species to further the cause of Alaitoc; it was another to sacrifice eldar, even if they were only Exodites. There may have been greater risk in an orbital attack, but it was the duty of the Aspect Warriors to face such dangers. The farmers lying dead in the ruins of their homes had made no such commitment.

Yet, it was the farseers that could foretell the perils facing the craftworld, and if this was the best course of action he was in no place to resist their judgement. He was glad he did not have to deal with the vagaries of divination. He had a clarity of purpose it was hard to argue against: kill the enemy. The fulfilment of that simple goal brought him contentment, often joy.

His prey had taken up a position in the ruins of a meeting hall, on the debris-strewn floor of the second storey. The squad's fire screamed out over the ravaged fields, covering their comrades as they took up defensive positions against the eldar attack. Their attention was focussed outward, unsuspecting of the Hidden Death that came at them from behind.

Morlaniath trod gently across a ramp of broken stone, careful not to move the smallest grain of debris. Crouched at the sill of a shattered window, he set eyes on his prey once more. The sergeant stood with one foot up on the lip of a wall, directing the fire of his squad. The white edging of his shoulder pads and the cross symbol they enclosed could be seen in the shadow of the ruin. Bursts of muzzle flare illuminated his craggy face as he stared intently out across the fields.

With a nod to his squad, Morlaniath slipped through the remnants of the window and across the rubble-strewn street, gliding between patches of burning material and smoking corpses.

They were halfway across the open space when the prey suddenly glanced down at his left wrist: Morlaniath could see a red light winking quickly on a device attached to his arm. To Morlaniath it seemed as if the sergeant turned slowly in his direction, raising his pistol to fire, mouth opening to bellow a fresh order even as his other hand raised the Space Marine's helmet towards his head.

The Striking Scorpions needed no command. They leapt forward at full speed, entering the bottom storey of the building occupied by the Space Marines. Riethillin and Lordranir sprinted up the stairway while Morlaniath led Irithiris, Elthruin and Darendir up the slope of a collapsed floor, into the heart of the enemy squad.

Harsh light blazed as the Space Marines unleashed the fury of their bolters. Darendir was in their line of fire and was torn apart, fragments of armour and body tumbling down the floor-slope. Morlaniath tossed a handful of small grenades, each exploding into a white-hot cloud of plasma that sent the Space Marines reeling back. He charged through the dissipating mist, the *Teeth of Dissonance* carving into the chest of the closest enemy. Blades screeched as they hacked through the gold-embossed eagle on the warrior's plastron. The Space Marine twisted away, almost wrenching the weapon from Morlaniath's grasp. The exarch ducked beneath a fist almost as large as his head and kicked his foot against the Space Marine's stomach to wrench his biting blade free. He lithely twisted aside as the Space Marine tried to bring an armoured elbow down on the exarch's shoulder, the *Teeth of Dissonance* cutting into the flexible armour behind the warrior's left knee.

The Space Marine toppled as the lower half of his leg spun away, his weapon blazing as his finger instinctively tightened on the trigger, the flare of the bolts disappearing into the darkening sky. Morlaniath drove the point of his blade into the faceplate of the Space Marine's helmet, the whirring teeth cutting through the grille-mouth until blood sprayed heavily and the Space Marine fell still.

Something slammed into the exarch's back and he felt ribs fracturing. Morlaniath snarled in pain and his mandiblasters spewed an arc of energy as he twisted with the force of the blow to confront his new attacker. The Space Marine ponderously swung overarm with a long combat knife, the blow falling wide as Morlaniath slipped aside. The exarch rained down three blows on the arm of the Space Marine, the last severing his wrist so that hand and knife fell to the blood-spattered floor.

The rune of fate danced across the exarch's vision and he plunged past the wounded Space Marine to attack the sergeant. His prey raised a chainsword in defence, the *Teeth of Dissonance* deflected away in a storm of sparks. Morlaniath adjusted his attack, feinting towards the sergeant's gut before bringing his blade down hard against the side of his head. The teeth skittered across the rounded helm, shards of armour splintering, but the blow did not bite home and the *Teeth of Dissonance* rebounded off the Space Marine's helm and shoulder pad.

The Space Marine clubbed down with the butt of his pistol, catching the exarch on the left shoulder. The eldar's arm went numb and his fingers lost their grip on the *Teeth of Dissonance*. Something sent grinding pain along his spine when he stooped to recover the fallen weapon. A booted foot crashed into his chest, lifting Morlaniath fully off his feet, pain flooding through every part of him. He felt his heart rupturing from the blow, his lungs filling with blood.

This cannot be, he thought distractedly. He coughed and blood filled his helm. Even his eyes hurt as he watched the sergeant turning away with a snarl of contempt. Morlaniath held on for a few moments longer to see Ethruin pounce.

As ETHRUIN, HE saw his exarch fall. Ethruin surged forward, triggering his mandiblasters to scorch the eyes of the sergeant, blinding him. His blade found the Space Marine's throat, ripping open the flexible protective collar, biting into windpipe and arteries with a solid thrust. Blood frothed from the wound as the sergeant fell back, crashing through a window to the ground below.

With their target dead, the eldar withdrew into the night, the Hidden Death taking the armoured body of their fallen exarch with them.

MORLANIATH SNAPPED BACK to the present with a fierce growl. Such were the convoluted strands of fate that the farseers had to follow, with lives and spirits overlapping one another across the skein of time. There were no such machinations to contend with in this battle. The goal was simple. Slay the humans and drive them from Alaitoc.

Nothing else mattered.

THE DOME OF Midnight Forests was dark, lit only by the glow of Mirianathir. Beneath the ruddy shadows of the lianderin, the Alaitocii gathered. Grav-tanks prowled along the pathways while scores of Wave Serpents shuttled back and forth delivering squads to their positions. The eldar had forsaken any defence of the dockward corridors, knowing that the Emperor's Space Marines excelled at such close quarters fighting. Swooping Hawks and Warp Spiders harried them, hitting and retreating, drawing the human forces on towards the forest dome. Here the eldar would make their next stand, able to rake fire across the wide clearings from the cover of the scattered woods. Every valley would become a killing field, every brook and meadow a graveyard for the invaders.

The Hidden Death were joined by Fiorennan and Litharain from the Fall of Deadly Rain shrine – the only survivors from the squad. Five of them had been scythed down by rockets during the initial Space Marine assault, caught as they cleared the Imperial landing craft. The exarch and three more of his warriors had died trying to fall back, cut down as the Space Marines drove into the eldar. Aranarha's armour had not been recovered and the loss hung heavy in his warriors' minds.

'What if they desecrate his suit?' asked Fiorennan. 'What if they break apart his spirit stones? He could be lost to us forever!'

'It is unwise to dwell, there are many such fates, but not all come to pass,' Morlaniath assured them. 'The enemy come fast, with no thought of the dead, he will be overlooked.'

'Out of spite and ignorance, they could cause harm they do not understand,' argued Fiorennan.

'Aranarha is lost, for the moment at least, we cannot change his fate!' snapped Morlaniath. Talk of the eternal death displeased the exarch. If Alaitoc was to fall, then all of his kind would finally die, the infinity circuit would be raped of its power and She Who Thirsts would feast heavily. He shuddered. No mortal creature scared him, not even the Emperor's Space Marine abominations, but everlasting torture consumed by the Great Enemy was a doom best not contemplated.

'Do not countenance death, dispel thoughts of defeat, think only of winning. Morai-heg was fickle, but it is in our hands, to shape our own future. Responsibility, to create our own fate, lies within our own grasp. To kill and not to die, to slay and not to fall, this is the end we seek.'

In silence, the Striking Scorpions stalked between the towering trees to their allotted position. As they flitted through the shadows, an enormous Cobra anti-grav tank slid past along a broad road, a nimbus of blue energy playing around the muzzle of its distortion cannon. The leaves trembled and grass flattened at its passing, though it made no more sound than the hum of a honeywing. The Hidden Death followed close behind until the Cobra turned off the road into a bowl-shaped clearing ringed with ancient lianderin.

This too was the Hidden Death's appointed place. Morlaniath quickly scanned his surrounds to get a sense of the geography. The clearing was like an amphitheatre on three sides, shallow-sloped and rimmed with trees. It opened out into a broad valley that led towards the docking bays, along which the enemy would have to advance.

Something amongst the trees caught Morlaniath's eye; a large statue entwined with the branches of a lianderin looking down the length of the valley. The statue would provide valuable cover if needed, while the trees gave ample shelter to circle behind a foe that entered the dell.

More figures converged on their location – two Vyper jetbikes appeared from the trees on the far side just ahead of several squads of Guardians clad in blue and yellow. They were followed by figures almost twice as tall, which strode silently through the undergrowth, eyeless, domed heads turning left and right as they picked their way forwards: unliving Wraithguard. Within the armoured shell of each was encased a spirit stone containing the essence of an eldar drawn from the infinity circuit. Morlaniath's thoughts grew heavier upon seeing the artificial bodies of the Wraithguard: even the dead had been roused to defend the craftworld. The exarch could feel the undead spirits touching on his senses, bringing with them the dry emptiness of the infinity circuit, leaving a trace of bitterness in the exarch's mind. Psychic energy coursed through their construct bodies and writhed within the wraithcannons they held.

Behind them came a coterie of seers – three warlocks carrying glittering spears and a farseer armed with a rune-carved witchblade.

Our fates share the same path again for a while.

Morlaniath looked over towards the farseer and recognised Thirianna. She raised her witchblade in salute.

'Is this coincidence, or a machination, brought about by your hand?' the exarch asked.

I am not senior enough to influence the judgement of the autarchs. Some have fates closely entwined; others have strands that never touch. We are the former. Do you not remember where you are?

Morlaniath looked around, reliving moments from his many lives, seeking a memory related to this place. His eyes fell upon the tall statue, of an eldar warrior kneeling before the goddess Isha, catching her tears in a goblet.

'I PRESENT *The Gifts of Loving Isha,*' he announced with a smile.

There were a few gasps of enjoyment and a spontaneous ripple of applause from all present. Korlandril turned to look at his creation and allowed himself to admire his work fully since its completion.

IT WAS A recent memory, yet no closer and no further than any other. His was an existence spread across all of Alaitoc and a hundred other worlds.

'I remember clearly, when disharmony reigned, when my spirit was split. This was my new birthplace, the path leading from here, which brought me full circle. It is no more than that, a place in a past life, of no special accord.'

Many new paths sprang from this place. Some for good, others that led to darker places. Your work began those paths, even if you did not intend it. We are all linked in the great web of destiny, the merest trembling on a silken thread sending tremors through the lives of countless others. Just a few cycles ago a child sat and stared at your creation and dreamed of Isha. He will be a poet and a warrior, a technician and a gardener. But it is as a sculptor that he will achieve great fame, and in turn will inspire others to create more works of beauty down the generations.

'I need no legacy; I am an undying, eternal warrior.'

No creature is eternal: not gods, not eldar, not humans or orks. Look above you and see a star dying. Even the universe is not immortal, though her life passes so slowly.

'What will become of me, have you divined my fate, looked upon my future?'

We all have many fates, but only one comes to pass. It is not for me to meddle in the destiny of individuals, nor to look into our own futures. Trust that you shall die as you lived, and that it is not the True Death that awaits you, not for an age at least. Your passing will bring peace.

'I suffer many deaths, I remember each well, never is it peaceful.'

An explosion rocked the dome, a plume of smoke billowing from the rimward edge above the trees as human explosives tore through the outer wall. Flocks of birds erupted into the dark sky with screeches and twittering, and circled above the trees in agitation. The crack of Space Marine bolters and the zip of lasers echoed in the distance.

'The enemy are upon us!' Arhathain's voice was quiet but firm in Morlaniath's ear. 'The next battle begins. Do not sell your lives cheaply, nor forget the artistry with which we fight. The day has not yet come when the light of Alaitoc will be dimmed.'

THE HIDDEN DEATH waited, concealed beneath the trees. Their swords and pistols were of no use in the battle being waged, and so the Hidden Death waited for the enemy to come into the trees where the

Striking Scorpions would excel. Or, Morlaniath hoped, he would get the command to move along the valley to deal a deadly blow to a force already torn apart by the rest of Alaitoc's army.

Arhulesh fidgeted with his bandaged arm, Elissanadrin whispered quietly to herself. Bechareth crouched beside the bole of a tree, staring intently down the valley towards the enemy. Waves of anger poured from Fiorennan and Litharain, touching the minds of the others. Morlaniath fed on the rage their exarch's death had unleashed, drawing it in as one might take a draught of refreshing air.

Nothing could be seen of the humans save for the flash of explosions. Their gunfire became a constant rumbling, mixed with the clanking of combustion engines and grind of tracks. Filthy smog stained the air above their advance, smoke from dozens of exhausts carpeting the treetops.

The padding of feet caused Morlaniath to turn. A squadron of war walkers advanced quickly into the clearing, the bipedal machines making no more noise than an eldar on foot. The cloven feet of the machines left shallow indents in the earth as they stalked forwards on their slender, back-jointed legs. The closest pilot, his open cockpit enclosed in a shimmering energy field, looked towards Morlaniath and raised a hand in greeting. The exarch nodded in return and watched the machines break into loping runs, turning rimwards to head into the trees lining the valley, weapon mounts swivelling to keep balance.

A ripple of explosions tore across the left slopes of the valley, still some distance away. Morlaniath traced the trajectory of more shells as they plunged down into the shallow-sided gorge, judging the artillery pieces that launched them to be at the far end of the valley: far too distant to be viable targets for his squad. With growing impatience he saw columns of human vehicles crushing trees beneath their bulk, forging up both slopes in an effort to gain higher ground. Squat tanks with large turrets lumbered at the heads of the columns, their large bore guns spewing fire and smoke every time they fired. Falcons and Vypers slid effortlessly between the trees, ignoring the lead tanks to fire at the clanking transports sheltering behind them. Detonations racked the columns and the tanks slewed to a stop, their turrets swinging ponderously to track their elusive targets while infantry spilled from their burning carriers.

The flicker of Warp Spider jump generators sparkled in the distance as they closed in on the debussed infantry. From beyond the valley walls, doomweavers – gigantic versions of the Aspect Warriors' deathspinners – sent immense clouds of monofilament wire into the air above the valley. The Warp Spiders disengaged and the Vypers broke free as the deadly wire descended, so thin it sliced branch and bone alike.

Behind the lines of halted tanks more vehicles appeared, painted in the red and white of the Space Marines. They charged fearlessly up the valley past the halted advance, ignoring the brightlance bursts and pulse laser blasts screaming around them. With them came attack bikes, three-wheeled contraptions with heavy weapon-armed sidecars. Bursts of plasma and laser criss-crossed between the two forces. More Space Marine tanks crashed forwards like mobile bunkers, the flash of lascannons erupting from armoured sponsons. The eldar withdrew again, leaving the shattered wrecks from both sides burning on the hillsides.

BEHIND THE SHIELD of the Space Marines' vehicles, human tanks advanced again, hundreds of soldiers following behind. From left and right explosions and other sounds of war echoed across the dome. The Emperor's warriors pressed forwards on a broad front, starshells hanging in the air to illuminate their path, the roar of great guns booming out above the splintering crash of falling trees and the crackle of flames.

Beside Morlaniath, the Cobra lifted effortlessly from the flattened grass, arcs of energy coruscating along its distortion cannon, throwing dancing shadows across the clearing. The lead Space Marine tanks were almost three-quarters of the way along the valley. Lascannon blasts stabbed from them into the darkness, setting fire to trees, gouging furrows in the ground as the enemy sought the elusive eldar.

With a thrum that set the ground shaking, the Cobra opened fire. The air itself screamed as the distortion cannon tore at its fabric, a rent appearing in the air above the closest Space Marine vehicle. The gap widened into a whirling hole framed with purple and green lightning, its depths a swirl of colours and reeling stars. Even at this distance, Morlaniath felt a slight nausea tremble through his body and a burning in his spirit stones. The warp rift tugged at his spirit, immaterial fingers prying into parts of his mind locked away behind barriers learnt as a child. Tempting whispers and distant laughter echoed in the exarch's thoughts.

The Space Marine tank was dragged to a stop by the implosive energies of the warp hole, its tracks grinding vainly through the soil, smoke belching from its exhausts as the driver gunned the engine in an effort to maintain traction. With a drawn-out creak, the vehicle lifted from the ground, tipping backwards, stretching and contorting as the breach into warp space opened wider. Rivets sprang free and disappeared into the ravening hole, followed quickly by the tangled remains of the gun sponsons. An armoured figure was drawn out of the top hatch and spun crazily into the maw of the warp a moment before the tank slammed upwards and was sucked into the spiralling vortex. With a crack like thunder the vortex closed, sending out a shockwave that sent a nearby Space Marine transport slamming into a tree with a shower of wood splinters and leaves.

The clearing fell still again as the Cobra's cannon recharged. Undaunted, the humans continued their advance, almost reckless in their haste to close. The whine of descending shells caught Morlaniath's ear and he looked up to see several black shapes falling from the flickering skies. Their trajectory was taking them somewhere off to his right and he followed their fall until they disappeared into the trees a moment before a series of ground-shaking detonations. Flames and smoke leapt into the air. Amidst the flash and turmoil, the exarch saw eldar bodies being tossed like leaves on the wind.

Lascannon blasts flashed across the clearing, shrieking off the Cobra's curved hull. The super-heavy tank lifted again as more power surged along the length of its main gun. Again came the scream of tortured reality and the concussive blast of the warp vortex forming. More than a dozen armoured figures and a pair of troop transports were sucked into the energy maelstrom, their forms thinning and twisting before they disappeared from sight while raw psychic energy forked to the ground from the breach's undulating rim.

Morlaniath strode to the statue and pulled himself up onto Isha's knee to gain a better vantage point, looking past the bulk of the Cobra. He felt that it would soon be time to act; he chafed at being a witness to the battle so far and longed to let the *Teeth of Dissonance* cut a bloody path through Alaitoc's foes.

Wrecks and bodies littered the valley floor, but the Space Marines had gained the higher ground to either side and from their vantage point their tanks poured chattering fire into the tree line. Within this cordon, batteries of self-propelled guns lumbered into position, bringing them into range of the dome's heart. A least twenty tanks grumbled towards Morlaniath's position, painted in the same grey as the soldiers' fatigues. Four brightly-coloured Space Marine transports charged ahead of the advance and would be at the edge of the clearing shortly.

Morlaniath flexed his fingers in anticipation and was about to lower himself to the ground when something crashed through branches behind him, their snapping audible above the din of war. He turned to see a trunk bending and then cracking

violently under some unseen pressure. The ground
trembled slightly from a massive tread, and a patch
of earth sank, squashed by a tremendous yet
invisible weight. Craning his neck, the exarch looked
up and saw a shimmering presence, a vague outline
of contortion against the dark red of the dome's sky.

Holofields shimmered and Morlaniath found
himself staring up along the giant, slender leg of a
Phantom Titan, half again as tall as the lianderin
trees. The Titan was like a giant rendition of Korlandril's sculpture of Eldanesh, its slender limbs and
narrow waist a perfection of proportion and design.
For all its beauty, it was the perfection of destruction
embodied by the Titan that impressed Morlaniath
more. Instead of arms, the immense walker had two
elegant guns, each longer than a grav-tank. From the
Phantom's right shoulder hung the ribbed barrel of
a tremor cannon; from the left a lance-like pulsar.

A flurry of missiles streaked from shoulder-
mounted pods either side of the swept dome of the
Titan's head, engulfing the enemy tanks in a curtain
of plasma blossoms. The air shimmered around the
vane-like holofield wings splayed from the back of
the Phantom, blurring its shape unto a dazzle of
fractured images as the Titan took another step forwards. A broad, clawed foot swung gracefully over
the clearing to find purchase beside the Cobra, the
massive machine's tread delicate for its size, dex-
trously avoiding the eldar warriors in and around
the dell.

Bending one knee slightly, the Titan swung its
tremor cannon into position, aimed along the left-
hand valley slope. Even within his suit, Morlaniath

felt a compression of air around him a moment before the weapon fired. A bass growl reverberated in the exarch's gut, swiftly rising in pitch to a shriek that tightened his throat and set his ears ringing, until it scaled higher, out of the range of even an eldar's hearing. He traced the path of the sonic pulse by the dancing of air molecules: overlapping sine waves of near-invisible energy that ended in the midst of the advancing humans. Where the line touched, the ground erupted, a huge gout of earth and rock rupturing into a widening crack that zigzagged along the hillside. Tanks shook themselves apart as the beam crossed over them; Space Marines were flattened inside their armour; unarmoured soldiers were torn limb from limb by the disharmonious sonic energy coursing through their bodies.

The whine returned and descended to a low rumble as the weapon powered down. There was no respite from the Phantom; more clusters of missiles streamed from its shoulder pods while its pulsar unleashed a glittering salvo of laser energy that tore along the front squadron of tanks, punching through armour, exploding engines and melting the crews inside. The Cobra fired again and the valley descended into an anarchy of swirling vortexes, wailing sonic explosions and the steady strobe of the pulsar. Shells screamed in return, flashing past the wavering image of the Titan to crash into the trees beyond the clearing.

Morlaniath climbed down from the statue, his excitement at the prospect of combat dissipated by the arrival of the Phantom. What use were mandiblasters and biting blade when compared to the awesome energies being unleashed upon the enemy? He rejoined the rest of the Hidden Death, who stood under the shadows of the trees watching the carnage in the valley.

'Do you think any will reach us here?' asked Elissanadrin.

'Not while we have our tall friend watching over us,' said Arhulesh, looking up at the Phantom Titan. 'Oh…'

Morlaniath looked to see the Titan turning away, its outline refracting into a shimmering cloud as the holofield cloaked its movements. In a few strides it was gone, lost past the canopy of the trees. With a whisper, the Cobra followed, sliding between the thick boles of the lianderin. Clearly their weapons were needed more elsewhere. Morlaniath brightened at the prospect that the battle was not yet over.

The exarch directed his gaze back to the valley. He could see red-armoured figures moving between the smoking wrecks and grey-clad soldiers taking up positions in the rents and craters torn into the ground by the Titan's weapons. Though the heaviest enemy vehicles had been destroyed, more of the gangling Imperial walkers advanced through the shattered stumps of the lianderin. Light anti-grav skimmers in the colours of the Space Marines streaked through the air, moving out to the flanks of the advancing force.

'They are needed elsewhere, but enemies remain, our blades will taste more blood,' said Morlaniath. He wondered whether to await the enemy attack, or to head out into the valley to take the fight to the foe. He felt the touch of Thirianna's mind in response to these thoughts.

Arhathain is mustering forces for a counter-attack along this axis. We wait for the reinforcements and then we will advance.

'Make ready your wargear, more warriors arrive, we shall be fighting soon,' the exarch told his squad.

They waited patiently, keeping an eye on the invaders as they approached along the valley, more circumspect than in their initial charge. Morlaniath saw squads of Imperial soldiers digging defensive positions into the hillsides: heaping up the earth to make barricades for trenches and mortar pits; creating semicircular redoubts for their anti-tank weapons; erecting spindly communications masts for their commanders to talk with each other. It was clear that they had abandoned their foolish hope of sweeping away the Alaitocii with a single attack and were now preparing to hold the ground they had taken.

'Their strategy is false, a folly of battle, to think that ground matters,' the exarch remarked to his squad. As he spoke, he pointed out the growing system of works. 'Their minds think in straight lines, seeking grand engagement, counting only in numbers. Our way of war is swift, the fast and fluid strike, not tied to a sole place. They hope we will attack, throw ourselves on their guns, to drive them out of here. We will be more patient, we have the advantage, Alaitoc is our home. Their presence is fleeting, it cannot be sustained, without food and water. They defend an island, cut off from their supplies, and we will rule the sea.'

'Perhaps their attacks are meeting with more success elsewhere?' said Litharain. 'They make solid their position knowing that advances are being made on other fronts.'

Morlaniath directed a beckoning thought to Thirianna. The farseer acknowledged the question and crossed the clearing to speak directly with the exarch.

'We have abandoned the Dome of Lasting Vigilance, and the humans control more than a quarter of the access ways to Alaitoc's central region.' Her voice was quiet, her tone non-committal. 'We still hold the domes around the infinity circuit core. It is Arhathain's wish that we drive these humans from this dome so that we can mount an attack on the flank of their other forces, severing them from their landing zone in the docks.'

'The enemy prepare, waiting is a peril, how soon do we attack?' said Morlaniath.

Thirianna said nothing for a while, her head cocked to one side as she communed with her fellow seers.

'The counter-attack is almost ready,' she said eventually. 'The humans' rough defences will be no obstacle. They think only of left and right, forwards and backwards. They still forget that we do not have to crawl along the groun–'

The farseer stopped and turned her gaze beyond Morlaniath. The exarch knew what had interrupted Thirianna, for he felt it too: a sensation in the blood, a quickening of the heart.

The Avatar was approaching.

Its presence joined the minds of the hundreds of eldar converging through the trees around

Morlaniath, linking them together in one bloody purpose. The exarch saw Guardians and Aspect Warriors advancing through the woods around him, heading for the valley. Far above, Swooping Hawks circled in the thermals of the burning tanks while Vampire bombers with wings like curved daggers cruised back and forth awaiting the order to strike.

Amidst the increasingly strong background throb of the Avatar, Morlaniath felt something else touching upon his spirit, something cold, yet keen and familiar: a direct call to him unlike the burning beacon of the Avatar's presence. He scoured the trees looking for the source. In the shadow of a split lianderin trunk, he saw a pair of yellow eyes flash. From the darkness appeared Karandras, oldest of the Striking Scorpion exarchs.

The Phoenix Lord stalked forwards, his helmet turning slowly as he looked at each of the Hidden Death in turn. He stopped a short distance away, gaze directed towards Bechareth. Morlaniath felt a quiver of worry. Did Karandras sense something of Bechareth's past? Did the Phoenix Lord realise he had once been counted amongst the most hated foes of the Striking Scorpions? The Shadow Hunter stared for a long time, the only movement the dancing reflection of flames in the lenses of his heavy helm and the slow flexing of his power claw. Anxiety flowed from Bechareth, his shoulders hunched, fist clenched tight around the hilt of his chainsword

'You will join me,' said Karandras, turning to Morlaniath. His voice was as of many speaking in unison, deep and full of power. Every syllable resounded through Morlaniath's mind like they were his own thoughts given life by another. The exarch breathed out slowly, struggling to remain calm. 'Serve as my guard.'

'It will be our honour, Hidden Death stands ready, for the Shadow Hunter,' replied Morlaniath, briefly bending to one knee in deference. As his psyche touched upon the Phoenix Lord's, Morlaniath felt a huge depth opening out beneath him, a bottomless well of life and death. Morlaniath was old, almost as old as Alaitoc, yet the creature that stood before him was even more ancient.

'Your shrine has done well, it is a pride to the Aspect of the Striking Scorpion,' the Phoenix Lord said, gesturing with a nod for the Hidden Death to follow him into the trees.

'The teachings are not mine, the wisdom is from you, I am the messenger,' said Morlaniath.

'Yet the message can become confused, distorted by the passing of ages, from lips to ear to mind, and on to fresh lips. The ideals of the Striking Scorpion remain strong on Alaitoc. It is not so in all places. It is to your credit.'

The Phoenix Lord led them away from the others, the presence of the Avatar receding as Karandras forged on through the trees towards the enemy. A blur of shadow followed Karandras, an aura of darkness that surrounded the squad even when they crossed paths and clearings. Its tendrils lingered behind, caressing the trunks of the trees, lightly striking the Aspect Warriors that followed. One diaphanous trail passed across Morlaniath's arm, chill to the touch. It came from the darkness between stars, the shadow of the deepest void. The tendril dissipated into the air and the sensation passed.

The crack of breaking twigs and the crunch of footfalls rang through the trees. To the left, three of the Imperial walkers advanced quickly through the woods. They lacked the grace of the eldar war walkers, strutting forward on their servo-powered limbs, swaying awkwardly from side-to-side. They were about twice Morlaniath's height, the leaves brushing the top of the pilots' open cockpits. Each was armed with a multiple-barrelled weapon that swung back and forth as the driver scanned the trees for enemies. Smoke drizzled endlessly from twin exhaust stacks mounted on an engine behind the cabin, leaving a sooty stain on the foliage of the lianderin.

More trampling alerted the squad's attention to another squadron passing to their right. Immobile, they waited for the reconnaissance sweep to pass by and then moved on again, heading close and closer to the human line.

KARANDRAS BROUGHT THE squad to a halt beneath the eaves of the woods, within gunshot range of the leading human squads. They squatted in the shadows and watched as several squads of soldiers fanned out into the woods, though none turned their eyes upon the Phoenix Lord and his companions.

The slope of the valley was a scene of crude industry, the humans digging-in like parasites on Alaitoc's flesh. Many of the soldiers were engaged with shovels and picks whilst their officers stood around, shouting orders or berating their men. A few sentries stood guard, but it was not these that drew Morlaniath's attention.

In front of the progressing defences were thirty Space Marines, each squad stood beside a slab-sided transport. They held their weapons ready, their helmeted heads turning with metronomic precision as they patrolled the hillside, watching the woods for any threat. At the near end of their line stood another walker, different in design from those that had passed earlier. It was almost as tall, but far broader, almost square in shape, painted in the red and white livery of the Space Marines. It was mostly thickly-armoured hull on squat legs flanked by two massive shoulders; from the right a short arm extended tipped with a claw wreathed in crackling energy; from the left protruded a short-barrelled weapon fed by several fuel tanks that reminded Morlaniath – in a very crude and human way – of the fusion guns used by the Fire Dragon Aspect.

'Which ones are we after?' whispered Arhulesh.

Karandras kept his gaze ahead as he replied, raising a finger of his claw to point at the Space Marines.

'The hardest prey makes for the worthiest prize,' said the Phoenix Lord.

'What will be our approach, the ground gives no cover, our enemies alert,' said Morlaniath.

'There will be a… distraction,' replied the Phoenix Lord in a mellifluous tone. Morlaniath detected a hint of humour.

They waited in silence. Above, the Swooping Hawks continued to circle slowly out of range of the enemy. Morlaniath detected the faintest of compression at the back of his skull, the passing touch of an immaterial presence. He knew that it was a leftover trail, a collateral effect of a Warp Spider's jump generator being activated not too far away. Not for the first time in his long existence, Morlaniath wondered what manner of eldar would become a Warp Spider, willing to expose themselves to the perils of warp space. There was a violent darkness in the core of every exarch and Aspect Warrior, but the Warp Spiders balanced on a precipice of self-destruction. They were not only risk-takers, they had a bleak outlook on life, rarely mixing with warriors from other shrines.

'Be ready,' warned Karandras, driving away Morlaniath's pondering. He had some inkling of what was to be expected and looked up into the sky. In the flickering, dim light of the humans' starshells, winged shapes swooped down from the heights of the dome. The shriek of the wind from their wingtips grew in volume as the Vampires dived, six of them in a V-formation.

A cluster of spheres arced down into the human soldiers as the Vampires swooped overhead. No mundane detonations rocked the valley: each sonic bomb exploded above the defence lines to send out rippling shockwaves. The sonic pulses pulverised bodies and barricades – expanding, ethereal globes of devastation swept across the hillside to create a screaming storm of debris. Morlaniath saw soldiers lifted into the air, their fatigues ripped from lacerated bodies. Those at the outer edge of the sonic eruptions fell to the ground with blood streaming from ears, eyes and mouths, crimson seeping from the pores in their skin, bursting from ruptured blood vessels.

The Space Marines turned as the Swooping Hawks descended in the wake of the bombing run, their bolters rising towards the flying Aspect Warriors. Karandras was already out of cover and dashing along the crest of the hill towards the enemy. Morlaniath pounced after him, the rest of the Hidden Death close on his heels.

A Space Marine gunner sitting in a hatch atop one of the transports spotted the Striking Scorpions and heaved around his pintle-mounted weapon. Bright flares streamed towards the squad as the Space Marine opened fire, his twin-barrelled gun spraying explosive bolts. Two rounds streaked past Morlaniath and he heard a scream of pain. Glancing back, he saw Elissanadrin writhing on the ground, right arm missing below the shoulder, a gaping hole in the side of her chest. In a moment, the exarch took in the frothing blood, splinters of bone and spurting arteries in the wounds. More bolts whined past. There was no time to spare for the fallen warrior. The exarch surged after Karandras, the *Teeth of Dissonance's* blades spinning up to full speed, powered by Morlaniath's growing rage.

Karandras cut to the right and plunged into the closest Space Marine squad as more bolter shells whickered past. With two steps, Morlaniath leapt up the sloping front of the transport, biting blade level. Without breaking stride, he bounded past the gunner, the whirring teeth of his blade sweeping through the Space Marine's neck as the exarch dashed past, thick blood spattering on the white hull of the vehicle. Swift retribution for Elissanadrin's death sent a thrill through the exarch as he ran across the engine grille and jumped down to rejoin his squad.

Four Space Marines lay at the feet of Karandras, their armour carved apart by his sword and crushed by his power claw. The Phoenix King's mandiblasters unleashed a torrent of blasts that hurled another foe from his feet, his armour shattering from the pulses of green energy.

The Hidden Death joined their Phoenix Lord in the melee, pistols singing, chainswords screeching. A bolter shell flashed across Morlaniath's vision, the flare of its propellant almost blinding him, his helmet lenses polarising to avoid permanent damage to his eyes. He instinctively ducked and spun, lashing out with the *Teeth of Dissonance*, the blade crashing against an armoured leg. A fuzzy red shape stumbled back to his right. Morlaniath drove forwards, angling the point of his biting blade high, catching the Space Marine across his heavy shoulder pad. The exarch fought back a brief flash of not-Lecchamemnon's death with a feral snarl.

'Destroy the invaders, set free your enmity, let the red river flow!'

Morlaniath launched himself at his foe, mandiblasters crackling into the Space Marine's eye lenses. With a growl, the exarch smashed the roaring teeth of his blade across the Space Marine's gut, slicing through pipes and cables in a spray of electrical sparks. The Space Marine swung his bolter like a club, Morlaniath catching the weapon on the armoured guard of his sword. The strength of the blow forced the exarch back three steps, but in a moment he regained his balance and sprang again, ducking beneath the Space Marine's outstretched arm, the *Teeth of Dissonance* tearing a furrow through the ribbed armour protecting the warrior's exposed armpit. Blood spewed from a severed artery, bathing Morlaniath's legs as he spun behind the Space Marine.

With a shout, the exarch hammered the biting blade into the vents of the Space Marine's power plant backpack. Fractured energy cells discharged their contents in an arc of bluish light, mirrored by a flurry of laser fire from the exarch's mandiblasters. Coolant hissed in a cloud from the Space Marine's ravaged armour, frosting across Morlaniath's left arm. The thin layer of ice crystals flaked to the floor as he brought back his sword for a final blow. The Space Marine turned lopsidedly towards the attack, to be met full in the face by the teeth of Morlaniath's weapon, which sheared through the helm, removing the top of the Space Marine's skull. As the Space Marine collapsed, Morlaniath delivered another burst from his mandiblasters into the exposed brain matter, reducing it to steaming grey slurry.

A shadow loomed over the exarch and he saw the blocky shape of the Space Marine walker towering above him. The metal beast had its massive hand upraised, energy crackling between long claws. The exarch lifted up the *Teeth of Dissonance* to parry the attack, but knew he did not have the strength to fend off such a blow.

Something hit the exarch hard in the side, pushing him out of the way of the claw's lighting-wreathed descent. Morlaniath rolled to the side, Bechareth between him and the walker, a moment before the claws slashed down, cleaving away the side of the Aspect Warrior's helm before parting the left arm from his body.

Karandras leapt across Bechareth as he fell, his powered claw raking trails of ceramic splinters from the walker's armour. Morlaniath was filled with the urge to drag Bechareth to safety, instilled in him by a thought from the Phoenix Lord. He could do nothing but act in tune with the compulsion. He held the *Teeth of Dissonance* in his left hand and grabbed Bechareth by his remaining wrist, hauling him from under the walker's clawed feet. The walker's fist caught Karandras in the stomach, glittering fingers punching out of the Phoenix Lord's back.

Morlaniath looked down at Bechareth's face, almost a mirror image of the first time they had met, the Striking Scorpion's eyes staring from a mask of bright blood. Morlaniath saw the hatred and anger of an Aspect Warrior in that gaze, but sensed something behind the war-mask.

The exarch understood why Karandras had sacrificed himself to save Bechareth.

'You must survive this war, move on along the Path, find the peace that you crave,' Morlaniath whispered. 'Fight the darkness in you. Prove that the Path is right, that Khaine does not own us!'

Bechareth's hand flapped against Morlaniath's arm, seeking to grasp him. He fell back with a shuddering gasp, eyes fixed on the exarch.

'I will,' said Bechareth, lips twisted with pain.

Morlaniath nodded and turned back to the walker, which was lumbering after the rest of the Hidden Death as they retreated down the hill. The exarch took two steps after the mechanical beast, eyeing the vulnerable pipes and exhausts jutting from its back.

He stopped, gaze drawn to the body of Karandras lying just ahead. The Phoenix Lord's armour was rent open from stomach to throat, but there was no blood splashed, no organs ripped apart. In the gouge, a galaxy swirled; motes of light circled around a central brightness, each a spirit of Karandras.

Morlaniath was entranced. He could feel the faint beating of a heart at the base of his skull. It grew in strength as he approached the rent form of Karandras, drawn closer by an irresistible instinct, filled with the same external purpose as he had been when he had dragged Bechareth to safety. He was not in control of his body and watch in detachment as Morlaniath knelt beside the fallen Phoenix Lord, dragged deeper and deeper into the circling lights. The call of Khaine waxed strong, roaring in the Morlaniath's ears to the drum of the heartbeat.

He reached out a hand to touch the glittering stars.

WITH A WRENCH, Morlaniath felt himself drawn from his weak physical vessel, every part of him: Morlaniath, the First, the Hidden Death; Idsresail, the Dreamer; Lecchamemnon, the Doomed; Ethruin, the Dark Joker; Elidhnerial, the Weeping One; Neruidh, The Forgiver; Ultheranish, the Child of Ulthwé; Korlandril, the Artist.

Not-Korlandril was but an atom in the star of Morlaniath, and Morlaniath nothing but a star in the whole galaxy that was Karandras. Countless essences, endless voices drifted slowly together.

Spirits from across the galaxy, of warriors born on every craftworld in every age, and the spirit-parts that made them, and the memories of those other spirits that had touched them, stretching out, far out into the infinity of the universe, all connected, all brought together in this one body.

Morlaniath fragmented, became his parts, each seeping away into the glitter of the Phoenix Lord's essence. The silence of space greeted them. Not for them the life-in-death of the infinity circuit. Not for them the ravages of She Who Thirsts. Here they would end, truly and forever. Only Karandras lived on. Briefly, Korlandril lived again, and then was gone.

Peace.

HE HID BEHIND the tumbled arch of the old temple, shivering in his nakedness. Hunger gnawed at his gut. His limbs trembled with weakness, his breath wheezing in his throat. And the pain inside, the throbbing in his heart and head, the needles of agony that coursed through his mind, stretching him in all directions, more unbearable than any physical pain.

A foot scraped on dusty stone and he shrank bank further into the shadows, eyes desperately seeking an escape. There was none, he was trapped. Through the tears, he saw a figure silhouetted against the light from outside the shrine.

'Do not be afraid,' the stranger said, his voice quiet but strong.

He remained as still as death, holding his breath. The stranger crossed the bone-littered floor of the temple with easy strides, his green gown flowing behind him. The stranger's eyes were unlike any he had seen before. They were empty of hatred, empty of lust, empty of jealousy and malevolence.

He flinched as the stranger reached out a hand. He pushed himself back until his spine was against the cold wall. There was nowhere else to hide. The stranger smiled, but there was none of the leering desire he usually associated with such an expression.

'What is your name?' the stranger asked. His voice was low, calm, not screaming, not shouting.

'Karandras,' he whispered back, his voice barely a breath.

'Karandras? That is a good name, a strong name.'

'What do you want with me?'

'I want to help you.'

'Where are you going to take me? The others wanted to take me into the dark web, but I ran. I was scared.'

'You were right to be scared. The others are not to be trusted.'

'Trusted?'

'I will teach you about trust. It is a good thing. Come with me and I will teach you many things.'

'What will I learn?'

'You will learn not to be afraid. You will learn about happiness, and peace, and balance. Do you want to learn these things?'

'I do not know… What are they?'

'They are what will make us strong again.'

'Will you teach me how to hide?'

'There are no places left to hide.'

'Will you keep me safe?'

'Nowhere is safe.'

Karandras considered this for a moment.

'Will you protect me?'

'Better than that, I will teach you how to protect yourself. I will teach you how to fight.'

Karandras reached out and hesitantly grasped the proffered hand. The stranger's grip was firm but gentle. He allowed himself to be lifted to his feet, his head no higher than the stranger's chest.

They turned towards the door together and walked across the light, Karandras's hand in the stranger's.

'Where are we going?' the boy asked.

'To a place where my friends are waiting. To a place where you can learn how to fight, to battle the enemies of the body and the spirit.'

They reached the cracked steps of the doorway, the harsh light causing Karandras to blink heavily, tears in his eyes.

'Who are you?' he asked.

'I am Arhra. I am your new father.'

WHITENESS FADED AWAY to the colours of life and death. Karandras pulled himself to his feet, his armour fusing the wound that had allowed his energy to escape. The Phoenix Lord looked down at the empty suit of the exarch that had given him this new life. He felt nothing of the eldar that he had been. There were no memories, save his own. There was no spirit, save the one he had been born with.

He was Karandras, and Karandras alone.

He looked around, assessing the raging battle. The Alaitocii were fighting hard and driving the humans from the dome, but the fate of their craftworld was far from decided. Karandras stooped to pick up his chainsword, reassured by the feel of it in his fist. The Striking Scorpions who had joined him were retreating back to the woods, carrying two of their wounded number between them. The Phoenix Lord turned his back on them and headed after the Imperial Dreadnought that had killed him. The Phoenix Lord felt the thrill of retribution singing through his body.

ANOTHER WAR, ANOTHER death. Such was to be his fate, until the final battle, the Rhana Dandra, when all things would end.

ABOUT THE AUTHOR

Gav Thorpe has been rampaging across the worlds of Warhammer and Warhammer 40,000 for many years as both an author and games developer. He hails from the den of scurvy outlaws called Nottingham and makes regular sorties to unleash bloodshed and mayhem. He shares his hideout with Dennis, a psychotic mechanical hamster currently planning the overthrow of a small South American country.

Gav's previous novels include fan-favourite *Angels of Darkness* and the epic Sundering trilogy, amongst many others.

You can find his website at:
mechanicalhamster.wordpress.com

WARHAMMER
40,000
A SPACE MARINE BATTLES NOVEL

HELSREACH

AARON DEMBSKI-BOWDEN

Buy this
series or read
free extracts at
www.blacklibrary.com

UK ISBN 978-1-84416-862-0 US ISBN 978-1-84416-863-0

HUNT FOR VOLDORIUS

ANDY HOARE

Coming Soon

UK ISBN 978-1-84416-513-1 US ISBN 978-1-84416-514-8

WARHAMMER
40,000

A SPACE MARINE BATTLES NOVEL

THE PURGING OF KADILLUS

GAV THORPE

Coming
Soon

UK ISBN 978-1-84416-896-5   US ISBN 978-1-84416-897-2

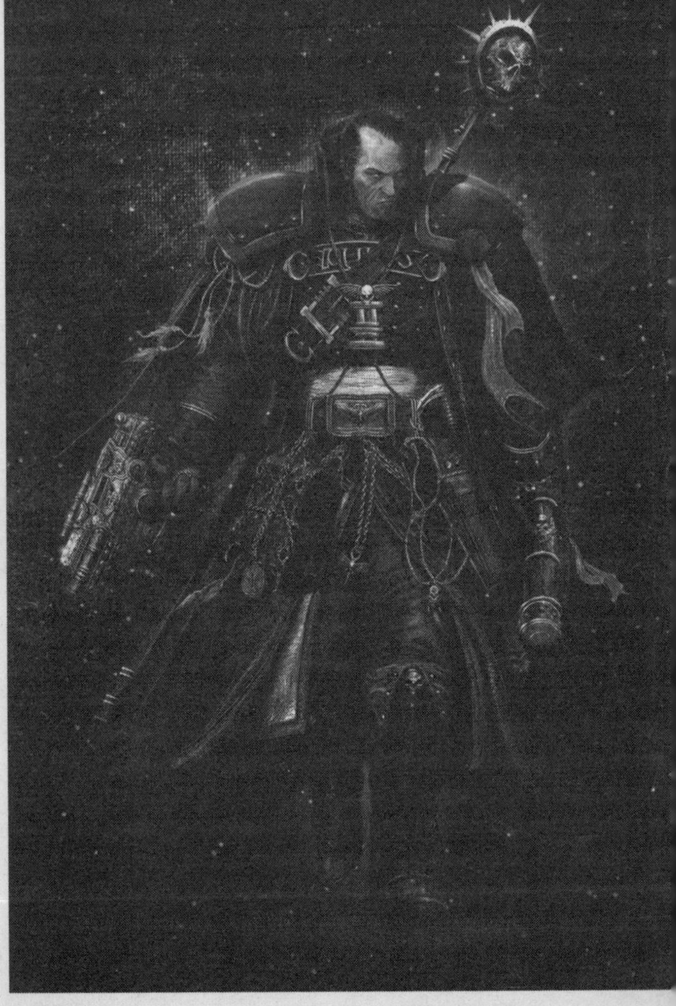